WHAT PEOPLE ARE
ABOUT HELIACA

The characters [in *Heliacal Star*] were a labor of love for the author. Readers can identify with them because there were both heroes and villains . . . The author writes with a wealth of knowledge about horses; [my] understanding has grown dramatically. For those who enjoy a blend of romance, horse racing, suspense, and crime fiction, Victor Bahna's *Heliacal Star* is highly recommended.

—*City Book Review* Seattle (★ ★ ★ ★ ★)

Filled with unexpected moments and thrilling revelations . . . *Heliacal Star* is an exhilarating and emotional novel centered on the rich history and thrilling atmosphere of thoroughbred racing. It offers gripping moments of suspense that build at a great pace as the plot thickens, keeping readers on edge. A compelling blend of sporting action, thrilling danger, and heartfelt moments.

—*Readers' Favorite* (★ ★ ★ ★ ★)

The fast-paced world of horse racing serves as the background to this entertaining novel. The plot of the narrative is straightforward; the dialogue is well-written and authentic. Author Victor Bahna tells a compelling story from start to finish.

—*City Book Review San Diego* (★ ★ ★ ★ ★)

Drawing on his own experience and love of the sport, Bahna captures the essence of the racetrack, smartly contrasting the quieter side of the landscape—the morning dew, the smell of liniment, and the sound of hoof beats with the excitement of race day. With a well-crafted, action-filled plot and solid characters, Bahna's work should appeal to both equine and non-equine enthusiasts alike.

—Blue Ink Reviews

HELIACAL STAR

HELIACAL STAR

VICTOR BAHNA

Heliacal Star

© 2024 Victor Bahna

This novel is a work of fiction. The names, characters, and incidents portrayed in it are the work of the author's imagination. Any resemblance to actual persons, living or dead, events, or localities is entirely coincidental.

Published by Victor Bahna

victorbahna.com

Kirkland, WA

Hardcover: 979-8-9882771-2-5

Paperback ISBN: 979-8-9882771-1-8

Ebook ISBN: 979-8-9882771-0-1

Cover design by Sarah Flood-Baumann

Interior design by Liz Schreiter

Edited and produced by Reading List Editorial

ReadingListEditorial.com

To retired thoroughbred racehorses everywhere, especially Rooster City, a valiant competitor, winner, and carrot-consuming champion!

AUTHOR'S NOTE

Thoroughbred racing is one of the oldest, richest, and most traditional of sports. Legendary tales connect its origins to ancient Greece, when horse-drawn chariots sped around oblong hippodromes. The first documented horse racing can be traced back to England nearly a thousand years ago, during the reign of Richard the Lionheart. In North America, the first known races date to the mid-1600s on Long Island, only a few miles east of present-day Belmont Park.

Intelligent, regal, and athletic racehorses throughout the United States selflessly train to compete at peak performance for their owners, trainers, jockeys, and fans at racing venues daily. Throngs of crowds cheer and scream for victory as the thoroughbred racehorse thunders toward the finish line, but few will consider the welfare of the horse once his racing career is over. All racehorses, no matter how well they run in their heyday, ultimately retire from racing due to age, injury, or poor performance. The most accomplished ones retire to the breeding shed, while less successful runners may have second careers in trail riding, jumping, dressage, or showing. Others are turned out to oversize pastures under the watchful eyes of caring and loving owners.

Several national and local charities actively and enthusiastically work to protect retired racehorses, but some unfortunate equines become lost, discarded, and forgotten. This group of unwanted horses may land in unkempt round pens littered with feces surrounded by the stench of ammonia from urine-filled puddles, en route to their final destination—a slaughterhouse.

PROLOGUE

C'mon, mama. Just a little push." The farm manager kneels behind the prone mare and pulls. The first two hooves appear, followed by a nose. Lying on her side, the mare grunts and pushes just a minute or two more, until the entire foal is visible. There is no need for more human intervention. It's a textbook natural birth.

"He's a colt. Time of birth is 4:37 a.m., March 20, 2013," the mare manager notes to her foaling attendant and assistant.

It was early 2012 when a six-year-old mare named Giant's Quest easily triumphed in a race at Aqueduct Racetrack to boost her career purse earnings north of $400,000. In the days following the race, the mare's veterinarian observed a small pool of fluid accumulating around her right front ankle, accompanied by a lame walk, indicating a high potential for injury if she continued to race. Given her age and estimated value as a broodmare, the trainer and owner retired her from racing.

Deciding on the right stallion for a first-time broodmare owner involves many factors, including statistical analysis, pedigree science, visual inspection, farm location, and stud fee. There are as many theories about proven methodologies for breeding champion racehorses as there are champion racehorses, all seemingly backed by at least one compelling statistic to validate the theory du jour.

The owner of this broodmare consulted with several bloodstock agents and specialists regarding her breeding prospects and ultimately landed on a promising young stallion standing in Kentucky, for a modest stud fee.

Within his first thirty minutes, the newborn colt stands, and within the first two hours of his life, he begins nursing. As the foaling attendant applies a mild soap to the mare's vulva and hindquarters, the foal turns his head, showing a distinctive white marking resembling a star on his forehead.

The foaling attendant says, "Hey, look! A star has been born!" She nicknames the foal Polaris; however, his officially registered name will not be determined until a future date.

At eighteen months of age, life for the colt is forever changed when he leaves the familiar surroundings of the only farm he's ever known. In a half an hour or so, he arrives at the pristine grounds of Keeneland. There he's led under a green-and-white canopy and over a manicured path toward the newly painted barns and thousand-plus stalls situated on the backstretch. Over the next two weeks, more than four thousand thoroughbred yearlings will pass through the on-site auction ring, attracting million-dollar bids from billionaire buyers, all of whom hope to discover a future Kentucky Derby winner.

In the days leading up to the auction, several prospective buyers, agents, and trainers traverse the grounds to inspect the well-conformed and personable dark bay colt unofficially named Polaris. On-site veterinarians apply their tools of the trade to confirm and reaffirm both the soundness and health of the colt. Well-compensated veterinarians carrying portable radiograph machines perform on-demand X-rays and probe for hidden bone fragments or other potential deformities not otherwise visible in his knees, forelegs, pasterns, or fetlocks.

One prospective buyer is an investment banker from New York named Alex Sherman, who's accompanied by veteran trainer Ted Bouchard. Like thousands of other prospective buyers, Sherman arrived at Keeneland with lofty aspirations to buy a champion racing prospect. Prior to arriving at the sale, he secured a preapproved credit allowance of a half-million dollars.

On the first day of the two-week auction, the dark bay colt unofficially named Polaris nickers while being escorted from his stall and led across the pathway to the entrance of the walking ring a few hundred yards ahead. His dappled coat sparkles under the late-afternoon sun, and his groom sprays a cool dash of water over his neck, back, and mane, accentuating his shine. Surrounding the walking ring are hundreds of horsemen crowded together for a final view of the yearlings as they march through the walking ring. Alex Sherman and Ted Bouchard are among them.

As the dark bay colt enters the auction ring, Sherman twitches and paces, jockeying for a prime viewing spot, with a clear line of sight to the bid spotters. Sherman gulps and clears his throat.

The bidding opens at $25,000 and increases in increments of $25,000 until it hits $425,000 in just a matter of moments, at which point only Sherman and one remaining bidder are locked in competition. Sherman raises his right arm and points at the spotter, declaring his bid for $450,000, but he's usurped only seconds later by a higher bid. Although nearing his preapproved credit allowance, Sherman pumps his arm once again, eclipsing the previous bid to reestablish himself as lead bidder at $500,000. The bidding pauses. Large droplets of sweat accumulating across his forehead, Sherman glares at his rival, who stands motionless. The bid spotter holds up two fingers in his left hand and five on his right to solicit a raise of $25,000.

The other bidder remains statuesque, and the auctioneer glances at the multiple spotters surrounding the ring. He announces, "Going once, going twice . . ." and raises his gavel, but fails to strike down when the underbidder raises his arm at the last possible second.

Now beyond his credit limit, Alex Sherman wipes his brow, shrugs, and looks toward Bouchard, standing nearby. Ted immediately nods, and Alex pumps his arm to reestablish a leading bid of $550,000.

The auctioneer again looks across the pair of bid spotters, and announces, "Going once, going twice . . ." and pauses to look around. He hammers down his gavel and declares, "Sold!" Sherman is the winning bidder and new owner of the young dark bay colt with the notable white star marking on his forehead.

———

It is tradition in racing for some owners to name and register a yearling based on the sire and dam names. Sherman jots down a few names derived from the colt's dam name, Giant's Quest, and his sire, Pioneer of the Nile.

Giant Pioneer . . . Pioneer Quest . . . Nile Quest.

He draws a line through each of the names and sketches a star, similar to the marking on the colt's forehead. After staring at his drawing for a moment, Sherman draws an approximation of Egypt around the star, with a north-south line representing the Nile River. He googles *ancient Egypt*, *Nile*, and *star*.

He reads about the "heliacal rising" associated with the star Sirius in ancient Egypt. The rising occurs when Sirius becomes visible, shortly before sunrise, after being hidden by daylight before the solstice. It's a new beginning and Sherman pens the name: Heliacal Star.

Sherman submits the name to the Jockey Club Registry, and his newly acquired yearling, previously nicknamed Polaris, is officially registered as Heliacal Star.

CHAPTER 1

PRESENT DAY: JUNE 2018

Standing inside the small, chilled, and dimly lit office at the rear of his butcher shop amid the earthy scent from dry-aged meats on nearby hooks, Tony Kaufman wraps his right arm around Larry Lonsdale, pulls him close, and says, "What do you mean? Are you telling me some random prick overheard your conversation at the racetrack this morning? Tell me exactly what this asshole heard."

Although younger, bigger, and stronger than Tony, Larry Lonsdale offers no objection to the pointed question as he shrugs his brawny shoulders. "Don't know, boss. I heard this noise when I was talking to our trainer. When I looked around the corner, I saw him running away and took off after him. He must have heard me coming, 'cause he was tearing ass out of there."

Tony releases his hold and pokes his bony finger into Larry's chest. "And where is this guy now?"

Larry lowers his head and mumbles, "He got away."

Tony slaps his hands and stomps his right foot on the ground.

"Shit, Larry! What the fuck is wrong with you? Tell me you at least got a good look at him?"

Larry keeps his head low. "Sorry, boss." He looks up, as if remembering. "He was definitely a skinny guy and about six foot. Quick little mother."

Larry glares at Tony, tightens his right hand, punches it into his left. "I was about to catch him when this frigging horse literally comes out of nowhere and runs me over."

Tony stares back, stiff in posture and offering no reaction or response.

Larry explains, "By the time I regained my balance, he was long gone. I walked the entire barn area for over an hour, but there was no hide or hair of him. He simply disappeared."

Tony's eyes narrow, and his forehead tightens as he abruptly turns from Larry, an indication it's time for Larry to stop talking, as judgment will now be passed.

After a long silence, Tony approaches Larry and speaks in a slow and deliberate tone. "Okay, Larry. You did your best, but we need to flip the script now. If this asshole really overheard you, then he knows about the fix. Instead of throwing the race, we're going to win it now. You tell McGee we made a change in plans. If our horse wins, you're safe. If not, we'll be having a different conversation."

Larry sighs as Tony says, "And Larry, don't fuck it up this time."

CHAPTER 2

A gentle breeze teases. It's a moment of temporary relief during an otherwise uncomfortably hot June afternoon. Ten horses march in a choreographed manner toward the starting gate. A piercing pain disables Matt Galiano, forcing him to hunch over while standing inside the main grandstand of Belmont Park. His nerves are fried. His favorite racehorse, Heliacal Star, is the number-four horse in the upcoming race.

From a lifetime of watching and wagering on horses, Matt understands many variables will factor into the outcome of any race on any given day. The post position, pace scenario, competition, break from the gate, and talent of the horse are all key factors. Each jockey will vie for position throughout the race and be forced into split-second decisions, ultimately leading to victory or defeat. For Matt, there are few things in life that unleash the intensity, suspense, and uncertainty of those moments just prior to a race. There's nothing in the world quite like the anticipation of anxious adrenaline, followed by the eruption of unbridled euphoria the instant victory becomes apparent. Every wager becomes a real-time pass or fail as winners are immediately paid and losers sulk and discard their now worthless vouchers.

Cashing a winning ticket instantaneously rewards the victors as the losers regroup and prepare for the next race and a chance at redemption.

Known as "Beautiful Belmont Park," the historic racetrack on Long Island stands less than fifteen miles from midtown Manhattan. The racing oval, also nicknamed Big Sandy, is North America's largest, stretching a mile and a half, or twelve furlongs. The oversize track complements an imposing grandstand, which accommodates over thirty thousand screaming spectators. The lush green grass course glistens in the sunlight of the late afternoon. The general admission area behind the grandstand, known as the backyard, opens from the rear façade of the main building with views of overgrown ivy reaching skyward and shadowing a portion of the grand windows that stretch to the roof of the four-story edifice.

In the glory days of yesteryear, horse racing was widely known as the Sport of Kings, complete with formal and influential gatherings at Belmont Park, an embodiment of elegance and grace. The men, donning splendid hats and pinstripe suits, and women, dolled up in glamorous dresses, came together for the prestigious ritual of race day. Belmont Park was the place to be for affluent New Yorkers.

Since Belmont Park first opened its doors, tuxedos and ascots have been swapped out for jeans, T-shirts, and baseball caps. Yet the pomp and circumstance of horse racing carries forward from generation to generation, as if frozen in time. Just as it was a century ago, each horse is escorted by its groom from their stable to the paddock prior to each race. The paddock area includes a sandy horse-walking ring around a magnificent century-old

Japanese white pine. As the horses enter the paddock, it signals the start of pre-race pageantry, roughly twenty minutes ahead of post time.

The atmosphere surrounding the paddock is typically festive. This is the same hallowed ring where legendary superstars such as Secretariat, Seabiscuit, and Man o' War once paraded as throngs of eager spectators gasped.

On this late June afternoon, the grooms lead their hopefuls single-file into the paddock. Awaiting the horses are gentlemen trainers in ties and blazers, lady trainers in long skirts, and color-fully outfitted jockeys. Riders and trainers are entrenched in deep discussions regarding their upcoming race strategy. Alongside the trainers are wealthy owners, some eavesdropping on the con-versations, seeking the perfect moment to interject with their unsolicited and unwanted expertise. Although some owners have never ridden a racehorse, they still feel emboldened to instruct the jockey on how he or she must perform. The jockeys are good sports, accustomed to the prolific ignorance and wealthy arro-gance of some owners as they smile encouragingly and humor them with reassuring nods.

As each horse makes its final pass in the paddock for the sur-rounding spectators, the jockeys are hoisted atop their mounts, indicating post time is nearing. At Belmont Park, the horses cir-cle in post-position order over the walking path before exiting the paddock and continuing on the sandy path through a tunnel that bisects the grandstand. Bettors standing behind protective glass are drawn to the parade of horses and a final chance to observe the thoroughbreds up close before they amble onto the track upon exiting the tunnel.

As the first horse emerges from the tunnel and enters the racetrack, the track bugler trumpets a familiar fanfare to inform spectators of the horses' trackside arrival. A murmur of enthusiasm builds among the owners, gamblers, trainers, and spectators. Some succumb to personal superstitions while others indecisively fret over their racing program in a desperate and final effort to predict the winning horse or combination of horses that will finish in first, second, and third.

Several minutes after walking onto the track, the horses are loaded into the starting gate in numerical order. Heliacal Star is the fourth horse to be loaded into the starting gate. Matt Galiano is fully aware it's the dark bay gelding's first race since suffering a devastating injury last October at Belmont Park. He glances at the tote board and notices Heliacal Star is the public's second betting choice at odds of 3–1. The odds are lower than Matt anticipated, given the lengthy time off the horse required following his injury last year.

Matt feels sorry for anyone who placed a wager on Heliacal Star today, considering his insider knowledge. For the past two years, Matt has intently followed the horse's career, and he's well aware of his talent and capabilities. Even with his prior injury, Matt believes he could easily win today's race, but he also knows victory is not on the agenda.

As always, Matt did his homework today. He diligently studied the past performances of each horse and carefully observed their movement, disposition, and appearance as they walked inside the paddock. Heliacal Star appeared strong, cool, and confident while the other horses seemed skittish, hot, or nervous by comparison. Yet, for the first time since discovering Heliacal Star,

Matt did not wager on him today. If not for certain mitigating circumstances, Matt would be full of enthusiasm, anxiety, and energy as the horses enter the starting gate.

Today's conditions are anything but normal. His normal excitement for Heliacal Star has been replaced by concern, trepidation, and outright fear. He is uncomfortable and feels paralyzed by his inaction as the tenth and final horse loads into the starting gate.

Matt's fear turns to nausea as the track announcer proclaims over the loudspeakers, "It is now post time!"

CHAPTER 3

Inside his spacious living room, Tony Kaufman sits on the sofa, eyes closed, legs stretched out, and feet comfortably resting. His fingers caress the stem of a snifter containing Hennessy XO cognac. The transporting music of Verdi's *Il Trovatore* is interrupted by a light tap on the door, disturbing his meditative state. Tony gestures for the professionally dressed gentleman standing in the doorway to come forward.

The man approaches Tony, leans in close, and speaks softly. "It's almost time, sir."

Tony sits upright, places his fingers on his lips, and whispers to his guest, "Listen for a moment," as he swirls the cognac in the snifter.

Tony stands up, stretches his arms, and says, "You can feel her passion at your core. Leonora has offered to sacrifice herself to save her lover, who has been condemned to die, rather than marry another." He sips his cognac and stares at his guest. "We are the same. Our passion will drive our success, or we will die in pursuit."

Tony lowers the volume and says, "Thank you," and his guest leaves.

Tony Kaufman is a gangster, a chronic gambler who always plays the odds in his favor. He cheats to win, whether it involves stealing insider knowledge, buying off players, influencing referees, or fixing races. Those who believe there's no such thing as a sure thing have never met Tony Kaufman. Slight and grandfatherly, Tony doesn't look like a ruthless psychopath, but that's exactly what he is.

Today promises to be a good day for Tony, as the fix is in for the eighth race. A victory has been guaranteed. Should his team fail, the consequences will be swift and severe. Tony squeezes his right hand into a tight fist and turns it, as if tightening his grip on destiny.

It's post time at Belmont Park, and his eyes fixate on Heliacal Star standing in the starting gate.

CHAPTER 4

It was two years ago at Belmont Park when Matt first noticed the horse, or, more accurately, the horse first noticed him.

Matt was handicapping an upcoming race and studying the past performances of the entries. A deep analysis failed to produce an obvious choice, and he concluded that making any selection would be difficult, given the lack of differentiation among the contenders.

To choose the right horse for his wager, Matt needed to get a closer look at the physicality and behavior of the entrants as they marched from the backstretch toward the paddock. He located an acceptable spot along the first of four railings in a tiered row, with a clear line of sight into the paddock, to view the contenders.

To narrow his choices, he evaluated the behavior, attitude, and athleticism of each horse as they were saddled and prepped for the race. The first horse, he noticed, produced a white foamy sweat down his neck, an indication of anxious or nervous energy. The second one dropped his head, walked slowly, and stopped frequently. He reminded Matt of a lazy old dog, a horse that would prefer to graze all day long versus race competitively. A third horse caught his attention when he nickered and reared his forelegs, displaying evident signs of athleticism combined with attitude. Moments later, the trainer of this third horse quickly dropped to the ground, barely avoiding an unprovoked rear kick while tightening the horse's saddle. The fourth horse, and betting favorite, displayed a dull coat that seemed to match his personality, as he appeared to lack any demonstrable interest in his groom, trainer, or the other horses in the paddock. Without a standout in this group, Matt lacked any motivation to wager.

Resigned to skip the race, Matt suddenly caught a glimpse of another horse. As he homed in on this potential new contender, he immediately noticed the horse's dappled coat shining brilliantly in the afternoon sunlight. The horse moved with a long stride and occasionally transitioned into a light hop while being led around the ring by his groom. To Matt's experienced eye, he appeared eager to race. In spite of the horse's subpar race record, Matt's interest in this horse was piqued, solely based on his visual observations.

As Matt maintained a watchful eye on the horse, he sensed a hidden elegance and budding level of confidence he could not objectively quantify. Upon noticing a marking resembling a star on the horse's forehead, Matt realized the horse had stopped and was looking directly at him. It was a fleeting moment, but it mesmerized Matt, causing him to drop his racing form to the ground.

Still eyeing the horse, Matt squatted and picked up his racing form. As the jockeys greeted the trainers, Matt noted the horse was draped in an orange saddlecloth and a black number seven. Matt reopened his racing form and remembered eliminating number seven as a contender based on his poor racing history. He made note of the horse's name, Heliacal Star. The horse was three years old, lightly raced, and had never finished better than fifth. He had not raced in over six months and had been recently gelded, which Matt figured was a tactic used by the trainer to improve the horse's focus. His morning line odds of 12–1 foreshadowed his likely status as a longshot come post time.

Intrigued by Heliacal Star, Matt peeked at the tote board, which showed his odds had already changed to 18–1, even longer than his morning line odds. Based on his handicapping experience, Matt understood a longshot was an indication of low confidence from the general public and other handicappers. Not many bettors were wagering on this horse.

As Matt continued to observe Heliacal Star in the paddock, the horse again stopped. Once again, the horse appeared to be staring at Matt.

This time, Matt felt an oddly genuine bond as their eyes locked. Unwittingly, Matt said his name aloud, "Heliacal Star," loud enough for a nearby gambler to offer his unsolicited opinion.

"Are you kidding me? You're seriously thinking of betting on that broken-down maiden? Trust me, he'll be lucky to reach the wire before the next race starts!"

Taking a step closer to Matt, the gambler lowered his voice and said, "Listen, kid, I've got a tip for this race. Spot me a ten, and I'll give you the winner, guaranteed!"

Matt brushed off the gesture, but his new acquaintance continued, "Oh, what the heck, you look like a good kid. My tip is for the number-six horse. He can't lose. Trust me, I heard it directly from the barn. Next time, though, it'll cost you twenty."

Matt smiled and feigned enthusiasm. "Thanks for the tip! I'll take another look at the six."

Given his experience around the racetrack, Matt knew when someone was bullshitting him. He figured this self-appointed tipster was acting like a bigshot to garner attention while lazily selecting the post-time favorite as a means of convincing Matt he was a legit insider. Matt waved him off and returned his attention to the paddock as the jockeys mounted their horses and led their mounts over to the walking ring for a final pass. After the unsolicited tip, there was no chance Matt would wager on the six horse.

The first of several horses moved forward and into the tunnel, but when Heliacal Star approached the end of the walking ring, he stopped and tipped his head downward while looking in Matt's direction. Ignoring the multiple prompts from his jockey to move along, Heliacal Star stayed put, only ten feet from where Matt stood. The horse stared at Matt, lowered and raised his head twice, then spun around to acquiesce to his jockey's instruction. As Heliacal Star walked through the tunnel on his way to the main track, Matt stood in stunned silence and struggled to make sense of the uniquely odd gesture. He convinced himself it wasn't a mere coincidence but an unmistakable sign to place a wager on Heliacal Star.

The tipster from moments earlier tapped Matt on the shoulder. "Hey, that was weird. That seven horse seems to have a thing for you." Then he laughed while holding up six fingers as he walked away. "Remember, bet on the six."

Matt turned his attention to the tote board showing Heliacal Star's odds had jumped to 25–1, even longer than just moments earlier. He reached into his pocket and pulled out three twenty-dollar bills and a five.

He ran up to the teller window, slammed his cash on the counter, and declared, "Sixty-five dollars to win on number seven."

The teller looked up for just a second, then mumbled, "Number seven?"

Matt nodded, and his wager was official. He grabbed the voucher from the teller, stuffed it inside his pocket, and skipped ahead to the front side of the racetrack.

Gambling wise, the day so far had been disastrous for Matt after a combination of close calls, near misses, and astonishingly bad luck. A terrible ride by the jockey caused his first loss, followed by an apparent win in the next race, until the finish line photo ultimately showed another horse winning by a head bob. In the race that followed, the reins on the horse he'd bet on snapped halfway through the race, causing the jockey to lose his footing and the horse to finish last. In the race previous to Heliacal Star's, Matt's horse won by three lengths, leading to a celebration of fist pumping from the surge of adrenaline associated with victory. In this case, Matt was prepared to collect on multiple wagers, as he won the exacta for picking the first- and second-place finishers in order, and the trifecta bet for selecting the first-, second-, and third-place finishers in order. He was calculating the amount of his big payout when the *Inquiry* sign flashed on the tote board. The jockey from the runner-up horse had claimed foul against the winner, Matt's selection. The complaint was sent to the racing stewards to assess the validity of the claim and determine if the winner should be disqualified.

The wait was agonizing for Matt as the television monitors around the track continuously replayed the point of alleged contention. It was replayed at normal speed, then fast-forwarded, then slowed down, rewound, and replayed again and again. Matt's neck grew stiff and cramped from staring at the monitors, hoping for no disqualification. To pass the time, he stepped away, paced, and sat down. He shuttled his attention between the replays and the still-blinking tote board, an indication the stewards continued to deliberate. Debates broke out around him. One group was insistent on disqualification while others were adamant no foul had been committed and no change should be made.

When the jockey's claim was finally upheld by the stewards and the winner disqualified, Matt's wagers instantly flipped from winning to losing. He slumped onto the floor and watched in disbelief as the television monitor replayed the confirmed violation yet again. In the course of a few minutes, his mood traversed from elation to concern to frustration and finally aggravation, best described as utter disgust. With a few remaining dollars in his pocket, he dismissed any obvious thoughts of quitting for the day and elected to remain for one more race, in hopes of salvaging his otherwise unlucky day at the races.

He pulled out his voucher, which showed his sixty-five-dollar win bet on number seven. With nobody else nearby, he chuckled. "Why not Heliacal Star?"

In the moments prior to the start of the race, Heliacal Star's odds jumped once again, this time to 30–1, eliciting thoughts of self-doubt accompanied by a desire to take a break from gambling, presuming this horse with huge odds could not prevail.

Rather than watch the race at the rail from ground level, as he had for the previous races, Matt opted for a bird's-eye view atop the mezzanine in a superstitious ploy to desperately alter his luck.

Among the conveniences of modern times is the ubiquity of streaming horse races on the internet, reducing the need or desire to attend in person. As Matt looked out upon the general seating area of the mezzanine, his options appeared unlimited within a tranquil ocean of seats spanning the grandstand, which sat virtually empty. It was a stark contrast to his own memories of yesteryear when such seats sold weeks in advance and entire sections were filled to capacity. On this day, there were only a handful of individuals seated among the thousands of otherwise empty chairs. Sitting high atop the grandstand flooded him with memories from his preadolescent years when he regularly attended the races with his dad.

Taking a seat, Matt observed the horses complete their warmups on the track before loading single-file into the starting gate. Once loaded, the track announcer's voice echoed throughout the grandstand, "And they're off!"

Matt immediately spotted Heliacal Star break from the gate with the bright orange saddlecloth. The horse gained a forward position early but then lost ground down the backstretch and fell behind until he was trailing the entire field after only a quarter mile into the race.

As Heliacal Star wallowed double-digit lengths behind the leader, Matt sighed and stared upward to the sky. He threw both arms into the air and eased deep into his seat, no longer interested in the debacle unfolding on the track. He yanked the voucher from his pocket, held it high above his head, and said to himself, "Hi, Matt. I'm Heliacal Star. You should bet on me. I'm going to win at long odds today."

He muttered to himself, "What was I thinking? I should have listened to my tipster friend and bet on number six."

Matt peeked down on the action with a perverse curiosity to see how far behind Heliacal Star was trailing. Several horses were bunched at the back of the pack, but none appeared to have the orange saddlecloth. In disbelief, he caught a glimpse of Heliacal Star speeding past several horses while rounding the final turn. At that moment, the track announcer bellowed, "And here comes—oh my, Heliacal Star. He's absolutely flying!"

Matt gripped his voucher and stood up. "C'mon, man. Let's do this!" As the horses approached the wire, he was jumping up and down. "C'MON, HELIACAL STAR! GO, BABY. RUN 'EM DOWN. GO . . . GO . . . GO!"

The number six was still leading, but Heliacal Star was closing fast with every stride!

The two horses engaged each other at the top of the stretch, head to head and nose to nose as they battled for the lead. They looked inseparable, running stride for stride as the finish line loomed closer. "C'MON, BABY. ONE TIME. ONE TIME!"

Heliacal Star pinned back his ears, dropped his head, and seemed to pull ahead, but his foe rallied and drew even once again. As they crossed the finish line, the announcer frantically said, "Too close to call. IT'S A PHOTO FINISH! Hold all tickets."

Matt did not need to wait for the photo or the announcement. He knew Heliacal Star had won, and a minute later, the official photo confirmed it: Heliacal Star had bested his foe by the tip of his nose. The tote board showed the result was official, and Matt screamed with joy, "YESSSS! HELIACAL STAR! YES!"

His hands shaking from excitement, he stared at his ticket, showing his wager of sixty-five dollars to *win* on number seven. He kissed it and said to himself, "This has the makings of a beautiful friendship."

The final odds for Heliacal Star had closed at 37–1, and Matt collected nearly $2,500 off his hunch wager. His mood was immediately lifted by his change in luck on what had become a stunningly profitable day.

Matt ran down the escalator and positioned himself just outside the Winner's Circle for a close look at the winning horse. He arrived just in time to see Heliacal Star enter the Winner's Circle alongside his owner, Alex Sherman, and trainer, Ted Bouchard.

In that moment two years ago, Heliacal Star instantly became Matt's all-time favorite racehorse.

CHAPTER 5

At thirty years of age, Matt Galiano has been a horse-racing enthusiast since childhood. Unlike the cigar-smoking, down-on-his-luck horse player trolling through the grandstand or the pompous aristocrat wagering at the elitist Turf Club while gorging on caviar and champagne, Matt fails to personify such racetrack stereotypes.

At six foot one and of slender build, Matt blends into the crowd of racing fans with an almost boyish look, nostalgic baseball cap, and pair of well-worn jeans. He favors the classic rock T-shirt to formal attire and dons a pair of tattered work boots to complete his ensemble.

As a youngster, Matt was slightly overweight and uninterested in sports or exercise. However, since he embarked on his career in construction, and most recently as an elevator installer, he's transitioned from a chunky kid into an athletic adult thanks mainly to his daily routine of lifting, carrying, and hauling heavy and bulky equipment.

An unattached male, Matt is committed to his job and advancing his career. His daily schedule consists of getting up before dawn and spending his evenings reading, listening to podcasts, or streaming movies and shows. His friends and co-workers constantly encourage him to join them clubbing, but Matt will only occasionally oblige. His appealing shyness garners curiosity from the ladies, in contrast to his extroverted friends who overtly seek attention from the opposite sex.

In spite of his physical appearance, pleasant personality, and approachability, Matt has yet to experience a serious or long-term relationship. His sexual experiences have been limited to superficial attractions. Once the initial sparks diminish, a predictable and unemotional breakup inevitably follows. Without a serious girlfriend, Matt has learned to be comfortable managing his daily routine without rehashing previous flings or fantasizing about potential ones.

The one consistent love in his life is an unreserved enthusiasm for thoroughbred horses and the challenge that comes from handicapping the races. He experiences an unparalleled excitement when visiting the racetrack and considers this vice of choice as his escape from the realities of everyday life. Since his dad passed many years ago, Matt has attended the races often, to the chagrin and angst of his short-lived girlfriends, who had shown little interest in his favorite pastime. At the track, Matt can flee the doldrums of life and concentrate on the thrill of the moment.

Handicapping horse races has become a skill Matt has honed over thousands of hours poring over racing forms, watching live races, and analyzing probabilities based on statistical inference. Refining his analytical skills over the years has provided Matt with a distinct handicapping advantage over the amateur or casual racing fan.

Matt's love of racing began at an early age, on Long Island, as he grew up about a dozen miles from Belmont Park. Matt's dad frequented the races along with his uncles and cousins, as they shared a common obsession with gambling, especially when it involved horses. As a preteen, Matt would constantly badger his dad to bring him to the races. His mom was vocal in her opposition—she didn't want her son to start gambling—but his dad eventually relented and allowed the enthusiastic young boy to tag along with him.

Following his inaugural visit to Belmont Park at just ten years old, Matt was instantly hooked and loved watching the horses race. Young Matt's initial love evolved to a fixation. While sitting on Santa Claus's lap one late November afternoon, he asked for a racehorse, dreaming of becoming a jockey one day.

While the majority of kids his age learned about reading, writing, and arithmetic, Matt taught himself basic statistics and learned to interpret the myriad of data presented in the daily racing form. He became a natural and enthusiastic statistician, and regularly picked winners based on his developing skills. When his dad boasted about Matt's race-picking talent to his uncles and cousins, Matt felt proud. In 1999, Matt was thrust into the role of family hero after correctly picking the winner of the Belmont Stakes. A horse named Lemon Drop Kid defeated a big favorite named Charismatic, after the latter had won the both the Kentucky Derby and Preakness Stakes and seemed poised to win the Triple Crown. Matt was only eleven when he correctly selected Lemon Drop Kid. Following the race, Matt's dad hoisted the young boy high off the ground and labeled him a genius and chastised his uncles and cousins, who had questioned his son's advice.

Energized by his father's praise, Matt obsessed over race-horses. He immersed himself in racing statistics, studied pedigrees, and learned about stallions who sired the best grass, dirt, or mud runners. He explored commonalities of precocious juveniles and conformational differences between sprint or route runners. Each day became another opportunity to incorporate the results of the previous day, update his handwritten notes, and refresh his statistics on horses, jockeys, and trainers.

Saturday afternoons became ritualistic as Matt accompanied his dad to the racetrack every week. Matt leveraged Friday evenings to study the racing form and determine his selections for the next day's races. He and his dad started with a track-side breakfast, then hung around the track to watch the horses gallop, jog, and exercise. To Matt, those Saturdays at the track were the highlight of his week. The jockeys often stopped before mounting their horses to offer a friendly greeting, toss over a set of goggles, or tell a story about the horse they sat atop. After breakfast, Matt rode on a backstretch tram for a guided tour of the barn and stable area while his dad entered the grandstand to meet privately with his business associates.

As he grew older, Matt learned his family was unlike the families of his other classmates. His dad did not work nine to five, commute to an office, or wear a uniform. It also was relatively common for the local police to appear at their front door. Matt eventually learned his uncles were not blood related but considered close friends of the family, which in Matt's world seemed normal, as they frequently visited.

One day, Matt inquired about his father's profession and why the police visited so often, prompting his mother to inform him about their ongoing interest in the family. She gushed about his dad's penchant for making money and how the police always reacted by fabricating charges out of spite and jealousy. She told Matt the FBI questioned anyone who made money freelancing and about how they sought to punish hardworking Americans, especially those who wagered on horses. Matt believed these tales and despised both the police and the FBI throughout his childhood.

At age fourteen, Matt's life changed dramatically and forever. It was early autumn, just prior to the leaves turning color, and Matt had attended the races with his dad that morning, as they did each Saturday. That night, he was awakened by an unfamiliar noise emanating from the kitchen. He followed the noise into the kitchen and saw his mom with her head bowed, uncontrollably sobbing. At her side was one of the police detectives who regularly questioned his dad. The officer slowly approached Matt with his shoulders sagging and said, "I'm very sorry, son."

Matt was confused and asked, "What do you mean? Why are you sorry?"

His mom walked over, pulled Matt close, and cried on his shoulder. Matt's stomach instantly knotted into a painful bulge. Realizing his dad had not returned from his business meetings that night, Matt feared the worst, dropped to the floor, and wept at his mom's feet.

The authorities never found the people responsible for killing his dad. After a while, they stopped looking.

Later that day, his uncles, cousins, and other relatives arrived at his house to share their condolences, but after the funeral, they stopped visiting altogether. Matt fell into a deep depression and no longer attended the races or socialized with friends and schoolmates. His heart ached. Every night, he pleaded with God to bring his dad back, and he contemplated suicide as a means of being reunited once again. At the same time, Matt's mom was heartbroken, compelling him to cease any thoughts of self-harm, as taking his own life would only exacerbate her pain and suffering. He found strength in his dad's words from long ago to never give in or quit. In spite of his commitment to press forward, Matt's sadness persisted, especially on Saturdays. His self-pity was overwhelming at times, and he was convinced he would never feel happiness again.

CHAPTER 6

The track announcer proclaims over the loudspeakers, "It is now post time!"

Looking down at the starting gate, Matt is all too aware of the race fix. His focus remains on Heliacal Star inside the gate. As the second betting favorite, the public is showing confidence in the talent of this horse. Regardless of what the public thinks, Matt knows Heliacal Star is going to lose this race today.

A few days ago, Matt inadvertently overheard a confidential conversation regarding Heliacal Star. Matt surmised the fix was a calculated ploy to artificially inflate the horse's odds for future races and set up a windfall wager at long odds down the road. He initially considered, and even intended, to share this knowledge with the racing authorities but argued with himself that getting involved could bring trouble or unwanted attention.

Looking down at the starting gate, Matt's stomach grows queasy as one the horses rears up and is backed out of the starting gate, causing a delay. A second horse reactively rears as his jockey jumps off, undoubtedly an act of self-preservation. The uneasy and fluttering sensation in his gut intensifies as Matt senses the manifestation of his own guilt and regret.

Attempting to calm himself, Matt unsuccessfully tries to slow his breath and relax. Instead, his pulse and breath quicken, and his thoughts turn to his fondness for Heliacal Star, further deepening the sense of guilt. As the final horses are reloaded into the starting gate, Matt is convinced it's not too late. He leaps up and dashes out of the grandstand.

Hurtling down the escalator, Matt hears the ring of the starting bell, signaling the race is now underway. At eight furlongs, the equivalent of one mile, the horses will cross the finish line in roughly a minute and thirty-five seconds. There is no time to lose.

Darting at full speed across the ground floor of the grandstand, past the paddock, and through the backyard, Matt glances at the television monitor. The horses are more than halfway to the finish line, and Heliacal Star is currently in the lead. Matt figures they purposely positioned the horse on the lead as part of their nefarious plan. He assumes they'll burn his energy early and he'll be too tired to finish strong in the final furlong. If they make losing appear too obvious, it could lead to unwarranted scrutiny. With little time remaining until the horses cross the finish line, Matt accelerates his gait and sprints toward the racing office, at the far end of backyard. He plans to tell the racing officials what he knows.

As he bursts into the racing office, Matt is out of breath and his clothes are drenched in sweat. All eyes turn to him as he looks around for an official. On the television monitor, Heliacal Star crosses the finish line, easily winning the race by ten lengths. Matt stares at the screen, shocked and confused. He bends down, drops his hands to his knees, and shakes his head, trying to process what just transpired.

Returning his attention to the monitor, he watches the full replay of the race. Heliacal Star just won, and there is no longer anything newsworthy to share with the racing official. Instead, he turns away and slinks toward the exit. Reaching for the door, Matt suddenly spins around as a booming voice shouts out from behind the counter.

"That's enough!"

The racing official slams his hand on the desk and says, "Leave *now*, Kristine." The racing official is responsible for the rules and ethics around the racetrack, and the gal arguing with him is a young trainer, standing inches from his face. Matt recognizes her.

She screams, "It doesn't matter. That horse won because some asshole fixed the race. What are you going to do about that?"

The official steps forward and bumps her with his oversize chest, sending her backward. He responds with a booming retort, "First, you tell me he's going to lose, and now you're accusing Ron McGee of fixing the race to win?" He holds up his hand, cutting himself off, and continues in a more measured tone, "Get out of here. Go!"

Stopping a few feet from the doorway, Kristine addresses the attentive group of onlookers, "How does that slogan go? See something, say something? Not around here. Don't bother with these officials. They may have ears, but they sure as shit aren't listening!" She slams the door hard upon exiting the office.

Inside his living room, Tony Kaufman beckons to the man who just left his office, points at the monitor, and says, "Looks like our man McGee came through. Send him a few steaks from the shop along with the usual amount."

He turns off the monitor, turns up the operatic music, stretches out his legs, and takes a sip of cognac.

CHAPTER 7

It was only a few days ago when Matt Galiano met first Kristine "Kris" Connelly, on what would have been his dad's fifty-eighth birthday. It had been nearly sixteen years since his father was murdered.

Matt had the day off from work and rose early. He considered phoning his mom. Given the gap in time since they last spoke, it was a fleeting thought. Their relationship had never really recovered after she'd given him little choice but to move out shortly after his father's death.

After being estranged from his mother for many years, Matt felt hurt she never attempted to reach out or apologize for abandoning him. Yet, he retained a modicum of guilt from the absence of a mother-son relationship, or perhaps it was simply self-pity. Matt assuaged his conscience through logical rationalization. His multiple attempts to make amends in the past had only resulted in disappointment as she was too sloppy and inebriated to carry a coherent conversation after a breakfast consisting of one part orange juice, two parts vodka, and three parts misery. It had been a decade since he last phoned her, and the prospect of a peaceful reunion grew more daunting each year.

Instead of calling his mom, Matt drew upon fond memories of spending so many pleasant Saturdays with his dad at the racetrack. His birthday happened to fall on a Saturday this year, which prompted Matt to start early, enjoy a trackside breakfast at Belmont Park, and watch the horses warm up. He envisioned his dad joining him in spirit, smiling and cheering, like the old days.

When he arrived at 7:30 a.m., the racetrack was already alive with horses, trainers, workers, and riders engrossed in their morning activities, as training hours begin before dawn. The airy scent of morning dew was a suitable companion to the sound of galloping ponies amid a backdrop of hushed chatter between riders and trainers. Reminded of the more innocent days of his youth by the sight of horses, smell of liniment, and sound of hoofbeats, Matt felt at ease and reminisced about simpler times when attending races with his dad meant everything to him. As he thought fondly of those days, he soaked in the atmosphere and lost himself in the pleasure of watching dozens of thoroughbreds exercising on the racing oval.

The public cafeteria serving breakfast was sparsely populated with only a handful of early morning railbirds. As he ordered a bagel and fruit cup, Matt caught sight of a weather-worn advertisement for a guided tram tour through the historical stable and barn area of Belmont Park. Matt had entirely forgotten about the backstretch tram. He recalled all those mornings riding on the tram, as a ten-year-old, while his dad remained inside the grandstand to meet his associates.

Strolling toward the pickup location, Matt arrived in time to see the multicar tram approach around the corner. Without hesitating, Matt found an available seat at the rear of the tram.

The vehicle had clearly aged in the decades since he last boarded, and it looked smaller and moved slower than he remembered.

A dad and his daughter and a young family were among several others to board. At its scheduled departure time, the tram lurched forward, leaving the curb outside the café en route to the backstretch. Over an antique intercom, the driver, who also doubled as tour guide, explained the history of the grounds and shared a story about the roots of horse racing in North America.

As the tram wandered through the expansive barn area, it occasionally stopped as the tour guide shared a quippy anecdote or pointed out the barn locations of the more famous names in racing, such as Lukas, Pletcher, and Brown.

One stop Matt remembered from childhood was the stall where Secretariat was stabled before infamously destroying his foes in the 1973 Belmont Stakes to secure the ninth Triple Crown in horse racing history. As they continued onward, the guide offered various factoids, many of which Matt already knew, including one about the oval being the largest in North America and the reason it was nicknamed Big Sandy.

A community unto itself, the backstretch of the racetrack is a bustling and self-sustaining environment with sixty-three barns as well as housing, a kitchen, a general store, a clinic, clergy, and childcare services. Throughout the area, grooms are constantly hand-walking and bathing the horses, while jockeys and exercise riders are guiding their mounts to and from the training track as trainers bark out instructions and entertain owners visiting for the day. With nearly two thousand horses on the grounds, a dozen or so equine veterinarians move quickly from barn to barn with endoscopes, radiographs, and a selection of medications to treat the myriad of conditions that may surface at any time. To the unfamiliar or untrained eye, the scene may look chaotic, but despite appearances, an underlying structure ensures everyone understands their role.

As the tram rolled forward, the grooms stopped, smiled, and waved to the youngsters onboard. Some of the exercise riders even volunteered to pose beside the tram while sitting atop their mounts, allowing the visitors to snap a photo or witness a thoroughbred up close.

As the tram bounced along, Matt was undeterred from studying his racing form while the guide spoke. He would occasionally glance up upon hearing an interesting fact, but otherwise he remained fixated on his racing program. Suddenly, he heard the guide mention the name of a familiar horse. Matt folded his paper and listened to the guide.

The tram had stopped at Ron McGee's barn, and the guide announced that former Stakes winner Heliacal Star was residing in this barn. Matt rolled up his racing form and waited for more information, but the guide moved on to discuss a trifecta he won back in '77 when Seattle Slew captured the Triple Crown. The guide asked the tour group a question about the number of Triple Crown winners. A young boy near the front of the car responded with the correct answer of thirteen Triple Crown winners and added a fact about the longest Triple Crown drought being thirty-seven years, between Affirmed in 1978 and American Pharoah in 2015.

Barely listening, Matt's thoughts turned to Heliacal Star. In the past two years, Matt had developed a strong affinity for the horse. He made it a point to watch all his races, either live or via simulcast. Matt had been aware of an injury the horse suffered a year earlier but had not been thinking about Heliacal Star until the tour guide's comment.

As the tram pulled through a quiet section of the backstretch, Matt pondered the likelihood of getting an up-close glimpse of his favorite horse. While the other riders on the tram seemed preoccupied by the guide's accolades about the Cornell Ruffian Equine clinic across the street from the eastern edge of the backstretch, Matt snuck off the tram and backtracked to the previous stop at Ron McGee's barn. As he walked through the barn area and passed several grooms, traffic officers, and trainers in golf carts, nobody paid him any attention.

Approaching McGee's barn, Matt felt out of place and worried about getting caught meandering from stall to stall in search of Heliacal Star. Expecting to be stopped and asked for access credentials, he arrived at the barn without inquiry. He paused for a moment, looked around, and peeked into several stalls, hoping to spot the distinctive marking on the horse's forehead. Matt wondered if the horse would stare at him and make eye contact as he did two years ago. After peeking into each of the stalls on the south end of the barn, Matt proceeded to the north end but halted around the corner as he heard a raspy voice. Matt had never been to McGee's barn before, yet the voice sounded eerily familiar. Matt leaned forward to catch a glimpse of the man speaking. In an instant, he recognized the man behind the voice. Matt stood there, paralyzed.

It was unmistakable. Seeing "Louisville" Larry Lonsdale unlocked a frightful memory from his past. Matt fully understood the necessity of avoiding a reunion with Larry to protect himself and his well-being. He needed to slip away, unnoticed.

Seeing Louisville Larry shook Matt's psyche and assaulted his memory as his brain spiraled back to an unpleasant time when he served as a bookmaker for the Kaufman clan. At that time, Matt was the brains of the operation while Louisville supplied the muscle, earning his nickname from his frequent use of the brand-name baseball bat to fulfill his enforcer duties. It was a relationship that ended badly for Matt. In the decade since their last encounter, Matt was aware Louisville had been arrested multiple times, and presumed he was still behind bars. Looking at him from afar, he could see that Louisville had aged some but still looked imposing as ever.

Louisville was talking to Ron McGee, whom Matt also recognized from his knowledge of racing personalities.

"Listen, McGee." Larry's voice pierced through Matt's soul. "This horse is going to lose his next fucking race . . . you understand me?"

Although Matt was desperate to dash away, he was also mesmerized by the conversation. Against his better judgment, he planned to remain still without making a sound, then sneak away after they finished talking.

"Hey, fucko, you got this?" Based on the tone of Larry's voice and his choice of words, it was obvious that Louisville hadn't changed much over the years.

Matt heard a mumbled response from McGee.

"Good boy, Ron! Oh, and don't fuck it up. Remember, Heliacal Star loses his next race, or you know what will . . . " Matt knew there was no need to finish the sentence. He had said enough already.

Matt could only assume the Kaufman syndicate was involved, given Louisville's prior relationship with them. Worst of all, this abysmal scheme involved his favorite horse, Heliacal Star. Matt was tempted to confront Louisville right then and there to stop him from destroying the integrity of the horse. However, he also knew such an encounter with Louisville Larry would be akin to a suicide mission, and logic prevailed over emotion as Matt refrained from advancing around the corner.

When the conversation between McGee and Larry seemed to end, Matt waited a few moments to ensure they were done. Should he anonymously inform the racing commission about these terrible plans? Matt heard approaching footsteps coming from the direction of Louisville and McGee. He feared it was one or both of them rounding the corner, and he felt little choice but to flee immediately.

As Matt turned to run, Louisville emerged from around the shed row corner. "Yo, asshole!"

There are few things on earth that could genuinely frighten Matt to his core, but Louisville Larry was at the top of the list. Matt darted away, and the chase was on.

With his assailant close behind, Matt accelerated as fast as his legs could take him.

Louisville was gaining on him. "Hey, shithead, just wait till I catch your sorry ass!"

A rush of self-preservation bolstered Matt's stamina as he found another gear and quickened his pace over the open horse path.

Sprinting over the path, Matt spotted a trio of horses being escorted and coming toward him as they returned from their daily workout on the track. He ran toward the horses, flailing his arms wildly in the air and yelling. All three horses immediately bucked, reared, and nickered in response. As they bolted down the pathway, their riders screamed at Matt while grabbing for their reins. Matt ducked out of the way to avoid getting kicked or stepped on and kept running without breaking stride. Still close behind, Louisville Larry angled himself off the path as the streaking horses approached him. Larry jumped to the left as one of the oncoming horses darted right and ran directly into the large man, spinning him backward and onto the ground.

Hearing the thud from behind, Matt stopped, turned around, and smiled with relief as he witnessed Larry lying flat and moaning. As Larry started to rise, Matt took off running and crisscrossed through several barns until his legs could no longer carry him. He dropped his head and bent over to catch his breath. There was no sign of Louisville. For the moment, he felt safe.

He wandered to the nearest shed row, which appeared unoccupied, given there were no grooms or horses present. He poked his head into a few stalls and confirmed they were empty. Unsure of where to go and afraid of another chance run-in with Louisville, Matt ducked into an empty stall. A cushion of loose hay was strewn across the ground, and it smelled like ammonia, but it was quiet and safe. Matt moved to the rear of the stall and slid his back against the wall until he was seated atop the hay. While not exactly the Turf Club, Matt was confident Louisville would never find him squirreled away in this equine hideaway.

After several minutes of peaceful silence, approaching

hoofbeats and the sound of people talking could be heard. The voices didn't resemble Louisville or McGee, but Matt stood up against the wall as a precaution.

Suddenly, the daunting shadow of a large horse appeared inside the small space. He was being led into the stall by a young blonde woman. Matt stood rigid against the back wall, and the horse pinned his ears and reared up, clearly agitated by the presence of a stranger in his stall.

The confined space offered no escape as the horse stood between Matt and the door. Unable to run, Matt turned away, dropped to the ground, and curled himself into a tight ball to brace for impact. Cowering on the ground, Matt heard the young woman who was leading the horse jerk the lead rope and retreat with the horse from the stall.

As the horse and shadow both vanished, Matt mustered his courage to look up. To his relief, the stall was empty once again.

He wiped his forehead and was thankful for not getting stomped on. As he moved cautiously toward the stall door, the young woman hollered, "Whoever you are, get the hell out of my stall!"

Covered with loose hay and embarrassed about creating a disturbance, Matt yearned to rejoin the tram or simply go home. He'd spent the better part of an hour being chased before landing inside a pungent-smelling horse stall. Exhausted yet relieved, Matt was happy to oblige and exit the stall.

The young woman motioned for Matt to move away from the stall door while she maintained a tight hold on the energetic gray colt, preventing him from bolting forward. Once Matt was clear, she led the colt inside and closed the latches to safely secure him. She then turned to Matt with her arms crossed, head tipped to the side, and glared at him.

Matt approached with his hands outstretched. Before he'd taken five steps, he felt a hard pop explode across his jaw. He staggered back several feet from the force of the blow, his legs wobbly and head dizzy. He touched his mouth and felt blood oozing across his lips.

"You stupid son of a bitch!" the woman said. "You're lucky my colt didn't send you to the hospital!"

Unprepared for this confrontation, Matt could understand why this woman was upset by his unexpected intrusion. She moved to within inches of Matt's face, poked her finger hard into his chest, shoving him back, and asked, "Who are you and what are you doing in my barn?"

She was gorgeous, athletic, and seriously angry.

Matt pleaded, "I'm sorry. I'm sorry. Please, let me explain."

She took a single step back, allowing Matt a chance to wipe his chin and take a breath.

He continued, "Wow, that was one helluva punch!"

She took another step back and spoke in a more subdued tone, "I'm sorry I hit you." She paused and continued, "I was only reacting. At least I think I'm sorry."

She offered Matt a tissue and continued, "There was a loose horse running around the backstretch this morning, and . . ." She stopped, flipped her hair back, and said, "Wait a minute, why I am explaining myself to you? Who are you, and what are you doing here?"

"Matt Galiano, eternally grateful you saved me from your horse."

He extended his hand, and she obliged with a surprisingly firm handshake. Matt was captivated by her intense green eyes and shoulder-length blonde hair jutting out of her helmet.

"Kristine Connelly."

The woman grabbed another tissue, moved up to him, and pressed it firmly over his bloodstained chin. "Let me take a look at this." Matt managed a weak smile, and his pulse quickened. "I'm afraid you're starting to swell up. Guess I hit you harder than I realized. Sorry about that. I have ice inside my office." She pointed to her office a few stalls over.

He nodded and followed her to the office.

After collecting himself, Matt finally stammered out, "So . . . um . . . you work here?"

Kristine turned and smiled. "This is my barn, and these are my horses," she said, pointing at the stalls down the shed row.

Matt noticed three photos taken from the Winner's Circle tacked on the wall with names he did not recognize. Alongside the horse photos were pictures of what he guessed were friends or family members. The coatrack included a few sets of reins hung next to a partly broken chair and well-worn desk covered with scattered racing programs. A handwritten training schedule sat atop the papers with the names of twelve horses written on them.

She asked, "Would you like a bottle of water?"

Matt declined. She handed him a bag of ice, then removed her riding helmet, dropping her golden blonde ponytail to just below her shoulders.

Kristine sat down and leaned forward with her elbows on her knees. "Okay, Romeo, now fess up: Why are you here?"

With his stomach still fluttering, Matt relayed the events of his day, starting with his dad's birthday, breakfast at the track, the tram ride through the backstretch, and the excitement that followed. He talked about his personal interest in Heliacal Star and the reason he felt compelled to sneak off the tram.

Kristine appeared to listen intently. Matt explained, "Heliacal Star is my all-time favorite horse, and when the tram driver mentioned he was in the stall around the corner, I had this unexplainable urge to get a closer look at him." He shrugged. "I know, it was stupid."

"I know that horse, Heliacal Star. He's a nice horse. I was Ted Bouchard's assistant a couple of years ago when he first trained him. He went . . ."

"What?"

She took a shortened breath, looked away, and exhaled. "I was just thinking about the horse you mentioned being moved from a good guy like Ted Bouchard to a shit stain like Ron McGee. I also worked for McGee a long time ago. It was before I worked for Bouchard. Let's just say Ron McGee is a professional asshole."

Matt looked around the office, at nothing in particular, and then remembered. "Oh shit, it was Ron McGee he was talking to."

She asked, "Who was talking to McGee?"

Matt inched closer to Kristine, still feeling paranoid from his earlier experience. He spoke so softly that only she could possibly hear him, even though nobody was nearby. "McGee was talking with Larry Lonsdale, aka Louisville Larry."

Kristine stood up, hands on hips, and laughed out loud. "Louisville Larry? Seriously, are you for real, man?"

Jumping up, Matt shushed her and looked all around, as if expecting someone to be listening in the shadows. He placed his hands on her shoulders to encourage her to sit. Kristine obliged, shook her head, and said, "Listen, Matt, don't bullshit me."

Matt shushed her again, and spoke softly, "Please. I swear this isn't bullshit. It was Louisville. I know, 'cause I used to work with him a long time ago." Matt inched close enough to smell the scent of track soil mixed with her sweet perfume and whispered, "I overheard Louisville Larry instructing Ron McGee to throw an upcoming race involving Heliacal Star."

Without hesitation, Kristine responded, "McGee is a first-rate asshole, and I wouldn't put it past him. What exactly did you hear?"

The ice inside the bag had melted, and Matt noticed it was dripping. He stood up, cupped the bag in both hands, and looked for a safe spot to place it. "Can I just leave this outside the door?"

Kristine took the bag, dropped it outside, and returned with a gauze pad and bandage. She placed the gauze gently over his injury and pressed on the bandage firmly.

"That should hold it for a bit. I'm sorry again about . . ."

"Don't worry about it. You had good reason. I'm impressed by how hard you punch. Shit, if you had thrown another, I would've been down for the count."

She smiled wryly and said, "You know, I could have hit you harder, but I suppose I was in a charitable mood. That first punch was just to grab your attention."

Matt could not remove his eyes from her. "It worked. You definitely have my attention now."

"Okay, I want to hear more about your story." Sliding her

fingers through the curly bangs of her blonde hair, she sounded serious. "You overheard this Louisville goon talking to shithead McGee."

Matt said, "I was afraid that Louisville would catch me eavesdropping, so I panicked and took off. Next thing I know, he was chasing me. I finally lost him and looked for a safe place to hide. I thought your stalls were unused, and here I am."

Kristine stood up and paced a few times, then sat for a moment with her arms folded and said, "If this goon is such a threat to you, why didn't you just go to Security?"

Matt responded, "Louisville Larry works for the Kaufmans." He waited for a reaction, which did not come. "You know, the *Kaufmans*—as in the Kaufman crime family?"

She stood up. "Get out of town!"

Matt responded, "So now you know why I had no choice but to run."

He tapped the bandage on his chin, turned to her, and said, "I totally deserve this, and I'm sorry I surprised you this morning. I'll get out of your hair."

As Matt spoke, he secretly hoped she would ask him to stay. He extended his hand and said, "No hard feelings?"

Gripping his hand, she continued, "I'm no fan of Ron McGee. Perhaps there's something we should do about this. How about you and I meet later today? I'll clean myself up. We can meet by the paddock after the races and grab a bite to eat if that works for you."

Matt felt airy. "I'd love that."

CHAPTER 8

Returning to Belmont Park later that same day, Matt was confident Louisville Larry would be long gone, and he was anxious to see Kristine. Concerned she may have second thoughts given their awkward introduction, he arrived at the paddock thirty minutes early. A short time later, Matt spotted her after the last race of the day. She was wearing a short-sleeved, floral-patterned dress with a pair of pink studded cowboy boots.

Matt was entranced. "You look fantastic."

She stepped back a step and curtsied. They both chuckled.

She asked, "How does pizza sound? There's a good place just up the street."

Matt nodded. "Perfect!"

She looped her arm through his, smiled, and said, "I'll drive."

In the car, Matt asked, "So . . . do you have a boyfriend? Husband?"

She burst into a spontaneous laugh. "Ha! I'm up every morning at four thirty, work seven days a week, and usually smell like horseshit. Not exactly what most guys are looking for, even if I had the time."

Matt laughed along with her. "Maybe you just haven't found the right guy yet."

She responded, "So, what's your story? Are you saying you're the one for me?"

Matt enjoyed the banter. "Well, I do get up pretty early in the morning."

She winked. "We got off to a rocky start this morning, but maybe there's hope for you yet."

After ordering at the counter, they took their pizza to a table near the rear of the restaurant. After looking around and confirming the nearby tables were empty, Matt spoke in a hushed tone. "I have no doubt it was him. Louisville Larry."

"Was he seriously going to hurt you?" she asked.

Matt explained while Kristine ate, "Listen, his nickname is 'Louisville' because of his skilled usage of a baseball bat while delivering a hard message. He can be very persuasive and has a famously bad temper. People don't cross him."

Kristine placed her elbows on the table, leaned close to Matt, and whispered, "And you know this goon how?"

Matt pushed himself deep into his seat. "The less you know, the better. Louisville is a major asshole, but he's my problem, and you needn't get involved. I'll deal with him on my own."

"What makes you think I was trying to get involved in your business?"

Matt didn't want to blow their first date, if that was in fact what this was, but he struggled to find the right words. "I'm sorry, Kristine, but you don't know me."

She leaned forward. "You came to my barn, talking about this idiot who's in cahoots with Ron McGee and planning to illegally fix a horserace. You can't just leave it there, Matt. I understand you have issues with this thug, but I've got no love for McGee, either, and would love to see that asshole go down in flames!"

Matt thought about her comment for a moment. She was right; it felt awkward and improper to leave the topic of Louisville hanging out there, especially since he raised the topic in the first place. He wanted her to like him. "It had to be almost ten years ago when Louisville was convicted for assault with a deadly weapon. I assumed he was still in jail, that is, until I saw him talking to McGee today." While he hadn't considered or planned on divulging elements of his former profession, he saw an opening for another get-together. "How about I tell you more about Louisville when we have a bit more time, and then you can tell me why McGee is such a shithead. Deal?"

She cracked a subtle smile and nodded. "Deal."

CHAPTER 9

Several hours prior to the race featuring Heliacal Star, an unassuming Ford Taurus sat camouflaged among the other vehicles in the local Starbucks lot. FBI Special Agent Carlos Anjero glanced at his watch for the fourth time in the past ten minutes. He reached for and fumbled his cell phone before catching it to swipe for new messages. Nothing. He increased the volume on his ringer to max.

Across the parking lot and inside the bustling coffee shop, there was an eclectic group that included a yoga mom and her kids, a middle-aged man in a tailored suit and tie, a bearded hipster tapping on a keyboard, an elderly couple talking, and an overweight middle-aged man showing an obvious interest in the yoga mom. Anjero closed his eyes, tapped his fingers, and counted down from 60 to 59, 58 . . . to . . . 25, 24, 23 until a tap on the window interrupted him.

Anjero stopped counting to roll down his window. "Where have you been the last thirty minutes? I was down to my last twenty seconds."

The man jumped into the passenger seat, turned to Anjero, and said, "Are you going to be a prick to me today? Cut me some fucking slack. I had to take care of some shit back at the track. I also need to bring you up to speed on some new developments."

Anjero replied, "Do I really care, Larry?"

Louisville Larry pointed his index finger at the special agent and said, "Listen, you want to nail Kaufman, right?" Anjero nodded and Larry continued, "When I was at the track a couple of mornings ago, you know, talking race strategy with my trainer McGee, I caught this idiot listening to our conversation. At least I think he was listening. As soon as I realized this, I took off after him and was about to catch him when some crazy fucking horse charged at me out of nowhere and knocked me over."

Larry leaned toward the special agent with a slight grin. "That crazy horse knocked the wind out of me. My head felt dizzy, but I managed to catch my breath. I looked around and saw a handful of grooms standing over me. One of them helped me up, but my legs went wobbly and I lost any chance of catching that asshole. My body still fucking hurts from that idiot horse."

Anjero's face turned red. "I don't need to remind you, it's best for both of us that you remain out of trouble. I took a huge career gamble getting you released early from jail, and I can't keep bailing you out whenever you lose your temper. We had an appointment, and you owe me. Frankly, I'm running out of patience with you."

Larry lost his smirk.

Anjero continued, "You've already wasted half my day, and I've got nothing to show for it except a story about you screwing around on the track, playing with horses. What's going on, Larry? You can't play it both ways. Are you going to give me something I can actually use, or do I send your ass back to jail?"

Anjero shook his head and said, "If that was a few days ago, you still look like a mess. I guess that horse really busted you up pretty good! Maybe you'll think twice next time, but I doubt you will."

Larry waved his right arm. "Listen to me. Tony Kaufman has a thing for racehorses and loves to gamble, but only when the odds are stacked in his favor. He's the one who set me up with this scummy trainer, Ron McGee."

Anjero offered a subtle nod and eyeballed the parking lot as Larry continued. "This may sound silly, but listen to me. Tony also loves to mess with people's heads. So, get this: he tells me to ensure McGee loses a couple races with this horse to make it seem like the horse is no good. Our plan is for this horse to run badly in subsequent races by purposely holding him back."

Anjero squinted from the sudden glare of sun, which appeared through the car window. "Where are you going with this story, Larry? I'm not a horseplayer or racetrack guy."

Larry explained, "Every time the horse loses, his odds go up for the next race. Let's say he starts out with odds of 3–1 the first time he races, but he runs poorly. The next time he races, his odds will go up to 8–1. After a few more poor races, his odds will start reaching 20 or 30–1. When his odds become this overinflated, we'll let him run his best, and Tony Kaufman cashes out with a bundle. You see, Kaufman owns the guy who trains this horse because he owes Tony, meaning he's got no choice but to follow my instructions as Tony's representative. Tony may even give out the horse to a few of his associates as a favor."

Anjero asked, "What do you mean, 'give out the horse'?"

Larry answered, "He'll share his insider knowledge as a

tip from the barn. It gives him more credibility, and he figures whomever he tells will owe him a favor in the future."

Anjero lowered his head and rubbed his temples. Larry asked, "What do you think?" There was a long silence until Anjero finally sat up, turned toward Larry, and slapped the steering wheel.

"Okay, Larry. This may work. They got Capone on tax evasion, and race fixing comes under federal jurisdiction. I'm going to need more than circumstantial evidence to make this work. I want to put a wire on you and get Tony Kaufman on record talking about this fix."

Larry turned ashen and raised his arms above his head.

"What's the matter, Larry? I need concrete evidence. Right now, your word equates to shit."

Larry leaned in. "I didn't finish. It's important. This idiot who heard me talking with McGee may have overheard our plan. I don't know for sure, but he was close enough to make me paranoid, and Tony called off the plan."

Anjero's face reddened again as a vein popped out on his forehead. "What kind of shit show is this, Larry? I thought you had something I could use. You best produce something, or I'm going to cut you loose, and you can kiss your privileges good-bye!"

Larry lowered his arm around the special agent and whispered, "Listen, something big is going down, and I swear I'll get you something you can use. You've got my word."

Pushing Larry's arm off, Anjero said, "Okay, Larry, I'm listening, but I'm also running super low on patience right now."

Placing his hand on the door handle, Larry said, "When I told Kaufman about this guy overhearing our plan, he told me to flip the script, and I instructed McGee to ensure the horse—Heliacal Star—wins today instead of losing. This is a better plan anyway."

Anjero grabbed hold of Larry's arm and leaned to within inches of his face. "Where exactly are you going with this?"

Larry smirked. "Don't you get it, man?"

The vein on Anjero's forehead pulsated. "No! Please explain it to me!"

Larry continued, "Tony should have ripped my head off for messing up his original plan. Instead, he acts nonchalant, like no big deal. This means something else, much bigger, is about to go down. I've been around Tony long enough to know when something big is about to happen. I don't know what it is, but it will be big."

Anjero sat back, looked away from Larry and across the lot. He said, "Okay, Larry. Give me some details. I need dates, players, what, and how! And you're going to wear a wire. I'm not fucking around with you anymore. I need to see real proof."

Larry nodded. "First, I need this horse to win his next race. Once he wins and Tony cashes out, then I'll get closer to him."

Anjero shrugged. "I'll be watching. You best not fuck this up."

CHAPTER 10

After the eighth race, Louisville Larry greets McGee inside the Winner's Circle with a giant bear hug as Heliacal Star is escorted by his groom, with his jockey proudly beaming atop. The winning photo is taken, and Larry walks beside Ron McGee as they exit the Winner's Circle.

Larry whispers, "Are we okay? I mean, the race is official, right? So, we're clear?"

McGee places a finger on his lips. "Relax. We're fine." McGee brings Larry to a quiet area. "They have to collect a urine sample, but I guarantee they won't find anything. I've been super careful."

McGee lowers his head, avoiding eye contact, and says, "Listen, Larry, we need to talk about this horse. I'm glad we pushed for the win today because I can't keep him together much longer. He's already showing a little soreness, and it's just a matter of time before . . . " He stops, looks around, and says, "Can you ask your boss about jamming him in the next race? You know, run him for a tag in a cheap claiming race, and then he'll become someone else's problem."

Like many horsemen when starting out, Ron McGee began his career operating cautiously and earned a reputation of running his training program with integrity. The discipline and consistency he preached in his barn led to early success and winning percentages above 20 percent, an impressive stat for any up-and-coming trainer.

While successful on the track, it was well known, especially to those on the backstretch, that his life off the track was disintegrating. His conspicuous drinking binges and public gambling displays were telltale signs of a troubled individual. As his marriage dissolved, his drinking and gambling worsened and became obvious even to the casual observer. His bank savings fell victim to perpetual gambling, and after a lack of good fortune, he called upon the Kaufmans to cover his losses. To repay his debt, he discovered creative and subtle ways to alter the outcome of races, without regard for racing rules or the health of the horses. Larry Lonsdale became a conduit between McGee and Kaufman and reminded him that working for the Kaufmans allowed for zero input about the choices being made. If the boss needed to win or lose, McGee was relegated to the role of obedient servant. Larry ensured that McGee understood playing fast and loose with the rule book was not his or Tony's concern. All that mattered was earning money, no matter how it was accomplished. As their relationship evolved, Ron McGee impressed Larry with his understanding that it was far better to upset the racing commissioner than Tony Kaufman.

Larry taps McGee across his back. "You did well today. Tony will be pleased. About that next one, I'll pass along your request, and we'll be in touch."

CHAPTER 11

After watching Kristine exit the racing office, the official sighs at his desk, rubs his temples, and phones his old acquaintance. After several rings, the voice on the other line answers, "McGee here."

The pair first worked together back in the late seventies when both were assistant trainers for the same head trainer, and before McGee ventured out to manage his own stable. McGee has since experienced a successful career training horses, whereas his contemporary struggled with a winning percentage south of 5 percent. Struggling to sustain a living wage, the racing official made the transition to bureaucrat and was eventually promoted to his current role overseeing the track's racing operation.

During their brief conversation, the racing official relays his knowledge of the complaint lodged by Kristine Connelly against McGee and sternly warns him to keep his barn and nose clean. After assuring McGee about the lack of evidence supporting this serious accusation, the official alerts the trainer to watch his back, especially around Kristine Connelly or anyone associated with her.

Outside the racing office, meanwhile, Kristine turns to Matt, who chased her down after she slammed the door. "What in the world just happened? That horse was supposed to lose! Why on earth did he win?"

In an attempt to lighten the mood, Matts says, "I feel like a real jackass. Perhaps you have an empty stall where I can hide out for a while?"

Kristine is expressionless and Matt continues, "I'd prefer a stall without a live horse, you know, for the safety of both of us. I'll also take a heater, hot water, fridge, and of course, internet access."

Kristine smirks, taps him on lightly on his arm, and says, "You idiot!"

Relieved at breaking the tension, Matt is equally baffled by the result of the race. He was so certain Louisville Larry and Ron McGee were up to something, yet Heliacal Star won, and he did so convincingly. He wonders how and why he could have missed the mark on the race.

Turning to Matt, Kristine says, "You overheard them discussing some sort of plan to fix the race, but then why didn't it happen? Instead of losing the race, McGee's horse won by ten lengths, and now I look like a frigging excitable moron!"

Kristine lowers her head, kicks some dirt ahead of her, and starts to walk away.

Matt calls out, "Hey, Kristine. Wait!"

She stops and turns around.

"I *was* telling you the truth. I know what I heard."

"Then why didn't he lose, like you said he would? You told me the fix was in!"

Matt considers the possibility that McGee and Larry were

discussing a different horse, a different race, or maybe it was a different racetrack altogether.

"I wish I knew the answer, but I don't."

"I want to believe you, but . . ."

Not wanting to see her walk away again, Matt interjects, "I should have been the one in the racing office today, not you. When they loaded those horses into the starting gate, I felt an overwhelming sense of guilt and dashed down here to tell them myself. I had no idea you were going to be there."

As Kristine listens, Matt tries to come up with a plausible explanation. He knows the Kaufmans and how they never leave anything to chance. If Heliacal Star won the race, it must have been part of the plan. "The only explanation would be if they turned the plan around. Instead of throwing the race to lose, they had to have fixed it to win." He continues down his logic trail. "Because someone, namely me, overheard them talking about the fix. That must be it!"

Kristine is quiet and stares at Matt with her fingers pressed against her forehead. "Meet me at the barn in an hour." She hands him a temporary security badge for barn access. "You remember how to get there, right?"

Excited about the prospect of spending more time one-on-one with Kristine, Matt doesn't register that the man walking toward them from the main track is Ron McGee until he's upon them. "Stay out of my business, bitch!"

McGee puffs out his chest, jabs his finger into Kristine's left shoulder, and says, "You have no fucking idea what you're doing and who you're messing with. You're so far out of your goddamn league. Do yourself a favor and stay clear of me and my business!"

Kristine presses her right forearm across McGee's chest, pushing him back a step. She moves forward as he moves back. "I know what you did, motherfucker!" She shoves him, causing the larger man to stagger for a moment.

Regaining his balance, McGee reaches for Kristine's arm, but she slides out of the way, clenches her fist, and crouches into a defensive posture. McGee rolls up his sleeves, bends his arms, and positions both hands into a fighter's pose. "I dare you, bitch! I just need a reason to beat your ass right here, right now!" He brushes his arms and says, "Take your best shot!"

Any concerns Matt may have had about Kristine's ability to handle herself instantly evaporate. In this moment, he becomes more concerned about McGee's health should circumstances manifest into a physical conflict. Matt steps behind Kristine, wraps his arms around her torso, and pulls her away from McGee. As McGee unclenches his fists and drops his arms, Matt releases his hold of Kristine. He jumps in front of Kristine and turns his back toward McGee. "You made your point, Kristine. He's not worth it. Let it go."

McGee places both hands on his hips and says, "Hey, Connelly, who's your snitch?"

Matt refuses to turn around and confront McGee but keeps his attention on Kristine to ensure she doesn't take the bait and respond to his taunt.

Kristine charges at McGee but cannot get past Matt blocking her path. Flailing her arms around Matt, she yells out, "You suck, McGee!"

McGee stops, turns around, and says, "You should know, Connelly. You should know."

CHAPTER 12

After the last race of the day, the crowds have dispersed, and the stable area is quiet. All the horses are fed and have settled into their stalls for the night. The jockeys and stewards have retired for the evening, and a single groom remains to rake the grounds ahead of tomorrow's early morning activities.

At the eastern corner of the shed row, Kristine is inside her office, busily writing notes on a large notepad, as Matt taps and pushes open the door.

"Do you need more time?"

Without turning, Kristine says, "Hey, Matt. Just a sec. I'm finalizing the schedule for tomorrow. You want to look?"

Remembering Kristine's fiery mood during her argument with Ron McGee only an hour earlier, he opts to leave the subject alone for now and keep the mood light.

He glances at his watch. "Sure, why not?"

Matt stands behind Kristine's chair and looks over her shoulder at an oversize 12x18-inch pad as she makes handwritten notations. The leftmost column lists the name of each racehorse and their stall number, and the rows reflect days of the week, starting from the beginning of this week through end of next week. Each box is filled with a letter—*W*, *J*, and *G*—or a fraction, such as ½, ⅜, and ⅝.

Pointing to the chart, Kristine says, "This is my master plan for daily training. Every day, each horse needs some level of activity and intensity. The last thing I do before wrapping up is to update the plan for tomorrow. It changes daily based on how they perform each day. For example, tomorrow's plan is based on how well each horse worked today."

Matt nods. "I see. What do the letters mean?"

"*W* stands for walking, *J* for jog, and *G* means gallop. When I write out a fraction, it means I've scheduled the horse for a breeze, which is a timed workout. A half means he'll breeze a half mile, and 3/8 means he'll breeze three eighths of a mile. If the horse is sound, gaining, or staying fit, and has no aliments, I prefer to breeze them every seven or eight days, specifically when they're readying to race, such as a first start or coming off a layoff. The breezes build up their fitness and prepare them to race. If they're already racing, I may breeze them two to three weeks after a race or just gallop them. It really depends on the horse."

Although Matt has spent much of his life as a racing fan and handicapper, he'd never been inside a race trainer's office. Her simple, yet methodical, technique combined with a disciplined approach to training racehorses and overall diligence impresses him.

She lays down her pencil and proclaims, "I'm done. Do you want to grab a bite to eat?"

The casual Italian restaurant they decide on is crowded, but they're seated immediately. As they're escorted to the table by the hostess, Matt smirks. Sinatra's "Strangers in the Night" plays in the background. He sings aloud, barely audible, "Doobie doobie doo," and smiles at Kristine.

Since their brief yet spirited encounter with Ron McGee earlier in the day, Matt has showered, shaved, and dressed in comfortable black chinos and his favorite breezy, short-sleeved cotton camp shirt.

"You look nice, Matt," Kristine says, then assesses herself. "Me, on the other hand, I look a mess."

Matt hadn't given her attire a second thought. She looks great. As he looks across the table, he absorbs her natural beauty and is drawn in by her infectious charm, amplifying her overall attractiveness. He wonders to himself if she's really uninvolved, believing she must get constant solicitations, especially as a public persona.

As if channeling Matt's thoughts, Kristine continues, "This may sound sad, but my social life beyond the backstretch is mainly reserved for events involving old dudes who own racehorses. This includes a bunch shameless pigs who assume they're entitled to a piece of ass simply because they send me a horse to train."

"That doesn't sound like too much fun."

Kristine chuckles. "I can handle myself. But enough about me. What's your story?"

Matt loses the smile. "Right! I first started coming to Belmont Park with my dad as a kid. He and I were really close. One night, he went out and never came home. He was in business with some bad guys, and his lifestyle caught up with him."

"Wow." Kristine reaches across the table and lightly caresses Matt's hands. Her hands are soft, and her gesture is reassuring, easing his sense of vulnerability.

"Suffice it to say, I was a mess afterward, but I had a talent for handicapping horses, and betting on sports, so I became a sort of bookie for . . . " Matt drifts off and looks around the restaurant. "I worked for Kaufman, as a bookmaker."

He waits again for her reaction, concerned she may disapprove. Instead, Kristine squeezes his hand, encouraging him to continue.

"I was the front guy taking bets and managing the books while Louisville was the muscle and handled collections. Louisville excelled at his job. He was terrifying, even back then, but I maintained my distance and stayed in my swim lane."

Kristine listens intently.

"I must have been bored, numb, or just plain stupid at the time. The longer I worked for the outfit, the harder it became to discern right from wrong. I finally grew tired of dealing with Kaufman and decided to leave. I began by creating a fake persona, whom I officially added to Kaufman's books. Then I placed a few wagers under the fake name. Winning and losing. Made it seem legit, I thought."

Matt takes a moment to reflect on his admission, one he's never told anyone, as Kristine sits tall in her seat with her eyes laser focused on him.

"I bet on college football games. Modest wagers. The charade continued throughout the entire season."

Kristine coughs and interrupts, "If you were placing bets for this phony alias, what would have happened if he—I mean you—lost too much? Would you have been able to pay? It seems like a risky plan."

Matt shakes his head. "It was zero risk because I managed the books. In reality, I didn't place the bets until after the games were played, then I time-stamped them to indicate the wagers were made earlier. Thus, I picked and chose when to win or lose, but there was no actual gambling on my part."

Their food arrives, and after the waitress leaves, Matt continues, "The final week of college football season, I played a ten-team parley bet. This means all ten teams must cover the point spread, or the bet is lost. It's generally considered a sucker bet, as more knowledgeable gamblers understand the odds of cashing such a ticket are astronomically small, and this is reflected by the 500–1 payout if someone holds a winning ticket."

Kristine interrupts, "You didn't . . ."

Matt smiles. "Oh yeah, I did! I placed a fifty-dollar ten-team parley bet. You can do the math. The payout was twenty-five thousand dollars!"

Kristine drops her fork. "Oh shit, Matt, no!"

"Needless to say, the sizeable payout caught Kaufman's attention. In the world of illegal gambling, one doesn't survive by getting a reputation for welching, but the bosses wanted to meet this persona of mine in person to quote unquote 'congratulate him.'"

"So, what happened?"

"I convinced them to meet me at a crowded pub where I would introduce them to my friend. They agreed. I thought I fooled them, but I was very wrong.

"When I arrived at the pub, they wanted to meet the guy who'd placed the bet. I told them he was only comfortable interacting with me. They seemed to buy it. I showed them the winning ticket, and they handed me a sealed manila envelope with the cash inside. I grabbed the envelope, promised to deliver it immediately, and was anxious to get out of there once I had the cash. My plan was to use the money to relocate and get a fresh start elsewhere. They insisted on buying me a drink before I left the pub, but once I was finally alone inside my car, I ripped open the envelope. Inside it were hundreds of blank sheets of paper!"

She asks, "What? How did they know?"

He shrugs. "I sat there completely dumbfounded, just staring at the paper. I needed to get out of there. Louisville Larry came running outside with baseball bat in hand. He reached through my car window and muscled me out."

Kristine winces and Matt takes a sip of his drink.

"I remember this incredible jolt of pain shooting up my legs. My body went numb and my head turned foggy, but I could still hear Tony Kaufman yelling at Larry to finish the job." Matt curls his lips and creases his left eye while recalling Tony's voice from that moment.

"After that, I blacked out. Next thing I remember, I'm lying in a hospital bed. I wasn't sure if I was dead or alive when I woke."

Kristine's lips are tightly pressed, creasing the corners of her mouth. She says, "You're lucky they didn't kill you."

Matt says, "Super lucky. I was told the bartender immediately called the cops once he noticed what was going down in the parking lot. Before the police arrived, apparently Kaufman, Louisville, and the others took off, leaving me alone in a pool of my own blood."

Kristine slams her hand on the table. "Holy shit, Matt. I totally understand why you ran off when you saw Louisville the other morning. Did you tell the cops about what happened and press charges against Louisville or Kaufman?"

A wave of paranoia surfaces for the first time since he began talking. "Are you friggin' kidding? No way. I told them I had no idea who might have assaulted me. There were no fingerprints, evidence, or cooperating witnesses. Not even the bartender who dialed 911 would talk. Of course, the police knew it was Kaufman, but had I squealed, I never would have made the witness stand at a trial. It was colossally stupid of me to steal their money, but I was smart enough to pretend the attack on me never happened."

As they finish up dinner, Kristine says, "Hey, Matt, I almost forgot to thank you."

Matt is puzzled.

She continues, "I'm so glad you stopped me from completely losing my shit earlier today." The corner of her mouth quirks up. "As you might have guessed, I have a bit of a short fuse, especially with certain people."

Matt laughs at the comment. "Yeah, I suppose so. I'm sorry for mixing you up in this race-fixing bullshit and riling you up with McGee. You shouldn't get pulled into my mess."

"You listen to me, Mr. Galiano. I'm glad you got me involved. Believe it or not, you're not the only one with a score to settle!"

Delighted by her sassy response, Matt throws up his arms. "Whoa there, cowgirl! It's a deal. No more apologies."

Kristine peeks around the restaurant, leans over the table, and whispers, "I can only wonder what McGee did to that horse to bolster his performance today. I'm positive he did something, especially considering how easily Heliacal Star won. I know that SOB well enough to know he bends the rules."

Matt asks, "Don't they thoroughly test these horses nowadays?"

Chuckling at his question, Kristine leans halfway across the table. "Horse racing is highly regulated and loaded with post-race testing. The racing industry has seriously invested in protecting our racehorses over the past several years, but there remain a few gaps in the system. For example, they can only test for known medications, like clenbuterol—trainers use it to aid breathing and enhance muscle growth. One problem is some hormones are produced naturally in horses, like erythropoietin, which you may have heard of as EPO."

Matt asks, "EPO? Like an anabolic steroid?"

"Yep, it's a type of performance enhancer, very similar to the more recognized anabolic steroid used by athletes, like ballplayers. One difference, though, is that a horse will produce EPO naturally, and there is no effective way to discern if the hormone was injected artificially or produced by the horse . . . but that's not everything."

Matt nods, intrigued by her candid admission given the cloak of silence that typifies most public comments on the subject, given his lifetime of watching and wagering on horse races.

Matt asks, "So, let me understand. You think McGee gave Heliacal Star an EPO-inducing hormone that helped him win today?"

She nods. "I'm sure he did something. I wouldn't be surprised if he slipped him some sort of milkshake before the race!"

As both a racing fan and gambler, Matt is genuinely surprised to hear the controversial term aloud and is keenly interested to learn more. "I'm aware that some trainers have been accused of juicing the horses in the past, but I don't recall anyone ever being expelled or severely penalized for such accusations. Seems like it would be easy to get caught and just isn't worth the risk."

Kristine responds, "Let me explain. The concept itself is pretty basic. If you want to max out his performance, you funnel a combination of baking soda and water—this is the milkshake—directly into the horse's mouth before a race. This will boost his stamina and lactic intake. Traces of the milkshake will usually sweat away, in theory, by the time he arrives at the test barn after a race. To prove it, you pretty much need to witness them administer the concoction versus testing for it afterward."

"So I guess the officials aren't able to catch anyone, if they are doing this."

Kristine glances toward the ceiling and shifts in her chair. "Ya know, even when they do, the penalties are not overly punitive. Sometimes, they'll serve a brief suspension, pay a fine, or forfeit some purse money. Honestly, it's not enough as far as I'm concerned!"

"If the milkshake is so easy to administer and generally undetectable, then why doesn't everyone do it?"

Kristine's expression hardens. "Quite frankly, most of us on the backstretch deeply care for our horses. We are hardworking, honest people. So many of us grew up with horses and pay special attention to their welfare and safety. We need to preserve and protect our reputation and uphold the integrity of the sport. We also watch out for each other. But like any big business or large corporation, you're always going to find a few assholes, and ours is named Ron McGee."

Matt looks away to avoid eye contact. "Have you ever been tempted . . ."

Before he finishes his question, Kristine's pupils flare. "Real horsemen and women do not cheat."

Matt gulps and says, "I didn't mean to—"

She interrupts. "Sorry. It's a sensitive subject with me because I've run into so many people who believe a young female trainer is incapable of being a good horseperson. I'm glad there are more trainers like Ted Bouchard, who genuinely care about horses and understand the subtleties of training, and fewer shits like Ron McGee, who seem to care less about the horses. McGee carries a reputation for running 'em into the ground, and propping 'em up until they can barely walk. When the horse finally has nothing left to give, he'll get rid of him one way or another."

"If you know McGee is cheating, why don't the racing authorities just send out inspectors to check out his or other suspicious barns? What am I missing here?"

Kristine snorts. "Have you ever seen a horse suddenly improve by ten lengths after switching to a new trainer?"

Before giving Matt a chance to answer, she continues, "Of course you have, but unless the new trainer is some sort of genius, or the previous trainer was completely incompetent, this normally doesn't happen."

Matt considers her comment and nods in agreement. He says, "Based on my handicapping experience, I'd say there are a handful of trainers who seem to miraculously improve a horse's performance after acquiring them."

She swallows her breath and continues, "Don't get me wrong. I'm not saying it's *always* meds. Many trainers are simply excellent at their trade. It's certainly possible a new trainer could improve a horse if they discover something previously untried. For example, moving them from grass to dirt or vice versa, or from route to sprint. Other trainers may immediately drop a horse into a less competitive race. You following me, Matt?"

He nods.

She continues, "There are still loopholes that can be exploited by dishonest individuals. As for the inspections, you may see the authorities occasionally sweep the barns, but I don't think it's very random. It seems those we suspect the most possess an innate clairvoyance for predicting inspections and manage to avoid embarrassing discoveries. Personally, I'd prefer to see security cameras placed around the barn area."

Matt asks, "Suppose you have direct evidence McGee is cheating, why don't you just turn him in?"

Kristine's eyes widen and her mouth falls open. "Really, Matt? Did you not see what happened at the fucking racing office today?"

Matt shrugs and feels stupid for asking his question as he recalls the abject lack of respect the racing official showed her earlier today. "Good point."

"Truth be told, Matt, I should have handled myself a lot better today. I'm still new and trying to establish my business. If I'm going to be successful in this business, I need to act with more grace and endear myself to owners who may be willing to send me some horses to train. I don't suppose you'd be interested in claiming a horse for me to train?"

Matt is taken off guard by the question and suddenly envisions himself in the Winner's Circle at Belmont Park, receiving a silver trophy as the prestigious winning owner of a stakes race. He looks skyward and ponders, for perhaps the first time in his life, the possibility of owning a racehorse. He repeats her question in his head while contemplating the possibility.

Kristine taps the table. "Hey there. You still with me?"

Matt snaps out of his daydream, wanting to say yes to her question, but instead only offers a blank stare.

Kristine continues, "In all seriousness, I need to focus my energy on winning races and enticing wealthy owners instead of worrying so much about McGee and his antics."

Matt knows he doesn't fit the profile of a wealthy owner, nevertheless he remains intrigued by her question about owning a racehorse. He presumes such an investment would be well beyond his means but decides there's no harm in asking.

Matt says, "Let's pretend I'm a potential client." He clears his throat and lowers his voice, as if imitating a sophisticated aristocrat. "How much would such a racehorse cost me, kind lady?"

Kristine laughs aloud at his imitation. "Any racehorse on the grounds is going to run you about four thousand a month while he's in training. At Belmont, you can claim a racehorse for between ten and a hundred thousand dollars. However, New York is one of the pricier circuits. A lot of people actually get started in ownership through a syndication or partnership as it is more affordable than owning outright. You know this, I'm sure, as well as I do, but regardless of where you race, this is not a sport for the financially insolvent, penny-pincher, or quick-return investor."

Matt's imagination is running wild, even as he silently acknowledges he is incapable of such a large financial commitment.

Kristine's eyes flutter as she squeezes Matt's hand tightly. "I'm glad you were there today. You prevented me from doing something colossally stupid. If you weren't there, I'm not sure what would have happened."

Matt is touched and appreciative of her sincerity.

"Several years ago, when I was McGee's assistant trainer, I was cleaning up the tack room when I came across a small, unmarked bottle. I showed it to McGee, and he ripped it out of my hand, telling me it was none of my concern. I couldn't prove it, but I suspect it was some type of a potent nerve block. At that time, I heard a few rumors that he occasionally used frog juice."

Matt laughs. "Frog water? That's a real thing?"

"Frog juice, not frog water, and it's very much a thing. Frog juice is a powerful painkiller. It's more potent than morphine. In hindsight, I should have reported him to the authorities. I'm still mad at myself for being too passive at the time."

Matt thinks back to his days as a bookmaker when he worked for the Kaufmans. He was aware that certain trainers or barns would push the limits but never considered such a powerfully illegal painkiller, like frog juice, would be among their tactics.

Kristine continues, "Keep in mind, this was many years ago, and I never saw the vial again. I seriously doubt anyone could get away with using frog juice or cobra venom anymore."

Unsure he heard her correctly, Matt jumps in. "Did you just say cobra venom?"

"Yep, it's another powerful painkiller. I've never personally seen it and it's more likely a relic of the past, before the current regulations and well before my time in this business."

Matt can only shake his head at the thought of someone

using cobra venom to block pain or enhance performance and wonders if it seems stupid, bold, or a little of both.

Kristine says, "I know it's getting late, but I wanted to ask something before I forget. How come Louisville Larry and those guys haven't killed you yet?"

Matt says, "I honestly thought Louisville was still in jail. As for Tony, I'm small potatoes to him. Once Louisville left me for dead, I doubt he gave me another thought. Nevertheless, I've kept my distance from Kaufman and his cohorts. I know where he operates, and I've avoided those areas. Just seeing Louisville the other morning took me by surprise and genuinely scared the shit out of me. What a weird and shitty coincidence to run into him. I have no idea when or how he was released from prison."

Kristine stands. "Matt, tonight was great. Thanks again for everything, but my day starts before dawn. I've got to run."

Matt remains at the table after paying for dinner and harkens back to the altercation outside the racing office. He wonders if McGee was right. Kristine Connelly may be getting in over her head.

CHAPTER 13

After purchasing Heliacal Star at auction in September 2014, Alex Sherman moved the newly named horse to a renowned training farm known for preparing yearling racehorses in Ocala, Florida. During this important development period, the horse learns the basic skills of being a racehorse. His training will include being saddled, lunged, ridden, and galloped under saddle. Humane training practices, aptly labeled "gentling," have all but replaced the old-school ways of breaking the will of a horse in order to gain his cooperation. As a young colt, Heliacal Star excelled throughout his early training program.

Ocala is an inviting equine destination, specifically during the winter months. Hundreds of developing thoroughbreds are vanned to Florida from sales grounds in Kentucky, New York, Maryland, and Pennsylvania. During these early days of training, horses are segregated into different tiers that adapt to their individual skills and future racing potential.

Prior to any thoroughbred's career debut, hope springs eternal regarding racing potential. Heliacal Star was grouped with several other promising racehorses and placed in the highest tier by the farm manager, given his efficiency, stride, and attitude.

After arriving in Florida during the early autumn months, and following several months of training and routine, it was time for Heliacal Star to graduate from Ocala and begin his racing career in New York, one of the toughest racing regions in North America.

It was April 2015 when Heliacal Star first arrived at his new home on the backstretch of Belmont Park as one of two thousand racehorses stabled on the grounds. The high-priced yearling from 2014 was now a two-year-old as both Alex Sherman and Ted Bouchard were present to greet the new arrival on an overcast spring morning. As he exited the trailer, Heliacal Star strutted off the ramp, showing no indication of typical equine stress following the long journey northward. As he sauntered away from Sherman and Bouchard, he swished his tail and swung his hips, showing a glimpse of his athleticism and grace.

At fifty-nine years of age, the balding and overweight Alex Sherman appears as a polished-looking middle-aged man, conveying the image of one in possession of an oversize bankbook. On the morning of Heliacal Star's arrival, Sherman stood out from the backstretch workers in his custom-tailored pinstripe suit, silk paisley tie, and designer wingtip derby shoes. Heliacal Star represented a new and unique opportunity for Sherman to enter the ring of racing elites and compete with the best of the best for the most prestigious prizes on the ultracompetitive New York Racing Association circuit. It is one of a handful of racing venues where young horses will race to earn a spot at the next Kentucky Derby.

As the most recognized horse race in the world, winning the Kentucky Derby is considered the pinnacle of achievement for any racehorse trainer or owner. Legendary stories of horses purchased for a few thousand dollars, such as Seattle Slew, have inspired participants at all levels to play the racing lottery. The occasional David versus Goliath story emerges when a modestly priced horse bests those purchased for millions and perpetuates such dreams, no matter how improbable. Alex Sherman had never brought a horse to the Kentucky Derby as an owner, and Ted Bouchard had trained a Kentucky Derby entrant only once throughout his long career. Although unraced, Heliacal Star had already shown enough potential to offer them optimism, with enough class and quality to potentially earn his ticket to the Kentucky Derby and give them both the thrill of a lifetime.

As Heliacal Star was led to his stall, Bouchard nudged Sherman. "He looks the part. No promises, but I'd like to have him ready for a debut at Saratoga by July."

Sherman smiled broadly. "I can't wait, Ted! You be good to my boy, and we'll make history together!"

Sherman had been patently successful as an investment banker, yet struggled to show much success as a thoroughbred owner. Although his accumulated wealth afforded him the opportunity to own racehorses, the dream of earning a start in the Kentucky Derby on that first Saturday in May had thus far eluded him.

In his younger days, Sherman spent many teenage afternoons gambling on the races at Belmont and the Aqueduct but was never mistaken for an astute handicapper among his gambling cohorts. While friends buried their heads inside their racing forms, he instead placed lazy bets. Such wagers were mostly based on horse names, the color of jockey silks, short betting odds, or from harassing his handicapping-literate friends for tips on their researched selections. Like many who attend the races, he often departed with less money in his pocket than when he arrived.

Alex Sherman and his wife first met at college in Washington, DC. After graduation, they were married in a small ceremony on Long Island and began their life together. For much of their marriage, they've presented themselves as a personable, outgoing, and outwardly friendly couple, although Alex has shown bouts of aloofness and prudishness, especially since earning his significant wealth. Life turned sour for the Shermans a few years ago after the tragic and sudden loss of their daughter in a suspected homicide. Following this tragedy, Alex Sherman withdrew from social interactions and distanced himself from anyone attempting to console him or reach out. While keeping to himself outside his job, he rediscovered horse racing after months of watching simulcast racing on cable television as a way of passing the time.

For experienced trainer Ted Bouchard, Heliacal Star provided a renewed opportunity for racing glory and a chance to establish his legacy in the annals of racing history. It had been more than ten years since Bouchard's one and only entry in the Kentucky Derby. In recent years, his name has been overlooked by owners and racing correspondents in favor of a few upstart trainers.

A thoroughbred racehorse trainer of more than twenty-five years, Bouchard has experienced his share of thrills, from triumph and glory to gut-wrenching defeat. During that one and only Kentucky Derby, Bouchard's horse took a short lead at the top of the stretch and had the look of a winner, only to get passed in the final furlong by three fast-closing rivals, ultimately finishing fourth. On the final chart for the race, his horse lost by just a length.

Throughout his career, Bouchard has been known for running a disciplined barn and is a well-respected trainer among seasoned horsemen. The racing media, which exhibits a harsh bias against trainers unable to win at a consistent level, has been solicitous of him over the years. A quiet man, Bouchard is both intense and serious while training horses. He can point out subtle cues in the horse's stride that many others cannot discern during a breeze or workout. In spite of his younger peers gaining more success, Bouchard has remained true to his character and continues to compete without reliance on medications or gray-area training tactics.

As the young Heliacal Star settled into the barn early that April morning, Alex Sherman fed the horse a carrot, after which he and Bouchard got right to work mapping out a training plan.

CHAPTER 14

It was a warm summer afternoon on the first day of July in 2015 at the racetrack under scattered cumulous clouds amid a light breeze. Inside the paddock, Alex Sherman was dressed for the occasion in his tailored pinstriped suit, silk tie, and wingtips as he paced in a tight circle waiting for Heliacal Star to arrive. Of the twelve horses entered, Heliacal Star drew the fifth post position and was saddled in a green cloth on this day.

As each horse entered the paddock for the second race of the day, Sherman stopped pacing and located a position close enough to the saddling stall with a proximate view of his horse being prepped for his career debut. For owners of racehorses, the moments just prior to a race are always the most anxious and nervous. Visions of glorious victory are mixed with feelings of stress, anxiety, doubt, and concern. Winning is euphoric, while losing is a gut punch. Owners, trainers, and jockeys are superstitious, and everyone has a pre-race ritual. This is the time to rub a good luck coin, find a lucky spot, sit with a lucky friend, or wear that lucky sweater.

For Ted Bouchard and Alex Sherman, Heliacal Star's first race represented the culmination of their time, investment, and emotion in preparing him for his debut. It had taken several months of daily training, feeding, vet checks, and grooming to ready him for this moment. A win or strong effort would validate their first impressions and justify the money Sherman had invested in such a royally bred and well-conformed thoroughbred. To win, Heliacal Star would need to outperform several similarly well-bred competitors with classic pedigrees and wealthy owners, trained by the top conditioners. Once the horses crossed that finish line, a new pecking order would emerge based on the results. It had been a long ten months since Sherman had purchased Heliacal Star at Keeneland. This debut would represent his first serious test.

Inside the saddling stall, Bouchard was the vision of cool, calm, and collected, absent of expression or emotion, as he typically was while preparing his horse to race. As with every race, he methodically placed the saddling cloth atop the colt's back, then the saddle, cinch, tongue tie, and bridle. Alex Sherman waited on the grassy interior of the paddock with his eyes directed toward the activity inside the stall as several tiny droplets of sweat formed on his brow, undoubtedly the onset of pre-race nerves. As he waited for his horse to exit the stall, he fidgeted and continuously rechecked the odds on the tote board. The minutes before post time ticked by as the horses moved out of their respective stalls and were paraded on the walking path inside the paddock.

Neatly dressed in a dark-blue suit, white shirt, plain blue tie, and flat cap, Ted Bouchard's look contrasted the dirt and grime of his barn, where he'd spent much of his morning. As the groom led Heliacal Star over the circular walking path, Bouchard approached Alex Sherman, tapped him on the shoulder, and greeted him with a formal handshake.

In a hurried tone, Sherman asked, "How's he doing?"

Bouchard responded, "He's feeling good. He looks ready for this group."

A few minutes before post time, the jockeys reached their mounts inside the paddock. For this race, Bouchard selected one of the leading and more experienced riders at the venue. Their jockey approached them wearing the silks Alex Sherman had registered with the Jockey Club, which consisted of a royal-blue jacket with an oversize yellow star on the front and back and multiple white stars on each sleeve, and a yellow bowtie.

Jack Fernandez was a familiar presence among the elite jockey colony at Belmont and Saratoga and had been in the top tier for more than a decade. He is generally respected as an intelligent and strong rider. Fernandez is known for riding with a light touch and tremendous confidence and for showing no fear when pushing his horse through a tight opening where less courageous riders would opt for a more circuitous route. Although he had maintained a solid record over the years, he'd yet to earn an annual Eclipse Award as the best jockey of the year. If Heliacal Star could win a few prestigious races, it might promote Fernandez to contender for the prestigious Rider of the Year award.

On this day, Fernandez greeted Bouchard with a firm handshake and large smile, then greeted Sherman with the same. Bouchard turned to Fernandez and said, "There's plenty of early speed in this race, so keep him quiet and relaxed through the turn and finish strong."

Fernandez nodded as Sherman listened without offering any of his own guidance or instructions. The groom approached with Heliacal Star, and Fernandez grabbed the reins, allowing Bouchard to give him a leg up atop the hopeful two-year-old colt.

Heliacal Star hopped on his toes, indicating a healthy sign of excitement and readiness. Once Fernandez was aboard, he deftly guided the horse from the paddock through the grandstand tunnel and onto the main track.

Each horse is formally introduced by name, rider, trainer, and owner during the post parade, as per the centuries-old tradition of presenting each horse to the spectators on the main track. The tote board continuously updates the ever-changing odds until the horses break from the gate and no more bets could be accepted. The morning line odds for Heliacal Star opened at 12–1 but had fallen to 8–1 by the time he casually strutted into the starting gate. Earlier that day, Ted Bouchard had reserved a box seat with clear sight lines to the wire. He and Alex Sherman settled into their seats as the horses loaded into the starting gate. It was finally time for Heliacal Star to show the racing world his tremendous talent.

Sherman reached for his binoculars, peered out toward the starting gate, and muttered, "C'mon, Star. C'mon, baby. Let's make it happen today."

There was only a brief pause until the bell rang, the gates opened, and the dozen juvenile thoroughbreds blasted out of the starting gate. The track announcer proclaimed, "And they're off!"

Although he was instructed to lay behind the early speed of the race, Jack Fernandez struggled to contain Heliacal Star, who tracked closely behind a trio of speed horses vying for the early lead. Even with Fernandez visibly tugging on the reins in a clear effort to moderate his pace, Heliacal Star seemingly ignored his rider's commands and propelled himself to the front of the pack as the dozen thoroughbreds thundered over the backstretch.

From his reserved seat, Bouchard grimaced as the events unfolded on the track while Alex Sherman stood and shouted, "Go! Heliacal Star, go!"

As the horses sped down the backstretch and moved onto the far turn, Heliacal Star maintained a short but tenuous lead. Alex Sherman continued to watch through his binoculars. "C'mon baby, go . . . Heliacal Star . . . go!"

As the horses ran through the far turn, a trio of competitors surged forward, evaporating the lead Heliacal Star had enjoyed throughout the first half of the race. They moved alongside and battled Heliacal Star for the lead. Fernandez shook his reins vigorously to encourage his horse to fight on and repel the challenge. Rounding the turn and entering the final stretch run, the four horses were across the track, side by side and vying for the lead. Heliacal Star was closest to the rail, and Fernandez actively applied his riding crop as the other jockeys did the same. The sounds of Alex Sherman rooting for his horse were absorbed inside the eruption of crowd noise, which escalated into a deafening roar.

Valiantly trying to keep up, Heliacal Star begrudgingly yielded his lead and faded to fourth with a furlong remaining. A few more fast-closing horses caught him in the final stretch, ultimately dropping him to sixth place when he finally crossed the wire, nine lengths behind the winning horse.

His horse clearly beaten, Alex Sherman ceased his shouting and slumped into his reserved seat, dejected.

Bouchard turned to Sherman. "He tired in the last eighth of a mile and simply ran out of gas. He'll benefit from the experience and improve off this effort. Onward!"

Sherman slapped the racing program across his leg and tossed it on the ground. "Seriously, Ted? What was that? You told Fernandez to settle him, race off the pace, and finish strong, but instead this idiot puts him on the lead? Fire the jockey!"

Bouchard waited a long moment before responding. "Alex, the horse was simply too eager today. Fernandez had no choice. If you watch the replay, he tried to settle him, but Heliacal Star was too wound up and headstrong. If you want to blame anyone, you can blame me. The horse was overly amped ahead of the race, but he still ran well. Alex, this wasn't a bad debut race. Your horse has talent."

CHAPTER 15

Following his rendezvous with Louisville Larry, Special Agent Carlos Anjero logs into the FBI database to initiate a search on Ron McGee. There's nothing.

He opens an internet search window and taps out *Heliacal Star racehorse. Ron McGee.* After scrolling past a few advertisements, he locates an article from a national horse-racing trade publication. Anjero clicks on the link and reads the article, dated August 2017.

TRAINER RON MCGEE DISCOVERS SUCCESS IN HIS HELIACAL STAR

Saratoga Springs, NY–Winning the Grade III Utica Stakes at Saratoga Springs with rising star Heliacal Star has erased any doubts that seasoned trainer Ron McGee appears to have rediscovered his old touch. After years of personal struggles, including a highly publicized divorce and several appeals related to alleged infractions, Ron McGee has returned to his roots and is thriving once again with Heliacal Star after taking over the training duties of this now four-year-old son of Pioneer of the Nile.

Following a lackluster juvenile year in which Heliacal Star failed a top-three finish and underwhelming sophomore year with just a maiden victory to his name, owner Alex Sherman changed things up in moving his $550,000 yearling to the barn of Ron McGee. The move has paid off, as Heliacal Star won at first asking this year and kept improving with an allowance victory and decisive win in the Grade III Utica with regular rider Jack Fernandez aboard.

Following this latest triumph at Saratoga Race Course, McGee was highly appreciative of his new star: "He does everything you ask of him, in the morning, before the race, and especially during the race. He's truly a dream horse, and I'm blessed to train him. I wish they were all like him." For his part, Sherman indicated the move to McGee's barn was more of a hunch play than any one thing in particular. Based on the results so far, it looks to be a prudent move that has paid dividends for horse, trainer, and owner. They will undoubtedly be competing on a quest for more treasure in the weeks and months ahead.

After finishing the article, Anjero writes down a few notes on a scratch pad next to his computer.

Infractions = violations = cheating.

McGee connection to Kaufman? Larry is the middleman.

Alex Sherman role? Involved? Patsy?

Browsing the New York Racing Association web page, he locates the phone number for Ron McGee and dials. Anjero's phone is configured with block caller ID.

The phone rings three times without an answer and rolls to voicemail. Anjero disconnects without leaving a message. He writes McGee's phone number on his scratch pad next to his other notes.

He resumes his search on Heliacal Star and clicks on the next article, this one from October of 2017, two months after the previous article was written.

HELIACAL STAR INJURED IN
GRADE III ROOSEVELT

Elmont, NY–Four-year-old Heliacal Star, racing under the silks of owner Alex Sherman for conditioner Ron McGee, suffered an injury while racing in the Grade III Roosevelt Stakes at Belmont Park. Rider Jack Fernandez was tossed from the mount when the horse buckled and went down in the middle of the racetrack. He was fortunate to sustain only minor injuries from the fall. In a post-race interview, Fernandez indicated Heliacal Star felt strong and was sitting in a great stalking position when a horse from behind clipped his heels, causing him to stumble. A post-race examination discovered a non-life-threatening injury sustained to his right front leg. His prognosis for recovery is good following successful surgery, but his future racing career is not as certain.

Anjero continues to a third and final article that came up in his search, dated only a few months ago, from April.

FORMER GRADE II WINNER HELIACAL STAR RETURNS TO TRAINING

Elmont, NY–After what may have been a career-ending injury in October of last year, Heliacal Star, last year's Grade III Utica Stakes winner, is back in training at Belmont Park. This follows successful surgery and six months of rehabilitation at a farm in Upstate New York. After a thorough veterinarian exam, he was cleared to return to training in March of this year and was recently seen on the backstretch jogging at Belmont Park. According to his trainer Ron McGee, they will monitor his progress closely with hopes of returning in early summer to the starting gate. McGee has not commented on which condition he may seek for the now five-year-old, but he expressed satisfaction with his progress since returning to Belmont after six months off since his surgery in October.

Anjero adds to his scratch notes.

McGee is fixing races for Kaufman?
Relationship between Kaufman and McGee?

Anjero logs in again to the FBI database and this time initiates a search on Alex Sherman. The case file reveals that Sherman had a daughter who died during a suspected homicide back in 2013. After an investigation, there were no arrests or charges ever filed.

Throughout the investigation, homicide was never ruled out. Her autopsy also revealed the presence of a unique but unnamed designer drug, along with a type of heroin that matched a batch previously seized by the FBI from a street dealer they had picked up. There were six additional overdoses within three weeks of Sherman's daughter, and all six presented with the same unique signature of this unknown designer drug in their respective autopsy reports.

The dealer in custody was prepared to name Kaufman as the connection for the dope in testimony to a grand jury, but he never made it to the courthouse, and the case went cold without any other witnesses. The suspicious overdoses ceased afterward, and the mystery drug disappeared.

There was no additional information in the file regarding Alex Sherman.

Anjero adds a few more notes to his scratch pad.

Alex Sherman is the named owner of Heliacal Star.
McGee trains the horse. Why is Kaufman calling the shots on Sherman's horse?

He jots down his final entry.

Is Kaufman responsible for Sherman kid overdose? Wow!
Larry is holding out on me!

He pulls out his personal file on Larry Lonsdale, reviews his
arrest record, the early parole, and mumbles to himself, "That
son of a bitch has been playing me."

He reviews the details of two arrests for simple assault that
began as bar fights, three arrests for illegal weapon possession,
and one conviction for aggravated assault with a deadly weapon.
Larry's conviction would have kept him in jail through the present day, if not for Anjero's influence in gaining his early release.
Kaufman is suspected to be a top distributor in the Northeast
of methamphetamines, heroin, cocaine, and other various sub-
stances in addition to illegal bookmaking, loan sharking, and
prostitution. But even with the occasional dealer bust, the FBI
has yet to find any hard evidence or a direct connection to Tony
or his younger brother, Ken Kaufman. Several questions remain
unanswered by the Bureau, including where and how the drugs
entered New York, who supplied them, and how the cash was
being moved around.

Looking down at his scratch pad, Anjero circles Alex
Sherman's name.

He locates Sherman's contact information and dials the
number. Alex Sherman answers on the first ring.

Clearing his throat, Anjero says, "Hello, Mr. Sherman, my
name is Special Agent Carlos Anjero from the New York office of
the Federal Bureau of Investigation."

He pauses momentarily, then continues, "You're not in any trouble, Mr. Sherman, but I am investigating an individual with whom you may have a relationship. I would like to speak with you, as soon as possible, at our New York Federal Plaza office. Would this be possible, Mr. Sherman?"

Sherman doesn't respond. Anjero can hear him breathing, though.

Anjero asks, "Mr. Sherman, are you still there?"

Sherman answers, "Yes, sir. I work in Manhattan. I know where your building is located."

CHAPTER 16

Standing trackside under the early glimmer of summer dawn, Ron McGee stretches his neck, watching his horses train on the oval. His binoculars are zeroed on Heliacal Star as he enters onto the main track for his first workout since winning impressively a few days earlier.

After a brief gallop, the rider strides past McGee's vantage point, shakes his head, and points toward the hind end of the horse. He turns his mount around, stops, and addresses McGee. "He feels a bit funny from the back."

Turning away from the track, McGee takes several steps but abruptly stops upon hearing a familiar voice.

"What did he say? A little funny in the back? What does that mean, McGee?"

McGee spins around. "Shit, Larry! How long have you been here?"

Louisville Larry strides up to McGee, half grins, and says, "So tell me. What's the deal with my horse? I assume you've got something in your bag of tricks for whatever 'funny' means?"

The color drains from McGee's face. "Listen, Larry, please.

Heliacal Star ran a huge race on Sunday. Am I good with the boss now?"

Larry slaps McGee across his shoulder with an open hand, laughs, and pulls McGee into a tight headlock. "You came through, my friend. The boss surely appreciates your good work."

Releasing McGee, Larry slips a sealed envelope into McGee's jacket. Larry says, "That horse went off at 4–1 odds. It was a very nice score!" He points to the envelope, now sticking out of McGee's pocket. "Don't spend it all in one place."

McGee flashes a grin. "I'm glad the boss is pleased. This horse has some issues, though. I'm concerned he may not hold up much longer. I can prepare him for another race, but he's almost out of mileage. But don't worry, I'll have him ready within two weeks for his next race. When he leaves the post, he won't be feeling pain, or anything else for that matter."

Larry nods to show his approval, and McGee quiets as another trainer walks nearby. Once the area is clear, McGee steps to within a foot of Larry and says in a whisper, "Please tell your boss it needs to be a one-time deal because this horse won't be worth much after his next race . . . if you know what I'm saying."

"That's okay." Larry smirks. "I don't care what happens afterward, but the boss wants another win first, if you know what's good for you. The boss told me if you deliver another win, you'll clear your marker with Tony and can come off my speed dial."

Looking away and down, McGee kicks a small pile of debris surrounding his feet. "Are you serious? Is this for real?"

Standing in front of McGee, Larry raises his palms. "C'mon, Ron, we're reasonable people. Yeah! Hundred percent free and clear."

McGee nods. "Okay. One more win. You've got it. I'll need two weeks, though. Oh, since you're here, I think you may be interested in some info I recently learned about our snitch."

Larry leers at McGee. "Do tell!"

McGee asks, "Remember the guy who overheard us discussing race strategy? The one you chased at the barn that morning?"

Larry's eyes go wide as he clenches both hands into a tight set of matching fists, revealing his rippling triceps underneath his short sleeves.

Gritting his teeth, Larry asks, "I didn't get a good look at him. Who is it?"

McGee responds, "No, no, no. I don't know his name. What I do know is our snitch must have spoken to my former assistant because she ratted me out." McGee smirks and continues, "I was told by the racing official after the race. Her name is Kristine Connelly."

Larry paces in a tight circle. "Do me a favor, and poke around the barns. I'd love to learn the name of the shithead who overheard us. I've got a score to settle with that prick!"

The smile on McGee's face dissipates. "Hey, listen, Larry, I only know about the girl. As a matter of fact, she confronted me right after the race on Sunday. Now that I think about it, she was standing with some guy I didn't know or recognize."

Both men are silent as another trainer moves past. Additional horses enter the track as more trainers gather nearby.

McGee whispers to Larry, "Listen. I know this bitch well. She and I had it out a few years ago, and she still has a thing for me. If you ask me, she's a bit too righteous, but don't worry, 'cause I can handle her. It won't be the first time."

Larry nods. "Okay, McGee. I'll lay off the girl for now, but if she's our best link to this mystery prick, then I'm going to do what's necessary. Kristine, you said?"

McGee nods. "Yep. Kristine Connelly."

CHAPTER 17

For the past two weeks, Matt had been consumed with thoughts of Kristine upon waking, during breakfast, on the job, eating his lunch, on breaks, driving home, and falling asleep each night. Although they'd only met recently, Matt was hooked on her moxie, her looks, and her passion for horses. They made plans to meet up again immediately after their dinner at the Italian place, but Matt was unexpectedly pulled into mandatory overtime, effectively derailing their plans. When he finally got free, it was Kristine who bailed at the last minute when a horse in her barn presented signs of colic.

After their aborted attempts to get together, Matt's excitement grew at the prospect of finally seeing Kristine once again today. Matt envisioned an epic day ahead. To guarantee no last-minute surprises, Matt suggested they meet at the racetrack, then drive to Manhattan for dinner. A romantic dinner, he hoped.

Although Matt knew Kristine was a young and fledgling trainer on the New York circuit, he hadn't considered the extent of her struggles until reviewing her career stats online. She had an unflattering win rate of just 4 percent. He also noticed most of her horses were entered in the lowest-level races, an indication she lacked a top-tier horse in her barn. Yet, she presented herself as a supremely confident, intensely enthusiastic individual. He admires her unyielding optimism and courage, in spite of her struggles.

Maybe, he wondered, he should actually invest in a racehorse, with Kristine as his trainer. If so, how would they manage both a personal relationship and professional partnership? The relationships between owner and trainer are inherently intertwined, as horse racing is a social sport inside a broader entertainment business. In a sport where owners may impetuously change allegiances, a rival one day becomes a client the next, and vice versa. The trainer must continuously operate as a salesperson as an ancillary skill. Would a romantic relationship infringe or enhance her professional demeanor, and create inherent complexity? He harkens back to Kristine's comments about the unique challenges she's faced within a male-dominated sport. No surprise it's not easy to convince a wealthy ownership group, especially the old-guard set, to take a chance on an unproven young female trainer, given her view of some deeply entrenched biases.

But in spite of his good intentions, purchasing a racehorse isn't within his means right now. Maybe someday.

Matt picks up his racing form. As he thumbs through today's entries, he fixates on the sixth race, as Kristine Connelly is listed as the trainer of the one-horse in that race. Studying the race records for each of the horses entered, he believes Kristine's horse has a legitimate chance at winning. A tinge of excitement tantalizes him as he grabs a black Sharpie and circles the horse's name. He rubs his temples in an attempt to emit vibrations of positivity toward her horse, a superstitious gesture for sure.

Poring over the racing form, Matt scoffs upon seeing the name of the trainer for the number-three horse. McGee's entrant is the morning line favorite and the one to beat if Kristine's horse is going to earn victory today. Matt takes his Sharpie and draws a line through the name of McGee's horse, then raises both index and pinkie fingers to symbolically curse his chances. He closes his eyes and envisions standing next to Kristine in the Winner's Circle later this afternoon, while McGee watches and sulks in defeat.

Turning his attention to the next race, the seventh, Matt reflexively drops his program on the floor upon seeing Heliacal Star's name entered. The potential of a daily double, with Kristine's horse and Heliacal Star both winning on the same program, seems too good to be true. His heart quickens from the possibility of a spectacular day ahead. A quick glance at the clock indicates it is time to leave and finally meet up with Kristine after a long two weeks.

CHAPTER 18

Matt and Kristine had prearranged to meet near the paddock, just behind the grandstand, at thirty minutes prior to the first race. Excited about their date, Matt arrives at their rendezvous location twenty minutes early. He considered arriving even earlier and showing up at Kristine's barn, but decided it was best not to surprise her.

Waiting for Kristine to arrive, Matt attunes his attention toward the proximate crowd of bettors, fans, and regulars passing through the area. He watches an older man with a long and scraggly beard sit down on a nearby bench, never removing his eyes from his racing program. The man serves as a useful distraction. Observing him, Matt ponders his potential backstory. Is he a disgruntled lifelong gambler, perpetually trying to reverse his luck? Or perhaps he's a dressed-down genius, avoiding attention by camouflaging himself, while applying his absurd talent to select today's winners? Maybe he's just a racing fan. Another group of six, whom Matt surmises must be college-aged students, appears on the scene. The gents are carrying oversize beers, and the gals are sipping mixed drinks from souvenir glasses. Matt overhears one of the guys boasting about his skill after selecting three winners yesterday.

The group suddenly grows quiet and appears to be distracted by the appearance of an attractive, petite blonde ambling toward them. Glancing at his phone, Matt smiles while making note of her promptness. He waves to grab her attention.

Before she reaches Matt, Kristine is intercepted by the three college-aged guys who stand in a semicircle ahead of her. One of them moves a half step toward her, points at his program, and says, "Hey, gorgeous, I've got the winners right here."

Kristine flicks her bangs and leans forward to peer at his racing program. "In the sixth race today, what do you think of the number-one horse?"

The flirty guy sets his beer on the ground and frantically shuffles through his racing program. "You said sixth race?" Kristine nods and he says, "Hmm, nope. Don't think so. No way the one-horse wins today."

Kristine narrows her eyes. Shaking his head, the guy says, "Don't get me wrong. I don't mind the horse or even the jockey, but I would never bet on his trainer. The number-three horse is a better bet, and I'll tell you why."

Placing her hands on her hips, Kristine says, "Please, do tell."

He says, "You see, his trainer, Ron McGee, has an excellent winning percentage. If McGee was the trainer of the one-horse, I'd bet on him."

Kristine flutters her eyelashes and says, "But I really like the number-one horse because he's trained by a girl!"

The guy draws a long breath, and says, "How about you and I hang out today, and I'll help you win a ton of money.

Guaranteed! I'm an oracle of the racetrack, baby." The guy extends his hand toward Kristine. "Jarod."

Shaking his hand, she says, "Hi, Jarod. It's nice to meet you. I'm Kristine."

Matt laughs. Jarod is wincing from Kristine's clenching handshake. "Wow, Kristine, you have one serious handshake!"

"It's Kristine Connelly, actually. Just like the trainer!"

Jarod's mouth drops open, and he takes an oversize step backward.

Kristine continues, "I'll even give *you* a tip for the day. The one-horse in the sixth race has been training lights out for the past few weeks. Make a big wager on him, that is, unless you *don't* want to win a bunch of money."

Kristine waves good-bye, turns, and strolls away from the group.

Matt is delighted after watching Kristine leave the group of arrogant college students in stunned silence. He overhears one of them saying, "Jarod, you're such an idiot sometimes!"

Matt points at his program, showing her the page with her horse's name circled. He says, "Hey there, gorgeous. I've got the winner picked out right here!"

She gently pokes her finger into his chest. "Ooh, a betting man!" Her face glowing, she says, "I suppose you know I've got a horse in the sixth today?"

Matt laughs. "I do! And as far as I'm concerned, your horse has a solid chance today. I'm totally psyched!"

They stroll toward the grandstand. An elevator carries them to the restaurant on the top floor of the clubhouse, where Matt reserved a table for the day.

As they ride the elevator, Matt tells her, "I have to admit, I was getting pretty jealous of your new friend when he was flirting with you."

Kristine looks sensational in her skinny jeans and pink tee underneath an oversize sport jacket. Her jeans are neatly tucked inside a pair of red studded cowboy boots, and she radiates a magnetic combination of sexy and stylish.

Although Matt had experienced his share of trials and tribulations with various women over the years, Kristine seemed so different from the girls he usually met, most of whom seemed more interested in posting selfies on Instagram than actually connecting with him. He was captivated by her looks, but equally drawn to her pragmatism, intelligence, and self-confidence.

As they are seated, Matt orders a vodka tonic and Kristine a club soda with a slice of lime. While fixating his gaze on her, Matt asks, "What are you thinking about right now?"

She eyes Matt and says, "I'm just happy to finally be here with you. Believe it or not, you've found a way to pull me out of my shell, and it feels nice." She looks over at herself. "I mean, look at me! I guarantee you this is not my typical look, especially here at the racetrack."

Matt feels at ease while Kristine continues, "As a woman in a male-dominated sport, I try to carry myself in a super professional manner. I don't let my hair down very often." She shrugs. "But I don't care today."

Her words reinforce his own feelings. "Good. You look fantastic!"

She says, "Okay, let's take a look at your racing program."

Matt open his program and Kristine slides her chair next to him and points to the name of a horse entered in the third race.

"Right there," she says. "Tony Tornado! That's Ted Bouchard's horse."

"Wait a sec. I remember. You worked for Bouchard, right?"

She smiles reassuringly. "Look who was listening!"

Matt continues, "Ted Bouchard once trained Heliacal Star, before McGee got his hands on him."

Kristine slaps her hand on the table. "I just don't get it. Why would anyone move a horse from such a great trainer like Bouchard to a piece of shit like McGee? I don't care what the stats say. You can't sell your soul to the devil. Ted Bouchard is the best trainer I've even been around. He's taught me more than I could have learned in a lifetime from someone else."

Matt is tempted to press the topic but fears jeopardizing the good vibes. "I don't mean to offend your guy Bouchard, but you have to admit Heliacal Star has been crazy good since McGee started to train him."

Kristine scrunches her face and scoffs. "Anybody can get lucky with a good horse, even a dickhead like McGee."

Clearly, Kristine is not letting go of her animosity for McGee, and Matt elects to change topics altogether.

He turns to her. "Did I mention that I met him last year?"

"You met Ron McGee last year?"

"No, no, no, I met Alex Sherman, the owner of Heliacal Star. Actually, I've met him twice. He seemed like a good guy, a bit aloof perhaps, but that's another story for another day."

Matt grabs his racing program and points to the name Tony

Tornado. "What can you tell me about Bouchard's horse in this race today?"

Kristine looks at the form and says, "Bouchard really likes this colt. He's raced just one time and should be on the improve. I like him to win today."

Matt is hypnotized by the sensuality of her voice along with the sweet scent of her hair and warmth of her breath. Matt remains still, enjoying the moment and anticipating her next move.

He clears his throat and says, "He told you that, um . . . " but cannot remember the name of the horse. "Um . . . what's his name, Coronado?"

Kristine chuckles. "Not Coronado. Tony Tornado! I watched him train the other morning. He looked really good."

The track announcer is speaking in the background to inform the crowd about post time for the first race. Matt looks up, not realizing how quickly time is passing.

Matt shifts the conversation to the sixth race. "What about your horse? Should I bet my paycheck on him?"

In a deadpan voice, she stares blankly at him. "Only if you want to become wealthy, Mr. Galiano!" She smiles wide. "He's been training beautifully ahead of this race today. If we get a good trip, I think we're going to surprise a few of these fans today, like my new friend Jarod."

When the horses for the next race parade inside the paddock on the closed-circuit screens in the clubhouse, Kristine says, "Hey, I need to scoot back to the barn and prep my horse for the sixth. Come meet me at the paddock beforehand. We can watch the race together. Hopefully, we'll get our picture taken in the Winner's Circle this afternoon!"

Matt stands up as Kristine disappears. As he watches, he cannot stop himself from smiling, considering how perfectly the day has gone. He briefly glances at his program to make his selection for the next race, but since Kristine gave him a tip, there is no need to handicap the race or consider another horse. Matt heeds Kristine's advice and pulls a hundred-dollar bill from his wallet to wager on Tony Tornado.

Approaching the self-service terminal, Matt checks the odds on the tote board. Tony Tornado is currently 5–1, and Matt foresees his wager transforming into $500. He inserts the crisp bill into the machine and bets it all on Tony Tornado. A paper voucher emerges, and Matt snatches it. With Kristine on her way to the barn, he walks by himself toward the closed-circuit monitors across the restaurant and near some oversize windows with a view to the racetrack down below.

Matt bumps into a brawny man approaching from the opposite direction. Sidestepping just before contact, he avoids a serious collision but is still thrown off-balance and spun around. Matt turns to apologize and freezes in place before his words of apology emerge.

The larger man stares at Matt for an extended moment and finally says, "Hey, I know you!"

Though Matt instantly recognizes the man, he freezes in place, praying for anonymity in hoping to avoid an unwanted reunion. The man grins broadly and slaps his open palm across Matt's shoulder, jolting him two steps forward. "I'll be damned. If it isn't my old buddy Matt Galiano! It's been a long time, friend! Hey, about that last time, no hard feelings, eh?"

Wanting to escape, Matt feels trapped. Louisville Larry drapes his beefy right arm across Matt's shoulder and says, "Come with me, buddy. I'll buy you a drink. What happened between us in the past is ancient history, as far as I'm concerned."

Knowing firsthand how Larry and his cronies operate, Matt is skeptical, but he understands refusing would be tantamount to an act of defiance. Larry squeezes Matt's shoulder to the point of discomfort, as a means of insisting there's no option. Matt surmises any attempts at fleeing the scene will be easier once the big man is relaxed. He offers no resistance to Louisville's offer.

At the bar, Louisville says, "Shit, Matt. It's gotta be about ten years, right bro?" He laughs out loud. "I gotta say, you look a lot better today than the last time I saw you!"

Increasingly paranoid, Matt fears that Larry may already know it was him on the backstretch a few weeks ago. Not knowing and trying to keep his cool, Matt remains quiet, listening for clues that may reveal Louisville's motivation for such feigned friendliness.

Louisville finally releases Matt from his hold and asks, "What's the matter, Matty? Cat got your tongue?" Matt shrugs but remains quiet. Louisville continues, "So, killer . . . you know, I honestly never thought I'd see your ugly mug again, but I gotta say, seeing you today totally makes my day!" Larry snaps the voucher out of Matt's hand. "I see you're still gambling." Clenching his jaw, Louisville says, "Hope you're not stealing from the till this time around."

Matt stiffens, afraid of saying anything that may trigger the larger man, yet feels some relief that Louisville has not mentioned the chase on the backstretch.

Louisville looks at Matt's voucher. "Tony Tornado, eh? If memory serves me, you always had a knack for picking the ponies." He flings the voucher back to Matt. "I bet on Tony Tornado, too. Maybe he's named after someone we both know!" Larry lets loose an uproarious laugh.

Matt plans his escape, hoping not to offend or trigger Louisville. Breaking his silence, Matt points across the room and says, "Hey, Larry, it's really nice to see you again and catch up on old times, but I'm heading over there to watch the race from my lucky spot. It's almost post time, so if you don't mind."

The intimidating hulk grabs and squeezes Matt's left shoulder. "Nonsense! We're going to watch this one together. Right here. After all, we both bet on the same horse!" Matt understands, all too well, that an argument with Larry will inflame the situation. Reluctantly, Matt nods in agreement.

Larry tugs on Matt's sleeve. "Come with me. I want you to meet someone."

The mere thought of associating with one of Larry's associates makes Matt nauseous. On a day that started perfectly, he now finds himself in the midst of a bad dream. As they move down the bar, Larry shouts. "Hey, Ron, get your sorry ass over here. I want you to meet an old friend of mine."

Matt sees the unmistakable profile of Ron McGee. It was only two weeks ago when Matt stepped between Ron and Kristine during their heated and intense confrontation. If Louisville was not already aware of Matt's association with Kris, McGee would surely recognize him as her friend. At that point, even Larry would logically finger Matt as the guy he chased through the barns.

McGee greets Larry and offers Matt his hand, squinting through a beam of sunshine streaming through the oversize bay windows. Matt shakes McGee's hand to acknowledge the gesture, but immediately turns his head to avoid eye contact and inhibit recognition.

Larry throws his beefy arms across both their shoulders and says, "Ron McGee, this is Matt Galiano. He's an old acquaintance of mine." Larry eyes McGee. "And I'm sure this man needs no introduction, being such a brilliant trainer. I wanted to introduce you to Matt because he's a huge racing fan. I bet he doesn't know you and I co-manage a horse." Larry chuckles. "Technically, my team calls the shots, and Ron follows my orders."

Still squinting, McGee looks at Matt and says, "You look kind of familiar. Have we met before?"

A sinking sensation consumes Matt. Once McGee connects him to Kristine, Larry is going to inflict some serious bodily harm upon him. Trying his best to hide his trepidation, Matt shrugs and remains silent, afraid his voice will trigger unwanted familiarity.

Lifting one arm off Matt's shoulder, Larry pulls McGee tight to him with his other arm. "You see, Matty boy has always been somewhat of a racetrack junkie. I'm sure you've seen this bum hanging around here before."

Matt nods in agreement with a tentative feeling of relief as McGee has yet to recognize him or associate him with Kristine from their encounter a few weeks ago.

Larry calls out, "Hey, Galiano, what are you drinking?"

Knowing his charade will only last until McGee recognizes him, Matt is desperate to find a way out before it becomes too late. Simply excusing himself and walking away would be a sign of disrespect, and insulting Larry is not a viable option. As he scours his brain for an out, Matt partially turns his back to the bar and shields himself to reduce the probability of sparking McGee's memory.

Larry orders a round of tequila shots, and the bartender obliges with a quick pour. Bracing for one of Larry's heavy pats across his back, Matt faces the big man and lifts his glass. Larry raises his glass and says, "Here's to old times! Drink up, Mr. Galiano!"

With no alternative, Matt downs the shot, triggering a burning sensation in his throat and causing his body to tingle. As the alcohol settles, Matt comes up with a plan to effectively excuse himself and wishes he'd thought of it sooner. Just before he tells Larry of his need to use the restroom, Matt's phone beeps with a text from Kristine. While he was downing the shot of tequila, Matt failed to notice Kristine return to their table.

Matt cups the phone and curls into a crouch, his back to Larry and McGee. He reads her text.

Hi Matt. I returned to the table to grab my program but don't see you. I'm heading to the barn to prep for the race now. See you then.

The racetrack bar stands next to the down escalator. He finally spots Kristine across the room looking at her phone. His eyes remain fixated on her as she looks up and notices Matt staring at her from the bar area, with Louisville and McGee smiling and chuckling behind him. Shaking her head, she slowly backs away and moves toward the escalator.

Matt waves his hands to indicate it's not what it seems, but Larry grabs Matt by the shoulder. Time for another round of tequila shots. Larry yanks Matt back to the bar, and Kristine eyeballs him as she rides down the escalator. Trapped, Matt complies, having experienced Larry's explosive temper in the past. Based on the expression of disgust he witnessed on Kristine's face, he must find a way to explain himself.

As he downs the shot, his phone alerts him to an incoming text message. A message from Kristine: *You asshole.*

Larry surprises him by gripping his arm, causing Matt to drop his phone. Larry glares. "Now you're going listen to me, Galiano, 'cause it's been a long, long time."

Matt says nothing.

"I should have finished that job on you when I had the chance. My loss is your gain. Just remember, it's never too late, and I don't like you."

Larry laughs. "Get your ass out of here, and if I see you again around here, I won't be so nice next time. Got it, asshole?"

Matt sucks in a breath and gathers himself, as he knows Larry can literally smell fear in others. He flicks his arm to shuck Larry's grip, picks up his phone, and slowly turns and walks away.

Descending the escalator, Matt catches the replay of the last race. Tony Tornado has just crossed the finish line to win. After the encounter with Louisville Larry, Matt had all but forgotten about his wager on the horse. He pulls out his voucher, made only thirty minutes ago, but seemingly from a different day, different week, and different year. Kristine's prediction was right. It's a coup for Bouchard, but that's no longer important. Matt needs to make things right with Kristine and, more importantly, protect her from Louisville Larry and the Kaufmans.

CHAPTER 19

Think, Matt, think!" he mutters to himself. It's only a matter of time before McGee will remember his face, connect him with Kristine, and inevitability share this knowledge with Larry. After an amazing start to the day, Matt's been drawn into a dangerous situation, while Kristine is oblivious to the seriousness of this burgeoning threat. Knowing Larry, and how his threats usually turn to actions, Matt can ill afford a second encounter.

Nausea settles into his gut as Matt contemplates the situation and the potential danger it may pose for Kristine if Louisville were to connect the dots between her and McGee after the confrontation he witnessed the other day. He feels a need to locate and warn her without causing undo panic. He stares at her last text, calling him an asshole. He must convince her of the truth and ensure she grasps how circumstances may take a perilous turn.

Matt leaves the racetrack grounds and walks to the parking lot, a relatively quiet area, to gather his thoughts and plan ahead. He texts Kristine.

I'm sorry, I'm not going to make it to the paddock.

He deletes the message and taps out a new text.

Something came up. Can't make it to the paddock. Very sorry. I'll explain later.

He stares at his phone for a few seconds, deletes it, and taps out a new message.

It's not how it looks. Really. Let me explain. Not here. Dinner?

He sends the text and paces in the parking lot, hoping she understands. A moment later, his phone dings with a response.

You fucking kidding me? Eat with your buddy McGee.

Matt knows he needs to regroup. He taps out a reply.

We need to meet. I've got the goods on them. I'll see you in the paddock.

Not waiting for a response, he reenters the racetrack, looking in all directions for any sign of McGee or Louisville Larry. The tote board indicates it's post time for the fifth race, meaning Kristine will be headed to the paddock in the next ten minutes to prepare for the sixth race.

Matt finds an isolated area with a sightline to the horses, grooms, and trainers as they enter the paddock. The heat and humidity of the day have intensified, and sweat pours down his face as butterflies dance in his stomach and he anticipates the sight of Kristine. What to say?

After just a few minutes, the horses for the sixth race approach the paddock. Matt searches for Kristine among those entering and immediately spots her leading the one-horse. Halfway to the entrance, Matt freezes, noticing Louisville Larry several feet ahead of him. Concealing himself among the other spectators encircling the paddock, Matt sees Louisville greet Ron McGee. With all the excitement from Louisville and the drama with Kristine, Matt had forgotten McGee's horse was also entered in the same race. He stands frozen in place and watches McGee and Louisville meet with a few suspicious-looking characters.

He glances toward Kristine and notices her attire has changed, as she now sports a navy striped skirt, hemmed just above her knees, and a matching blazer.

Weighing his options, Matt opts to act versus continuing to hide in the shadows. He draws on his inner strength and convinces himself that neither Louisville Larry nor McGee are going to intimidate him. If they want a piece of him, he'll no longer back down. His most important job is to shield Kristine from the threat Louisville represents.

Inside the saddling ring, Kristine is preparing her horse but notices Matt and gestures to the security officer to permit Matt inside. As Matt enters, she offers him a sideways glance and returns to her saddling activities. McGee and Larry are in conversation among themselves. *So far, so good,* Matt thinks.

Prior to each race, owners and their guests stand on the manicured grass lawn within the perimeter of the circular horse path. A row of open-ended saddling stalls stands across the path at the south end of the paddock. As Matt moves to the designated area for the one-horse, Kristine is inside the saddling stall. In spite of the circumstances, the moment is surreal. Matt is standing inside the paddock for the first time in his life after spending a lifetime observing horses from the other side. He takes a moment to eye the crowd of spectators.

Matt peeks to his left where Larry and McGee are huddled at their designated spot on the lawn for the number-three horse. As Matt is standing in the spot for the one-horse, his foes are only twenty feet away. Aware of their proximity, Matt turns his back to them and drops his head, hoping to hide in plain sight.

Her horse saddled, Kristine exits the stall and hands the lead rope to her groom to escort the horse across the walking path. She saunters over to Matt and sinks her hands into her skirt pockets.

"Why did you come here, Matt?" She points toward McGee. "I think your friends are over there."

"I swear it's not how it looks. Can we talk later?" Matt ignores her attempted provocation.

Kristine appears to ponder his question while staring at him for a long moment. She breaks the silence and points. "Who's the big dude hanging out with Ron McGee? You were pretty chummy with him at the Turf Club!"

Concerned by the volume of her voice, Matt squats down, wraps his arms around his legs, and drops his head in an attempt to hide in the open space. Picking up his head a moment later, Matt finds Louisville Larry and Ron McGee, who must have heard Kristine, looking right at him.

"Shit!" Matt mumbles to himself.

Larry runs a finger under his chin and mouths, "You're dead, motherfucker!"

The jockeys stream into the paddock, breaking the tension, and Matt notices a security officer monitoring them. Refusing to allow the terror of the situation to dictate his actions, Matt boldly takes a step toward Louisville. The bigger man laughs out loud, turns his back to Matt, and raises his right middle finger as he walks away.

Matt looks toward to Kristine, who raises her eyebrows but is otherwise silent.

As Kristine provides instructions to the jockey, Matt is aware it's the only time rider and trainer will discuss race strategy, and for only a few seconds. As Kristine engages the jockey, Matt glances in the direction of Louisville, who is in conversation with McGee's jockey and group of friends. The threat, at least for the moment, appears to have subsided.

Once the jockey is hoisted atop his mount, Kristine walks in step with the horse as they move toward the tunnel en route to trackside. Kristine is suddenly several steps ahead of Matt, and he runs up to catch her. McGee and his clan are just two horses behind as the group parades through the tunnel.

"Seriously, Matt," Kristine says, "what the fuck is going on with you?"

Breathing heavily and sweating profusely, Matt looks over his shoulder and spots McGee walking behind them with Louisville at his side. Keeping pace with Kristine, Matt leans into her. "That big guy is Louisville Larry. By now, I bet he knows I'm the guy he chased around the backstretch."

As they exit the tunnel and appear at the opening to the main track, the jockey steers the horse onto the main oval, and Matt walks with Kristine into an open area near the railing, until they reach the stretch run where several fans are viewing the horses marching in the post parade.

Only minutes till post time, the race itself could not be further from his mind. He grabs hold of Kristine by her wrists and looks her in the eye.

"I'm really sorry, Kris, but my life has gotten rather messy right now. You totally don't deserve this, but you also should know I really like you. I'm afraid my problem will become yours somehow, and I really don't want that to happen."

She lowers her head. "I'm not sure what to think, Matt. You could be sincere, and I may have overreacted, but I don't know what's going on. I'd like to believe you."

Hearing Kristine's willingness to listen, a major concern has been alleviated. He hugs Kristine and says, "Well, at least you didn't hit me this time." Still concerned about a potential confrontation with Louisville, he asks, "Don't let go, but take a look behind me. Is Louisville Larry there?"

She whispers in his ear, "Yes."

Matt stiffens. He takes a step back, gulps hard, and turns around to confront his assailant.

CHAPTER 20

Before he can shake off the impact of the first blow, Matt's head is trapped in Louisville's viselike headlock. Unable to free himself, an intense pain sears across Matt's neck, and his legs grow wobbly from the intense pressure. A small crowd forms in a circle around them as Matt drops to his knees. Louisville releases his hold, leaving Matt motionless and supine on the ground. In a single motion, Louisville wraps his oversize arms around Matt's chest and hoists him into a sitting position. Matt is at Louisville's mercy while being dragged backward across the floor. Feeling helpless, Matt wonders, *Where are the cops or Security?*

Suddenly, Kristine dives on top of Matt's legs and wraps her arms around his waist, slowing down Louisville's momentum. As Louisville tugs at them, Ron McGee grabs Kristine by the shoulders and yanks her backward and off Matt.

Standing above Kristine, McGee points down and laughs. "What are you doing, little girl? This is men's stuff. Let the boys have some fun!"

Ted Bouchard stands nearby and offers Kristine his hand. "Are you alright? What's going on here?"

McGee bumps Bouchard away and hovers above Kristine. "You want to finish what you started outside the racing office? Oh, I know it was you who ratted me out about Heliacal Star! How did that work out for you?"

Staring at Kristine, McGee's arms are crossed as he scrunches his eyebrows and snarls. She jumps to her feet and charges toward him.

Standing several inches taller than Kristine, McGee pushes her back a step. "Go ahead, bitch, take your best shot!"

Ted Bouchard waves on the Security outfit, who are now running toward them. He addresses Kristine. "Don't do this. He's not worth it." McGee pokes Bouchard in the back. "Get lost, Ted. This is not your fight."

Kristine takes a step back, and McGee steps around Bouchard. "And just how well do you know your new boyfriend . . . Matt, right? Matt Galiano?"

Kristine advances toward McGee, who continues to taunt her. "In case you don't already know, your boyfriend is a thug who hangs out with thugs." He laughs. "Matt and Larry are old buds. This scene was just an act. Galiano is with us, you stupid bitch!"

Kristine's face reddens, and she strikes him in the gut with her clenched fist. He lurches forward. With his legs quivering, Kristine follows with a second cross to the left side of his cheek, snapping McGee's head to the right and causing him stagger.

Before he falls, Kristine grabs hold of McGee's face with her left hand and reaches back with her clenched right fist. The security officers finally arrive and grab Kristine by the shoulder. She releases her grip, spins around, and raises her fist at the officer.

Ron McGee crumples to the ground. Kristine freezes in place with her arm cocked above her head.

Bouchard shouts, "Stop it, Kris!"

She stares at Bouchard and nods in agreement. Looking at the bloodied McGee lying on the ground, she says, "I need to get out of here." The security officer escorts her away.

CHAPTER 21

Matt is dragged across the grandstand floor to a remote area, away from the escalating conflict between Kristine and McGee, which is grabbing the attention of the nearby crowd. Groggy but cognizant, Matt braces as Louisville swings his heavy right boot directly into his exposed right side. He tries to swallow the pain but gasps from the force of the blow, forcing out a raspy grunt.

Louisville points down at him. "Shut the fuck up!"

Louisville lifts Matt to his feet. Weakened by the kick, Matt's legs are shaking, but he forces himself to remain upright. The hulking man moves around and stands inches from Matt's face. "You're a sneaky little shit!" Without hesitation, Louisville unleashes a powerful jab into Matt's stomach, instantly dropping him to the ground.

As Louisville hovers over him, Matt squeezes his eyes shut and raises his right arm as a shield from the anticipated assault of fists and fury. Nothing happens as five, ten, and twenty seconds pass. Matt slowly lowers his arm, opens his eyes, and notices Louisville is several feet away and speaking to a pair of uniformed individuals.

Matt struggles to his knees and pushes himself to his feet.

Louisville approaches with the individuals, who Matt now recognizes as the security detail.

The first officer appears to be about forty, an inch shorter than Larry and lean and muscular in stature. The second officer looks about half the age of his partner and stands quietly, observing the interaction. Louisville throws his arm across Matt's shoulders and says, "Hey, Matty, tell my new friend we're just goofing around."

The older security officer addresses Matt. "I'm not buying it. A serious fight just erupted inside the grandstand and several people frantically pointed me over here, telling me you're also being assaulted." He turns his attention to Larry with a serious scowl. "What exactly is going on here?"

Matt realizes that Louisville was trying to downplay the situation and convince the guard there is nothing going on. He also understands that fingering the hulking goon could enlist additional law enforcement. If so, the situation would only escalate once word reached Kaufman, turning a bad situation even worse.

A few curious spectators have now gathered behind the officers, who are keeping them from advancing farther. Matt looks around, avoiding eye contact with the older officer. "Yeah, you can say . . . listen, I really don't want to cause any trouble, officer."

Matt removes Louisville's thick arms from his shoulders and looks at the officer. "Let's just call it two guys goofing around?"

The officer stands statuesque. "You sure you don't want to press charges?" Matt jams his elbow with a subtle force into Louisville's ribs, causing the large man to reflexively bend forward. "Hundred percent sure, but I really gotta run now."

The officer sighs. "If you change your mind and decide to

pursue this matter, our office is located in the southeast corner on the first floor of the grandstand. You're free to go."

Matt darts away, leaving Louisville with the two officers. He reaches the trackside rail before stopping to look around for Kristine, but there's no sign of her anywhere.

He remembers Kristine's attempt to help him when Ron McGee suddenly intervened and wonders where she may have disappeared to. Standing trackside, Matt looks at the giant monitor near the tote board, showing a live video of a horse entering the Winner's Circle. He instantly recognizes the red saddlecloth emblazoned with the number one. Kristine's horse has just won the sixth race.

CHAPTER 22

Matt watches the monitor showing Kristine's horse winning at long odds and earning her a long-awaited trip to the Winner's Circle. Her prediction of victory proved accurate, and Matt wonders if Jarod and his college buddies were sage enough to cash a winning ticket. Matt knows Kristine earned this victory through diligence and discipline. He's thrilled for her accomplishment and sends her a congratulatory text.

Inside the Winner's Circle, Kristine pumps her arms, congratulates the jockey, and rubs her hands across the neck of her winning horse. She poses for the customary photo at the hind end of the horse and flashes a triumphant grin for the camera. A security officer stands nearby at the entrance to the Winner's Circle. The winning celebration is short-lived as the jockey dismounts and her groom takes the reins to escort the horse onto the track in the direction of the test barn.

As the team disbands from the Winner's Circle, Kristine scrolls on her phone through multiple congratulatory messages and stops at Matt's text.

Congrats on the big win!
She taps out a reply.
What happened? R U ok?

As the live video on the monitor pans away from the Winner's Circle, Matt is reassured by Kristine's concern. He weaves through the crowd at the rail and beelines his way toward the Winner's Circle. A hundred feet from his destination, he abruptly stops and looks around. It's imperative he remain vigilant, keep a low profile, and stay out of sight.

He taps out another text to Kristine.

I was saved by Security but still need to lay low. I'll find u later.

With a healthy crowd of spectators milling about, Matt shudders at the thought of Louisville Larry potentially spying on him from among them. His face goes flush from a sudden wave of anxiety, exacerbating the sweltering heat and humidity of the day.

He dips his head and slips both hands into his front pockets, touching the voucher from his earlier wager on Tony Tornado. He pulls out the ticket, runs to the teller window, and collects his cash. With several hundred dollars in hand, he heads for the track gift shop on the second floor of the grandstand. Inside the small shop is an elderly woman slumped behind the counter and a couple bickering over which souvenir coffee mug to purchase.

Matt squeezes past the young couple and grabs an extra-large forest-green T-shirt featuring the racetrack logo and a matching baseball cap. He places the shirt, cap, and a hundred-dollar bill on the counter. As the elderly woman rings him up, Matt rips off the tags on his newly purchased items, removes his shirt, and puts on the shirt and matching cap.

Behind the counter, the woman frowns while shaking two twenties and a five-dollar bill. "Your change, young man?"

Matt awkwardly says, "Oh, thanks. Really. I apologize

for . . ." He looks up and doesn't finish his sentence. "Can I trouble you for a bag?"

Matt tosses his old shirt inside a plastic shopping bag and departs the shop, looking slightly different from when he entered. He hopes the subtle transformation will suffice in preventing Louisville or McGee from spotting him in the crowd.

Matt determines it would be best to leave the track before the crowd grows thin. Knowing there is a distinct possibility that Louisville is searching or, worse, waiting for him in the parking area, he strategizes a plan to exit unnoticed. Matt maneuvers himself into the middle of a crowd near the railing. Leaning over the rail, he watches the monitor showing the horses load into the gate for the seventh race.

Watching the horses break from the gate, Matt's mouth drops open as the track announcer calls the race with Heliacal Star taking the lead. He suddenly recalls his favorite horse had been entered in the seventh race today. Heliacal Star leaves little doubt, winning by six lengths and striding away at the finish line. Matt is happy for the horse; this day played out as he hoped, with both Kristine and Heliacal Star winning. On the monitors adjacent to the tote board, he watches the livestream of the horse entering the Winner's Circle along with his trainer Ron McGee and owner Alex Sherman. To Matt's disgust yet simultaneous delight, he also sees Louisville Larry standing among them.

Matt looks skyward and says, "Thank you, Heliacal Star. I seriously owe you one!"

With little time to waste, Matt rushes through the grandstand, past the paddock area, and through the exit to locate his car in the parking lot.

He takes a long look in all directions, opens the driver-side door, and slumps deep into the seat. Safe for the first time in hours, Matt closes his eyes and wipes his forehead. His shirt is soaked with perspiration, but he doesn't care. Turning the ignition, Matt exits the parking lot, lowering the cap over his forehead as he drives. Once clear of the racetrack and on the turnpike, he screams in relief, having escaped the violent wrath of Louisville Larry.

Parking his fears for the moment, Matt's thoughts shift to Kristine. The possibility of her becoming a pawn in his personal war is a scenario he can neither ignore nor deny. Her welfare and well-being must take precedence above all else and trump his personal feelings for her. He swallows hard, and his eyes well up. Matt has made up his mind.

Safely distanced from the racetrack, he pulls over and taps out a new message to Kristine.

Kris, please forgive me, but I can't see you again. It's for your own good.

Matt sends the message and stares at his phone for several minutes, then deletes her contact information.

CHAPTER 23

Alex Sherman stands alongside Ron McGee in the Winner's Circle as Heliacal Star enters it for the second time in June. Today's victory also gives the horse two wins in two races since returning from his injury. Sherman appears quiet and subdued as the winning photo is taken, offering no smile and none of the typical exuberance of winning owners after such victories.

Standing on the opposite side of McGee is Louisville Larry, joining Sherman inside the Winner's Circle. After the photo is taken, the horse is escorted out of the Winner's Circle. Larry wraps his oversize arm around Sherman and says, "Mr. Sherman, congratulations on the victory! Well done, sir! McGee has a few of my horses in my care, and he invited me here today. Hope you don't mind that I crashed your photo? We didn't see you earlier in the paddock, so Ron thought it would be okay."

Sherman nods, and Larry continues, "Truth be told, I'm a big fan of Heliacal Star, at least since McGee started training him. You could say I've taken a rather special interest in him. Seriously, I hope you don't mind me standing with you for the photo?"

Sherman nods again and shakes Larry's hand again.

Gripping Sherman's hands, Larry says, "Hey, I just won a few hundred bucks on your horse. How about I buy you a drink to celebrate?"

Sherman looks back toward the track as both Heliacal Star and McGee move out of view.

Larry prompts, "What do you say, Mr. Sherman? Just one drink. On me. Seems Ron is headed to the barn, so it'll just be you and me."

Sherman nods. "Why not? Let's grab that drink. Sorry I missed you in the paddock earlier. I was running behind and barely made it here for the race. A drink sounds pretty good right now."

As they approach the bar, Larry is greeted enthusiastically by a group of friends with a series of high-fives and fist pumps. One of them shouts, while waving a few hundred-dollar bills, "Nice tip, Larry. Frigging Heliacal Star, baby!"

Larry winks. "What did I tell you? I hope you all were smart enough to make a big wager." He pauses and looks at Sherman. "That is, smart enough to wager on Mr. Alex Sherman's incredible horse, Heliacal Star!"

Addressing his group of friends, Larry says, "Gentlemen, and I use the word loosely, it is my pleasure to introduce you to Mr. Alex Sherman, the owner of Heliacal Star." He waves to the bartender and says, "Bring him anything he wants!"

Sherman orders a vodka soda with a twist, and Larry gestures for them to sit at an unoccupied table, only a few feet from the bar area. Sherman follows Larry, and the pair toast to the winner of the seventh race. The vodka perks up the previously reserved Sherman as he starts to ruminate about his horse and the torch he once carried for Heliacal Star, after purchasing him at auction for $550K.

Larry quips, "Holy shit, man! You paid more than a half-million dollars for him! No wonder you had high hopes!"

Sherman says, "I'll tell you something, Larry. I've been a highly successful investment banker, managing funds worth millions of dollars, but I've never been as nervous, anxious, or excited as when I placed the winning bid on Heliacal Star and purchased him as a yearling."

Larry holds up his glass and says, "A toast, my friend, to your horse, Heliacal Star. He may not have won the big one, but he's surely brought you to the Winner's Circle many times!"

Sherman downs his beverage in a single swallow and salutes Larry. "Here here!" He looks at his emptied glass and hands Larry a fifty-dollar bill. "That was exquisite. Let's get one more." Larry refuses the money, but Sherman insists.

Returning with their drinks, Larry chuckles and asks, "You say you're an investment banker? No kidding? I notice you dress fancy, but no offense, I didn't envision you as some super-rich banker."

Sherman sips from his glass and speaks with a slight slur. "I consider this place"—he points to the area all around—"my escape from the rest of the world. But enough about me. You look familiar. What is it that you do, Mr., Mr. . . .?"

Larry answers, "Lonsdale. Larry Lonsdale."

"Of course. Mr. Lonsdale. So, how do you make a living, Mr. Lonsdale? Do you have an office in Manhattan?"

Larry bursts out laughing. "Dude, take a look at me! Do I really look like the Manhattan office type?"

Sherman joins his laugh. "Okay, I give up, what do—" he starts, but stops talking midsentence as a trio of attractive ladies catch his eye. The first wears a short sundress and stilettos, the second lady leaves little to the imagination, wearing skintight yoga pants and a halter top, while the third is a leggy display in form-fitting denim short shorts and flowing auburn hair. As the three ladies move toward the bar, they slink past Sherman, one brushing him and causing him to blush as he excuses himself. Men hush as several maneuver around the three ladies.

After accepting one of multiple offers to pay for their drinks, the ladies grab their cocktails and find an open table near Sherman and Larry. Larry waves the trio over, encouraging them to join him and Sherman.

Catching the attention of the auburn in short shorts, Larry flexes his arms as they rest across the table. His biceps obligingly bulge under his short-sleeve shirt, and he smiles while watching the girls ogle his muscles. Larry stands and addresses the auburn, "What's your pleasure today, sweetheart?"

She smiles approvingly as her two friends join her. Alex Sherman silently rises from his chair and watches Larry take the lead.

The auburn sits close to Larry, strokes his bicep, and points to her drink. "You can buy our next round, big boy!"

Larry stands, whips out two hundred-dollar bills, and escorts her to the bar. Her two friends follow close behind.

Watching Larry escort the attractive auburn and her friends to the bar, Sherman leans deep into his seat, gulps his entire drink, and chews on the remaining ice cubes in his glass.

A few minutes pass, and Larry returns to Sherman. He leans in close and says, "It's showtime, my friend. These babes are fucking gorgeous and looking for a good time tonight." Sherman squints, looks in the direction of the ladies, and shakes off Larry's offer.

Larry smiles. "Oh, I know what you must be thinking. No, no, they're not ladies of the night. Nobody's paying for sex if that is what worries you, my friend. So, are you ready to have some fun tonight?"

The paunchy Alex Sherman grabs his empty glass, swirls the remaining cubes, and tosses them in his mouth. He kicks away his chair as he stands and follows Larry to the bar. At the bar, Sherman hails the bartender for a refill.

Larry throws his arm around Sherman's shoulders and says, "Ladies, allow me to introduce you to my close associate and acquaintance, Mr. Alex Sherman. You see, Alex is an investment banker by day and the owner of Heliacal Star, the horse who just won the last race! Here's to Mr. Alex Sherman, a true winner!" Larry, holding up five fingers for five champagne flutes, calls to the bartender, "Bring us your finest champagne!"

The bartender opens a bottle of Dom Perignon and fills each flute generously. Larry offers the auburn, now pressing herself into him, the first flute. He hands a champagne-filled flute to each of her friends and one to Alex Sherman before taking the final glass for himself. Larry raises his flute and says, "To Heliacal Star! A beautiful horse and a winner today!"

All five clink their glasses and drink in unison.

Larry again raises his flute. "Hold up a minute. Another toast to one beautiful horse and three beautiful ladies!"

The auburn girl throws her arms around Larry, pulls him in tight, and kisses him passionately. Larry slowly pulls away to glance and wink at Sherman. The other two ladies slip in tight to either side of Alex Sherman.

On Sherman's left, the girl in the sundress caresses her mouth over his ear and whispers in a sultry voice, "Don't be nervous, sweetie." She traces his face with her finger while stroking the back of his head. As he turns to her, she presses her tongue inside his lips. Her friend on his right is pressing her finger on his thigh and slowly moving it up his leg. She pulls Sherman away from her friend, gently twisting his head. Positioning her index finger between his lips, she says, "Congratulations, darling, on the win today. You're cute, baby!"

Sherman's breath becomes rapid as the girl in the sundress presses her lips on the back of his neck while the other is massaging his thigh. She methodically moves her hand up and says, "Ooh, I don't think he'll need any Viagra tonight." She places her fingers on his pants zipper.

Sherman grabs her hand and pulls it off. He drops his head and takes several steps away from the bar. Turning around, he faces the group and takes a long breath, then another and yet another. He moves back a step and says, "My God, you're the most beautiful ladies I've ever been around, but . . . " He pauses, looks at Larry, and continues, "But this is just not me. You see, I'm a married man and have never cheated on my wife. I'm just . . . I'm sorry. I'm really sorry."

One of the gals walks up to Sherman, pecks him on the cheek, and says, "You really are very cute, baby." She smiles and blows him a kiss. "It's too bad. We had some big plans for you tonight!"

Sherman stares at all three of them for several more seconds, turns, and leaves without looking back.

Larry moves up to the pair of gals who were all over Sherman. "Well?"

The girl in the sundress says, "He was definitely hard. Must be very loyal to his wife." She looks at herself. "I mean, he turned this down!"

Larry finishes his champagne, kisses the auburn, and says, "Thanks, babe, for doing this today. Sherman definitely seems to be straitlaced and serious." He laughs out loud. "You almost had that poor bastard selling his soul. Perhaps next time he won't be so intimidated!"

Larry's phone vibrates, and he excuses himself. "Let me take this." He picks up his phone. "Oh, hey, McGee, what's up? I'm at the bar with the girls. Come join us. They're pretty horny tonight and were just jilted by your client a few minutes ago."

On the line, McGee gasps. "Larry, you didn't. Shit, why did you do that? Alex isn't a bad guy. Wow, I give him credit, though. He must have some very strong willpower. On the other hand, I've got a weak mind. I'll see you soon."

Larry says, "A couple of photos of this Sherman guy with my girls, and we'd have ourselves a sucker to buy us some horses. Oh well, you better get here fast. These girls are getting plenty of loving looks from the crowd around here."

McGee says, "Let them know I'm coming."

"Anything going on at the barn?"

"That's why I was calling. Heliacal Star tied up after the race today. He had muscle cramping, and it took him an extra-long time to cool out this afternoon. Hopefully, it's nothing, but I'm going to pump him with a shit ton of electrolytes and keep a close eye on him over the next couple of days. We may only have one more shot with him."

CHAPTER 24

After celebrating her earlier victory and giving an official statement regarding the fight with McGee to track security, Kristine Connelly returns to her barn to wash and groom her horse. Her phone has been lighting up with congratulatory texts from Ted Bouchard, his assistant, her family upstate and several acquaintances from the racetrack. She acknowledges them all with a smiley face, along with a horse and heart emoticon and the word *Thanks*.

After blanketing the winning horse, she hands the shank and lead rope to the groom to hand-walk him in the shed row for another twenty minutes. She walks to her office, shuts the door, and stares at her phone and the latest text message from Matt.

Kris, please forgive me, but I can't see you again. It's for your own good.

She stares at the message until the screen times out and goes dark. Kristine sits still for several minutes, then responds to Matt's text.

WTF Matt?

Kristine exits the office, takes the shank from her groom, and leads her horse down the shed row. She walks him for another thirty minutes, only stopping when her groom interrupts to ice his legs. Placing the horse's forelegs into prefilled ice boots, he says to Kristine, "¿Todo bien?"

She replies with an empty stare, "Huh?" He points to the ice boots, and she says, "Oh, okay. Yes, gracias."

The groom asks, "¿Estás bien?"

Kristine says without expression, "Yes, I'm fine. I'm just thinking is all. Estoy pensando."

As the groom returns to the horse, Kristine reenters her office and answers a few more congratulatory texts. Scrolling through her contacts, she stops at Matt Galiano's name and presses the green icon to ring his phone.

After three rings, she hears his voicemail. She hangs up without leaving a message and redials. No answer again. This time she leaves a message. "Hello, Matt . . . This is Kris. Of course, it's Kris, who else would I be? I honestly don't know what's going on with you, but I believe you, Matt, and I'm here for you. Perhaps you got spooked by those goons today. I'm not afraid of them. At least tell me what's going on."

Across town, Matt's phone is ringing. He glances at the caller ID, which shows a phone number he recognizes as belonging to Kristine. As he approaches a red light, he grabs his phone and is about to answer, but declines. Moments later, his phone rings again. He looks at the number until it stops ringing. A few seconds later, his phone chirps, indicating a new voice message.

Fighting his temptation to respond, Matt is torn between his feelings for Kristine and his deep concern and obligation for her safety should they remain involved. He knows Louisville Larry will never go away. The strength of his feelings and inherent difficulty in letting her go are not his priority. He convinces himself a clean break is the best and only choice to protect her from his sins of the past. He listens to her voicemail, draws in his breath, and reaffirms his decision.

After taking such a bold and decisive action, Matt realizes his abruptness may cause Kristine some short-term pain, but if he tries to explain his reasoning, he's afraid his resolve will weaken. Yearning for her, he rests his head on the steering wheel.

A horn blares from behind, jolting Matt upright. He drives aimlessly for another thirty minutes, debating the merit of his arbitrary decision to ghost her. Her voicemail message only makes his decision harder. He cannot deny, even to himself, his feelings for her.

He pulls into his driveway and approaches his front door but does not enter.

He picks up his phone, stares at the missed calls on his display, and shuts his eyes. And then, unlocking his phone, Matt returns his last missed call.

CHAPTER 25

After a formal greeting from Special Agent Anjero, Alex Sherman sits inside a conference room at the Lower Manhattan FBI office. The room is unadorned, with four office chairs surrounding the small, bare conference table with floor-to-ceiling windows facing the hall corridor. Sherman adjusts his chair, places his elbows on the table, and tilts forward.

Anjero sits across from Sherman. "Thank you, Mr. Sherman, for meeting me today. To be clear and put your mind at ease, I'm not investigating anything related to you. I'm specifically interested in an acquaintance of yours."

Sherman sweeps his hand across his balding head, tugs on his collar, and looks across at the special agent.

Anjero continues, "I'm interested in Ron McGee. I'm aware his trade is training racehorses. This includes a horse you own named Heliacal Star. Can you tell me how you became associated with Ron McGee?"

Sherman asks, "Are you seriously investigating Ron McGee? What did he do?"

After realizing modest success with a few partnership horses, Alex Sherman ventured out on his own and purchased several yearling and two-year-old horses. Although his purchases were considered modest by general racing standards, Sherman found success after a couple of wins using Ted Bouchard as his trainer. The wins came at the claiming level, which comprise the majority of races in North America but are not intended for the best racing prospects, as the top-flight horses race at elite levels.

When the hammer fell for Heliacal Star at the annual Keeneland sale in September of 2014, Alex Sherman was overtly expressing a desire to compete among the most affluent in horse racing and those willing to drop several hundred thousand dollars or more on a single racing prospect. Such expenditures come with lofty expectations, including the potential to compete in the biggest races at the most prestigious racing venues throughout the country.

Despite his impressive pedigree and lofty sales price as a yearling, Heliacal Star failed to win or finish in the top three during a trio of races as a juvenile two-year-old colt. Some young horses, regardless of their pedigrees, may require additional time to mature and fulfill their potential as superstars. After a disappointing first year on the racetrack, Ted Bouchard turned Heliacal Star out to pasture to mature, develop physically, and grow into a potential top-flight racehorse.

After a full winter off from racing, Heliacal Star returned to the racetrack as a newly gelded three-year-old in 2016. The minor one-way surgery meant Heliacal Star could never become a stallion, thus dashing any hopes of a breeding career after racing. Sherman initially voiced opposition to Bouchard's suggestion but eventually relented at the insistence of his trainer after the latter claimed such surgery would improve his focus for training. Heliacal Star responded with perceptible improvement, and he broke his maiden but fell short of winning consistently during his sophomore three-year-old season.

The dream of a Kentucky Derby or Breeders' Cup faded into the rearview as Bouchard dropped him to compete against less accomplished foes for lower purse money. After a shouting match with Bouchard about Heliacal Star's three-year-old campaign, Alex Sherman made the decision to fire his longtime trainer. He moved his elite purchase to the barn of Ron McGee.

In this game replete with big money, big egos, and big expectations, the virtues of patience and understanding are supplanted by an insatiable desire for immediate successes and quick returns, especially for those making substantial investments. Replacing and scapegoating trainers when initial expectations are dashed is a common practice exercised by persnickety owners.

Although Ted Bouchard had enjoyed a long and successful career as a thoroughbred trainer and had been the only trainer Alex Sherman had ever employed, Heliacal Star was transferred without incident or complaint from Bouchard's stable to Ron McGee. It was also during this time when various trade articles surfaced regarding Bouchard's lost touch, citing his declining winning percentage and shrinking stable. He was criticized as being too old-fashioned and overly conservative in his training methodology. Bouchard's winning percentage had fallen below 10 percent for the first time in his career. Conversely, Ron McGee was ascendant, and he challenged the top racehorse conditioners with an exceptional win rate of 25 percent. By any measure, Sherman's decision to change trainers from Bouchard to McGee was a sensible and logical one to anyone competent at reading a racing form.

Sherman looks across at Special Agent Anjero and says, "I met Ron McGee for the first time about two years ago, in late 2016, when he took over training for Heliacal Star. I was brash and frustrated. No, I was angry with Bouchard and decided a change of scenery and a different approach would unleash my horse's potential. I studied the statistics, which took me to Ron McGee, who was doing well on paper. I phoned him, and he seemed both eager and genuinely excited to train my horse. Unlike some super trainers who manage stables with hundreds of horses, McGee only has about fifty horses in his barn and was very approachable."

Anjero interjects, "What do you mean by super trainer?"

Sherman says, "There are a handful of elite trainers who condition the classiest horses purchased by the wealthiest owners. Along with a small number of jockeys, these trainers are racing's human celebrities. They're called super trainers because they manage massive stables with hundreds of horses competing at venues from coast to coast, aided by an army of assistant trainers. They win a lot of races and charge a high day rate in addition to some pricey veterinarian bills—or so I've heard. Of course, I can't speak from personal experience, but any trainer with so many horses across multiple racetracks isn't realistically spending much attention on my one horse, unless he's a superstar."

After moving from Bouchard to McGee, Heliacal Star resurged on the Belmont oval. Sherman was rewarded for his decision, as Heliacal Star won his first start for McGee as a four-year-old. When midsummer racing transitioned from

Belmont to Saratoga in July, his good fortune continued.

To anyone with deep roots or just a passing interest in horse racing, Saratoga Race Course is regarded as the premiere racing oval in North America. The nineteenth-century venue is the oldest in the United States, dating to the mid-1800s. Each year the Saratoga racing meet attracts the top trainers, richest owners, and top horses across North America and across the world. Among its nicknames is the "Graveyard of Favorites," as it was the only venue where both Secretariat and Man o' War lost as heavy betting favorites. Its historical significance is complemented by the presence of the National Museum of Racing and Hall of Fame, located across Union Avenue from the main entrance of the historic racetrack.

To both the casual and serious racing fan alike, Saratoga is an annual celebration of the racehorse, its history, and tradition. Upon entering the grandstand, visitors are greeted with several bands playing upbeat jazz. The famous Big Red Spring within the grounds is one of several natural springs inside the city of Saratoga Springs. At the racetrack, the horses are the true celebrities, as they saunter past curious onlookers en route to the oversize paddock for pre-race preparation. The paddock itself is a meticulously decorated private area where the horses prepare for battle. For more than a century, a bell has rung through the grounds for the sole purpose of informing everyone the next post is seventeen minutes away.

With a widening grin, Sherman says to Anjero, "Ah, Saratoga. The summer of 2017 was nothing short of a magical for me with Heliacal Star. I have Ron McGee to thank for that. He won my first and *only* stakes race at Saratoga that summer. It was beyond incredible. Just the excitement alone from the crowd screaming alongside of us when he finished first was such an indescribable feeling. My wife and my . . . "

His smile fades. He looks down and away from Anjero and says, "My wife and my younger daughter." Sherman rubs his eyes. "We were so happy that day."

A seasoned federal agent maintains a certain empathy based on their experience for those who have unexpectedly lost loved ones. Anjero remains quiet as a show of respect and allows Sherman time and space to work through his obvious emotions.

Sherman looks up. "I'm sorry. I didn't expect to react like this, but being here brings back memories of my first daughter, whom we lost in 2013. The FBI . . ." Sherman trails off as he stares at Anjero. He points at the agent, wrinkles his forehead, and says, "The FBI opened an investigation into her death." He rises, leaning forward on his hands. "Were you aware of that?"

Anjero looks across at Sherman. "Yes. I was aware of your daughter's suspected homicide, and I'm very sorry. I know the case is still open, and it remains an active investigation."

Sherman nods, and Anjero continues, "I have read through your daughter's file and understand you provided a detailed statement, but it may be helpful to listen to your story directly. Of course, if this is too upsetting, I totally understand . . ."

After a long pause, Sherman says, "My youngest daughter was entering her sophomore year at NYU . . . The shock from that phone call . . . It was exactly 7:32 a.m. when my wife picked up the phone. The police discovered her body discarded in an alley on the Lower East Side."

He stops for a moment and looks at Anjero, who signals for him to continue, "They told us she was brutally assaulted." He looks down and away from the agent and mumbles, "I know she was murdered."

Anjero is taking notes as Sherman looks up. "The autopsy determined the cause of death was a lethal injection of some undetermined designer drug. Agent Anjero, I know this will sound cliché, but my wife and I were close to her. She was not a drug user." Sherman rubs his eyes again and continues, "In the months that followed, we asked her friends, her college room-mates, and anyone that knew her. I'm convinced some asshole must have drugged and assaulted her, then left her to die in the middle of that alley."

"Thank you for sharing, Mr. Sherman," Anjero says. "As I'm sure you know, your daughter's wasn't the only suspicious death that year. You may have read or watched news stories about drug cartels operating out of Canada and local organized crime distributing designer drugs around the city. They are careful in covering their tracks, but we are determined to reveal, catch, and arrest them."

Sherman looks up. "So, why this sudden interest in Ron McGee?"

Anjero replies, "It may be nothing, but we suspect he may be a link or participant in a crime syndicate we are investigating." He pulls out a photograph and shows it to Sherman.

"Have you ever seen this man with McGee?"

Sherman only looks briefly at the photo. "Yep. I've seen him. In fact, I met him after the races just yesterday. Name is Larry Lonsdale, and he's apparently something of a ladies' man."

Sherman's face flushes. He continues, "He's a big guy. Why? What's his deal?"

Anjero says, "His name is Larry Lonsdale, but he also goes by the moniker 'Louisville' Larry. He's a member of the Kaufman crime syndicate. We've had surveillance on him and recently spotted him with McGee. Thank you for confirming their association. Do you know the nature of their relationship?"

Sherman looks up. "Lonsdale was already in the Winner's Circle after my horse won yesterday. He told me that McGee trains a few horses for him and said he was big fan of my horse."

"Thank you again for confirming their association. To preserve the integrity of our case, I'm going to ask that you keep the details of our conversation private and just between us. We'll be in touch."

CHAPTER 26

In the three days since Heliacal Star paraded inside the Winner's Circle at Belmont Park for the second time in June, the elegant thoroughbred had yet to return to the racing oval to be jogged or galloped and been confined to his stall. As he's done each morning for the past three days, Ron McGee enters the stall and places his right hand on the horse's front left knee, holds it for a moment, and slowly slides it down till he reaches his ankle and pastern. He lifts Heliacal Star's right front hoof and inspects his sole with a hoof pick. Repeating the same inspection on his right leg, McGee shakes his head and asks the groom to bring him a halter.

After slipping on the halter, McGee slowly walks Heliacal Star out of his stall and down the shed row. After just a few steps, the limp is noticeable in the left front foreleg. McGee halts, massages the back of the horse's leg, just below the knee, and returns Heliacal Star to his stall.

Inside the stall, McGee phones his veterinarian.

"Hey, Doc, McGee here. The swelling and heat are down considerably from a few days ago, but he's still lame at the walk. Call me when you get this message."

As McGee leaves the stall, he watches Heliacal Star ignore

any discomfort he may be feeling as a new bundle of timothy hay is hung outside the stall. Watching the horse graze, McGee phones Alex Sherman, who answers after a single ring.

"Hi, Alex, McGee here."

Sherman says, "Hey, Ron. Hey, who is your acquaintance Larry Lonsdale? I met him the other day after Heliacal Star's race? Man, he had some gorgeous gals around him!"

McGee chuckles and says, "Yeah, Larry is certainly one of a kind. He's a truly interesting fellow, but I didn't call to talk about him. I called to give you an update about Heliacal Star. It looks like he aggravated his front left foreleg during the race last Saturday. When I looked at him on Sunday, there was a fair bit of heat and fluid in his leg. My vet checked him, and we gave him some bute and pumped him with electrolytes and amino acids. The swelling and heat are considerably better since Sunday, but he wasn't moving too well a few minutes ago when I took him out for a walk."

"Shit!" Sherman shouts in the phone. "What's the problem this time? What's your plan?"

McGee says, "I'm sorry, Alex. This horse has a litany of issues, and given his age and history . . . I gotta be honest with you: he's close to the finish line regarding his racing career."

"No! C'mon, Ron. Don't feed me that line of bullshit! I've just watched him win two in a row. He looked fantastic in his last win!"

McGee asks, "Are you familiar with the horse's suspensory ligament?"

Sherman is quiet, and McGee continues, "Picture a taut rubber band that stretches down the back of the horse's leg, starting at the knee and traveling to just above his ankle. Call that his ligament. If the rubber band or ligament becomes too stretched out, it may eventually snap. Even if it doesn't snap, it will never regain its original tautness. You can think of the rubber band as analogous to the suspensory, except it also attaches to important structures in the lower portion of the leg. Your horse pulled his suspensory. It's not a good injury for any horse to sustain, and especially a racehorse. I'm afraid to tell you this, but he's never going to be the same racehorse again."

Sherman interjects, "So, what's the plan? Are we turning him out to pasture, letting this shit heal, and then assessing the situation in a couple of months? I get it. I've been through the drill before."

"Alex. You're not listening to me. This is not the type of injury that improves, even after time off. Think about the physics . . . his front legs are repeatedly absorbing the force of eleven hundred pounds while cruising at high speed. A little rest won't hurt, but you'll be spending money all along. I guarantee we can cut your losses by dropping him into a claiming race now, especially while he's on a winning streak."

Sherman is silent.

"I'm sorry, Alex, but Heliacal Star is not the same horse he was last year. Shit! He's not the same horse he was three days ago!"

Sherman is abrupt. "What exactly are you suggesting?"

"His last two races were very good visually. Prior to this, he's had extended time off following his injury from last year. Thus, we should be uncompromising in order to lure someone to our bait. If we're not aggressive, there will be hesitation. If it were entirely up to me, I'd drop him into a cheap claiming race and get rid of him now before it's too late."

Sherman says, "Just to be clear, you want to enter him in a claiming race for say, twenty thousand dollars, and you expect someone will drop a claim and scoop him up?"

"Yup, that should do it. Maybe even $12,500 or $16,000."

Sherman responds, "I want to ensure I'm really getting this. You're telling me I should enter my horse, who just won $50,000 in purse money, in a race where he could be sold for $20,000? The same horse I paid over a half-million dollars for is going to be dangled for less than five percent what I paid, and you consider this a sucker bet? Wouldn't such a move raise several red flags, even if someone were baited? What am I missing here, Ron?"

In a sharper tone, McGee says, "Alex, I've been in this game a long time, and I'm trying to help you. Honestly, your horse isn't worth the twenty thousand, based on what I'm seeing. You're only going to get this one chance to dump him, salvage a return, and get him off your books. After his next race, nobody's going to want to touch him."

Sherman remains silent, and McGee continues, "Yes, of course it's a red flag, but this place has many hungry owners and obedient trainers, and I guarantee somebody is going to bite. They always do. Some may guess we're just trying to steal a race by placing him so aggressively. If they believe that and call our bluff by submitting a claim, they'll be wrong."

"I see," Sherman says. "Does this have anything to do with that Larry Lonsdale fellow?"

McGee says, "What? Where did that come from? No, of course not! Are you with me on this, Alex? If so, I'll get him ready in a week or two."

Sherman says, "Wait! I thought he couldn't walk? How is he going—"

McGee interrupts, "I'll worry about getting him ready. All you need to know is that he'll look the part during the post parade."

"I'm not sure I like this plan, Ron. I know it'll cost me more, but I think we could turn him out for six months and see how he does."

"Relax, Alex. It's just one more race, and then you needn't worry about him anymore. I know you invested a lot of money in him, but he's not getting better, and you'll be spending a lot more money in the days and months ahead if you don't get rid of this problem now."

After his sizeable investment, Sherman had been unable to regain any practical return while he continued to pay for boarding, training, veterinarian, and equine hospital bills, which were sometimes, but not often offset by the purse money. For many owners, there is a point at which pragmatism replaces optimism.

McGee presses. "Alex, I'm not trying to pull any punches here. I'm trying to be your advocate and do what's best for my client. You had a nice run with this horse, but it's over now."

There is silence on the other end of the phone. "Can you still hear me, Alex?"

Sherman says, "Fine. Do it. Let's get this over with."

McGee ends the call and walks to his barn office. He waves at the two grooms standing nearby, hands one a twenty-dollar bill, and instructs them to return in fifteen minutes with coffee from the kitchen. Once the grooms are gone, McGee is alone in the barn. He unlocks a cabinet above his desk, grabs an unlabeled bottle and clean syringe, and scurries to Heliacal Star's stall. He gently taps the horse on his neck and injects the loaded syringe. "This will make you feel better, big guy, but remember, it's our secret."

McGee phones Larry, who promptly answers, "What's up, McGee? You got another tip for me?"

"As a matter of fact, I do."

Larry sounds enthusiastic. "The boys were pretty happy about the last one. You did well. What do you got this time?"

McGee looks around, covers his mouth with one hand, and speaks softly into the phone. "I'm bringing Heliacal Star back quickly. There's a race in the condition book for July 4th. Remember when I told you he was cramping after his last race? Well, he's literally on his last legs. The entire planet is going to bet on him in this next race, and it's going to be an epic sucker bet. He's going to run like shit, if he finishes at all. You and your boys can bet on it!"

CHAPTER 27

Matt tosses in his bed as he tries to sleep but is unable to shake off the guilt from enlisting Kristine in his escalating fight with the ghosts from his past. Throughout the night, he navigates through sorrow, remorse, and selfishness, until finally landing on a satisfactory justification. Perhaps cognitive dissonance is a tonic to rationalize his decisions, but he can't fight or deny his desires in ultimately surrendering to his affection for Kristine.

As the early light of morning peeks through the shades, Matt's heart warms with thoughts of Kristine's charismatic smile, infectious laugh, and soft lips. It has been nearly a week since his aborted date with Kristine at the racetrack. It has also been a week since he has seen Louisville Larry or Ron McGee.

During the past week, Matt has remained vigilant about his personal safety by avoiding locations where he might encounter Louisville. To reduce the probability of an unwanted encounter, he has stayed home throughout the week except while working. When he and Kristine finally spoke on the phone last week, Matt encouraged her to maintain a low profile, in the event somebody was snooping or spying.

When Matt finally climbs out of bed, he's excited for his

plans to meet Kristine again tonight. Training hours at the racetrack open at half past five each morning, and since he's up and awake, Matt decides to surprise Kristine with an early morning visit. Without security credentials to enter the stable area, he dresses quickly and drives to the track, entering via the public grandstand. A short walk to the rail places him near a group of early railbirds watching the horses train. Matt looks in all directions for Kristine, hoping to catch her or one of her horses training on the main track this morning, but there is no sign of her. As a precaution, Matt wears his forest-green T-shirt and matching green cap pulled low over his forehead and a pair of oversize sunglasses. While not the most clever or masterful of disguises, Matt is confident it'll be good enough to fool McGee or Louisville should they happen to amble nearby the rail this morning.

All morning, Matt notices celebrity trainers and enjoys his view of the dozens of horses jogging, galloping, and sprinting on the track. To the untrained eye, the scene plays out as organized chaos, with dozens of horses moving at different speeds and in different directions, but everyone appears to know the rules and there are no mishaps or accidents. Time moves quickly as Matt is immersed in his admiration of the athleticism, power, and grace of the thoroughbreds in training. After spending years analyzing and wagering on these horses, Matt has never taken the time to appreciate the inherent beauty of the equine breed or consider them as anything beyond a means for gambling and entertainment. Perhaps it's the lack of sleep or maybe it's Kristine's influence, but as Matt continues to watch the horses train, the more he admires them as magnificent and majestic animals, moving dutifully and in harmony with their exercise riders.

His mind wanders to a time mostly forgotten, and he wonders if training horses has changed all that much from a century ago when the racetrack originally opened. Of course, there had to be horses, riders, and trainers and perhaps a mechanical stopwatch to time their breezes. While conveniences like mobile phones, simulcasting, radiographs, veterinary medicine, and digitized racing forms have modernized the racing game, he imagines the fundamentals of equine science in terms of training a successful racehorse have remained mostly intact over the past hundred years. After all, he rationalizes, horses are physical beings who require repetitive training to build fitness, strength, and stamina, then as much as now.

After several hours, Matt remains stationed at the rail, but still has not seen Kristine, or McGee for that matter. The number of horses on the track is dwindling until none remains, meaning the main track has closed for training for the day.

As the final horse leaves the track, Matt notices two gentlemen in golf shirts and khaki shorts approaching the stable area. As the two men converse with each other, Matt runs up behind them, keeping just a few feet of distance to avoid their attention. They reach the guard booth, are waved through, and continue walking.

Matt sneaks closer, pretending to be with them, but the security guard in the booth is not fooled and stops him from entering the stable area.

"Hold on, son. I'll need to see your security credentials."

Matt sifts through his wallet, looks up at the guard, and shrugs without producing the required document. He hands a driver's license to the guard. "I must have left my racing license at home. Will this work?"

The guard is terse. "I'm sorry, sir. In order to gain access to the stable area, you're required to carry an updated horseman's badge with stable access." The guard takes Matt's license, and continues, "Mr. Galiano, are you here to visit anyone specifically? I can write you a day pass."

Matt exclaims, "Great! Yes. I'm here to see Kristine Connelly."

The guard pulls out a clipboard and runs his finger down a sheet with several names and numbers on it and stops. He repeats, "Kristine Connelly?"

Matt nods, and the guard steps into the security booth and dials a number from his landline.

A moment later, he says to Matt, "I'm sorry, but my call went directly to voicemail. I tried twice, but there was no answer. I can't allow you through."

Matt planned to surprise Kristine without calling or texting ahead of time, but his plan is clearly not working, and his eyes feel heavy from his limited sleep. Instead of arguing with the guard, he decides to return home. He waves to the guard, thanks him for his help, and returns to his car.

An overwhelming fatigue suddenly takes over as Matt settles in at home. He yawns a few times and picks up his cell phone, intent on phoning Kristine, but the yawns keep coming. Lying down on his couch, Matt rests his eyes and drifts into a deep sleep until he's awakened by a loud chirp coming from his phone. Groggy, he reaches for the phone and reads the notification from a new horse racing app he just downloaded.

The time on his phone indicates he's been asleep for more

than three hours. As he awakens, his energy returns. Matt taps the notification and opens the app.

It shows the upcoming entries for the races on July 4th:

1ST RACE: CLAIMING PRICE $20,000
6F FOR COLTS AND GELDINGS 3 AND UP.
PURSE: $42,000

PP	HORSE	A/S	JOCKEY	WGT	ODDS
1	HELIACAL STAR	5/G	J. FERNANDEZ	123	--
2	ROOSTER CITY	7/G	J. JOSE	123	--
3	KEN'S HARD ROLL	4/G	L. ANDERSON	...	

Matt rubs his eyes and rereads the entries a second and third time.

Speaking aloud to himself, he says, "What the heck? Did McGee really enter Heliacal Star in a low-level claiming race?"

Based on Heliacal Star's last two races, Matt figures the horse must be worth at least four or five times the amount he's being offered, based on the claiming value, as a condition of entry.

As a lifelong racing fan, Matt knows there are generally two reasons a trainer will drop a horse into a race substantially below his perceived market value. In one case, an owner may be trying to dump the horse by offering him at a highly discounted price to improve the probability a claim will be made. This could be the consequence of a horse not fitting a program, an issue with soundness, or a lack of confidence in the projected future perfor-mance of the horse. Each owner may differ in terms of reasons to cull a horse from their stable. Another reason is when an owner is bluffing or looking to steal an easy win against softer competition. If the drop is so precipitous to look suspicious, others may get spooked and stay away, even if nothing appears physically wrong with the horse. This second scenario is more likely to occur at smaller racing venues where there is a limited number of trainers and fewer dollars available to make such claims.

Matt knows Heliacal Star's last race was against tougher company and earned his owner more than $40,000 for the victory. Doing cursory research on the internet, Matt learns Alex Sherman paid more than a half million for him as a yearling, and his career earnings to date have surpassed $200,000. Matt wonders if Heliacal Star no longer fits Sherman's program, although such a big drop in class certainly looks suspicious. Matt argues with himself that even if the horse has a health issue, such a large discount relative to his potential market value seems excessive. Assuming he were to be claimed, the new owner could simply run him back and win at the same level to recover the initial capital investment and then some.

Another oddity about the race piquing Matt's curiosity is the fact that Heliacal Star is being entered so soon after his last race. The most common interval between races is at least three or four weeks. It has been just a week since Heliacal Star's last race, and returning him on such short notice is a super aggressive tactic given the day-to-day rigors of training a racehorse.

Throughout his life, Matt never considered owning a racehorse. After Kristine mentioned the possibility, and given his fanatical affinity for Heliacal Star, he figures this may be destiny reaching out to him. He envisions owning Heliacal Star, pictures

Kristine as his trainer, and daydreams about celebrations together in the Winner's Circle. Yet, to satisfy his starry-eyed fantasy, he would still need to raise twenty grand, which may be inexpensive by thoroughbred racing standards but represents an insurmountable obstacle given Matt's personal finances.

Without any collateral, even a bank or personal loan is not a realistic option. No one in their right mind would lend him the cash to purchase a racehorse. As he scavenges his mind for potential options, a farfetched yet viable idea suddenly pops into his head. As he plays out this scenario, he wonders if Kristine will find his creativity, decisiveness, and boldness impressive or irrational and compulsive. Scrolling through his phone contacts, he stops on a specific name. After taking several short breaths, he dials the number.

Matt clears his throat. "Hello, Mr. Sherman. This is Matt Galiano. I hope you remember me. We first met at Saratoga and then at Belmont last year."

CHAPTER 28

Matt? Oh, Matt Galiano, yes, of course! I recall you're quite fond of Heliacal Star. Saratoga and Belmont. Yes, I remember you."

In just hearing Sherman's voice, Matt reminisces about their first encounter last summer at Saratoga Race Course.

It was August of 2017, almost a year ago, when Matt drove the hundred miles to Saratoga Springs from Long Island, arriving at the fabled track an hour ahead of post time for the first race.

Throughout that year, Matt had cashed multiple tickets by wagering on Heliacal Star, and he was pumped to watch and wager on him at the Upstate venue. Although Matt was not directly affiliated with the horse, he likely felt as nervous as anyone connected to Heliacal Star prior to the race. After arriving at Saratoga, Matt buried his head in his racing form and analyzed a myriad of possible outcomes for the race. The exercise was academic, as Matt had already decided before even opening his form as to the winner. He marched confidently to the betting terminals and placed his wager.

Since his first encounter and winning wager on the horse at Belmont Park a year earlier, Matt maintained a sense of pride for

Heliacal Star. The race at Saratoga presented an opportunity for his favorite horse to lift his stature with the racing world. Winning a graded stakes race at the most important racing venue in North America would establish his ranking as one of the top racehorses in the country. Matt showed no hesitation when exchanging his wrinkled hundred-dollar bill for a betting voucher.

Pleasant summer afternoons at the historic Upstate racing venue habitually lead to swelling crowds, and this day was no exception, as all picnic tables and open spaces throughout the backyard were densely occupied by hundreds of groups, extended families, and several large parties enjoying a day at the races. As one of hundreds of interested onlookers, Matt darted through a narrow opening to reach the white wooden fence outlining the horse path. His timing was ideal, as Heliacal Star was approaching, with Ron McGee leading the larger-than-life racehorse on the horse's left flank. Walking several steps ahead of McGee was a middle-aged man in a sage-green double-breasted linen suit, paisley print silk tie, and Stetson straw fedora. Based on his attire, Matt deduced the well-dressed man was the owner of Heliacal Star, Mr. Alex Sherman, as listed in the racing program. Observing the horse dance gracefully across the pathway, Matt assessed Heliacal Star as strong and confident.

As McGee escorted the horse past where he stood, Matt hollered out, "Looking good, Heliacal Star!" Ron McGee did not turn, break stride, or adjust his hold, but Sherman turned back, glanced at Matt, and tipped his hat while walking down the path en route to the paddock.

Minutes later, a bell rang seven times and echoed throughout the paddock, indicating post time was scheduled in seventeen minutes. The sound of the bell sent a chill down Matt's spine accompanied by excitement, anxiety, and impatience. Matt paced as the thoroughbreds were saddled and could only manage a distant glimpse of Heliacal Star, while standing outside the paddock. Ron McGee aided the jockey atop Heliacal Star, and both horse and rider strode out of the paddock and toward the main track. The post parade was forthcoming, and Matt sprinted trackside, hoping to catch a view of Heliacal Star on the track.

As Matt edged along the railing to improve his view, he unwittingly bumped into a man walking toward him. Matt exclaimed, "I'm sorry, sir, excuse me . . . "

He recognized the man in the fancy attire and straw fedora as the one who'd just escorted Heliacal Start down the pathway minutes earlier.

Matt cleared his throat. "Excuse me, sir, are you the owner of Heliacal Star?"

Sherman offered a half smile and nodded.

Matt extended his hand. "I'm a huge fan. Good luck today . . . sir, Mr. Sherman."

Sherman took Matt's hand. "Thank you, young man. I hope you put a little something on him, 'cause he's looking good and ready to fire a big one today!"

Still shaking hands with his eyes widened, Matt said, "You bet! I absolutely love Heliacal Star." Sherman released his hand and Matt continued, "I gotta tell you something. Your horse showed me the eye of the tiger last year. It happened at Belmont in the paddock just before he broke his maiden. I made a nice little profit on him that day!"

Sherman chuckled, as Matt rambled. "I know it sounds odd,

but I swear he gave me this look I've never seen before or since. It was like some sort of magical sign, and the rest is history!"

Sherman's smile broadened. "Nice work, son. I remember that day, too! You won't get those long odds today, but I'm sure you can still make a profit on him. Nice to meet you. Say, what's your name?"

Matt extended his hand again. "I'm Matt. Matt Galiano. Best of luck, sir!"

"Back at you, Matt."

Heliacal Star did not require their additional well wishes, as he was superior to the competition in securing his one and only graded-stakes victory by five lengths, making both Matt and Alex Sherman winners for the day in their respective ways.

Matt's daydream is interrupted by Sherman's voice on the other end of the phone. "What's on your mind, son?"

Matt clears his throat and draws in a deep breath. "If you don't mind me asking, why did you enter Heliacal Star in a claiming race on the Fourth of July? Before Sherman can respond, Matt continues, "I'm sure you must remember me from last year? I was with you when Heliacal Star got hurt!"

Matt reflects on his only other meeting with Alex Sherman, last October at Belmont Park.

The cold and drizzly day on Long Island starkly contrasted the toasty sunshine of Saratoga two months earlier. As the drizzle transitioned to steady rain, most of the crowd scurried under a nearby awning or found cover inside the grandstand building. Matt could have cared less about the weather and remained out in the pouring rain at the rail to secure a prime viewing spot for the upcoming action on the track. He watched intently as

Heliacal Star was loaded into the gate as the betting favorite of the nine-horse field.

After breaking sharply on the sloppy racetrack, Heliacal Star shot forward and took a leading position along the rail, which was uncharacteristic of his recent races. As he continued down the backstretch, several horses loomed to his outside. One of them suddenly darted left and directly in front of Heliacal Star. The action caused Heliacal Star's jockey, Jack Fernandez, to pull back on his reins and caused the horse's head to rise sharply. The next second, Heliacal Start ducked down, popped his head high, and lurched forward upon clipping heels with the horse who'd cut him off just a moment earlier. Heliacal Star staggered, buckled his front legs, and rolled forward onto the ground, tossing jockey Fernandez in the process. The two horses immediately behind Heliacal Star leapt over the fallen horse but couldn't avoid contact as they also stumbled and fell forward. The remaining horses swerved around and maneuvered past the three fallen horses, narrowly escaping disaster.

Fernandez was tossed over the rail, sparing him from serious and potentially fatal injuries, as he could have been trampled by one of the trailing horses. Once all the horses were clear, the jockey stood on his own accord and approached his fallen mount. Heliacal Star had pushed himself to his feet but avoided putting weight on his right foreleg. Fernandez grabbed the reins and lifted the injured leg to protect it from further damage. The racetrack ambulance arrived within seconds of the spill, along with a vet ambulance. Matt watched Heliacal Star load onto the ambulatory van from where he stood across the racetrack near the finish line. He feared the worst.

Unable to watch, Matt turned his back to the track and instantly recognized Alex Sherman running toward the rail. Dripping wet, Sherman leaned over, slapped his program to the ground, and punched his hand in the air. Sherman pulled up a pair of binoculars strapped around his neck and looked across the track. The ambulatory vans collected all three injured horses and were moving down the track. A moment later, Sherman's phone rang. As he turned to answer, he looked directly at Matt, standing in the rain near the rail.

Sherman lowered his phone and yelled out toward Matt, "Hey! I know you, right?"

Matt nodded.

"Do you have a car nearby?"

Matt nodded again, and Sherman grabbed Matt by the wrist. "Would you drive me to the barn?"

As they strode toward Matt's car, Sherman spoke into his phone. "I'm on my way. I've got a ride. I'll find you . . . " There was a pause, then, "What was that?" Another pause and, "Okay, got it!" Sherman stopped, pocketed his phone, and mumbled to himself, "Damn it! This accident is going to cost me a shit ton of money!"

Sherman clenched his jaw and wrung his hands. "Well, at least they're not going euthanize, but he's being rushed to the clinic for emergency surgery."

Matt's eyes welled as he considered the potential fate of the horse. "Oh man, I was afraid . . . " He asked, "Did they say what happened or how badly he's hurt?"

Sherman rocked his head side to side.

"You still want me to drive you?" Matt asked.

Sherman coughed and cleared his throat. "If you don't mind, I would appreciate the lift."

As Matt drove to the stable area, the guard recognized Matt's passenger and waved them inside without any credential checks. Sherman directed him to an area where an assistant trainer jumped into the backseat of Matt's car and pointed them to the equine hospital across the street from the eastern border of the grounds.

At the hospital, the trio were escorted into a waiting area outside a surgery room as the attending equine surgeon approached them. The scene felt surreal, as Matt could see Heliacal Star through a Plexiglas wall, which Matt surmised was presurgery. The horse was standing in an oversize boot covering the bottom of his front leg.

Unsure of his place among Sherman and McGee's assistant trainer, Matt took a step back and stood in the background as the surgeon approached. Addressing Sherman, the surgeon said, "My exam revealed a medial apical fragment of the right proximal sesamoid and suspensory desmitis. We'll give him a general anesthetic and remove the fragments. The surgery should be routine, and he'll be standing post-op." He points to the horse through the Plexiglas. "I'd put his chance of returning to racing at about fifty-fifty, but he should recover in terms of a return to general health."

Standing next to the surgeon, McGee turned to Sherman. "Alex, we're fortunate it wasn't a basal or midbody fracture of the sesamoid, or he would have required screws and his career would be over."

Not wanting to interfere or look like an interloper, Matt

kept his distance from the group as they discussed the injury but was fascinated by the conversation. McGee never seemed to notice Matt standing nearby. Sherman looked at Heliacal Star through the Plexiglas and said, "Sorry, Ron, all this sounds like a foreign language to me. Can you explain it to me in layman's terms?"

McGee thanked the surgeon, who politely excused himself. McGee and Sherman walked, and Matt followed several feet behind the pair. McGee said, "In layman's terms, he broke a small bone in his right front ankle and damaged an associated ligament attached to it. They'll remove the bone fragment and observe him overnight. If there are no complications, he'll be released to me in the morning."

As they continued to walk outside the clinic, Sherman said to McGee, "Got it. I suppose this is going to take a while. Will he rehab at the track? Will he ever race again?"

McGee placed his hand on Sherman's shoulder. "Alex, he'll be moved to a nearby farm for rehabilitation. If you have no objections, I'll put him on a van as soon as he's released. He'll be limited to his stall for sixty days and require frequent bandage changes. After that, he'll graduate to hand-walking for another forty-five days. If all goes well, he'll spend time in a small round pen for another thirty days. If he continues to progress, we'll turn him out another forty-five days before we bring him back to the track and put tack on him. Let's give it six months. Bottom line is, it's too early to call, but I've seen horses return to the races from far worse injuries."

Matt returns to the present, with Alex Sherman on the other end of the line. "Based on what happened last year; as you know, I was there. Are his legs okay?"

Sherman says, "Matt, I think you're a good guy, and I never properly thanked you for helping me when Heliacal Star went down last year. Of course, I cannot ethically divulge our strategy, but let's just say I still believe in this horse and may not fully agree with McGee's decision to enter him in a cheap claiming race. Why do you ask?"

Matt's mind spins while considering the possibility of claiming Heliacal Star, except for the matter of the $20,000 required ahead of the race. The question from Sherman prompts a vision of himself and Kristine hoisting a trophy overhead to the cheering crowd surrounding them.

Sherman asks, "Matt, you still there?"

"Yes, sir. Sorry. I was thinking about your question." Unable to contain himself any longer, Matt says, "I think I'd like to claim Heliacal Star in that race on July 4th!" Matt pauses, still unsure about how far-fetched it is for him to own a racehorse. He swallows hard and continues, "I don't have the claim money, though."

Sherman asks, "Do you have a trainer and owner's license?"

Matt expected Sherman to press him about the money and is caught off-guard by the question about prerequisites. "Kristine Connelly is my trainer, but I'm not yet licensed . . . Is that important?"

"Okay, Matt, here's what you need to do. You talk to Ms. Connelly, who will undoubtedly have a horseman's account with the racing association and be licensed to own horses. If she is serious about training this horse, then I'll lend you the money. Consider it my way of saying thanks for your help last year, and as a means to keep tabs on the horse, should you get him. To be clear, this will be a loan and not a gift. It'll be a legal no-interest loan, with all the paperwork notarized. You'll pay me back in full based on the terms in the loan. Before you make the final call, be aware that monthly training and vet bills can be burdensome, especially if you're tight for money. However, if you agree, I'll send you the paperwork and wire the twenty thousand to Connelly's account on Monday and you can put in your claim for Heliacal Star on Wednesday."

CHAPTER 29

After his call with Alex Sherman, Matt immediately phones Kristine.

She answers on the first ring, and he says, "I've got some big news for you."

Matt pulls up an online version of the racing form and reviews the past performances of Heliacal Star to refresh his memory regarding the horse's career to date. As he reviews the stats, Matt realizes he could author the full racing history of this horse based off his memory alone.

Matt says, "I'm going to claim Heliacal Star this Wednesday, the Fourth of July. And you're going to train him!"

Kristine immediately responds, "Whoa, Matt Galiano. Let's back up the truck a minute. Only a week ago, you told me we couldn't see each other. You remember being dragged across the floor at Belmont by your former associate, right? Now, all of a sudden, you're hellbent on claiming a racehorse and sending it to my barn? Do I have this right?"

Matt cannot suppress his smile, knowing Kristine is surely teasing him.

He responds, "Well, yeah. That sounds about accurate."

"Okay, wow! How much is the claim? Are you even licensed?"

Matt responds, "I'm not licensed, but I've got the money covered. I'm finalizing the legal paperwork as we speak for a zero-interest loan to cover the claim, which is twenty thousand! It's all aboveboard, legal, and legit. I swear."

Kristine is quiet as Matt continues, "And regarding last week, I really am sorry. I will admit, I was shaken up. I don't want to see you get involved with my personal shit. Louisville and Kaufman are from my past and are my problem. I'll find a way to deal with them on my terms. I must admit, after ten years of avoiding them, I'm tired of hiding."

"Good for you, Matt!" exclaims Kristine. "For the record, I'm not scared of Louisville, and if he's your problem, then he's my problem, too. Got it?"

Kristine's conviction and unwavering support grabs Matt by surprise. Unbeknownst to her, she's become his inspiration to finally resolve any prior grievance with Kaufman and Louisville, one way or another.

Kristine interrupts, "Wait, who is this horse you're about to claim?"

Matt shouts, "It's Helical Star!" He repeats, "Heliacal friggin' Star! McGee entered him in a claiming race on the Fourth of July. Oh, by the way, I need you to drop the claim for me, because I'm not licensed!"

After sharing the details from his phone call with Alex Sherman, Kristine says, "Matt, you are aware of the cost of upkeep for a racehorse, right?"

"C'mon Kris, how much can it be? I mean, I know it's twenty grand to buy him, but I've got that covered. And besides, this horse is a money-making machine. I've been reading through his past performances, to be absolutely sure, before making this big decision. Do you know Heliacal Star has earned more than five times this claiming price in just the past year alone? I'm sure he's going to win back the twenty grand in one or two races, especially if you're training him."

Kristine responds, "I appreciate your certainty, Matt. I wish all my owners were this confident, and I wish it were this simple. Before you drop the claim, understand the training and vet work for a horse at the racetrack is not cheap. This endeavor may cost up to four thousand per month. Heliacal Star may have been a great horse, but there's a reason they're entering him in a cheap claiming race. As much as I'd love to take one from McGee, I don't trust that shady asshole for a single second. Something doesn't add up. Do you really have the money to risk?"

Until Kristine's sobering dose of reality, Matt hadn't seriously considered the monthly recurring expenses of owning a racehorse. He calculates that, at four thousand per month, Heliacal Star will need to win or place second on a regular basis, just to earn enough for ongoing expenses. This would be in addition to paying back the twenty thousand he'll owe Sherman. If something did go awry, impacting his ability to run, Matt could quickly find himself sinking into a deep hole of debt.

Struggling to rationalize his impulsive decision, Matt says, "Um, I hadn't really thought about everything. It just . . . it just feels like my destiny to own this horse. I believe that Heliacal Star and I have a mystical connection!"

After a lengthy pause, Kristine finally says, "Okay, I've got an idea. How about we find you a few partners and distribute the risk? I don't know anyone offhand, but I'm guessing my old friend Ted Bouchard may know of some people potentially interested in a shared ownership. Even better, and as you already know, Ted previously trained Heliacal Star before McGee took him. He'll be able to share his firsthand knowledge about this horse."

CHAPTER 30

The morning of the Fourth of July starts with bright sunshine and a warm, light breeze nudging the shades above Matt's open bedroom window. The fragrance of sweet morning dew consumes the room. *Today could be the day,* he thinks.

It's late morning as Matt arrives at the track, well ahead of the first race. Looking across the bleachers and beyond the grandstand, he notices a few hard-core gamblers screaming at the simulcasted races streaming from overseas. He watches a few early arriving fans stake out prime trackside real estate for the day, taking residence across several benches. Hustling to the racing office, Matt grabs an information pamphlet and thumbs through the contact information.

He finds and dials the number he was seeking.

After the first ring, a voice answers, "Bouchard."

Matt stammers, "Hello, Mr. Bouchard. My name is Matt Galiano. I'm a friend of . . . Kristine. Kristine Connelly. She said she would call you about a claim we're making today."

Bouchard is polite and speaks with a slight French accent. "Hello, Monsieur Galiano. Kristine tells me you're planning to claim my former horse, but she says, how do I say . . .

you're bourgeoisie and not made from money."

Matt smiles to himself at the comment and is excited by the hope that Kristine's plan for a partnership plan may actually come to fruition. Doing his best to maintain his cool and seem credible, Matt replies, "No, I'm definitely not made of money! I'm hoping you know someone who might be interested in partnering with me on this claim today."

Bouchard responds, "Perhaps. Find me near the paddock about twenty minutes before race one. I'll introduce you to *des amis*, some friends, looking for action."

Considering Kristine's earlier skepticism regarding McGee's motives, Matt wonders if Heliacal Star may have some underlying issues, which prompted McGee to run him for a claiming tag. Unsure of the protocol or appropriateness of asking pointed questions, Matt wonders if Bouchard has knowledge of the injury the horse suffered last year. Bouchard has already offered to bring a few potential investors, which is more than he initially expected, but obtaining even more insider knowledge about the health of the horse would be reassuring.

Given the risk and his personal stake, Matt says, "Mr. Bouchard, Kristine has the utmost respect for you and your knowledge. If you don't mind me asking, could there be something wrong with Heliacal Star? I mean, why would McGee run him so cheaply and well below his market value? Is this too good to be true?"

Bouchard sighs. "Monsieur Galiano. I appreciate your concern, but it's been a while since I trained him. If he is the same horse I trained, then of course I would not hesitate to claim him. But a lot may have happened since I trained him and he was injured last year. As for McGee's motivation, you'll have to decide for yourself. If you drop a claim, I'm sure you won't be alone. Several trainers will be shaking for this horse."

Hearing the phrase *shaking for this horse* gives Matt an opening to showcase his racing knowledge. He says, "Shaking is how racing officials will determine who owns him if more than one person makes a claim, right?"

Bouchard says, "Yes, after Kristine drops the claim, there is no rescinding it, even if the horse runs poorly or gets hurt. If other trainers also drop a claim, the racing secretary will assign each claimant a lottery ball, put them in a jug, shake it, and pull one out to determine who wins the horse."

Matt thanks Bouchard as they end the call. He grows anxious to find Kristine. With just an hour until the first race of the day featuring Heliacal Star, he arrives at the paddock to meet her. His emotions oscillate between excitement, happiness, and terror as he anticipates following through with dropping a claim on Heliacal Star. He paces furiously as the beaming Kristine approaches, smiling from ear to ear.

Increasingly nervous as the first race draws close, Matt asks, "Why are you smiling?"

She moves close and says, "You're cute, Matt Galiano! What do you say we grab a beer before the race?"

Matt is quick to agree, knowing a beverage could serve as a useful tonic to combat his nervous energy. One becomes two, and his enthusiasm grows at the mere prospect of becoming the new owner of Heliacal Star. Before she arrived at the paddock, Kristine filled out all the paperwork and dropped the claim ticket with the racing secretary. Toasting to the possibility of horse ownership, Matt's suddenly hit with a panicked thought. "What happens if the claim ticket is not filled out correctly?"

"Trust me, Matt, I triple-checked everything to ensure the form was filled out precisely. I also verified with the bookkeeper, and they confirmed Sherman's money has been deposited into my account, thus we have sufficient funds to satisfy the claim. We're all set!"

Finishing his drink, Matt's nerves are settled, and he points out the time, indicating it's time to rendezvous with Ted Bouchard.

Returning to the paddock, Matt cannot suppress his smile. His confidence is buoyed as the oversize tote board shows Heliacal Star is the overwhelming betting favorite to win the first race at Belmont today.

At exactly twenty minutes till post time, Matt looks around for Ted Bouchard. Instead, an uneasiness strikes him as he spots Louisville Larry enter the paddock alongside Ron McGee and Alex Sherman. Matt keeps his focus on Heliacal Star, who struts, head raised high while walking over the circular horse path. Louisville is festively dressed for the Independence Day holiday in a red, white, and blue Tommy Bahama print shirt, khaki shorts, and classic Panama hat. By contrast, McGee is dressed in a pair of rugged blue jeans, black T-shirt, and sneakers. Sherman appears in a classic dark pinstriped silk suit, wearing a solid bumblebee-yellow tie. Matt watches the immoral pair and Sherman from a safe distance. He wonders if Sherman knows about Louisville and his association with organized crime.

Another minute passes, and Ted Bouchard approaches. To

stay out of sight, Matt turns his back to the paddock and extends his right hand to greet Bouchard.

"Hello, Mr. Bouchard. It's nice to meet you in person."

Bouchard returns Matt's handshake. "Bonjour, Mr. Galiano."

Kristine interjects, "Please, guys. Enough of the formalities. Ted, this is Matt, and Matt this is Ted!"

Bouchard chuckles. "Okay, Kristine, we'll be casual."

Bouchard turns to Matt. "I have good news . . ." He pauses, looks at Kristine, then back at Matt. "Three of my guys expressed an interest in your claim today. Thus, you can split ownership four ways. They were just here a minute ago but are probably at the bar by now. If you win the claim, let's meet up, right here after the race."

Matt reflexively smiles. "Wow! I don't know how to thank you, Mr. Bouchard. I mean, Ted!"

Surging with energy, Matt turns to Kristine. "Today is definitely going to be our day! I can totally feel it!"

The horses exit the paddock and move through the tunnel and toward the main track. Matt fixates on the tote board and the always changing odds. With ten minutes until post time, Heliacal Star remains the overwhelming favorite, as his odds have dipped below even money. Matt slides up to Kristine, coils his arms around her waist, and squeezes her tightly. He gazes into her blazing green eyes and kisses her.

Matt traces his finger over Kristine's cheek. "I don't think I've ever felt so alive before."

She places her index finger across his lips, hushes him, and whispers, "You're going to remember this moment forever."

As Matt dwells on the significance of her comment, Kristine

nudges him. "Hey, we can't miss the big race. Let's watch away from the crowds."

Walking toward an open area on the east end of the grandstand, Matt feels amazing. His head, heart, and feet float with an unprecedented lightness, lifting his body and soul.

The latest click on the tote board continues to show Heliacal Star as the odds-on favorite, and the overwhelming public choice to win the first race. The horses finally move into the starting gate and the track announcer declares it's post time. Once the horses are loaded safely, the gates fly open, and they're off.

His heart beating at a furious pace, Matt focuses on Heliacal Star in the red number-one saddlecloth. After breaking slowly out of the gate, Heliacal Star settles for a stalking position two lengths behind the early leader. The horses race over the backstretch, and Heliacal Star is unhurried, relaxed, and poised. Grabbing hold of his tightly rolled-up racing program, Matt taps it across the side of his leg. "C'mon, baby!"

Heliacal Star tugs forward and effortlessly pulls into the lead by one, then two and three increasing lengths as he enters the one and only turn for the race. Matt quickens his tapping and says, "That's it, baby. Bring it home now!"

Heliacal Star rounds the turn, and Matt has visions of a smashing victory as the horse extends his lead from three to six lengths. The track announcer says with emphasis, "Heliacal Star has shaken loose and takes a commanding lead, now by eight lengths!"

Among the others screaming throughout the grandstand, Matt is shouting at top volume.

An eighth of a mile to the finish line and well ahead of the pack, Heliacal Star takes an awkward step and his gait immediately slows. His insurmountable lead rapidly evaporates as several horses are suddenly closing fast. What seemed like a guaranteed victory a mere moment ago has turned into a desperate stretch to the finish line. Matt yells, "No, no, no!" He points at the jockey. "Look, he's not even trying."

Stunned by the events unfolding in front of him, Matt fears something terrible is amiss. The first horse reaches the finish line, and several others have now passed the fading and limping Heliacal Star, who finally reaches the finish line in seventh place, a dozen lengths behind the winner. All the horses gallop beyond the finish line, except Heliacal Star, who is noticeably lame and stops just past the wire.

Dumbfounded, Matt turns to Kristine. "What just happened?"

Her smile from moments earlier has vanished, and her eyes go vacant. She shrugs and points toward the racing office, to learn the fate of their claim.

As they arrive at the racing office, it is overcrowded with individuals whom Matt assumes are owners and trainers. Matt overhears one of them saying, "Sure as shit hope my number doesn't come up. Guess we now know why that fucker McGee dropped him into a claiming race!"

The racing secretary looks around the room and says, "Okay. Everyone is here for Heliacal Star. We're going to have a nine-way shake for him."

Matt calculates that, being one of nine participants, he has an 11 percent chance to win the claim. He's torn, as he still wants to win the claim but worries about the horse's future after watching the debacle unfold on the racetrack. Kristine warned him ownership has risks and could become a financial nightmare if the horse is unable to compete. On the other hand, owning Heliacal Start would still feel like a dream come true. As he waits for the racing secretary to initiate the shake, he realizes he forgot to wager on Heliacal Star. Perhaps it was an unwitting, yet fateful sign indicating the horse wasn't meant to win today. Still, Matt knows this horse can overcome adversity, and once Kristine has the opportunity to train him, he'll show his mettle. He's convinced it's still his destiny to win the shake and own the horse.

The racing secretary loads the lottery balls into the shaker and assigns a different number to each trainer, announcing everyone's number aloud. Kristine and Matt have been assigned the number-six ball. After a brief pause, it's time for the draw.

The secretary shakes the container and pulls out the winning number.

CHAPTER 31

The loud chatter inside the racing office goes eerily silent as the racing secretary drops the winning lottery ball on the table after the shake. Scanning across the room, Matt observes several trainers turning away or looking down while others are grimacing in anticipation of the outcome. He momentarily shudders from the possibility that either McGee or Louisville could be inside the racing office. Although he vowed not to hide any longer, Matt is still relieved not to see either of their ugly mugs in the room.

The racing secretary holds the winning lottery ball in the air. Matt crosses his fingers on both hands and tightly squeezes his eyes shut, hoping the number six is called. If so, he'll become the proud new part-owner of his favorite racehorse!

The racing secretary holds out the winning lottery ball and looks around the room. In a raised voice, he says, "There were nine claims made for Heliacal Star. The winner of Heliacal Star in this shake is the number five. Paula White, come claim your prize."

Disappointed, Matt lowers his head. He's the only losing claimant in the room not showing relief. His perfect day is no more as Heliacal Star will be moving to another barn and new owner, but not to him or Kristine Connelly. After losing the shake, Matt understands the loan of $20,000 will be returned to Alex Sherman as one of the conditions of the loan. Thus, even if Matt wanted to make an on-the-spot offer to Paula White, he could no longer afford the asking price, no matter how desperate she might be to sell.

Lifting his head, Matt looks around the room and notices Ted Bouchard wiping his brow and mouthing, *Whew*.

Matt turns to Kristine. "Paula White. Who is Paula White? I've never heard of her."

Emerging from the crowded room is a gray-haired woman in loose-fitting jeans and old cowboy boots, pushing her way toward the racing secretary's desk. She is muttering to herself in a scratchy, garbled voice. "Oh crap! I guess I win the broken-down horse lottery." She snatches the winning claim from the racing secretary, turns around abruptly, and marches out the door.

Kristine laughs, turns to Matt, and says, "That, my friend, is the ever so elegant Paula White!"

Matt shakes his head, unsure of what he just witnessed, still stung from losing the shake.

Kristine says, "Holy moly, Matt. You really dodged a bullet today." She laughs. "And of all people, this poor horse is going to the barn of Paula White!"

Matt feigns a smile, grabs his mobile phone, and looks up the Wiki page for Paula White. He reads the following:

> Training racehorses since 1987, Paula White has experienced all levels of racing success from low-level claimers through graded-stakes horses. She has won

more than eight hundred races throughout her career with victories in Pennsylvania, Maryland, New York, New Jersey, and Delaware. Her home since 2014 has been Upstate New York, two hundred miles west of the historic Saratoga Race Course.

Her most successful horse was graded stakes winner Clandestiny, who won the New York Cinderella Stakes in 1994 as a juvenile filly. However, most of her success has been at the claiming level, as competing with the top echelon of the racing elite has eluded her throughout her career.

Paula is considered by her peers as an old-school trainer who is often spotted under saddle, galloping her horses in the early mornings. Over the past five years, Paula's winning percentage has dropped from 16 percent in 2012 to 7 percent in 2017. Her career winning percentage is 13 percent from more than six thousand starts.

As a younger generation of owners and horsemen have emerged and become prominent, Paula White has trained fewer horses after once peaking with more than sixty horses in her care in 2000. She has less than a dozen in her stead in 2016. While many trainers and syndicates actively embrace social media channels and have a web presence, Paula has shown no internet presence to date.

Since 2010, Paula has also been an outspoken critic of the overuse of medications and performance-enhancing drugs in racing. She is an active supporter of retired and off-the-track thoroughbreds and equine therapy and actively supports thoroughbred aftercare and local farms for rehabilitation. Paula promotes and remains involved with several equine retirement charities.

Kristine taps his arm. "Hey, Matt, show's over. Let's get out of here."

Matt thinks out loud while turning off his phone. "Do you think Paula White would consider selling Heliacal Star to me, if I could come up with the money?"

"Really, Matt? Are you serious?"

Matt smiles. "We're talking about Heliacal Star!"

Kristine leans in close and whispers softly, making it difficult for Matt to hear. "I don't like to speak about other people, and I don't know Ms. White very well, but that woman is a trip. She's got a trashy mouth and something to say about everything and everybody. Rumor has it she doesn't like the younger generation. You know, people like you and me."

As Matt is listening, he considers calling Alex Sherman to inquire about another loan for a private purchase.

Kristine continues, "A couple more things. Paula is based in northwest New York State, so it's likely she'll be moving Heliacal Star out of here to where they run cheaper races. If you really want him, I suggest you show a little patience. Based on his performance today, she'll drop him in a lower claiming price next time he races. I'll bet you'll nab him for half the value of today's claim in just a couple of weeks. Losing this shake may have literally saved you ten grand!"

Matt is sure Alex Sherman could help him out again if he asks. As he ponders his options, he holds Kristine's hand as they leave the racing office. She reciprocates with a gentle squeeze in return. They amble toward the barn area, and Matt succumbs to the realization that claiming Heliacal Star wasn't meant to be, at least not today and perhaps for good reason. Smiling once again at the prospect of owning Heliacal Star down the road, he stops sharply and turns toward Kristine.

"What if . . .?" Matt stops himself. He hesitates at the thought of saying something stupid. Kristine prompts him to continue, and Matt turns away. He drops his head. "What if he was really injured badly out there today? What happens if he never races again?"

Kristine draws a long breath, exhales audibly, and says, "If he can't race again, his options may be limited. As a gelding, he can never breed. Given his history of injuries, he's probably not a good candidate for jumping or any sort of stressful competition. I don't know his demeanor, but many thoroughbreds are retired as trail, rehab, or leisure riding horses. For example, some have long second careers as lesson horses, 4-H projects, or are used for therapy with people suffering from PTSD or who have autism. I've even seen retired thoroughbreds used for prison rehab and reform. If racing for him is really over, I suppose there would be several options available to him."

Considering her response, another thought enters his head. "What's the deal with the old adage about poor performers or broken-down horses going to the glue factory? Is that just a euphemism?"

Kristine says, "Yes and no. There is a controversial cottage industry associated with unwanted horses of all kinds, not just thoroughbreds. As for retired racehorses, there has been a rapid improvement in awareness and increased efforts taken to protect them, including fines and penalties imposed for violators, but . . ."

She pauses, looks intently at Matt, and continues, "Unfortunately, there are still some former racehorses that end up in what is called the slaughter pipeline. It's not exactly the old glue factory, but it's the same end. For what it's worth, I've heard Paula does a lot of work with charities and rehabilitation for retired racehorses, so your boy should be safe even if he never races again."

Matt is relieved for Heliacal Star, although the words *slaughter pipeline* strike him as harsh and frightening, especially given Kristine's matter-of-fact tone.

Afraid of how she may respond, he reluctantly presses the topic. "What exactly is this slaughter pipeline you just mentioned?"

Kristine explains, "Around ten years ago, the United States banned all domestic horse slaughter, but it's still legal in Canada and Mexico. In theory, a racehorse could end up at one of those slaughterhouses in Quebec, Alberta, or Mexico. An unscrupulous individual may come across a former racehorse at an agricultural auction if the previous owner is intent on dumping the horse to avoid paying for ongoing expenses."

Matt is listening intently and nods as he considers the surprising ease with which this sinister act seems to happen.

He asks, "If such an unscrupulous buyer purchases a horse at this auction, how do they legally transport them to Canada or Mexico, if horse slaughter is not legal in the US, or is the transport also illegal?"

Kristine continues, "Technically speaking, the US did not outlaw horse slaughter. What they did was stop funding the USDA inspectors for horses at American slaughterhouses. So, without qualified inspectors, there's no actual slaughter occurring in the US today. However, this doesn't prevent some people from transporting unwanted horses across the border; hence, the pipeline. One of the biggest agricultural auctions for selling used racehorses to these unscrupulous individuals, called 'kill buyers,' is located in Pennsylvania."

Matt is stunned.

Kristine says, "Look, it was way worse ten years ago. Racehorse trainers and owners are now severely penalized if any of their horses are identified at one of these auctions or sold to a kill buyer. These horses are often identified by rescue charities after inspecting the racing tattoos under their lips, but this is far from perfect and not always the best deterrent."

CHAPTER 32

Before the first race today, Ron McGee informed Louisville Larry with certainty that Heliacal Star would lose. With his insider knowledge, combined with the near unanimous public sentiment in making Heliacal Star the overwhelming favorite, Larry managed to spread several large wagers on the other horses at very long odds. When Heliacal Star lost as McGee foretold, Larry found himself holding several winning bets, amounting to a substantial profit from the race.

Late in the afternoon, Larry arrives among the growing crowd at the annual Fourth of July block party. For several years, Tony Kaufman and his younger brother, Ken Kaufman, have hosted a blockbuster Fourth of July bash in the same Queens neighborhood as their shop, courtesy of Kaufman Meats. Using this guise, Tony and Ken have successfully endeared themselves as civic celebrities in sponsoring burgers, hot dogs, sausages, and summer salads along with overfilled trash cans stuffed with ice, ales, and soft drinks. For this year's celebration, a supersized tent on the north end of the sectioned-off street is abuzz with activity, featuring an arts and crafts station of face painting, origami projects, and patriotic coloring books. A live band is playing on a makeshift stage at the south end of the block. Everyone is looking forward to the fireworks show this evening, which promises to be on par with any professional show.

The typically reclusive and unapproachable Tony Kaufman is highly visible on this day, greeting neighbors and acknowledging their gratitude for his generous contribution to the community. Comfortable temperatures and blue skies have encouraged a historically large gathering.

As the second-in-command for the family, Ken Kaufman maintains the job of overseeing logistics for the Fourth of July festivities. He'll conduct secret discussions with the local authorities and ensure they obtain permits for the block party. As a gesture of his gratitude, Ken generously provides a sizeable donation to the benevolent associations and various political action committees for local legislators representing the district. A relaxed group of officers goes mostly unnoticed as they intermingle among the locals.

On the blocked-off street, Louisville Larry locates Tony, who suggests they walk to a quiet area. As they meander through the crowd, Tony is stopped frequently by drunken and appreciative partyers reaching out to shake his hand. The pair snakes through the crowd until they are alone in a side alley.

Although no one else is around, Tony speaks softly, "What does McGee know?"

Handing him the cash profits from his wagers on the earlier race, Larry whispers in response, "McGee told me which horses to bet and assured me Heliacal Star would lose today. As expected, we also lost Heliacal Star in a claim today. McGee's a good insider. He's been solid for us this year."

Tony nods and takes the money but offers no comment.

Larry continues in a whisper, "We also have him wrapped around our finger. If the racing officials ever discover the antics he pulled with this horse, his career will be over. We have him, and he knows it."

Tony smiles, taps Larry on his back, and says, "You did well today, Larry." He returns a fraction of the cash to Larry and then a second, smaller fraction. Pointing to the second one, Tony says, "Give this one to McGee. Tell him it's a token of my appreciation for his loyalty and good work."

Kaufman is standing close enough to hug Larry, and whispers, "Inform McGee that I don't care he lost the horse in a claim today. I'm not yet done with him."

Larry nods.

Tony continues, "As for you . . . no more careless bullshit. You almost got caught when some asshole overheard you talking to McGee, right? We cannot leave such things to chance in our business."

Larry nods affirmatively.

Tony is curt. "Just remember to keep your fucking head clean and stay out of trouble."

Larry nods again, but his mouth is ajar.

Tony prompts, "What's the problem, Larry?"

Larry stumbles over his words. "I think—" He stops, takes a short breath, and continues, "I think I know who the asshole is that overheard me talking to McGee."

Tony stands expressionless as Larry continues, "It happens to be your former bookmaker, Matt Galiano."

Tony snaps, "I thought you took care of that problem years ago? What the fuck, Larry?"

Larry mumbles, "I did, except he got away from me. I honestly don't know how he survived the assault because I doled out a massive beating that day. Anyways, I assumed he disappeared. I went to jail and I hadn't seen or heard from him since, until I managed to chase him around the backstretch. Of course, I didn't know it was him at the time, but I saw him again at the racetrack a few weeks ago with his rat girlfriend."

"This is not a positive development, Larry. Not good."

"What do you want me to do, boss?" Larry asks.

"Right now, nothing. I need you to lay low. His time will come, but we need to be absolutely sure we're taking no undue risks. I need you to avoid unwanted attention." Tony pokes his finger into Larry's chest and whispers, "What do you know about a potential rat in my org talking to the feds?"

Larry stares blankly at Tony. "You shitting me?" Tony folds his arms, cocks his head to the side and glares at the large man. Larry shrugs and shakes his head. "I have no fucking clue, boss. But if there's a rat, I'll take care of it."

Tony peeks down the block, then whispers into Larry's ear, "No, I'll find the rat and take care of him in my own way. Remember, no bullshit from you. No fucking side jobs. I'm serious. You hear me?"

Larry nods and Tony continues, "As for that asshole Galiano, I'll give you the job, but not right now. Only when the time is right."

An approving smile emerges across Larry's face. "Yeah, Tony. Of course. No problem."

CHAPTER 33

Frustrated by the absence of updates about Heliacal Star, Matt phones Kristine, as he's done each day since the horse was claimed by Paula White. Although he knows she'll have nothing new or noteworthy to share, he is pacified by the sound of her voice. Kristine has reminded him each day that losing the shake was a genuine blessing, yet Matt won't let it go. His desire to own this thoroughbred has only grown more resolute over the past several days.

As Kristine picks up the phone, Matt skips past the usual formalities. "Okay, Kris, I know we've been through this before, more than a few times, but I'm telling you, I'm not giving up. There hasn't been one scintilla of information about Heliacal Star since he was claimed. I've searched the internet, been on all the racetrack and internet gambling sites, and there's not a single mention since he was claimed Wednesday. That was three days ago!"

Kristine responds, "Yes, Matt, I'm quite aware. Let me check the calendar. Ah yes, it's one more day since yesterday. You remember yesterday? That's when you said he was claimed two days ago?" She sighs and says, "Although it's against my better judgment, I'm going to send you Paula White's contact information. This way, you can speak with her directly!"

Matt smirks and mutters, "Progress at last!"

Kristine is laughing. "Now, I want you to stop asking me about the horse and just deal with Paula!"

"Perfect. I'll be sure to tell you all about my conversation with her when I see you tonight. Thanks for the help!"

Matt is pleased with himself for pressing Kristine. He remembers his first and only impression of Paula from the racing office: she was cantankerous, unapproachable, and seemed unfriendly.

His phone beeps with a text from Kristine: Paula White's contact information and a snarky emoticon of a gray-haired lady.

Matt jots down the number on a note pad, writes out the name Heliacal Star and the number ten thousand. He gazes at his pad and musters up the courage to make the call.

His anxiety spikes. Paula's phone rings several times before she answers, "Yeah, who is this?"

Matt is taken aback by her abrasiveness and goes silent, unsure of what to say. He hadn't necessarily expected a warm and friendly hello, but he also didn't expect hostility. Fighting the urge to hang up and forget about Paula White, he remembers his purpose is to inquire about Heliacal Star.

Clearing his throat and speaking in his most polite and respectful tone, he says, "Am I speaking with Paula? Is this Paula White?"

Paula is terse. "Yep. Who wants to know?"

Matt bites his tongue and continues to be polite and respectful. "Hello, Paula, my name is Matt Galiano and I noticed you claimed a horse at Belmont Park last week."

Paula interrupts, "Matt who? I never heard of you."

Matt swallows hard and continues, "I'd like to make an offer to buy him—"

Paula cuts him off. "Save your breath, honey. I assume you're talking about Heliacal Star. He's no good. Broke down. Trust me, you don't want him."

His early nervousness is supplanted by a wave of irritation after only a few seconds of interacting with this ornery woman, but Matt fights his impulses and maintains his composure. "Yes, ma'am, I'm aware he might have been injured. I was also at the racetrack last Tuesday and watched his last race."

Paula says in a more conciliatory tone, "Listen, sweetie, I don't know you, but I don't envision this horse racing anytime soon, if ever. As I said, you're asking about a severely broken-down gelding with his best racing days behind him. Or is this news to you?"

Matt had not anticipated such brutal honesty or the dismal appraisal. He assumed Heliacal Star sustained some injuries, but he's also witnessed him bounce back from worse-looking situations and presumed a full recovery was a given. Based on her assertions, Paula White seems declarative about Heliacal Star's doomed career. Matt hadn't considered any scenario in which this horse would never race again. He wonders if she may be mistaken or trying to scare him off, but his thoughts wander to Kristine's assertion about dodging a bullet after losing the shake.

Wanting to learn more but hesitant to poke and potentially upset her, Matt's voice is shaky. "What exactly . . . what I mean is, what specifically happened to him?"

Paula's voice softens. "Listen, sweetie, first, let me apologize if I came across rough when you called. I get crackpots calling me all the time, but you sound genuinely concerned."

Marginally vindicated, Matt graciously accepts the olive branch. "Thank you, ma'am."

Paula continues, "I need to send Heliacal Star for rehabilitation. He'll need to be stall bound for at least sixty days. At the rehab center, they'll have the proper facility and staff to ensure he heals from his injuries. I've been in this game a long time and will tell you not many horses return successfully from this type of soft tissue injury. I expect with time, he'll heal just fine, but as far as competitive racing goes, I wouldn't bet much on it."

Matt cannot help but believe Ron McGee had full knowledge of Heliacal Star's condition prior to his last race. He understands why McGee dropped the horse so dramatically to a less competitive race after winning against much tougher foes for substantially larger purses. These new facts are too coincidental, initiating a surge of outrage toward McGee for his part in willingly and purposely destroying the horse's career and threatening his health. Matt's anger extends to Alex Sherman, who encouraged him to claim the horse through a no-interest loan.

Matt asks, "Do you think McGee may have known about these issues before the race?"

Paula snaps at the question. "Of course that cocksucker knew! I'm just the moron who took the bait and claimed the broken-down horse. I honestly should have known better!"

In spite of Paula's initial terseness, Matt finds himself enjoying the conversation while adjusting to her salty personality. Her brutal description of Ron McGee feels oddly comforting.

To reciprocate with his own honesty, Matt says, "I'm not too proud to admit this, but I also participated in the lottery of suckers who were shaking for the horse."

Paula laughs and says, "I'll raise a toast to your good fortune, son."

After finding some common ground, Matt continues, "I also have to agree with you about McGee. He's nothing but a dirty scoundrel and cheating asshole."

Paula says, "I'm glad we both agree about McGee. As for Heliacal Star . . . at the very best he may end up as a cheap claiming horse, but he'll never return to the form you remember from his best racing days. McGee ruined him. I wouldn't be surprised if he never races again. If so, I'll find him a second career as a riding or trail horse somewhere. Anything else you want from me today?"

Unhappy to admit it, Matt begrudgingly acknowledges to himself that Kristine was right about losing the shake, as it turned out to be a genuine blessing in disguise. At the same time, he feels strongly that Heliacal Star is a resilient racehorse who will complete an unprecedented comeback by overcoming such improbable adversity. Thinking about his unique connection to the horse, Matt is convinced he can return to the races and be wildly successful once again.

Unwilling to end the conversation, Matt continues, "This may sound crazy to you . . ."

Paula prompts, "Go on . . ."

Matt clears his throat. "First, I want you to know I appreciate everything you've shared with me today. I respect your opinion and appreciate your candidness. Given all the above, how much would you expect someone to pay for the horse right now?"

As the words leave his mouth, his heart thumps. Matt braces

for an answer, staring at his notepad with the number ten thousand written down.

Paula coughs into the phone several times. "If you're some sort of kill buyer, I've gotta hand it to you regarding your creativity and ingenuity. Nice try, pal, but you're wasting your time and mine, and I don't have time for your shit!"

Matt cries out, "Wait, what? Kill buyer? What do you mean?"

"Okay, I'll play along," she says. "I paid twenty grand for this horse. Do you think I'm going to give him away now? How about you make me whole and wire me the full twenty grand? Shit, you were willing to pay it a few days ago when you dropped a claim, right? Give me twenty grand, and he's yours as soon as I receive the funds."

Matt continues to stare at the number on the pad.

"Are you serious? Twenty thousand? You just said he would never race again."

Paula sharpens her tone. "How do I know you're not a clever kill buyer trying to swindle me to make a quick dollar? How can I be assured you're going to spend the time and money to properly rehabilitate this horse and give him the care he needs? How do I know you're not going to abandon him or ditch him or shop him off to another kill buyer in six months?"

Matt remembers the short exchange with Kristine about kill buyers and the slaughter pipeline. At that time, it was an academic conversation, but as Paula White is now accusing him of being such a person, the harsh reality of Heliacal Star potentially meeting such a fate horrifies him.

Matt's emotions get the best of him. "Stop it! I'm not a horse killer. To be perfectly honest with you, I never even knew about kill buyers until Kristine explained it to me a few days ago. I love horses, and I love your horse, and I phoned you with all sincerity. Of course, I would love to see him race him again, but even if he never races, I'll take him injured with a poor racing prognosis."

Paula asks, "Is the Kristine you refer to Kristine Connelly, by any chance?"

Matt meant to reference Kristine earlier in the call but was thrown off by Paula's initial terseness. "Yes, ma'am. Kristine Connelly. She'll become his trainer and be hands-on regarding any rehabilitation needs."

Paula says, "Why didn't you tell me about Kristine up front? I don't know her personally, but she has a solid reputation among the community. In fact, now that you mention her, I remember seeing her in the racing office when I claimed the horse."

By merely mentioning Kristine, Matt senses an instant credibility boost, prompting a renewed sense of optimism.

He emphasizes his relationship. "Yes, Kristine was with me at Belmont last week. I also remember seeing you after you won the shake. Does this convince you I'm not some crazy kill buyer?"

Paula says, "Okay, Matt. Let's walk through the math. A kill buyer could spend up to a thousand dollars for a horse to make a profit."

Matt tries to break in. "Um . . . " but Paula continues before Matt can interject. "Now, I'm not calling you a kill buyer, but hear me out. If you offered, say, six thousand dollars, then I might be convinced of your genuine interest in the welfare of this horse regardless of his racing future. Of course, I'd want to speak with Kristine as well to get her assurances."

The quote of $6,000 is less than his self-appraised $10,000

estimate, but this also predated any knowledge of the extent of Heliacal Star's injuries and his uncertain racing future. Matt internalizes the size of the bullet he dodged, given that he was prepared to borrow $20,000 for the horse. With the added discount, he's confident he'll convince Alex Sherman to lend him the money once again while shaming him about hiding the horse's health problems. Convinced that Heliacal Star will overcome his injuries and be competitive once again, he calculates the ongoing expenses and allocated time for Heliacal Star to fully rehab and return to the racetrack.

With a rush of impulsiveness, Matt says, "Ma'am, for six thousand, you've got yourself a deal!"

Paula coughs into the phone and says, "Okay, son, but we need to discuss terms before I'll agree to this deal."

Matt understands purchasing a racehorse will extend beyond a simple verbal agreement as he silently acknowledges Paula's motive for additional formality.

He asks, "Okay, what are your terms?"

"First, we do the deal here, where the horse is located. Once you arrive, I want to look you in the eye to ensure you're a serious buyer. If you're coming from Long Island, I'm about a six-hour drive."

As Matt calculates his availability over the next few days and the driving logistics, he says, "Absolutely! No problem. When do want me there?"

Paula says, "Let's see. How about we shoot for next Wednesday? If you can't make it, I'll know you're not serious. Oh, one more thing: I need to speak with Kristine Connelly, too. Have her call me."

Matt is miffed about Paula's continual assertion about him not being a serious buyer, but the conversation has already exceeded his expectations, and he decides not to be argumentative. After securing the funding from Sherman, he'll call in sick for a few days to free up his work schedule.

Matt says, "I understand, ma'am. Your terms are reasonable. I'm happy to say you've got yourself a deal. I'll see you next Wednesday."

Matt's pulse quickens as the call ends, and he daydreams of Heliacal Star thundering home across the finish line well in front of his competition. He imagines himself and Kristine celebrating and screaming for joy as the horse is wrapped in a victorious blanket of roses. He hears the track announcer echoing, "Congratulations to Heliacal Star, his owner Matt Galiano, and trainer Kristine Connelly for their impressive and courageous victory."

His snaps out of his musing and declares aloud to himself, "I can't believe it! I just bought Heliacal Star!"

Next up is getting his hands on the $6,000.

He grabs his notepad and excitedly jots down some information.

Helical Star!
Owner = Matt Galiano. Trainer = Kristine Connelly
Wednesday
Need $6K ASAP and $10K for expenses. Ask Alex Sherman.
Injury? How much does rehab cost? Does he need surgery?
= Kristine

Matt puts his pen down, scrolls through his phone contacts, and stops at the name Alex Sherman. Without hesitation, he dials the number but is sent directly to voicemail. He decides not to leave a message and instead hits redial. Voicemail again. This time, he waits for the beep. "Hi, Mr. Sherman. This is Matt Galiano. Please call me as soon as possible. I have a chance to privately purchase Heliacal Star, and I'm hoping you're still willing to loan me the money."

With a rush of adrenaline, he dials Kristine but goes to voicemail. Assuming she's still training horses this morning, he leaves a message. "Hi, Kristine. Matt here. Guess what? I did it. I really did it! I just bought Heliacal Star. Well, technically speaking! I verbally agreed to buy him. Oh, I need your help. Paula White needs to speak with you. Call me as soon as you hear this message."

His thoughts shift to his dad, his childhood, and attending the races together. His own love for horse racing was borne out his relationship with his father. The tough exterior his dad showed the world resulted in many things being unspoken, but Matt knew his dad deeply cared for and loved him. Those times at the racetrack continue to hold a special place in his heart. In this moment, he can feel the presence of his dad in the room.

His phone beeps, interrupting his thoughts with a text message from Alex Sherman.

Sorry Matt. In Africa. Cannot talk for two weeks. Shitty service here.

Engulfed by enthusiasm and consumed by unbridled optimism in spontaneously making the deal with Paula, Matt naïvely assumed Sherman would naturally offer him a second no interest loan. He had not thought of or considered the possibility of Sherman being unavailable to lend him enough funds to purchase the racehorse. He considers asking Paula for an additional two weeks, until Sherman returns, but only manages to stare at her phone number, failing to call for fear of appearing flaky or unstable.

He logs into his bank account and confirms what he already knows well: his savings account balance falls far short of the purchase price, less than $4,000. Staring at his bank balance glaring on the screen, Matt invents a scheme that will fund his dream.

CHAPTER 34

As she does most weekdays, Carol Chambers is driving her daughter Bethany, who volunteers with a local 4-H club at a farm near her home in Upstate New York. As school is closed for summer recess, Bethany's drop-off has been integrated into Carol's daily commute to her office, where she works as an administrative assistant at a local law firm. Bethany Chambers earns credits for the club on the farm by performing various chores such as mucking stalls, feeding horses, holding them for the farrier, and leading them to pasture. In return, the farm awards her two hours of instruction per week with a certified instructor for dressage lessons.

The forty-acre farm, Happy Trails North, is owned and managed by Carol's childhood friend, Amanda Casey. The farm offers stalls and pasture for horse boarding, injury rehabilitation, and rescue services, along with trail riding, dressage, and riding and horsemanship lessons. Happy Trails North serves as the headquarters for the local 4-H chapter.

At the law office where she works, Carol is generally known as a compassionate person with an affinity for saving abused and neglected animals. Among her experiences, she has volunteered at animal shelters, saved horses destined for slaughter from agricultural auctions, and led several fund raisers for the local chapter of the ASPCA. She suffered a personal tragedy when her husband lost his battle with cancer just three years ago. Afterward, Carol became deeply involved in the rescue of equines, especially those that had been injured or abandoned.

It was several years ago when Carol's husband was initially diagnosed with an aggressive and rare form of hypopharynx cancer, and amid her despair, that she discovered her calling through volunteer work with deprived animals. After he passed, she informed her friends and colleagues it was God's will to receive her husband at such a young age. Before his illness, her husband spoke fondly about his childhood on a farm where he rode and groomed horses. As he battled his illness, they spent quality time together visiting different farms. It's a time Carol references as being formative in attuning her to a spiritual connectedness around horses. This is when Bethany discovered Happy Trails North. Although Carol was not raised on a farm, she and her daughter spent significant time at Happy Trails North after her husband succumbed to his illness.

Through Bethany Chambers's association with Happy Trails North, Carol reacquainted herself with Amanda, the farm's owner. As Bethany's proficiency improved, she yearned for her own horse, but the recently widowed Carol lacked the resources to afford a horse for her daughter.

Upon hearing about Carol and Bethany's situation, Amanda Casey offered them a barter deal. In exchange for monthly boarding fees, Carol would volunteer twenty hours per week assisting Amanda by attracting business to Happy Trails North, along with performing barn chores, such as mucking stalls, feeding, blanketing, and walking the horses.

The mother and daughter traveled together to a local agricultural auction where Bethany selected an underweight but otherwise elegant Arabian. Carol outbid the others and acquired the horse for a modest price and vanned her to Happy Trails North. Bethany cared for the horse and nursed her back to good health and a normal weight over a six-month period.

As they approach Happy Trails North this July morning, Carol's cell phone rings.

One hand on the wheel, Carol reaches and fumbles her phone into her purse, barely maintaining control of the steering wheel. From the passenger seat, Bethany reaches into Carol's handbag and picks out the phone.

Handing her the phone, Bethany says, "I don't recognize the number, Mom."

"Just put it on speaker, sweetie."

Once on speaker, Carol says, "Hello. This is Carol Chambers."

A gruff female voice speaks on the other end. "Hi, Carol, my name is Paula White. I've heard about you and am interested in the rehab services at Happy Trails North. Was told to contact you. I've been looking for some new boarding options in the area, and your place seems to have a solid reputation."

As part of her barter arrangement with Amanda Casey, Carol has been promoting Happy Trails North Farm, spreading the word about the farm's rescue and rehab. Pictures on the farm's Facebook page show large stalls with turn-out paddocks, horses running in a pasture, and an expansive covered riding arena.

Carol has also posted a recent photo of herself and Bethany alongside her daughter's Arabian horse. The caption reads:

Need a new, safe, and warm home for your horse? Worried about expenses? Injured? Retired? We know you care about the welfare of your horse and need to find the right home. **We can help at Happy Trails North**. *We are experienced horsewomen, passionate about working to save horses. We'll do the legwork to rehome your horse. For qualified applicants, we'll even waive the first month of boarding.*

Since Carol posted her message eleven months ago, nearly fifty unwanted horses, who otherwise may have been lost, neglected, or sent to agricultural auctions, have landed at Happy Trails North. Amanda and her crew have had great success rehoming the discarded horses.

Carol responds, "Thank you, Paula, for your call and your interest. What information can you share about your horse?"

"Long story short, Carol," says Paula, "I'm a horse-racing trainer nearby, and you were recommended by one of my grooms for rehab services. I've got a banged-up gelding who needs immediate time off, stall rest, and proper care and attention. All my regular layup places are currently full or over capacity. Is this something you can accommodate on short notice?"

Carol pulls her car onto the gravel driveway for the farm. "Yes, I believe we can help. I just arrived at the farm now and will double-check our availability." Carol gestures for Bethany to run out and look for Amanda. "Of course, it depends on the extent of his injury. We offer rehabilitation services, but we're not a clinic or equine hospital, just to be clear."

"I don't need a clinic or hospital. I need to know if your establishment can be trusted, as racehorses are expensive investments and require excellent care. I've been training for more years than I want to admit and have seen my share of horses needing second chances or basic rehab and getting neither. Some owners are more interested in the almighty dollar and could give two shits about the horse once they stop earning. Pardon my language."

Her car now idling, Carol takes the phone off speaker. "Of course. We feel the same way about those irresponsible owners, which is why we do so many rescues!"

Among the horses currently on the grounds at Happy Trails North are paints, quarter horses, mustangs, draft horses, and even a miniature, but not a single thoroughbred. Creating a new association with the local racetrack could bring obvious benefits for the farm. On more than one occasion, Amanda had asked Carol to reach out to the nearby racetrack and build business for the farm while providing a soft landing for older racehorses. According to Amanda, the racetrack only publicly endorses a limited number of reference farms, but if Happy Trails North were to become one of them, it would boost their profile and ensure steady business.

Paula continues, "Here is the deal, Carol. I have a horse named Heliacal Star, whom I claimed last week downstate. Frankly, the scum who entered him knew he wasn't sound, but he ran him anyway." Paula mumbles something inaudible and continues, "He can't run a lick now and needs immediate care and attention. It'll be the basics. Stall rest, daily bandage changes, topical application, temp checks, antibiotics, limited hand-walking twice a day, and regular drop-ins from the vet."

Bethany approaches the idling car and shows her mom a thumbs-up. Carol says, "Okay, I just checked. We have an open stall here. We charge thirty dollars per day to board, and basic rehab will cost another thirty. We'll confirm the details once we receive your paperwork and veterinary instructions."

Paula says, "You'll receive discharge papers with specific instructions. I'll be checking on him regularly. Oh, I'll also need you to sign a waiver, and I presume you'll want me to do the same."

"Yes, of course. We look forward to seeing you and him."

Paula says, "One more thing, Carol. I'm going to require an in-person tour of your farm before I can drop him off. This weekend is not going to work for me, but how does Tuesday afternoon work for you?"

Farm tours are common. Carol has escorted many individuals around the property, answered questions, and reassured potential clients of the mission of the farm's advocacy.

As she watches Bethany disappear behind the barn, Carol says, "Of course! This Tuesday should work just fine. I'll also introduce you to the farm owner, Amanda Casey. I'm sure she'll be thrilled to meet you!"

CHAPTER 35

After printing out a copy of today's racing action, Matt snatches it off the machine and rushes out his front door. His first stop is his local bank, where he fills out a withdrawal slip in the amount of $3,000. Writing out the bank slip, his hand trembles, as he's never withdrawn so much cash. He approaches the teller and is informed of bank protocol requiring multiple forms of identification. Fumbling to pull out his driver's license and bank card, he hands them to the teller, who studies his identification for what feels like an uncomfortably long moment. She calls over to her manager and looks at Matt void of expression.

The bank manager grabs the identification, studies it, and looks over at Matt, who nervously taps his fingers on the counter. She initials the withdrawal slip without speaking, hands it to the teller, and walks away. Counting out thirty one-hundred dollar bills, the teller places the money into a small white envelope and looks up. "Anything else I can help you with today, Mr. Galiano?"

With the money in hand, Matt cordially smiles. He folds the envelope, stuffs it in his front pocket, and exits the bank.

Twenty minutes later, Matt enters the grandstand at Belmont

Park, just as the horses cross the finish line for the first race of the day. Matt finds a seat outside near the paddock and shuffles through his racing program.

At one in the afternoon, the heat of the sun is oppressively hot and complemented by haze and humidity, causing the dripping sweat down his back to stick to his shirt. The thick wad of cash stuffed inside Matt's front pocket is excessively uncomfortable, distracting his focus. He sits quietly to assuage the elements and assess the past performances for the upcoming race but cannot concentrate. Matt takes three measured breaths and instructs himself to remain cool.

Returning to his program, he pores over the glut of statistics regarding each horse but feels too stressed and scattered to strategize. Standing up, Matt slowly idles up to the paddock, seeking inspiration. As the horses walk across the path, Matt looks skyward, shielding his eyes from the bright sun.

"Show me a sign! I need to be sure this time. This is for Heliacal Star." He scans the paddock for something, anything, but nothing manifests.

Once the horses are led to the racetrack for the post parade, the sizeable crowd dissipates. Matt taps on his pants pocket; the wad of cash remains on his body. Matt reevaluates the merit and sanity of his idea. Arriving a short while ago with the intention to wager his savings, he's starting to feel a little desperate. He refuses to call Kristine for fear of looking stupid, irrational, or both.

He decides to contact Paula White and postpone their meeting until he can secure another loan from Alex Sherman. Aborting his plan releases a flood of relief. Without the added pressure, Matt picks up his racing program through a different lens. Turning the page to the third race, his pulse suddenly quickens and his heart skips a beat.

Fretting over his options, an older gentlemen sidles next to him and says, "Excuse me for the interruption, but you're looking rather serious, son. Have you picked out a winner yet?" Matt shrugs and dismisses the stranger by returning his eyes to his racing program. The older man continues, "Do you know the Ralph Waldo Emerson quote, 'Once you make a decision, the universe conspires to make it happen'? Good luck, son."

Perplexed by the interruption and the mysterious old man, Matt makes up his mind. He decides not to spend any more time deliberating. He came to the racetrack today on a mission, and it's time to man up! Matt draws a dark circle around the number-six horse in the third race, Tony Tornado. He remembers heeding Kristine's advice the last time he raced. Once he spotted the name Tony Tornado in his program, he knew it was fate.

The morning line odds on Tony Tornado are 3–1, making him one of the favorites for the third race. A crowd inside the grandstand is cheering, and Matt assumes they are cheering for the second race as he beelines to the nearest teller window. With his confidence restored from divine intervention, Matt removes the envelope and deposits the cash at the window. He counts out thirty hundred-dollar bills and instructs the teller, "Three thousand to win on number six."

The clerk looks up. "You sure?" Without looking at the teller, Matt points to the cash. The clerk pushes the money in a drawer, punches in some numbers, and hands a voucher to Matt. Anxious and excited, Matt tucks the voucher into his front pocket and walks away from the teller. He returns to the paddock area, where it remains quiet, takes out the voucher, and reads it to himself.

$3000 WIN #6 DEVIL'S FOLLY BELMONT 2ND RACE

Staring at the voucher for a moment, his knees buckle and his face goes flush. Matt is confused. Didn't he bet Tony Tornado in the third race? Devil's Folly is running in the second race. Matt rushes to the nearest monitor as the final horse for the second race loads into the gate. Bewildered, his brain is unable to process the words on his voucher. He rereads it.

$3000 WIN #6 DEVIL'S FOLLY BELMONT 2ND RACE

The starting bell rings, and the second race is underway. Matt stares blankly at the monitor as the track announcer exclaims, "And they're off!" The horses sprint out of the gate, and Matt is dumbfounded about what just transpired. He's sure he told the teller to place his bet on Tony Tornado, but as he replays the moment in his head, he cannot recollect ever mentioning the name Tony Tornado or specifying the third race.

Reality hits him. Matt has just wagered his life savings on the wrong horse in the wrong race.

CHAPTER 36

An old, mud-painted Dodge pickup with a horse trailer attached pulls into Happy Trails North. A youngish-looking driver in a pair of well-worn blue jeans, black T-shirt, and brown cowboy hat jumps out and pokes his head into the nearby arena. Inside, Carol Chambers is watching her daughter work with her horse under a trainer's supervision on dressage drills.

Clutching a folder, the driver approaches Carol. "Excuse me, ma'am. Do you know if there is a Carol Chambers here?"

Carol says, "Yes. That's me. Are you here for a tour of the farm?"

"No, ma'am. I'm here on behalf of Ms. Paula White. Did you receive a text from her? She informed me earlier that she texted you about dropping off a racehorse from her barn at the racetrack."

Carol says, "Yes, of course. I assume she completed his evaluation with her veterinarian at the track. Do you have his discharge papers and any additional vet care instructions?"

The driver hands over a folder. Carol opens it and removes a few papers and reads over them as the young man in the cowboy hat watches the activity in the arena. After a moment, he says, "Hey, she's pretty good with that horse."

Carol looks up. "Huh . . . oh, thank you. She's my daughter, Bethany. She loves her horse, and by the looks of it, I'd say the feeling is mutual." Carol takes another look at Bethany before returning to read over the paperwork.

She returns the papers inside the folder in the exact order she pulled them out and says to the driver, "These are very detailed instructions. We'll have no problem taking good care of her horse. Let's bring him inside where I've prepped a stall."

As she stands, she pauses for another look at Bethany and asks the young man to follow her to the stall area. Carol shows him the empty stall, deeply bedded in several layers of hay and with a pair of hanging buckets filled with water along with a fan propped up just outside the stall. On the outside of the door is a sticker that says *Quarantine*. This is standard protocol for any new horse arriving on the farm.

She asks him, "Will you take him inside the stall? I assume you have a halter and lead?"

He affirms this and walks to the van. Carol remains at the stall.

The young man opens the back door of the van, clips a lead rope to the halter, and leads Heliacal Star down the ramp. As he hobbles down the ramp, there are obvious signs of discomfort as he continues down the path. Carol opens the stall door and Heliacal Star enters, acting as if he's been there before.

Carol slides the door closed and latches it. She says, "Wow! He is striking and so well-behaved. Was he tranquilized coming over?"

"No, ma'am, he's normally this well-mannered. I'd call him

a perfect gentleman. No need for acepromazine or any other tranquilizer on such a short trip. He's been given two grams of phenylbutazone powder, which will help him with his pain and discomfort."

Once inside the stall, Heliacal Star walks in a small circle, sniffs the hay, takes a large drink of water, and lays down on the soft bed of hay. The driver hands Carol two bags, one small and one slightly larger.

He says, "The small bag contains his medications, and the larger one has some cotton wraps, vet wrap, stretchy tape, and a pair of sanitized surgical scissors. According to the discharge instructions, he's due for his next topical treatment in the morning. Oh, I almost forgot. His name is Heliacal Star."

Carol pulls out a carrot from a nearby bag and walks into the stall. Heliacal Star stands, moves up to her, and sniffs her hand as Carol offers the treat. The horse consumes it without hesitation in just a few bites.

She offers him a second carrot and whispers, "Hello, Heliacal Star. Welcome to Happy Trails North. We'll take good care of you here."

CHAPTER 37

The twisted irony of betting on a horse named Devil's Folly and putting his entire savings on the line is not lost on Matt as he dashes from the monitor to frontside to catch the race from the rail, still numb after realizing he bet the wrong horse in the wrong race. As the horses sprint down the backstretch, he focuses his attention on the race while his eyes become glued to the oversize high-definition monitor next to the tote board on the infield of the track.

Desperately searching for the number-six horse in the black saddlecloth, Matt's heart flutters with anxiety and abject panic as he finally spots Devil's Folly running well behind the race leaders. The track announcer confirms Matt's observation. "And a disinterested Devil's Folly lingers behind the field as they approach the half-mile pole."

Annoyed, frustrated, and angry, Matt stomps on the hard pavement, producing a painful reverberation up his calf. He yells out, "Shit!" It was only a short minute ago when he made the wager of his lifetime on Tony Tornado, who will easily prevail in the next race and would have converted his wager into a lottery winner, had he managed to bet on the right horse in the right race. Matt can no longer watch or listen; instead he silently sulks as he steps away from the rail and wanders away.

Had Matt actually read his racing program, he would have learned Devil's Folly is a seven-year-old mare with an unremarkable career to date. Her sire was a champion of the early nineties, named Devil His Due, and her dam was unraced. Devil's Folly began her uneventful career as a three-year-old in 2014 and has since run thirty-three times with three wins, nine seconds, and eight thirds. In her most recent races, she finished second three times and third twice. In all three of her wins, she rallied from the back of the pack, as her running style is to trail the field early, then close strong in the final furlong.

As Matt meanders, he is intercepted by a familiar face. Upon greeting him, Ted Bouchard says, "Bonjour, Matt. Did you bet my horse?"

Matt shrugs, unaware and uninterested, given his current state of mind.

Bouchard continues, "Keep your eye on Devil's Folly. She'll be closing fast."

Matt's head snaps up. "What? Did you just say Devil's Folly? Oh, I didn't know she was your horse. Oh, man. I just put my entire savings on her."

Bouchard points to the monitor. "Look! She's starting to move. This mare is sitting on a big race. Allez, Devil! C'mon!"

As the horses enter the final turn, Devil's Folly is widest of all as she begins to rally from the rear, double-digits' lengths behind the race leader. The wide turn requires her to cover extra ground and compromises her position, but Bouchard's words of encouragement have given Matt the tiniest scintilla of hope. He prayerfully watches as Ted Bouchard eyes the action, standing next to him.

Bouchard slaps his racing program and yells out, "Now, *fille!*"

As if jockey and horse could channel Bouchard's instruction, Devil's Folly quickly accelerates as she enters the stretch run, passing several horses and gaining on the leader with every stride. Upon realizing this horse has a legitimate chance of winning, Matt finds himself screaming as the horses race toward the finish line.

The track announcer exclaims with surprising enthusiasm, "Devil's Folly is closing fast on the outside and making a huge run!"

Yards from the finish line, Devil's Folly hooks up with the leader, and they race nose to nose and stride for stride with no separation between them. Both jockeys are riding vigorously to gain any possible edge, but neither horse yields to the other as they race in tandem across the finish line, too close for the naked eye to discern which nose crossed the wire first.

The track announcer exclaims, "Too close to call," and the tote board flashes the word *Photo*, indicating the racing officials must review a high-definition photo, taken electronically at the finish line, in order to declare the winner. If either horse shows a nostril in front of the other, it will be declared the winner. If there is no discernable separation between both horses in the photo, the race will be declared a dead heat, and both horses will be considered the winner.

Matt looks to Ted Bouchard, hoping the trainer's skilled eye will help him assess the outcome. The stoic Bouchard squints and says, "Very close. Je ne sais pas. I don't know." The monitors are replaying the final few frames of the race in super slow motion, but the order of finish is indistinguishable, even slowed down. As the replay is shown, the crowd sighs and *oohs* in unison.

A few guys standing behind Matt and Bouchard can be heard debating the results. One says, "It was definitely the seven-horse," and the other says, "No frigging way, my friend. I'd bet my wife it was the six."

The last ten strides through the finish line are repeatedly replayed at varying speeds, presenting a new form of torment for Matt. If the race is declared a dead heat, Matt will still win his wager. Matt stares at the monitor and prays for a favorable outcome. The seconds turn to minutes, and the minutes feel like hours as Matt's stomach is a bundle of knots. He whispers to himself, "C'mon. One time!"

The results are posted, with the unofficial order of finish showing on the tote board. A collective "Oooh" echoes as a winner has finally been declared. Matt looks at the monitor with disbelief. The seven-horse has won, and Devil's Folly has finished second. He falls to his knees and drops his head, stinging from the shock of agonizing defeat. His entire savings are gone. There are no do-overs or second chances. Matt has forfeited his dream of owning Heliacal Star.

If Devil's Folly had been declared the winner, Matt would have earned the cash to purchase Heliacal Star, with money to spare for rehabilitation and training expenses. He could have treated Kristine to a night on the town, and they'd be driving Upstate in just a few days to complete his transaction.

Curled on the ground with his head on knees, Matt feels a

tap on his shoulder. He looks up at Ted Bouchard, who says, "It's not official."

Matt gapes at Bouchard for a second, puzzled by his comment. After processing his meaning, he snaps his head up and flashes a look toward the monitor. The number seven is blinking. As Matt gawks in disbelief at the screen, Bouchard says, "There's a stewards' inquiry on the winner. If you watch the replay closely, you can see my horse is getting thrashed down the lane."

Matt looks to Bouchard. "Do you think it's interference?"

"Yes, I think so, but I'm biased, of course."

Another debate ensues from the same guys behind them, who previously debated the photo finish. The first one declares, "She's coming down!"

Matt is fixated on the replay of the stretch run showing on the monitor. Previously, he watched the replay to ascertain the order of finish. Now he watches in search of an infraction or violation that will compel the stewards to disqualify the winner and place his horse first. The replay is played, rewound, and repeated again and again on every monitor on the grounds. On the replay, both horses appear to bump each other multiple times while sprinting to the wire, making it difficult to discern mutual from egregious contact. Based on his experience, Matt understands a majority of the three stewards must determine that a foul was committed, enough to affect the order of finish and disqualify the winner.

The second guy argues with his friend. "No way, dude! They're both bashing each other down the lane. She's not coming down. I hope I'm wrong because I'll hit the exacta if she comes down!"

As long as the number keeps blinking, there remains a chance

Matt could still win his wager. One minute turns to five, and the extended wait consumes every ounce of Matt's paper-thin patience. Mesmerized by the constant replays repeating on the monitor, Matt grows confident they'll disqualify the winner and declare his horse the winner, given the amount of time the stewards are taking to make a decision. Potentially escaping the jaws of a devasting defeat, Matt's heart teeters on the scale of renewed hope. The number seven continues to blink on the tote board as the stewards deliberate.

Matt pulls himself away from the monitors to ask Bouchard his opinion, but the trainer has already left. Matt whispers to himself, "What is taking them so long?"

The murmur and chatter from the crowd converges into a collective "Oooh" as the tote board goes blank and the order of the finish is changed. Matt stares at the updated results in stunned silence. The number-six, Devil's Folly, has been declared the winner, and number seven has been disqualified and placed second!

A euphoria grips him as he grasps the utter gravity of this reversal. The track announcer on the public address system comes on. "Ladies and gentlemen, we have a change in the official order of finish. After reviewing the replay, the stewards have determined there was sufficient interference during the final stretch run to affect the outcome of the race."

The tote board flashes the word *OFFICIAL*, indicating the result is now final and irreversible. Matt walks to the Winner's Circle and spots Ted Bouchard, who looks up and winks after posing with Devil's Folly for the photo.

The tote board shows the payout for a two-dollar win bet is exactly eight dollars. Matt calculates his wager will pay him roughly $12,000. He'll collect enough to replenish his bank account and pay for Heliacal Star and his rehabilitation expenses. Matt's hands shake and his body trembles from the miracle that just transpired.

He sends a text message to Kristine: *YEAH BABY!*

Matt recalls his brief encounter with the old man prior to the race and his words, which made little sense at the time. He realizes his faith has been rewarded and the misplaced wager was indeed his destiny. He made his decision and somehow, someway, the universe really made it happen. He looks skyward and says, "Thank you, Dad."

CHAPTER 38

Unlike most Saturdays, Kristine Connelly is quick to complete her afternoon tasks at the barn. She instructs her groom to take over operations for tomorrow's morning activities and reminds him to take temperatures first thing, then inspect legs and feet. She asks him to prep the first group of horses for morning gallops on the track, as she expects to arrive late tomorrow morning.

He flashes a broad smile and says, "¿Cita esta noche, señorita?"

She places her hands on the groom's shoulders and grins. "It is that obvious? Yes, I have a date tonight!"

"Bueno! Have fun, señorita."

Since relocating downstate and spending most of her time at the barn attending to her horses, Kristine has not spent any time dating.

Inside her apartment, Kristine tosses several outfits onto the floor and picks up a black lace miniskirt. She slips into the skintight skirt, then rummages through a drawer full of blouses and stops on a hot-pink, short-sleeve, scoop-neck crop top. She spins around to view herself at varying angles in the mirror. After pulling on a pair of red spiked cowboy boots, she completes her outfit with a studded denim jacket. She fluffs her wavy blonde hair and adds a touch of blush and trace of lipstick.

Eyeing herself in the mirror, Kristine puckers her lips. "Better watch out, Matt Galiano, I am smoking hot tonight!"

Kristine arrives early at Mario's and locates a chair at the bar near the entrance. She looks around the room as the bartender approaches.

The bartender's mouth drops open. "Is that you, Miss Connelly? Wow! If you don't mind me saying, you look . . . incredible! Sorry, didn't mean to be . . ."

"That's okay. I appreciate the compliment." She flashes a slight smile. "Could you bring me a club soda with slice of lemon?"

The bartender attends to her order and the front door flies open, prompting Kristine to take a look toward the entrance. Ron McGee enters, approaches the bar, and yells toward the bartender, "Have you seen my friend Larry? Do you happen to know if he's here?"

Before the bartender has a chance to respond, a pair of muscular and heavily tattooed men approach McGee from inside the restaurant. The first puts his hand atop of McGee's shoulder and asks, "You McGee?"

McGee looks up at the muscle twins and nods.

Kristine sips her soda water while keeping her back to McGee and his associates. She whispers to the bartender, "Hey, I'm going to sneak inside and grab a table. If a guy name Matt is looking for me . . . " Louisville Larry is approaching the bar from the dining area. Kristine whispers to the bartender, "Plan B. I think I'll stay here for a minute."

Sauntering past Kristine's seat, Larry shouts over to McGee

standing on the other side of the bar, "I see my friend has finally arrived." Larry wraps his arm across McGee's shoulders and clenches his face with his fingers. "I see you met my friends. I'll formally introduce you." He points to the first of the brawny pair. "This is my man Frankie Fischer." He points to the other. "And that's his brother Johnny Fischer."

McGee pulls out an envelope from his back pocket. "And this belongs to you. I hope that—"

"Not now, Ron," Larry says as he looks at Kristine across the bar. "Hold your horses."

Leaving McGee alone with his strapping associates, Larry intercepts Kristine as she slides off of her stool and walks toward the dining area of the restaurant. He eyes her from head to toe. "Miss, let me buy you a drink!"

Kristine shields her face. "Um, thanks for the offer, but I'm meeting someone."

Larry steps in close to her and says, "I don't see anyone here. Perhaps your friend is lost or has other plans? C'mon, what's the harm in having a drink with a good-looking guy?" He chuckles and gestures to the bartender. "Bring this smoking-hot lady whatever she wants and a few glasses of Dom."

"Thanks, but no thanks."

Larry does not move. "Think it over, sweetheart. I just ordered us a round of drinks, and it would be a shame to turn ol' Larry down."

Kristine places a hand on her hip and shifts her weight to one side. "Sorry, but you're not my type. Can I go now?"

Larry's eyebrows rise. "You . . . oh . . . whoa . . ."

Kristine smirks. "You sure you want another drink? Your

breath tells me you've had plenty already!" She moves around him.

"Hello, Kristine."

Kristine spins around and finds herself staring at Ron McGee.

Her face goes flush and her breath quickens. Why did she decide on this place for tonight? It's not the first time it's been full of creeps.

McGee gulps down a shot of bourbon and looks her over. "I think we have some unfinished business. What do you say?"

Kristine shoves McGee, and Larry steps in. "Oh shit, I know you! You're that girl trainer from the racetrack—the one who ratted me out." Larry moves in close, snatches Kristine from the back of the neck, yanks her backward, and says, "And to think, I even offered to buy you a drink tonight!"

Kristine wriggles free, takes a step toward Larry, and presses her middle finger into his face. "Fuck you, Larry, and screw you, McGee!"

"Your big mouth almost caused some serious trouble. Nobody screws with Louisville and gets away with it!"

Kristine drives her boot directly into his groin. The large man screams out and staggers forward. The two toughs he walked in with, Frankie and Johnny, restrain her.

Larry struggles to his feet. "You're fucking dead now!"

CHAPTER 39

As eager as he was to message or call Kristine, Matt decided it would be more dramatic to surprise her in person. With incredible restraint, he manages to avoid contacting her all afternoon.

After hiding his cash under his mattress at home, Matt heads out to Mario's, blasting his music mix and feeling unstoppable. Bursting with excitement for his date with Kristine, he envisions caressing her face and staring into those beautiful green eyes. He contrasts his passionate feelings for Kristine with the ambivalence of previous dates and one-night thrills. Her beauty, intelligence, and charisma have opened up an entirely new world, and Matt can only smile to himself as he thinks about her.

As he enters the parking lot of Mario's, Matt anticipates an exciting evening and is convinced nothing can spoil his amazing day. His playlist blares on the car stereo. He sings aloud to "Don't Stop Me Now" by Queen, which magically channels his mood in this moment.

Singing inside his car, Matt notices a man bursting through the front door of Mario's and sprinting toward the parking area. Matt shuts off his engine and intercepts the man to ask about what's happening inside the restaurant.

The man is panting as he dials 911. "Hi, you need to send police and an ambulance to Mario's Restaurant and Bar. There's a bunch of thugs pummeling this poor young lady inside. If you don't get here right away, they're going to seriously hurt or kill her."

Matt immediately sprints toward the front door of the restaurant and smashes through the entrance, pushing the door into the backside of Frankie Fischer. Matt skips past the staggering brute and finds Kristine squirming on the floor with Louisville Larry hovering over her. Matt wraps his arm around the big man's neck.

Larry spins. Matt shouts to Kristine, "Get out of here! Now!"

Kristine crawls away.

Louisville's resistance wanes, and he drops to one knee, flailing. Feeling the bulky man weaken underneath him, Matt gains confidence he'll soon subdue the powerful hulk.

Suddenly, a powerful force throws Matt off Louisville. Frankie Fischer grabs Matt by the hair and slams his head onto the wooden floor, opening a gash across his chin and ear. As Frankie Fischer holds Matt down, Louisville delivers a violent kick to Matt's ribs. Matt screams and rolls onto his back. Frankie lands a punch to Matt's stomach.

His vision blurred, Matt hears the unmistakable voice of Louisville Larry piercing through the fog in his head. "Did you really think you would walk in here and beat on me? You're mine now! Once I'm finished with you, I'll take your girlfriend next."

No matter what happens to him, Matt desperately wants Kristine to escape. Matt is lucid enough to understand his attackers will offer no mercy. He lowers his hands, glares at his assailants, and forces a defiant smile. Spitting blood, he says, "Go straight to hell, Larry!"

Larry leans over. "You should've left well enough alone, Matty boy. This wasn't your fight. It was between me and your bitch girlfriend, but you had to be the hero. And that was a very bad idea!"

Louisville hoists him by the collar of his bloodied shirt. "You know, I have just one regret, Galiano. I should have finished you all those years ago."

Matt recounts the man from the parking lot as the faraway sound of a siren indicates the authorities may be coming. The sound of the approaching sirens grows louder. Frankie turns to Louisville. "Motherfucker! We gotta get out of here, bro. It's the cops!"

Propping up a visibly flaccid Matt, Louisville raises his left arm and hurls his clenched fist into Matt's unprotected face. The explosion of impact shatters inside his head. Then nothing but black.

CHAPTER 40

In Mario's parking lot, the flashing lights of the patrol cars present an ocean of blue and red on an otherwise dark evening. The responding officers are combing the lot and searching for evidence inside Mario's, which has been shut down for the evening.

The police responded within minutes of the first 911 call and asked those on-site to remain as eyewitnesses. Although many were present to witness the assault, nobody interviewed seemed to recall or showed willingness to share any details regarding the attackers. Without direct evidence or eyewitness descriptions, the only discernable information the police had was about an unprovoked attack on a female victim by multiple assailants. The bartender provided only a vague description of three large and burly Caucasian men with dark hair. Video surveillance from the restaurant was unavailable as the camera over the bar only served as a visible deterrent but was never activated.

After combing through the scene, lifting fingerprints from the bar area, and bagging potential evidence, the police seek out the two victims. The lead detective approaches the ambulance where a medical technician attends to one of them. The detective peers inside and approaches the technician. "Can I get a statement from him?"

The technician responds, "He not quite all there yet. When we arrived, he was unconscious and only awakened a few minutes ago. Right now, he doesn't even know his name, so he won't be much help at the moment. I'll let you know if things change and he comes around."

The officer nods and approaches Kristine as she sits inside a makeshift police tent. She is attended by a medical technician, who cleans and dresses the lacerations across her forehead.

The lead detective approaches. "Excuse me, miss . . . Are you okay to answer a few questions?"

The technician seals a bandage across her forehead and Kristine sits up. "Hi, I'm Kristine Connelly." She extends her hand toward the detective.

"Hello, Miss Connelly. I'm Detective Kruger, and I'd like to take a formal statement."

She nods.

The detective asks, "Do you know the men who attacked you?"

Kristine doesn't hesitate. "Without a doubt! One goes by the name Louisville Larry. Another was named Johnny, and I didn't catch the name of the third. I suspect they were at Mario's tonight to exchange money with a guy named Ron McGee, who trains horses at the nearby racetrack. I know him, because I'm also a trainer at the track and used to be his assistant."

The detective makes a note and asks, "Could you identify the men from a lineup?"

"One hundred percent! Just tell me when and where, and I'll be there."

After asking a number of other questions and getting Kristine's side of the story, the detective has heard enough. "Thank you, Miss Connelly. You've been extremely helpful. We'll be in touch."

CHAPTER 41

Sir, can you hear me?"

As he awakens, Matt feels a tingling throughout his body, yielding to an intense, stabbing pain emanating from his ribcage and crawling up the sides of his neck and across his forehead.

"Sir, can you hear me?"

The faint voice is more audible now, and Matt realizes someone is talking to him.

Matt slowly opens his eyes and shies away from the intense beam of a flashlight. Lost and confused, he looks around, trying to ascertain what is happening. His focus narrows in search of something, anything that may help him make sense of his situation as an intense pain throbs, impeding his concentration.

The voice returns. "Sir, if you can hear me, blink your eyes."

Matt obliges, keeps his eyes open, and focuses on a tall gentleman who leans over and flashes a light into Matt's right, then left eye. Matt recognizes the uniform of an emergency medical technician. He raises himself into a sitting position but retreats quickly. The pain pulsates unrelentingly.

The technician says, "Slow and steady breaths. It will reduce your discomfort."

Matt shutters his eyes and channels his energy toward his breathing. He inhales and exhales slowly and deliberately. He repeats the exercise and counts off ten breaths. The pain abates a bit. The image of an irate Louisville Larry suddenly appears in his mind. He flinches and breaks into a clammy sweat. The numbing pain intensifies as his adrenaline increases.

The technician interrupts, "Sir, do you know your name?"

Matt takes a moment to process the question. After a pause, he answers in a raspy voice, "Matt." He takes slow and measured breaths and speaks in rhythm to assuage the pain. "Matt Galiano."

"Do you know where you are?"

Matt darts his eyes across the parking lot and flashing lights. "Outside, parking lot?"

The technician continues, "Do you know which parking lot?"

His mind flashes with broken images of Louisville Larry and his goon squad and the interior of Mario's Bar and Restaurant. He remembers arriving at the restaurant for a romantic dinner with Kristine, but something is off.

Matt responds, "Is this Mario's?"

As he says the name of the restaurant, it triggers a replay of earlier events from the evening. He recalls arriving at Mario's to meet Kristine and witnessing a savage attack. Stretching his mind, he remembers intervening in the fracas but cannot retrieve what may have happened next. His mind shifts to concerns about Kristine as he fears for her health and safety.

Matt calls out her name.

He cannot shake the horrific image of Kristine getting pummeled by Louisville. He failed to protect her.

The technician says, "Mr. Galiano, Kristine is fine. Miss

Connelly is sitting nearby and anxious to see you."

An overwhelming relief neutralizes his aches for a brief moment.

The technician continues, "I have one more question for you before we bring her over. We found you lying on the ground, only a few feet from the main entrance. Do you remember leaving Mario's?"

Unable to remember much of anything, including the fight, Matt has no recollection of leaving Mario's or how he made it outside.

Matt responds, "No, I don't remember leaving Mario's."

The tech continues, "You were assaulted inside the restaurant and have likely suffered a concussion, which explains your memory loss. We'll administer a series of standard tests per protocol. We're going to take you to the nearby hospital, and they'll check you out, okay?"

The pain emitting from his midsection intensifies as he shifts his weight.

"Where is Kristine?"

The technician waves Kristine over and says, "I'll be nearby but will give you a moment of privacy."

Kristine appears and places her hand on his forehead. "Thank God you showed up when you did. Those assholes wouldn't have stopped if you didn't step in and rescue me."

Matt smiles, as she appears relatively unscathed. "Are you okay?"

She gently caresses his arm. "I should be asking you that question. I'm so glad you're up and alert. The technician said you took some nasty blows, but he expects you to fully recover. He called you young and healthy." She smiles. "I swear those are his words, not mine!"

Matt is sullen as he looks at her. "I'm sorry, Kristine, for getting you involved in my shit and this entire mess with Louisville. This is my fault."

Leaning in close, Kristine kisses him lightly on the forehead and whispers, "Mr. Galiano, you risked everything for me. I was in serious trouble in the moments before you arrived." She continues, "I don't want to hear about how this is your fault."

Kristine pulls back her hair, revealing a long bandage stretching across her forehead. She chuckles and points at the bandage. "This is my badge of honor. A technician cleaned me up and handed me an ibuprofen, and I'm as good as new!"

In spite of her encouragement and positive attitude, Matt cannot help but feel responsible for placing her in such a dangerous situation. The mental anguish of guilt parallels the physical pain he's experiencing, and he looks deep into her soulful eyes.

Kristine leans forward. "I'm in your corner, mister. Don't you ever fret about me." In spite of her reassurance and resiliency, his guilt stubbornly tugs at him. Kristine takes a step back and shouts, "Holy moly, Matt Galiano! There is not a single person on this planet who would have done what you did tonight! You just try and get rid of me now!"

Emboldened by her words, Matt cannot help himself from smiling.

The technician returns. "It's time to move you, Mr. Galiano."

Two more technicians approach, and all three lift the stretcher in unison and place Matt inside the ambulance. The primary tech says, "Since you're fully conscious and alert, we'll allow Miss

Connelly to accompany you on the ride to the hospital."

Kristine climbs in through the back of the ambulance and sits adjacent to Matt. The technician joins them inside as the other techs shut the back door from the outside. Once the stretcher is secured, the ambulance pulls away from Mario's.

An intensifying ache throbs in Matt's forehead as the ambulance moves out. Given the excitement, Matt hadn't considered requesting a pain reliever. He calls to the technician, "Excuse me, but my head is killing me. Can I get an aspirin?"

"I'm sorry, Mr. Galiano, but anything like ibuprofen or aspirin right now could mask concussion symptoms."

Kristine takes Matt's hand. "Everything is going to be fine. I know it. You're going to be okay."

The technician nods in agreement and says, "Focus on your breathing. We'll be at the hospital soon. Now, I'm going to replace the ice pack on your midsection. This will feel cold initially, but continue to focus on your breathing, and there is nothing to worry about."

Matt was unaware an icepack had already been placed on his midsection, but it explained the chilly feeling and numbness throughout his middle. Considering all his discomfort, he hadn't given thought to the odd sensation around his torso until just now.

CHAPTER 42

Matt's long night at the hospital began with a set of X-rays to check for fractures and a CT scan to assess swelling or bleeding. This was followed by a seemingly endless cycle of nurses waking him up for temperature and blood pressure readings along with periodic blood draws. Unaware of time since he drifted off to sleep, Matt notices Kristine sitting next to his bed as he opens his eyes.

With heavy eyes and an aching body, Matt is grateful and reassured by her presence. He fights off the obvious discomfort and twists his head toward Kristine. Groggy and disoriented, Matt slurs, "I can't believe you're still here. What time is it?"

Kristine smiles broadly. "It's nice to see you, too! I've been napping in the waiting room most of the night until they finally allowed me to see you about fifteen minutes ago. It's three in the morning."

Eyes half shut, Matt says, "I'm so exhausted, Kristine. Please tell them to stop with the nurse parade!"

Kristine shakes her head and mouths out the word *Sorry* as an overnight doctor enters his room.

The doctor approaches Matt's bedside. "Hello, Mr. Galiano,

I'm Dr. Grekin. I've been looking at the results of your tests. The good news is there are no signs of bleeding or swelling, but you suffered a few fractured ribs. We also diagnosed a sizeable contusion on your right leg."

Given the intensity and consistency of pain emanating from his midsection, the medical diagnosis is unsurprising.

Dr. Grekin continues, "You're likely going to experience soreness for at least a week or two, but you should see improvement every day. We're going to keep you here for observation since you experienced acute memory loss. The human body has a remarkable ability to heal itself, and you appear in good general health, which will expedite your recovery."

Matt asks, "Can I take an ibuprofen or aspirin?"

The doctor grimaces. "I'm afraid not yet. If nothing new arises, we'll write you a prescription for a pain reliever, and you'll be free to use over-the-counter ibuprofen in another six to nine hours."

Matt appreciates the concern and caution. He hopes the worst has passed as the overall intensity of pain seems to have subsided since he was admitted several hours earlier.

The doctor asks Matt if he has any questions.

Matt says, "Just one more question. Will you be putting a cast around my broken ribs?"

Dr. Grekin looks at him with a friendly grin. "Thankfully, we're no longer living in the twentieth century, meaning there's no need for a body cast. Before we release you, we'll provide you with a flak jacket for protection, which will restrict your mobility. You should limit your movement and physical activity for three to four weeks until those bones fully heal. You should feel a lot better in just a week or two. However, don't stop wearing the flak jacket until you have a full checkup with your primary doctor in four to six weeks."

As he walks toward the door, Dr. Grekin reminds Matt he'll be under nursing care for the next several hours and to expect continued periodic checks throughout the night.

As he watches the doctor exit his room, Matt returns his attention to Kristine, glad she's there. "So, where were we?"

Kristine scooches her chair close to Matt's bed and takes his hand in hers. "Just who are you, Matt Galiano?"

Caught off guard, Matt is unable to respond. His eyes grow heavier as the inevitable respite of sleep tugs hard. Although he can still hear Kristine's voice, her words are fading as he drifts into an overdue sleep.

Kristine continues to hold his hand as his eyes shut and he falls asleep. She says, "You're a special one, Matt Galiano. You might not know it yet, but you'll find out soon enough." She leans over, kisses him gently on his forehead, and whispers, "Soon enough. Good night, Matt. I hope your dreams tonight are pleasant ones."

CHAPTER 43

Larry Lonsdale was supposed to meet Tony Kaufman at precisely 9:00 a.m. Sunday morning to deliver the cash from McGee but failed to show. It is well-known among those in the Kaufman crew that it's best to show up on time when Tony Kaufman calls. If Tony wants to see you at 9:00 a.m., you don't show up at 9:01. It doesn't matter if you're sick or your car broke down. Tony's people make it happen.

Tony looks at his watch, and the time shows 9:45 a.m. No sign of Larry. He snatches one of several burner phones from his desk and phones his brother, Ken. "Where is that motherfucker?"

Ken says, "Apparently, there was a mix-up last night with our friend." Tony is silent, indicating Ken should continue. "He says it was a simple misunderstanding, and he apologizes for missing dinner last night. We're both heading to Grandma's house now."

As they speak in code, Ken refers to the names of relatives, such as Grandma or Auntie, to indicate he's traveling to see Tony. His reference to missing dinner last night is code for missing his morning appointment.

The last person who didn't show up to meet Tony Kaufman had been infamously reprimanded. After missing his appointment when his wife unexpectedly went into labor, Joey the Juicer was offered a new appointment with Tony at 6:00 a.m. the next morning. Joey arrived thirty minutes early this time, but Tony arrived later. Much later.

Joey waited obediently on the corner. As each hour passed, he stood in the same spot, as instructed by Tony, checking his watch throughout the morning and early afternoon. When nature called, he relieved himself in place rather than wandering off and risk disrespecting Tony.

Tony rolled up in his Lincoln Navigator at precisely two in the afternoon and invited Joey to sit next to him in the backseat. They drove from Queens to Manhattan, and throughout the drive, Tony did not speak to or look at Joey. After thirty minutes, the Navigator parked outside Sutton's Clock Shop, which was closed for the day. A burly gentleman in a custom charcoal suit approached their vehicle. Tony rolled down the rear window, and the man handed him a box. No words were exchanged. As Tony rolled up his window, the man retreated around the corner and disappeared from view.

The Navigator drove another thirty minutes from Manhattan into New Jersey. As was the case before, Tony kept his eyes forward and was silent throughout the drive. As the Navigator pulled into an abandoned parking lot, Tony opened the box to reveal a fully restored nineteenth-century Howard Miller mantle clock. The antique clock was slightly longer than a foot, about a foot high and nearly a foot deep. It weighed about five pounds.

Tony turned to Joey the Juicer and grabbed a fistful of hair in one hand while holding the clock in his other. In an instant, Tony smashed the face of the clock onto Joey's head, drawing blood from his nose and forehead. He came at him again, this time shattering the clock face directly across Joey's nose, causing a stream of blood to gush. He repeated this motion until both the clock and Joey's face were no longer recognizable.

As Joey faded to unconsciousness, Tony threw a bucket of ice water over his battered face to prevent him from passing out. Tony reached over the beaten man, opened the back door, and shoved him onto the pavement. Joey lay motionless on the ground. Tony threw a towel to his driver, who cleaned Joey up and returned him inside the vehicle.

Once Joey was back inside the car, Tony spoke to him. "Never forget how to tell time again." As the beating of Joey the Juicer became known throughout the organization in the days and weeks that followed, it served to reinforce Tony's reputation as a ruthless leader, intolerant of insubordination.

CHAPTER 44

Tony Kaufman is about power, money, and control. Tony and his brother Ken have operated their family's butcher shop on Long Island since they were young adults, immediately after their father was murdered. As the oldest and heir apparent, Tony learned from his father early in life that once power is obtained, it is best perpetuated through fear and intimidation, qualities Tony Kaufman has leveraged during his reign. For anyone foolish enough to cross the Kaufmans, misfortune is bound to follow.

Ken Kaufman arrives at Tony's office in the rear of the butcher shop after instructing Larry to remain in the front seat of his car. Tony greets Ken with a firm handshake and kisses him on both cheeks. Looking past Ken, Tony gestures to a heavily tattooed, overweight middle-aged man in a white tank top and jeans standing nearby. Following Tony's cue, the tattooed man goes outside and returns a few moments later with Larry at his side.

Tony's office is sparse and uninspiring. There are no windows, telephones, computers, or any electronic equipment, just a single desk and single oversize desk chair surrounded by three small guest chairs. Tony conducts his most private conversations here. As Larry enters the office, he is carrying a stuffed brown grocery bag.

A single framed photo hangs on the wall just behind Tony's desk, featuring a picture of his father standing beside the boyish-looking Kaufman sons. Across the desk on a small wet bar is a selection of liquor, including two bottles of aged single malt scotch whiskey, an unopened bottle of premium cognac, along with a bottle of Grey Goose, Patrón tequila, and a barely emptied bottle of Crown Royal.

Ken runs his hand on the underside of Tony's desk, then under the seat of each chair before tapping on the door to signal all clear. Before entering Tony's office, Larry hands his gun, cell phone, keys, and shoes to the overweight bouncer who escorts him inside. Ken pats down Larry and nods to Tony.

Tony settles back into his desk chair as Ken sits in one of the guest chairs. Larry remains standing. Getting the nod from Tony, Larry slowly approaches the desk and dumps the contents of the paper bag, which had been filled with rolls of US currency. Larry says, "It's all there, sir. Twelve thou."

Tony rises and leans forward. "What the fuck were you thinking, Larry?"

Larry lowers and turns his head.

"Look at me when I'm talking!"

Larry lifts his head.

"You stupid fucking idiot."

Turning to Ken, Tony's demeanor shifts. "How about you and I go for a quick ride? I think we need to take care of something." He points a finger at Larry and says, "Our friend will wait right here and consider his moronic behavior until we get back. We'll deal with him later."

Once Tony and Ken are gone, Larry is locked inside the room alone. Without any means of communicating, he is effectively imprisoned until Tony, Ken, or someone else unlocks and opens the door. Alongside the impressive array of liquor are requisite mixers, but given the circumstances and without access to a bathroom, there is no chance Larry will partake.

Inside his car with tinted windows, Ken assumes his typical driver role while Tony settles into the back seat. As they pull away, Tony says, "Just drive around the neighborhood. Nowhere in particular. I'm concerned about Larry. He's been a loyal soldier for almost twenty years, but . . . "

The car stops at a red traffic light, and Ken twists around the headrest to face his brother. "Larry's always been useful to us, but let's face it, there isn't much between his ears. Even so, it seems the few functioning brain cells in his head have gone on vacation the past few weeks, ever since he ran into that prick, Matt Galiano."

The traffic light turns green. "You're right about Galiano being a thorn. Larry should have finished him off years ago, but he botched that job, right?"

Ken nods while continuing to drive.

Tony continues, "Larry doesn't usually screw up his enforcement assignments, but we can't afford for him to be emotional. I told him to finish Galiano, but not now. Only when the time is right."

As he points the car toward Tony's place, Ken says, "What do you want to do with Larry? Not only did he risk drawing the attention of the authorities, but he disrespected you by missing his scheduled appointment."

Chuckling from the backseat, Tony says, "You're going to take Larry with you tomorrow, drive him Upstate, and cool him off. When you return on Tuesday, he'll turn himself in to the local authorities. This will keep him iced until we bail him out. Reinforce my message about cooling off for a bit on the Galiano job, which includes his troublemaker girlfriend, until I give the word. Right now, we need to avoid unwanted scrutiny or attention. Things will quiet down in a few weeks, and then he can do his job."

After dropping Tony at home, Ken returns to the butcher shop and unlocks the office door. Larry leaps to his feet as the door swings open.

Ken slowly walks over to Larry and pokes him in the chest. "I don't want to hear a fucking word from you." He pauses a moment as Larry stands motionless. "Your actions last night were colossally stupid, but consider yourself lucky because Tony's in a forgiving mood today. You've been with us a long time, and Tony appreciates your gesture." He points to the money, which remains untouched where Larry tossed it atop Tony's desk.

"Now, go home and clean yourself up. We have an important job together in the morning. I'll pick you up at seven a.m. sharp. You best be ready."

Larry says, "Yes, sir, boss."

CHAPTER 45

Matt drifts in and out of sleep as on-shift nurses periodically check on him throughout the morning for pulse, temperature, and blood pressure readings. As midday approaches with the sun shining through the hospital window, Matt is fitted for a flak jacket and offered prescription-strength ibuprofen and some water. Achy and uncomfortable, he accepts the tablets and swallows them down without hesitation and lays down to catch up from a night of broken slumber. Suddenly, his head snaps forward and he yells out, "Nurse!"

She rushes back into the room. "What is it, Mr. Galiano?"

A sudden panic consumes him, and beads of sweat form across his forehead. "How long was I sleeping? What time is it? Is it still Sunday?"

She responds, "Yes, Mr. Galiano. Today is still Sunday. It's almost one in the afternoon. Are you planning on going somewhere?"

Matt thanks the nurse, as the rush of anxiety dissipates as quickly as it arrived. He lays back down and considers the probability of meeting Paula White on Wednesday. Driving anywhere in just a few days seems unlikely if not impossible.

His thoughts turn to Louisville Larry and the threat he represents. Based on his own firsthand experiences, Matt expects Louisville will intensify his efforts against him and Kristine, especially since he failed to finish the job last night at Mario's. This represents strike two, and there won't be a strike three if Louisville gets his way. As long as he remains in the hospital, Matt is safe, but once he leaves, he fears he and Kristine will be hunted.

He pages the nurse.

As he waits, Matt obsesses about Kristine, her enchanting smile and the sweet fragrance of her perfume. The peril she faces gnaws at his conscience. Acting is critical. Where is that bleeping nurse?

Still waiting, Matt decides he and Kristine will flee Upstate, at least for a few days, and meet up with Paula White. The diversion will buy them extra time and space from Louisville, and a chance to concoct some longer-term options. Escape won't be easy, but they must remain a step ahead of Louisville until the police can track him down.

Dr. Grekin enters the room and reviews Matt's chart. He turns to Matt. "Surprised to see me? Your vitals look good. Did the nurse provide you with ibuprofen?"

Matt nods, and the doctor continues, "I expect you'll continue to feel soreness and discomfort for a while, but everything will heal with time. How are you feeling?"

Since the ibuprofen kicked in, his aches have marginally diminished. Anxious to be discharged, Matt adjusts into a sitting position while swallowing his breath to avoid grimacing or showing any display of obvious pain. He looks at the doctor.

"I feel better! Look, I can even move around a bit." He stands up and sits back down while biting his tongue to keep himself from grunting. "Don't get me wrong, everything hurts, but the ibuprofen is helping. I'm ready to get out of here, like now."

Doctor Grekin responds, "As I said yesterday, your ribs should heal nicely over the next four to six weeks. You must avoid physical activity or undue strain, or you'll aggravate your injuries and hinder the healing process."

Matt nods. "Fair enough."

Matt promises to follow the doctor's orders and restrict his movements, but his main concern is getting at least one bar on his phone and calling Kristine to warn her about Louisville and the threat he presents. They'll need to hide out somewhere for the next night or two before driving Upstate to meet Paula White on Wednesday.

As Matt stands to retrieve his clothes, Dr. Grekin says, "Not so fast."

Matt mumbles to himself, "Shit, I knew this seemed too easy."

The doctor shushes Matt and continues, "Before you go, there is an officer standing outside who needs to speak with you. We kept them away all night considering your condition, but they've waited patiently to speak to you."

Matt nods, and Detective Kruger enters his hospital room. With nothing to lose, he offers his full cooperation and willingness to appear at the station to positively identify his assailants should they find and apprehend Larry and his thugs.

As the detective leaves his hospital room, Kristine enters.

"I heard you're leaving and may need an escort?"

Seeing Kristine standing in front of him creates a tidal wave of relief, and Matt shows it by spontaneously smiling. An orderly arrives with a wheelchair and assists Matt into the chair. Kristine walks alongside as they move through the hospital toward the exit.

Matt stares at Kristine and whispers, "I was worried about you."

Kristine stops, steps in front Matt sitting in the wheelchair, and asks the orderly to hold up a moment. With her hands prominently on her hips, she says, "You were worried about me? Before you start worrying about me, let's put ol' Humpty Dumpty back together again."

"I'm serious, Kris. These guys won't stop."

Kristine steps to his side, and they continue moving toward the front desk for Matt to sign a waiver for his release. He lists Kristine Connelly as his designated driver. After thanking the orderly for his help, Matt slowly stands, grabs a walking cane, and hobbles out the automated doorway.

Once outside, Kristine looks in all directions, turns to Matt, and says, "What are our options?"

Although tacitly aware his dubious history could resurface at any time, Matt hadn't anticipated being in a serious relationship. He failed to consider how his dubious history might disrupt someone else's life in such a terrifying manner. Just days ago, the Kaufman crew was not his biggest concern. He believed Larry remained secured in jail and the Kaufmans had bigger concerns. After taking a severe beating for his actions years ago and never legally pursuing the assault with the authorities, Matt realized he'd been lulled into a false sense of complacency. In spite of the gap in time and absence of contact for several years, his past is rapidly resurfacing with a vengeance and dragging Kristine into the fight with him.

As Kristine heads off to the parking lot to retrieve her vehicle, Matt considers their options. Retaliation would be a suicide mission, as he would never get close to Kaufman, even if he somehow managed to take out Larry. His last attempt at swindling Kaufman with his betting scheme a decade ago didn't work out too well. Any bold action on his part would likely put Kristine in even greater danger. They could go into hiding indefinitely, but after spending ten years looking over his shoulder, Matt cannot force Kristine to alter her lifestyle and abort her livelihood. He knows of only one realistic and viable option to pursue.

Kristine pulls up in her vehicle to the designated pickup area. Matt looks around and carefully climbs inside the passenger seat, feeling thankful she doesn't drive a tiny sports car. He refuses her offer of help in order to show his ability to manage his own movements. In doing so, he surprises himself upon entering her SUV without too much pain or trouble.

As he closes the passenger door and settles deep his seat, Matt turns to Kristine.

"Are you okay, Matt?"

"Yes, I'm fine. I just need to manage my breathing for now. Hey, with everything else happening, I forgot to tell you something super exciting! Remember the text I sent you yesterday before Mario's?'"

Kristine nods as a subtle smile forms.

"It just so happens, I earned enough at the track yesterday to purchase Heliacal Star by myself! And the best news is . . . you're going to train him for us!"

Smirking, Kristine asks, "Matt Galiano, are you serious or delirious?"

Matt is amazed he managed to keep such big news under wraps for more than twenty-four hours, but then again, his circumstances were extenuating. He says, "It means you and I need to see Paula White Upstate on Wednesday. Besides, a road trip will give us a little space from Louisville, if you know what I mean."

Matt locks his eyes on hers. "There's also one more thing I need to do. Something I should have done ten years ago." He takes a long pause and finally says, "It's time I went to the authorities about Kaufman's operation."

CHAPTER 46

At the police station late Sunday afternoon, Special Agent Anjero is whispering quietly to himself, "Answer the phone, you stupid—" His call goes to voicemail. Turning to Detective Kruger, Anjero asks, "Are you sure it was Larry Lonsdale involved in the assault last night?"

Kruger nods and says, "Yup, but I can't arrest him until I get clearance from the FBI for some reason. So, here we are."

"I appreciate your cooperation, Detective. What can you tell me about the eyewitness accounts?"

Detective Kruger sighs and says, "Lonsdale allegedly beat some poor sap into pulp at Mario's last night. According to our notes, Larry was roughing up the female victim first, until the male victim allegedly jumped him."

Anjero's cell phone rings, interrupting their conversation. He excuses himself and slips into an unoccupied room.

He answers, "Special Agent Anjero here."

Larry is on the other end of the line. "Hey, boss. What's up? I'm returning your call."

Anjero asks, "I assume you know why I'm calling?"

"Oh, that. Yeah, okay. I fucked up last night. I had too much tequila and lost my cool . . . Listen, boss, I'm really close to Tony and will get you something if you can make this one go away."

Stepping into an unoccupied room and closing the door behind him, Anjero peers through the window and watches the activity inside the busy squad room. He closes the blinds and sits on the edge of the table.

Anjero raises his voice and says, "Do you think I'm stupid, Larry? At this very moment, I've got a local precinct full of detectives looking for your ass, right here, right now! And I gotta say, the way I feel right now, I'm compelled to let them have you." He puts down the phone, tilts his head back, and looks up at the ceiling for a moment. Returning to his phone, Anjero asks, "You still there?"

Larry grunts.

Anjero continues, "Whatever you have, it better be really good. Otherwise, I'm done with you after the stunt you just pulled."

Larry says, "If Tony finds out, I'll be dead anyway. I promise I'll get you the juice next week."

For Special Agent Carlos Anjero and the Bureau, Larry has been a reliable insider for the past two years, but the flow of information has tapered off over the past several months. The lack of intelligence of late has garnered the attention of Anjero's field director, who recently expressed concerns about the lack of actionable information. As Larry was the aggressor in this latest police inquiry and is now being actively sought for questioning and possible arrest, Anjero's supervisor will need to take action to protect their informant.

Anjero speaks slowly to Larry, "I'm out of patience with

you. I swear, this will be your last lifeline if you fail to produce. I'm out of town tomorrow, so meet me at police headquarters Tuesday afternoon. If you bring me something better than what you've been feeding me of late, I'll clean this up. In the meantime, I'll inform the detective in charge of your case you'll be here Tuesday to turn yourself in. Don't fuck this up, Larry. I'll ensure they throw everything they've got at you if you stiff me."

Anjero pops out of the room and locates Detective Kruger. "Call off your boys on this one, at least for a couple of days. I've arranged for your suspect, Larry Lonsdale, to turn himself in on Tuesday. When he gets here, he's all yours."

CHAPTER 47

Just after sunrise Monday morning, Ken Kaufman pulls up in his old sedan on a quiet stretch of Northern Boulevard. His unremarkable and unwashed car draws little attention in the neighborhood, as similar vehicles are commonplace.

It's been less than twenty-four hours since Larry was held prisoner in Tony's office, but in the time since, he's showered, shaved, and appears alert in a patterned linen shirt and khaki shorts. Larry paces in a tight circle outside of Starbucks as Ken arrives.

Ken lowers the passenger window and calls out to Larry, "Get in. We're heading Upstate."

As he gets in the car, Larry peeks into the backseat. "Where's Johnny and Frankie? They usually come on my jobs."

Ken does not respond.

Larry offers Ken a coffee from the Starbucks. "I can run inside and add cream and sugar if you want."

Ken takes the coffee, opens the driver-side door, and dumps it onto the street. "I'm not in the mood for your fucking coffee right now."

Ken navigates through Queens, across the Whitestone Bridge, and onto Hutchinson River Parkway, taking them north through the Bronx and into Westchester County. Larry fidgets in the passenger seat.

"You nervous about something, Larry? Maybe we should take a little detour. I think I know someone who wants to see you."

Ken navigates into the right-hand lane and sharply turns onto an exit ramp and comes to an abrupt stop on the side of an auxiliary road. He shuts off the engine. Larry stiffens in his seat and starts yammering as droplets of sweat form across his forehead.

"C'mon, Ken. I was jumped at that bar the other night. I'm telling you. This is legit. I went there to collect your money. That prick Galiano came out of nowhere and jumped me. Ask Johnny. Ask Frankie. I swear they'll vouch for me."

With both hands clutching the steering wheel, Ken turns his head slowly and faces Larry before erupting into an uproarious laugh.

"What? What's so frigging funny, Ken?"

Still laughing, Ken says, "This was Tony's idea. He could give two shits about your stupid fight, but he's still pissed to Hades that you stood him up." Ken stops laughing, and his smile disappears. "Now, if you miss another appointment like that again, we'll be pulling over for real. Next time, it won't be a laughing matter, Larry."

They drive silently as the concrete and steel facades of southern Westchester fade in the rearview and the parkway winds through scattered oaks and maples that dot the side of the highway. Larry fiddles with the radio dial and switches between multiple stations. The car does not have satellite, HD, or a navigation system, only an old-fashioned radio dial and CD player.

A known paranoiac, Ken has repeatedly refused offers to upgrade his audio systems and insists all passengers turn off smartphones and GPS devices so they can't be tracked. For navigation, Ken keeps paper road maps in his glove compartment.

Larry tunes in to a local news station. He lowers the volume and slumps low into his seat.

Ken says, "Something on your mind, Larry? Let's have it."

Larry sits up. "Just before the fight with Galiano the other night, I was with Ron McGee . . . you know, he's the racehorse trainer we own. There was this woman sitting alone at the bar—smoking hot. McGee recognized her—it was the bitch who ratted us out to the racing authorities. I wasn't sure if I wanted to bang her or toss her a beating, probably a little of both. I'm worried about this getting back to Tony . . ."

"Is that all of it, Larry?"

Larry continues, "You remember Matt Galiano from about ten years ago, right?"

Ken nods.

"Apparently, this hot bitch who ratted on McGee is banging Galiano. Can you believe it? Matt fucking Galiano. After all these years, he remains my one big mistake. While I'm busting my ass for you guys, he's living the high life with his hot girlfriend who has a thing for McGee! Small world, eh?"

Larry pauses for a moment as Ken offers no reaction, and continues, "So, I decided to teach this whore a lesson, when out of nowhere, Galiano leaps on my fucking back."

Ken says, "Sounds like self-defense to me. What choice did you have? You had to defend yourself."

"Damn right. I just wish I had more time to finish the job

this time around. Now, I've got a bunch of cops trying to break my balls and who knows what else."

Ken raises the volume on the radio. "Sounds like Matt Galiano and this girl present a serious problem for us."

Larry nods.

"I get it. You already have the job. You don't need to oversell it, Larry!"

Without hesitation, Larry says, "Of course! Yes! And I'll do it with great pleasure!"

Larry fiddles again with the radio dial, flipping between stations until he finds a classic rock station. He sings along with childlike enthusiasm to a Rolling Stones classic.

After the song ends, Larry lowers the volume and finishes his coffee. He says, "Hey, Ken, I've been curious, how's the butcher business doing these days? I figure it must be good given the heat this summer. I image lots of folks are having barbeques."

Ken peers at Larry with an awkward smile. "You freaking kidding me? You want to discuss the butcher shop and barbeque season?"

Kaufman's Prime Meats has provided the two Kaufman brothers with an essential and necessary front since Tony Sr. first opened the shop in 1975. As a cash business, it provides a viable and legal operation, perfect for money laundering. The aging brick facade, hanging meats in the window, and vintage red-and-white *Kaufman's Prime Meats* sign have become a staple of the neighborhood. For the locals, the shop supplies an ample supply of quality meats, six days a week, from 9:30 a.m. through 4:30 in the afternoon. Tony Sr.'s butcher shop is known from western Queens to eastern Long Island as the destination for the finest cuts of beef, plump sausage, succulent lamb, and specialty pork and veal cuts.

After Tony Sr. was assassinated in the late nineties, the younger Tony took up his late father's meticulous habit of sustaining and growing the operation. As business grew, he bought the building next door and doubled the store's footprint, then upgraded and modernized the butchery equipment.

A known germaphobe and neat freak, Tony regularly demonstrates painstaking conscientiousness by ensuring the grinders, choppers, blades, cutlery, and slicers are thoroughly cleaned and sanitized daily.

The local authorities have occasionally harassed the Kaufmans based on suspicions of criminal activity within the shop but have never discovered any evidence of foul play. By all accounts, the Kaufmans appear to be operating a legitimate, profitable, and successful neighborhood business.

Ken turns to Larry and says, "Let's just say business is good this year. That's all you really need to know."

"Sure, Ken." Larry pauses, then says, "Hey, this coffee is starting to rip through me. Where are we going?"

Ken asks, "Do you remember the turf wars of the late nineties?"

Larry nods, and Ken turns the volume up on the radio again.

"Years before you arrived on the scene, when my old man was still running things, he got pinched along with bosses from two other outfits. Turns out there was an informant working with the feds. This rat gained my father's trust and got inside our business."

Pausing a moment, Ken switches lanes and maneuvers

the sedan around a slow-moving utility vehicle. He continues, "Where was I? Oh yeah, the authorities pinched several of our guys, and we nearly lost our butchery. The feds offered Tony Sr. witness protection in exchange for names and connections, but my dad was old-school—gave them the finger and told them to fuck off."

Ken mumbles something under his breath and continues, "My dad was sent to Rikers to await trial but never made it. Just like that, they got him." Steering with his left hand, Ken genuflects with his right, taps his forehead, and points toward the sky.

Although there were multiple rumors regarding these turf wars, discussing the details was considered taboo in the presence of the Kaufman brothers.

Ken continues, "Of course, we knew who was behind my dad's assassination, and this triggered the war. Nobody trusted anybody. My father's mistake was trusting that scumbag informant. I know for a fact my dad never uttered a single word about anything or anybody. He would have served his time, like the loyal general he was. But a few assholes spread a rumor he was going to talk, and they silenced him. Alliances were made, sides were drawn, and things got nasty in a hurry."

A smattering of rain spits on the windshield, and Ken flicks on the wipers and the headlights. The rain accelerates quickly into a downpour, limiting his visibility. Ken grips the wheel with both hands and decelerates. Larry lowers the volume on the radio, and the pair drive silently under the symphony of the pelting rain for several minutes.

As the sudden rain shower slows to a drizzle, Ken loosens his grip on the steering wheel.

Ken says, "Turn up the radio. I think we're through the squall."

Obliging, Larry asks, "So, where are we going again?"

Ken says, "I'm getting there. Let me continue."

"Yes, sir."

"Back then, everyone was fair game, and it was impossible to know who to trust until Tony stepped up and took control. He was ruthless and eliminated those responsible for my father's murder. However, one of the collateral effects of the war was the loss of our distribution network. As we established new connections, we discovered a few partners in Canada, and they became our gateway for international imports and exports. However, we needed to ensure a foolproof border crossing to make Canada work. Flights were too risky given the prevalence of radar and air traffic control, so we opted for ground transportation."

Larry asks, "So, this brings us to . . . ?"

Ken says, "This brings us to our man, John Nanske. He's become our link to Canada, and he's the guy we're seeing today. You see, he carries our goods and cash in and out of the US from Canada and vice versa. The cash is then transferred to various offshore accounts. You see, Nanske's in the agricultural business, and he crosses the border regularly. It's also a damn good cover for our activities."

He looks at Larry. "Do you have any idea what can be transported across an international border without the risk of direct inspection?"

Larry shrugs.

"Livestock and horses coming from the United States and destined for slaughter in Canada. At the crossing, they review the paperwork, but since horses are no longer slaughtered in the United States, there's no questions asked. It's beautiful. Simple, low-tech, and amazingly effective."

Larry quips, "You putting me on?"

"Do I ever put you on? Listen, we've done our research on this guy. Apparently, slaughtering horses is illegal in the US, so this fucker has no other choice but to enter Canada to ply his trade. It just so happens whenever he hauls a truckload of horses across the border, he also offers us . . . let's just say, he provides an import-export service. Even if they were to inspect his trailer, there's so much piss and shit across the floor it wouldn't even matter. No trained dog would sniff or smell anything except the overwhelming stench of ammonia and excrement."

Ken laughs. "Nanske's been hauling livestock to Canada for over a decade, and get this—he's considered a trusted traveler. I wouldn't be surprised if the border agents knew him by name."

Ken goes on to share his perspective on kill buyers being opportunists collecting unwanted horses who may otherwise be neglected or abandoned. Until recently, there were several horse slaughterhouses located in Texas and Illinois, but everything changed in 2007, after the US passed an appropriations bill prohibiting funds for the compulsory inspection of the horses. Although the law was enacted in 2005, the slaughterhouses self-funded inspections until this was further prohibited by an amendment in 2007.

Without the ability to operate in the United States, kill buyers, like Nanske, turned to Mexico or Canada. Given the location of his farm, Nanske shifted his business to Quebec.

Access to Canada created unique opportunities. Ken and Tony met Nanske through a mutual contact associated with the meat distribution business.

Nanske had shared the logistical details of his crossing routine at the agricultural inspection station in Champlain, New York, with Kaufman, assuring him they don't unload horses for inspection. His trailer crosses the border without incident as long as he shows a licensed veterinarian-signed health certificate, called a Coggins certificate, and matching manifest.

Larry asks, "Why do you trust Nanske with our money?"

Ken smiles. "We checked him out. Since then, we've experienced more than ten years of flawless execution. I can assure you he understands that if he were to double-cross us, it wouldn't end well for him."

Larry asks, "So, why are you taking me to see Nanske?" He makes a tight fist with his right hand and punches it into his open left hand. "Are you expecting some trouble?"

Ken chuckles. "He's a total jackass, but no, he wouldn't dare give me trouble."

Ken lowers the volume on the radio.

"I can't hear myself think with that thing blasting. We've had a really good month, more than double our normal take. Tony wants me to stay with the money and personally hand it off to Nanske. You're only coming along because you're an asshole who screwed up on Saturday night, and I need company. After your latest outburst, Tony doesn't trust your temper."

"What do you mean he doesn't trust me?"

Ken continues, "He gave me explicit instructions to cool you out. In other words, I get to be your fucking babysitter. If you land in any more trouble with the police, you're going to bring in unwanted attention."

Larry's face turns a reddish hue and his brow furrows as he mumbles to himself, "I really hate that fucking guy, Galiano. He's a goddamn rat who thought he could fuck me up at Mario's the other night! Give me a fucking break."

After a brief pause, Ken says, "Relax, tough guy. Now is definitely not the time. There's too much shit going down, so keep everything in your pants until Tony gives the word. Got it?"

Larry looks out the window and nods slowly in agreement. A few minutes pass and Ken pulls into a public rest stop off the throughway, steps out of the car, and motions for Larry to come inside with him. The rest stop features a small gift shop as well as storefronts for fresh donuts, coffee, burgers, and pizza. Larry walks with Ken into a public bathroom with a long row of urinals and toilet stalls. He pulls out a plastic maintenance sign from behind the door and places it at the front entrance of the restroom.

After checking all the stalls, which are empty, Ken instructs Larry to move inside the toilet stall at the far end of the bathroom. Ken glances toward the entrance and removes a pistol from his belt. He points the gun directly at Larry's forehead. Ken motions for Larry to remain quiet and strip off his clothes.

Ken says, "Nothing personal."

Larry strips naked, and Ken tells him to turn his clothes inside out, shake them, and toss them out of the stall. Still pointing his gun, Ken removes Larry's wallet and dumps the contents onto the dirty bathroom tiles. Four twenty-dollar bills, three bank cards, a car key, and a driver's license spill out.

Ken conceals his gun and tosses the shorts and shirt to Larry. "Get your clothes back on. We need to get going."

Getting dressed, Larry eyes Ken.

Ken says, "We can never be too careful. Don't get huffy on me. Just get dressed, and I'll meet you at the car."

CHAPTER 48

The lanky Detective Kruger greets Matt and Kristine with a firm handshake as the pair enter police headquarters Monday afternoon. The detective navigates through a buzz of activity inside the squad room and escorts them to his desk in the rear of the station. They take a seat across the desk from the detective.

"Mr. Galiano. You said there was something else you'd like to share about your assault?"

Caressing Matt's elbow, Kristine's eyes are soft and compassionate. "Tell him just like you told me."

Matt slowly nods in agreement and turns to Kruger. "The attack on me and Kristine Saturday night wasn't just a random assault. I have every reason to believe my life and hers are at risk."

The detective pulls his chair forward as he sets his eyes squarely on Matt. "I'm interested. Please continue."

As Matt looks across the desk at the detective, an intensifying heat envelops him, causing a thin film of moisture to form across his forehead. Glancing down toward the floor, Matt takes a quiet breath to assemble his thoughts.

"As I told you before, my assailant is a man named Larry Lonsdale. He goes by the moniker Louisville, and he works as an enforcer for the Kaufman brothers. I assume you already know this."

The detective does not acknowledge the comment or alter his expression as Matt pauses for a moment to gauge his reaction. In the absence of one, Matt continues, "Louisville Larry assaulted Kristine with the intent to inflict maximum harm as an act of retaliation. He needs to be arrested for attempted murder. You see, she has direct knowledge of his involvement in a race-fixing scheme. Fortunately, I arrived in time to intercede and, well, you know the rest."

Detective Kruger maintains eye contact for a moment and glares at the bruises and marks across Matt's face and arms.

The detective turns to Kristine. "Miss . . . "

"Connelly," Kristine finishes for him.

"Miss Connelly, I presume you understand that race fixing is considered a federal offense." She nods as the detective continues, "If what you allege is indeed true, then I'll need to contact the feds. I presume you understand the burden of proof here is extremely high. You're going to need more evidence than hearsay or circumstantial details."

Matt interjects, "Excuse me, sir, but race fixing is not the full story. I have more."

As Matt is speaking, another officer approaches. Detective Kruger stands and introduces his captain. Matt approximates the captain to be in his midfifties, given his loosely combed jet-black hair, streaks of gray around and above his sideburns, and paunch in his midsection. For an officer, his untucked shirt is casual in the otherwise formal police setting. The captain pulls up a chair and kindly asks Matt to proceed.

Matt continues, "I used to manage Kaufman's gaming books until ten years ago when I permanently left the business. When I left, Louisville battered me in an alley and left me for dead."

The captain asks, "Have you spoken to anyone else about your experience, specifically to the Federal Bureau of Investigation?"

"No, sir. Never."

"Why are you coming to us with this information now?"

Matt lifts his shirt and rolls up his sleeves to show the extent of his bruising to the captain and the detective. After ensuring they've had a good look, Matt continues, "Louisville likes to boast about an army of women who can't keep their hands off him, but in reality, he lures them with drugs. You name it, uppers, downers, coke, psychedelics—whatever it takes. When I worked in the syndicate, I dismissed his bragging as him just boasting about his latest conquest. That is, until I read this story a few years ago about a series of girls being murdered. The assailant allegedly tied their arms and legs to bedposts with police-grade handcuffs." He pauses and asks, "You with me?"

They nod and he continues, "This was exactly how Louisville portrayed his sexual conquests, leaving out the part about killing them. Of course, back then, I assumed he was simply exaggerating. I honestly can't say for sure if he was involved in these murders, but it's surely worth investigating."

The detective responds, "Thank you for sharing. If memory serves, the FBI still has jurisdiction on those murders. If he is a suspect or on their radar, your information could lead to something. They'll find you if they have any questions. Right now, getting Larry Lonsdale locked up for aggravated assault might protect you. Are you willing and able to identify him from a lineup?"

Matt and Kristine agree.

The detective continues, "Good! We've obtained DNA samples from the scene. If they can be matched to Lonsdale, it'll be enough for an arrest, along with a positive lineup identification."

The captain turns to the detective. "Once you confirm the DNA matches, pick up this prick and then reach out to the OCU." He looks at Matt. "OCU is the Organized Crime Unit. They'll also be in touch with the feds."

The captain stands. "Thank you both."

Matt stands and shakes the captain's hand. "He won't stop until he kills both of us." Matt shivers, hearing the utter harshness of his own words. "You've got to do something."

The detective says, "We'll be in touch."

Exiting the police station, Kristine turns to Matt and says, "I suppose we're on our own for now!"

CHAPTER 49

After more than a decade of being too afraid to share his story for fear of retaliation, Matt finally found the courage to speak with the police. In spite of relieving his burden by revealing his deeply held secret, he remains abjectly frustrated from the apparent inaction by the police. Upon leaving the precinct, he feels depleted and drained.

"You okay, Matt?" Kristine asks.

As he leans onto Kristine for support, a ferocious hunger overcomes him, as neither he nor Kristine have eaten much all day.

"Hey, let's grab something to eat. I'm starving."

The police precinct is located near a rail station and large hospital with several restaurants and cafés within walking distance. Matt points to a small Italian eatery. They enter and are quickly seated in the corner in the back of the restaurant.

Matt and Kristine quietly study the menu, written in both Italian and English. Blankly staring past his menu, Matt cannot stop himself from worrying about their next move and ensuring Kristine's safety. He glances toward Kristine while knowing he's responsible for dragging her into this mess. He struggles with the irony of being so attached to Kristine while simultaneously feeling she'd be better off had they never met. He wonders if she knows just how deeply she's penetrated his soul. In spite of their obvious peril, Kristine continues to carry herself as the picture of poise and grace, showing no signs or signals of fear, instead projecting a sense of confidence, hope, and optimism.

Matt peeks over his menu at her and notices Kristine looking directly at him. She maintains eye contact, lowers her menu, and says, "I'm ready to order."

Not wanting to waste time, Matt selects the first item on the menu, not giving much thought to his meal. He wonders how things would have turned out had they first met at a different time in a different place.

Leaning forward, Kristine points to the side of her forehead. "Mr. Galiano, I'm pretty solid up here. If you think I'm going to let this flaming asshole get the best of me or you, then you don't know me very well."

Not wanting to show fear, especially given her apparent confidence, Matt says, "You're right. We're going to take that asshole down, but we also need to recognize he's an experienced hunter and we can't let our guard down. Not for one minute."

He considers his last comment, gathers his thoughts, and continues, "If I know Louisville, and I do, he'll be searching for us. We'll need to find a place to lay low for a while, at least until we figure things out."

She chuckles. "Are you trying to lure me on a romantic getaway, Romeo?"

Surprised by her quick wit, his face grows flush. "No . . . I mean, sure . . . I mean . . . . wow, if we ever get out of this, I'd love . . ." He regains his thoughts. "Hey, I'm being serious. Louisville won't stop. Do you have someone who can handle things at the barn, at least for a couple of days?"

"Not without notice. Sorry, but I'm it for now."

Matt thinks for a second. "Okay, first I need you to assure me you'll never be alone when you're at the barn. Keep your grooms, riders, and assistants close at all times."

After Kristine nods, Matt continues, "Do you own a gun?"

Kristine goes expressionless. "What? No, of course not!"

"I'm going to lend you one in case you need to defend yourself. I'm sure you won't need it, but if you see Louisville anywhere, make sure he notices the gun."

Kristine is silent for several seconds before slowly acknowledging.

It's not ideal, but knowing Kristine will have some form of protection offers a small semblance of reassurance. He's glad Kristine has street smarts. As the waitress arrives with their meals, Matt notices his companion's face has become ashen and tense.

He asks, "What's going on?"

She turns away and flicks her bangs away from her forehead. "You initially struck me as honest from our very first encounter, and I admire that, and frankly speaking, I find it sexy. I mean, you could have acted way differently after I hit you, but you didn't." She pauses to smirk. "Of course, you were hiding out in my stall and I had every right to . . ." Taking Matt's hand, Kristine says, "Seriously, though, it's also why I got so angry at you when I spotted you with McGee at the Turf Club that day. I felt betrayed and began to question my own judgment, but

I should have stuck with my intuition." She wipes a tear from her eye. "I liked you from the get-go . . . I hope I'm not being too mushy."

Matt nods. "No, of course not. I feel the same about you. What's going on, Kris?"

She looks at Matt for a protracted moment, inhales deeply, and blows out a lungful of air. "I've been holding this shit inside me for such a long time, I'm not even sure how to begin."

Matt is intensely focused on Kristine as she tilts her head and stares off for a moment.

"It was St. Patrick's Day four years ago. I was Ron McGee's assistant trainer."

Matt offers a reassuring nod.

She continues, "I was in his office and exhausted after a crazy busy morning. It was nonstop from the moment I arrived. We were shorthanded, and I jumped on at least five horses that morning. The last one reared up, kicked out, and dropped me hard onto the track before galloping away. I wasn't hurt, but the horse was loose, and I ran back to the barn. I remember it distinctly because that was the last time I've been thrown off a horse!"

She looks around, tips her head, and continues, "When I returned to the barn, there was no sympathy or concern for me. I mean, I could have been seriously hurt. Instead, I updated the charts, checked temps, and wrapped legs because I was McGee's only groom for the day."

"Let me guess, Ron McGee was nowhere to be seen?"

"It was way worse. That asshole was walking around with his precious Irish whiskey in a coffee mug. Remember, it was

St. Patrick's Day. Anyways, I'm busting my ass all morning while McGee was getting shit-faced."

Matt squeezes her hands from across the table.

She gazes at Matt and continues, "McGee had a few horses entered on the card, but given his morning of inebriation, it was a foregone conclusion I would be saddling horses for him in the paddock later that afternoon. On most days, I would just head home after training hours to shower and clean up, but I felt so wiped out, I fell asleep on the lumpy couch in his office. Next thing I know, McGee wakes me up, stumbling in piss-drunk."

Kristine sucks in a breath and continues, "I'm still half asleep on the couch when all of a sudden, that asshole leaps on top of me. He forces his hand on my mouth, pins my arm down, and starts to rub himself on me."

An intense anger builds as Matt's face reddens and he feels an impulsive urge to smash McGee's face into a thousand pieces, if only he was here right now.

Kristine continues, "You know, I can still remember the smell of his cheap cologne and his godawful body odor. His breath reeked." Kristine tightens her jaw and curls her lips as her voice trembles. "He started grinding on me like some sort of crazed animal. I pushed his head to the side and screamed, but he kept going. He called me his barn bitch."

Matt's unsure if he wants to say something, scream, or console her.

Kristine continues, "He was breathing so heavily, and I remember hoping and wishing he would die from a massive heart attack right then and there. Then, he pushed himself up and straddled me, grabbed my shoulders, and pinned me down on the couch. He leaned forward and pressed his gross tongue right on my lips. I spit at him, turned my head, and squirmed, but the fat shit was too heavy. He had all the leverage."

He knew Kristine had bad blood with McGee, but never totally understood why until now. Her unbridled anger and hatred suddenly made perfect sense.

"He grabbed his dick and tried to push it inside me, but I wriggled my right arm free and pounded my fist into his face. It stunned him for about a half second before he took a swing at me. I squirmed out from under him and kicked him in the gut with all my might. He gasped for air and started to cough. I pushed him onto the floor with his pathetic little dick hanging out of his pants. I lost all self-control, jumped on him, and wrapped my hands around his throat."

Her demeanor changes, and a twisted smile emerges. "I was straddling this cowardly asshole, my legs around his chest and hands around his neck, when he suddenly stopped fighting back. I wondered for a moment if I killed him. I ran out of the office and don't remember much after that."

He says, "I'm so sorry this happened to you, Kristine. I don't know what else to say."

Kristine says, "It was more than four years ago. I'm still not over it, but I take satisfaction in knowing he got a lot more than he bargained for."

Matt asks, "So why is he not in jail?"

Kristine smiles. "Mr. Galiano, you and I have a lot more in common than you realize. Just like you and Louisville, I never pursued the incident with McGee. It took me an entire week before I even returned to the racetrack. I thought about never returning, but I couldn't stay away from the horses. I love training and working with thoroughbreds too much and wasn't going to let a shithead like McGee ruin my career. Besides, I didn't think anyone would believe me, and I feared reporting on McGee would hurt my career."

Matt nods. "I suppose I can understand your reluctance."

"Since then, I've gotten harder, stronger, and more determined than ever to succeed. Don't mess with us farm girls. We bite back."

Matt asks, "You never told anyone at the track about what happened?"

Kristine shakes her head. "Of course, rumors were flying after McGee returned the next day with a black eye."

Matt asks, "I'm really the only person you've told?"

"Well, not exactly. I spoke to Ted Bouchard because I was ready to quit and return to my family's farm. He encouraged me to press charges. But I knew if I pressed charges, I would be blackballed on the backstretch. Bouchard offered me a job as his assistant trainer and mentored me for the next two years. In many ways, he shaped me into the person I am today."

Matt is impressed. Instead of shrinking from the trauma, she seemed to grow stronger and gain confidence.

As they finish eating, Matt's thoughts return to their dire need to find safe refuge for the night. One obvious option he considered was checking into a cheap hotel under a pseudonym, but the limited flexibility and dank accommodations were far from appealing, yet it now seems like the most viable option given their desperate situation.

As he ponders the thought of them holing up in a room,

Matt drops his fork and blurts out, "Wait a sec! I've got it!"

"You got what, Matt?"

"We'll head to my mother's house tonight. It's the last place Louisville would suspect, and even if he did, he wouldn't dare. Families are off-limits, even for Louisville. This is probably our safest option for the night."

Kristine sips her water. "Does she live nearby?"

It takes a moment to remember as Matt draws a map in his head. "Yep, she lives about twenty minutes away if there's no traffic. I've not seen my mother since I left her house more than a decade ago. It was before I worked for Kaufman, and she was drinking heavily. She was pretty depressed after my dad's murder. It was a lot."

He thinks about his dad for a moment and continues, "In hindsight, I didn't fully understand or appreciate her suffering. I was a blockhead and couldn't deal."

She asks, "Why didn't you go back or make up with her?"

"I called her several times after I left Kaufman, but we just got into the same old argument. She was drunk, and I felt like a shit. I still owe her an apology for walking out when I did. I'm sure she'll like you, and your presence will give me the courage to face her. We'll be safe there tonight."

As they sit inside Matt's car, he opens the glove compartment and pulls out a handgun from behind the registration papers. "The gun is registered and legal."

Kristine is staring at the weapon and turns her head away as Matt drops it into her purse.

"Shouldn't you call her first?"

"If I hear her voice on the line . . ." He trails off. "I've tried calling her in the past. No, let's just go. I hope she still lives there!" Feeling brave, Matt says, "It's about time we looked each other in the eye."

The drive is quiet and they pull up in front of a white two-story Cape Cod with a manicured lawn and flower garden in front. There is a hybrid car in the driveway and a light on inside the house.

As they exit the car, an uncontrollable nervousness consumes Matt. He tensely places Kristine's hand in his, and they slowly walk up the front path. The house, yard, and driveway all appear smaller than he remembers, but the house and neighborhood are familiar and strangely comforting. He swallows his breath as they reach the door. Kristine glances at him and reaches for the bell, as Matt stands statuesque and silent. A dog barks loudly and approaches the door followed by footsteps and a familiar, yet unfamiliar voice, "Who's there?"

He clears his throat. "Hi, Mom, it's Matty."

The door unlocks. Matt's mom appears older but does not look old. The dog stops barking. "Hi, Mom."

CHAPTER 50

Special Agent Anjero hangs up. The conversation with the captain of Nassau County police regarding Larry was revealing, but problematic. A single assault charge could be dismissed if he takes jurisdiction, but accusations of race fixing and other felonies could enlist other agencies and force Anjero's hand to drop Larry as an informant.

Larry had teased Anjero about some new insider knowledge regarding Tony and Ken Kaufman a few days ago, but has yet to provide tangible intel. Given Larry's position and tenure with Kaufman, his value as an informant has fallen short of expectations, and Agent Anjero is not a person known for patience.

During his call with Detective Kruger, Agent Anjero received assurances the local police would be staking out Larry's residence to arrest him for the alleged assault at Mario's. Kruger also shared his intent to obtain a sample of Larry's DNA in order to cross-reference it against previous evidence collected from cases gone cold. If the local police match Larry's DNA to such evidence from other felonies, it will not bode well for Anjero or his superiors at the Bureau. Agent Anjero phones Larry but is directed to voicemail. He hangs up without leaving a message.

If Anjero locates Larry before the local police, he can confront him about these alleged extraneous offenses. Such knowledge could then be used as additional leverage in pressuring Larry to give up useful details regarding Kaufman and avert any possible embarrassment or reprimand regarding his choice of informants.

CHAPTER 51

Following the disappearance and likely assassination of his father, Matt's mother struggled. One can never fully prepare for the unexpected loss of a loved one, even when someone's lifestyle presages it, as was the case for Mrs. Mary Galiano. Following his father's murder, Matt observed her self-medicate through alcohol and moping. Matt's father had always provided well for him and his mom and hid shoeboxes of cash throughout their house over several years. He squirreled away enough money to enable him and his mom to sustain a normal lifestyle long after his father's passing, which was helpful given that Mrs. Galiano had never earned a paycheck and lacked the skills and experience to land a decent job.

With his notorious background and dubious associations, Matt's father was never confused for a law-abiding citizen, but he always doted on Matt. After he was gone, Matt's mom wore black daily and was often spotted stomping around the block without purpose or destination. Neighbors tried to engage with her, but her dismissiveness caused them to retreat. After a few months, her proclivity for evening drinking extended to the afternoons and, eventually, the morning hours.

Matt watched her suffer and attempted to intervene many times, including a solicitation for professional help, but she rebuked his overtures. The more he interceded, the nastier she became. In time, Matt's concern about his mother's well-being flipped from compassion to resentment as she denied his attempts to help, while wallowing in self-pity. Unable to tolerate her constant moodiness and general unpleasantness, Matt stopped returning home after school. His mom showed no concern when he slept at his friends' homes for days at a time. When he would inevitably overstay his welcome, Matt slept outside in the park rather than share a roof with his unstable and inebriated mother. He learned how to be independent and take care of himself.

After leaving home permanently, Matt was a survivalist. He picked up used clothes from the local shelter, lost considerable weight, and grew his hair long. A few odd jobs earned him enough for sustenance, but this resulted in multiple absences from school, and his faltering appearance garnered him the reputation as a person to be avoided. Even teachers and counselors dodged him, and the school eventually ceased messaging his mom about his frequent absences, given her obscenity-driven diatribes.

Over time, Matt became increasingly gaunt and emaciated, which encouraged name-calling from schoolmates and several former friends. He pretended to ignore the harsh words and accepted his lot as an outsider while he hurt inside. One day after school, Matt was assaulted by a group of freshmen football players. Matt was propped up and tied to a tree with his shirt ripped open and the word *Loser* written in deep, indelible black marker across his chest. A teacher found him two hours after the attack, but Matt refused to name those who perpetrated the assault, in spite of its brutality. Instead, he felt a seething rage toward his mother for enabling his situation to deteriorate to such a low point.

Matt remembered the promise he made as a child to his dad to never get involved with drugs. When he made this promise, he could not have understood or appreciated the level of commitment it took. However, as his father was gone, this commitment provided Matt enough strength and courage to resist the lure of such demons. Immediately following the attack, he purchased new clothes, trimmed his hair, returned to school, and earned some cash clerking at a nearby delicatessen after school. He quietly returned to his mother's home at night to sleep and avoided her most days by leaving early in the morning.

Working behind the counter of the deli during the second half of his junior year, Matt was introduced to a businessman and regular customer, known simply as JP. Over time, small talk evolved into engaging discussions regarding the upcoming action on the racetrack as they found a common interest in horse racing. JP introduced Matt to a local bookmaker, and Matt subsequently placed a few wagers. After enjoying a few modest successes, Matt expanded his wagering to college and pro sports. It wasn't long before he mastered the stat sheets, formulated his opinions, and made smart selections. He started to make decent money to supplement his modest income from the delicatessen.

Matt rediscovered his passion for horse racing and obsessed about past performances and pedigrees. He learned about the jockeys and trainers. His self-confidence boomed as he continued to make smart wagers, earning enough to upgrade his wardrobe with name-brand gym shoes and rent a small place in town.

He moved out of his mother's house permanently.

Most gamblers are impulsive when it comes to wagering and eventually lose money over time, even after experiencing short-term success. Matt's consistent level of success was a notable anomaly and effectively gained him a reputation among the syndicate bookies accepting his wagers. The attention manifested into a formal request to meet those running the operation. Matt was reluctant, but they offered little choice and convinced him such a meeting served his best interest. After being grilled about his gambling prowess and condemned for cheating, Matt shared his wagering methodology and persuaded the syndicate to drop their accusations. Instead, they became impressed with his knowledge and offered him a job taking book for the syndicate. Matt agreed and thus began his life with the Kaufmans.

As he immersed himself into the world of bookmaking, setting and updating gambling odds, creating new, exotic wagers, and calculating usury interest schemes, Matt gained the reputation within the syndicate of a bookmaking brainchild. He was paired up with Larry Lonsdale, who was also just getting started with the outfit as an enforcer. Kaufman believed Larry would be the perfect complement to Matt's timid persona, given his brawn, temper, and savagery. Matt maintained the wagering lines, instilled tempting sucker bets, and ultimately chose which wagers to accept or reject. His ability to anticipate results and entice compulsive gamblers created a steady and largely predictable stream of revenue for the outfit. If there was an outstanding debt, Matt was first to approach the delinquent gambler and politely offer an opportunity to clear their debts without harm or harassment. However, if they refused or simply could not pay, Larry waited in the wings to steer them right. Larry openly craved any opportunity to inflict pain on others and seemingly enjoyed his role.

Matt remained employed as a clerk while working as a bookie for Kaufman, as the deli generated substantial foot traffic, serving as a front for his nascent gambling operation. Matt quit high school after his junior year to work full time at the deli. The money was flowing in, and he lacked any need or desire for his mother or her shelter. He drifted away and lost contact with his mother, and while he's attempted to reach out a few times in the years since, they have never have reconnected since he permanently left her house. He eventually stopped trying.

As she opens the front door, Matt immediately notices his mother is sober and appears to be healthy. He fretted about her reaction to his sudden appearance, partially expecting her to slam the door in his face.

After opening the front door, his mom takes a long look at him and darts forward to embrace him in a long-overdue hug. His mom takes a half step back and silently looks over her son, mouth partly open as if trying to speak, but struggling to find the right words. Moved and astounded, Matt could not have predicted such a strong reaction to his sudden appearance. So many years have passed.

"Matt, I'm so sorry. I was a shit to you for so long. I was too embarrassed and ashamed to reach out. I understand why you left. Believe it or not, your leaving was a major wake-up call, especially after losing your father. I've hoped and prayed almost every day you would return, and I'm so glad you did!"

She looks up at him and points to the obvious bruises on his face. "Oh dear, you're hurt. Are you in trouble?"

Matt says, "It's been way too long. I missed you too, Mom. I want to introduce you to," he pauses, looks at Kristine, and reassuringly smiles, "I want you to meet my girlfriend, Kristine Connelly."

Kristine extends her hand and is greeted by a hug in return.

"It's wonderful to meet you, Kristine. Please call me Mary."

The three of them move inside, and Matt wanders through the kitchen and dining areas, making note of the cleanliness of the household. His mom turns to him and says, "Don't worry, Matt, there's no alcohol in the house. I haven't had a drink in more than seven years. I work at the local supermarket and volunteer at the church."

Upon seeing her looking well and sober, Matt feels a twinge of regret for not returning sooner or checking in on her from time to time. A sense of relief based on her appearance and demeanor envelops him. In a strange way, he's grateful his extenuating life circumstances have steered him to her during this time of crisis.

Matt says, "I'm really sorry it took me this long. There were times I wanted to see you, but I was afraid you . . ." He cuts himself off, not wanting to revive or remind himself of the unpleasant memories he's acutely aware caused him to leave all those years ago.

He chooses a different set of words and finds it hard to control his emotions as he stumbles over his remarks. "I just didn't . . . I couldn't . . ."

Again, he stops without knowing how to finish the sentence. Instead, he brings the conversation to the present. "I bet you're wondering why we showed up tonight!" He points to his face.

"And you may be curious about these marks on my face?"

His mom nods, and Matt continues, "It's a long story." For the next few minutes, he brings her up to speed.

Mary Galiano turns off the lights, walks guardedly toward the front window, and takes a long look all around. She draws the curtains and says, "It's quiet out there, but no need to take any chances. Move your car inside the garage and get it out of sight. I doubt they'll look for you here, but you never know."

CHAPTER 52

Following a surprisingly restful night of sleep, Matt watches the early morning light ascend over the horizon as he chauffeurs Kristine from his mother's home to her barn at the racetrack. A relaxing and uneventful night helped ease the lingering discomfort from the injuries he suffered during his encounter with Louisville and his cronies.

The morning activities on the backside of the racetrack are well underway as Matt drops Kristine off at the barn. Matt exits the car and slowly walks with her toward the barn, paranoid about Louisville lurking about. With no apparent danger in the vicinity, Matt turns to Kristine, who offers a quick smooch on the cheek and strolls to the shed row to confer with the groom beyond her office door.

Matt slides up behind them and taps Kristine's shoulder.

She turns and winks. "You still here to protect me?" She points out the two grooms at her barn. "As you can see, I've got plenty of friends capable of babysitting me. Besides, if you were to stick around much longer, I'd surely get distracted. Seriously, Matt, I'll be fine. Will you come back to pick me up in a few hours?" He nods, and she kisses him on the forehead. "Don't worry, I'm good here."

Hesitant to leave, Matt also doesn't want to be overbearing. With the number of grooms, assistants, riders, and veterinarians surrounding Kristine and her promise to remain close to them at all times, he reluctantly agrees to let her do her job. Staring at Kristine, Matt reflects on the extraordinary events of the past few days, beginning with his all-or-nothing gamble, followed by the assault at Mario's, and then finally reconnecting with his mom for the first time in more than a decade. Throughout everything, his heart has been etched with the indelible imprint of the incredible lady standing in front of him. He pecks her on the lips, waves good-bye, and departs the barn area.

Driving back to his mom's home, Matt feels bolstered by the sudden and unexpected manner of reconciliation with his mom. Her turnaround, self-awareness, and full transformation since they parted so many years ago triggers a stream of remorse for failing to initiate contact sooner. His frayed nerves prior to ringing the doorbell last night were steadied by Kristine at his side. His trust in her is pure and genuine, especially after spending their first night together. Matt chuckles to himself at the irony of his circumstances. If not for the dire situation, everything else seemed to be going ironically well. Matt is full of confidence after finding his soulmate, bonding with his estranged mom, and purchasing his favorite racehorse. If he could only escape his formidable and unrelenting foe and the existential threat he represents, life would be ideal.

Matt considers the timing of his upcoming meeting with Paula White tomorrow to officialize the transaction for Heliacal Star. Following his go-for-broke gamble, he has cash in hand and just needs to drive six hours upstate to meet her. However, given the events of the past forty-eight hours, he's feeling unprepared for the extended drive. He grabs his phone to call Paula and postpone the meeting.

As he scrolls through his contacts, he reconsiders the road trip as a means to misdirect and create distance from Louisville. If Kristine joins him on the trip, they could also brainstorm ideas to derive a plan for their long-term preservation. He puts down his phone without making the call.

After speaking with the police yesterday, Matt is hopeful they'll locate and arrest Louisville while he and Kristine are away on their excursion.

The blare of a car horn jolts Matt out of his thoughts, and he reactively jams the gas pedal and drives off. Increasingly paranoid, he constantly looks through the rearview and sideview mirrors but does not notice anything nefarious. As he stops for yet another red light, he wonders if Kristine might consider permanent relocation as a means of retreat or escape. Starting over in another place, without Louisville's looming threat, could represent a new beginning for both of them. She can still train horses, including Heliacal Star, and Matt can easily transfer his professional construction job anywhere they land. Looking into the rearview mirror, he catches himself smiling at the notion of his unlikely, yet intriguing, idea.

Arriving at his mother's house, Matt pulls into the garage. Inside, Matt is greeted by the unmistakable aroma of sizzling bacon, scrambled eggs, and freshly baked bread, inviting his presence with a welcoming warmth. He is impressed his mom remembers that bacon and eggs are his favorite breakfast, especially when complemented by a slice of warm homemade bread. The moment prompts a fond memory of those Sunday mornings from yesteryear when his mom and dad were both around.

Too tempted to resist, Matt plucks a piece of bacon off the plate and quickly consumes it. His mom approaches with a cup of hot coffee. She also remembers his preference is coffee black, no sugar!

Instinctively, Matt kisses her on the cheek and embraces her.

"Mom, I'm sorry. I didn't know you . . . I'm just sorry it took this long."

She smiles. "I've lacked the courage, too, but have been praying to Saint Anthony and your father every night. Last night, my prayers were answered."

Additional words are unnecessary. As they sit down for breakfast, Matt momentarily forgets about his conflict with Louisville and spends the entire morning regaling his mom about Kristine.

Following a quick nap, Matt grabs his keys. "I'm off to pick up Kristine. If you don't mind, I'd like it if we could return here again tonight." His mom nods approvingly.

It's a short drive to the stable area, and Matt observes Kristine from afar before she notices him.

Kristine finally sees him. "And when did you arrive on the scene?"

Matt says, "Oh, I've been here for a little while. Are you ready to go?"

She saunters toward him and drops a towel on the ground without changing her stride. Reaching Matt, she throws her arms around his waist, pulls him tight, and initiates a long and luscious kiss.

She says, "Now, I'm ready."

As they clasp their hands together, the grooms applaud the pair from the shed row. Kristine's smile is radiant as she waves to the grooms before getting into Matt's car.

CHAPTER 53

On a misty morning in northern New York, a gutted trailer overloaded with horses approaches the Canadian Food Inspection Agency inspection station at the Champlain-St. Bernard de Lacolle, United States–Canada border crossing. John Nanske, a recognized kill buyer from Western New York State, is hauling his bounty of condemned horses before they'll face an inescapable fate at the slaughterhouse in Quebec.

There is high demand for horse meat outside of North America in places such as Japan, France, and Belgium. As a kill buyer, John acts as supplier for these countries by purchasing unwanted, undernourished, and oft-injured horses at auction and makes a modest profit. Since the United States government stopped funding the USDA inspectors at facilities within the States, all horses slaughtered and originating from the United States have been vanned to Mexico or Canada. In most countries, a horse previously given medications, such as Lasix or bute, is banned from use in the human food chain; however, these regulations are hardly enforced and easy to bypass when slipping unwanted thoroughbreds among the unfortunate lot.

The advent of social media has led to an increased awareness among several animal activist groups who regularly condemn Nanske and his kind. They'll cite the horrible conditions in which these horses live prior to shipment and dramatize the trauma of their final van ride. Some of the processing plants in Canada and Mexico with unflattering reputations for animal cruelty have emboldened these activists.

Nanske defends himself against such attacks by portraying himself as a simple middleman, not responsible for overbreeding or the consumption of the horsemeat. As part of a small group of unpopular agricultural farmers, he appears numb and indifferent to the various threats from activists but promotes himself and his trade as legitimate.

Every couple of weeks, John Nanske loads up his trailer in Western New York, usually during the early morning hours, and drives until he reaches the inspection station at the border. If the weather is good and the roads are clear, he'll cover the trip in approximately eight hours. Underneath the feet of the condemned horses is a false bottom, filled with airtight bags of laundered cash or illegal paraphernalia, courtesy of the Kaufmans. The smell of urine and feces discharged by the frightened animals creates a crude yet effective mask should any inspection sniffing dogs engage in a search.

Before loading his trailer, Nanske attaches a required USDA slaughter tag to each horse's mane, making it easy for any inspector or veterinarian to read. After recording the tracking number of each tag, he matches them to his own paperwork and loads the trailer. The first few horses will enter the van without much trouble, but as the space inside grows tighter, he'll resort to whipping and even applying a hot poker to encourage them all inside, regardless of how limited the space becomes. After being crammed inside the trailer, many of the horses can instinctively smell fear and whinny for help.

Driving alone and undisturbed, Nanske turns off his mobile phone, turns up the radio, and ignores any and all noises coming from the back of his trailer. After leaving his farm just past four in the morning, he arrives at the international agricultural inspection station before noon.

The crossing at Champlain is an especially useful one, as the on-site veterinarians do not typically unload his freight. Upon arriving at the crossing, the routine is predictable. He presents his driver's license and passport information to the border agent and pulls his van into the Canadian Food Inspection Station.

After presenting his credentials to the agent, he greets the inspector.

"Good morning, sir, and what is the purpose of your trip into Canada today . . . Mr. Nanske?"

Fielding the routine question, Nanske says, "I'm hauling horses to the slaughter facility in Quebec. They're all USDA tagged."

The inspector then may choose to spot check a few horses or count heads by peering through the rear windows of the trailer, thus validating the tags match the paperwork. He may also perform a cursory inspection of the cab, and John Nanske is always the cooperative professional, as the illegal payload is well hidden. The most important details are the veterinarian-signed Coggins certificates, which verify each animal has been examined and confirmed to be free of any communicable diseases, making them fit for transport across an international boundary.

Once the inspection is completed, the on-site veterinarian may perform another visual inspection of the horses from inside the trailer. However, as accommodations inside the rig are tight, he is normally satisfied with visual cues and paperwork. For the majority of his border-crossing trips, Nanske experiences few delays or issues.

The on-site veterinarian reviews the Coggins certificates, and the inspector reads the paperwork. "Everything seems to be in order, Mr. Nanske." He instructs Nanske about the compulsory requirements regarding his payload upon entering Canada.

The inspector continues, "We'll now seal your trailer. It cannot be opened until you arrive at the facility in Quebec. When you arrive, the horses must be unloaded immediately and slaughtered within four days."

An hour after crossing into Canada, Nanske arrives at the processing facility. The routine is similarly predictable as he drives to the receiving pens used for staging new arrivals. Nanske greets the on-site facility manager and checks in for his scheduled appointment. After a thorough review of his paperwork, the seal on the back of the trailer is broken. At this point, the facility operators are the only ones authorized to handle the horses. They unlock the doors and step aside as the stampede of frightened horses leap out of the trailer and run into the staging pen. This is the final stop for the condemned lot. The horses are funneled through the maze-like pen and into the final chute and shot in the head with a captive bolt gun.

As the horses enter the kill chute, the smell of death surrounds them, and their best hope is for a clean shot and instant death. It may take multiple shots along with violent thrashing before the animal finally succumbs to the inevitable, given that the original shape of the chute was never designed or intended for an equine head.

The handler will monitor the fallen horse until there is no life remaining. The once-majestic animal slumps down and is hooked and hoisted away to make room for the next one, now consumed by fear after witnessing the previous carnage. These once-mighty thoroughbreds, quarter horses, Arabians, and draft horses, originally purchased for tens of thousands or hundreds of thousands of dollars, have been whittled to wholesale and sold by the pound.

For these animals, once cared for and loved, there is no more pasture. Their fate was sealed the moment they fell into the hands of the kill buyer. For Nanske, the horse slaughter business has served as the perfect cover for his clandestine indiscretions, which have made him a wealthy man.

After the animals are unloaded, there is little time for Nanske to lose ahead of his next appointment near Saint Luc, Quebec, a short distance away. It takes just thirty minutes for Nanske to reach the inside of a nondescript and darkened warehouse, park his trailer, and wait inside his cab for his French-Canadian counterparts. The exchange is professional and efficient. No words are necessary.

Ski masks conceal faces, and dark clothes disguise the trio of individuals who swiftly move about and around the trailer. Nanske hears them complaining in French about the smell. The remainder of the time goes by without incident or issues. Minutes later, one of the French Canadians hands him a slip of paper with a phone number and three digits written underneath.

Nanske slips the paper into the glove compartment, and the back trailer doors close and lock as the garage door opens, exposing it to bright daylight.

By design, John Nanske does not possess any knowledge about the payload that now sits inside the false bottom of his trailer. Whatever has been dropped into the trailer has been tightly sealed and placed inside predetermined compartments. It was Ken Kaufman who made the decision not to inform his driver of the payload as a means of reducing anxiety and to ensure a consistent experience at each exchange. If the driver is unaware of his payload, Kaufman argued, he will not be nervous or tempted to disappear with the goods. Some payloads carry millions of dollars of goods or cash while others are empty and worth nothing. Nanske will get paid the same regardless of what he transports across the international border.

Nanske pulls out of the warehouse and drives to his final stop in Canada, a farm twenty kilometers to the southeast.

To retain his agricultural designation upon returning to the States, Nanske picks up several horses from the local farm. Most of these horses will remain on his Upstate farm for sixty to ninety days before returning to Canada for their final journey. The merry-go-round trip provides him with sufficient inventory to move regularly and cross the border with full loads, reducing any specter of suspicion.

On his return trip, Nanske pulls into a rest stop and removes the scrap of paper from the glove compartment with the three digits written on it. He powers up a burner phone and dials the number on the slip. It's just a single ring before he hears a voice. "Yeah, what are they?"

Nanske responds, "Four-eight-six."

The line drops. Nanske puts the burner phone in a paper bag, moves outside the rest stop, stomps on the bag, and tosses it into the garbage.

The sun has set over the rolling fields and farms in north-western New York, and it's been a long yet profitable day for John Nanske. He returns to his farm after dark, unloads the horses he just collected in Canada, and retires for the night.

CHAPTER 54

Driving eastbound, Ken Kaufman and Louisville Larry return to Long Island after fulfilling their task Upstate. They left Queens about twenty-four hours ago and covered more than six hundred miles round trip. The handoff of laundered cash, destined for overseas, was predictably uneventful. It took less than an hour for Ken and Larry to meticulously pack the cash in airtight bags and stuff them underneath the floor of John Nanske's horse trailer.

They pull off the highway and into a vacant parking area across from Belmont Park. Ken shoves Larry awake, as he nodded off a few hours earlier. "Wake up, dummy. I'm dropping you off here."

Ken continues, "You need to give a retainer to McGee to find a new horse, given his track record with Heliacal Star. Also, in case you have forgotten, you fucked up the other night. . . . " He pauses, clears his throat. "Remember, you got stupid and started a bar fight with your old buddy and his new girlfriend."

Larry lowers his head and looks down at the floor mats while acknowledging Ken's instructions.

Ken continues, "Once you finish with McGee, go directly home. The local police will receive an anonymous tip about your whereabouts. You'll comply without resistance when they arrest you. This is not the time for trouble or unwanted attention."

Larry lifts his head and looks at Ken as if to speak but instead turns away in silence.

Raising his voice, Ken says, "Larry, I swear, you best not fuck this up. Our guy on the inside will take care of you. He'll meet you inside the precinct and identify himself as your legal counsel. Just keep quiet, and don't say a fucking word unless instructed to do so. No more bullshit, you hear me?"

Avoiding eye contact, Larry says, "Okay, boss. I'll be good."

With no live racing happening today, the parking area is a sea of open spaces, except for a lone black sedan, which Ken pulls up alongside. He hands a set of keys to Larry and points at the sedan. In Ken's business, it's not uncommon to obtain a vehicle with clean plates for a unique and specific purpose. Once the particular assignment is completed, it's generally understood the car will be retrieved and taken to the chop shop to be painted, fitted with new plates, a new VIN, and new registration papers. Such practices make for extremely challenging investigations should the authorities determine such a vehicle was involved in some illegal activity.

Larry drives into the stable area and declares his presence with a series of horn blasts as he pulls into McGee's barn area. After spotting the hulking presence in the sedan, McGee scurries into his office and comes out a moment later. He runs up to the sedan, and Larry hands an unmarked envelope to McGee.

McGee looks inside the envelope and smirks quizzically before resealing it.

"McGee, we'd like to continue doing business with you,

given the success of our last venture. You know what this means, right?"

McGee nods.

"And in case you've forgotten how to behave, me and my boys will happily pay you a visit and repeat that little dance number you witnessed at Mario's the other night should it become necessary. My guys just love an opportunity to show off their unique skills." Larry laughs at his own comment.

McGee reaches out to shake Larry's hand but is greeted by a large plume of dust as Larry punches the accelerator and speeds off, causing several horses to whinny and rear.

Once he is out of sight from the barns, Larry puts the vehicle in idle. He grabs his personal car key, slides a slender cover off, and connects it to a USB wire attached to his phone. Throughout the ride upstate, Larry kept his car key in his pocket and recorded several hours of his conversation with Ken Kaufman. When Ken forced Larry to strip inside the rest stop, he never considered the car key would be a secret recording device. Had he done so, Ken would have returned to Long Island alone. Larry pockets the key and says to himself, "Who's the dummy now, Ken?"

Larry pulls the black sedan to the exit of the stable area and sits behind a car already stopped at the red traffic light. He squints at the two passengers in the car ahead of him, does a double take, and says to himself, "Well, I'll be son of a bitch!"

CHAPTER 55

Kristine slides next to Matt as he stops the car for the red light at the stable exit. Matt places his arm around her as he waits for the traffic signal to change to green, which is seemingly taking forever. A car pulls up behind them, and Matt takes a quick glance into the rearview mirror, immediately retracts his arm, and turns around for a better look through the back window. With the sun high in the sky, he swallows hard upon recognizing the clear profile of the driver sitting just behind them.

Although the traffic light remains red, Matt does not hesitate. He jams on the gas pedal and accelerates through the red light with an abrupt force that pins Kristine deep into her passenger seat. He makes an immediate right, screeching his tires, and ignores the blaring horns and colorful gestures coming from multiple drivers as he rushes down the turnpike. Switching lanes and weaving around cars, Matt jerks the steering wheel to the right, sending his vehicle flying onto the entrance ramp of the parkway. The move, however, fails to create any separation from their pursuer, as Louisville is tight on their tail and speeding onto the entrance ramp behind them.

Matt races his car down the ramp as Louisville closes the gap to within inches of his rear bumper. Without regard for his safety while merging into traffic, Matt presses the gas pedal to the floor and accelerates onto the busy highway.

The odometer shoots from sixty to ninety miles per hour, as Matt deftly navigates his vehicle around the traffic and defiantly switches lanes from middle to right, back to middle, and then through an opening in the left lane. Unable to create any separation from Louisville, Matt exits the parkway in a sudden and bold move by darting across all three lanes and barely making the exit ramp, knowing it'll be impossible for Louisville to follow. His respite is short-lived as, to his astonishment, Kristine shrieks that Louisville made the exit and remains in close pursuit. Securing the wheel with one hand, Matt frantically points to her purse with his other.

"The gun, Kris. Grab the gun!"

Kristine pulls the gun out just as Matt speeds over a deep pothole, causing her to lurch forward and fumble the gun underneath Matt's seat.

Instincts take over as Matt veers his vehicle over the curb and zooms past several stopped vehicles in driving over a grassy lawn that runs parallel to the exit ramp. Louisville follows in his car, but another vehicle pulls out, effectively cutting him off from chasing Matt's car. The break gives Matt time and space to speed away onto the boulevard, leaving Louisville well behind.

Matt turns onto a side street, looks at Kristine, and asks, "Did we lose him?"

Kristine looks behind them with a massive sigh. "Yeah. Thank God!"

With a chance to catch his breath and think, Matt reaches

below his seat and retrieves the gun. He hands it to Kristine and says, "Hang on to this until we know we're safe."

She takes the gun, looks back through the rearview window, and shouts out, "Oh, shit. No. No!"

Matt catches a glimpse of Louisville's car in his rearview mirror, just a block behind and approaching fast. He shifts gears and screeches his car forward.

As they accelerate down the side street, Kristine monitors Louisville through the rear window and screams as he closes the gap.

Just ahead, Matt notices an oblivious car pulling out slowly across the intersection. Leaning on his horn, a collision with the clueless vehicle appears unavoidable. Matt stomps hard on the brakes in a desperate attempt to avoid the inevitable.

Grasping the wheel tightly does nothing to help Matt control the vehicle as they violently spin through the intersection. Matt and Kristine are mercilessly pinned while the car spins uncontrollably. It's a moment of horror until the car finally comes to a halt. His fingers still wrapped around the wheel and feet glued to the brake pedal, Matt is disoriented and shaken but amazingly unscathed. As he regains his bearings and assesses the situation, he looks at Kristine.

She screams at him, "Drive. NOW!"

Once his car stopped spinning, it completely turned around and is now pointing in the opposite direction from which they were driving. Matt realizes his car is now directly facing Louisville, who is accelerating toward them.

Matt moves his foot from the brake to the accelerator. The car fishtails while lunging forward for several feet until the engine sputters and shuts down under a sensational plume of black smoke erupting from the hood. Louisville is barreling toward them, and Matt desperately turns the ignition key again and again, but the car does not start. Then, a thunderous explosion, the sensation of weightlessness, sounds of shattering glass, and shrieks of crushing metal.

CHAPTER 56

An eerie silence surrounds him as Matt looks out toward a grassy green pasture. It's bordered by a white-rail fence stretching to the extremes under a bright sun and perfect blue summer sky. A familiar-looking figure appears in the distance, charging toward him. Getting closer, the figure moves effortlessly while galloping down the hill, showing off his magnificent stride and graceful motion. Thundering up to Matt, the horse abruptly locks his legs and stops short with an eruption of dust and dirt, inches from Matt, who stands motionless. Upon recognizing Heliacal Star's distinctive white star, a sensation of warmth and perception of safety manifests.

Noticing a fresh carrot is protruding from his jacket, Matt offers the natural treat to his equine acquaintance. Heliacal Star bows his head and leans into Matt's shoulder before accepting the edible offer. After devouring the carrot, Heliacal Star spins around in a flash and accelerates rapidly beyond the hill from where he initially came, disappearing as quickly as he appeared only moments ago.

Matt feels a gentle finger caressing the top of his hand. The touch is familiar, comforting and reassuring. He turns and smiles as Kristine presses against him, showing off her angelic glow and magnificent radiance. He reaches for her soft blonde hair, shining fiercely under the bright sunlight. He is warmed by her presence and numbed to potential danger.

Remembering the automobile accident, Matt wants to ask Kristine what happened, but finds it impossible to speak. How did they get here? How did they survive the accident? What happened to Louisville Larry? The questions are vivid, but his voice remains muted as the silence permeates. The gorgeous blue sky rapidly turns gray, and a strong gust of wind ripples over the pasture with a swirling dirt funnel tearing up the beautiful grassy field. Matt senses a hidden danger lurking nearby as the intense storm barrels down upon him.

Matt turns around to shield Kristine, but she has suddenly vanished. He wants to run, but his legs are anchored to the ground and too heavy to lift. The white fence border that glistened in the sunlight only moments ago has become weathered, rotten, and worn. His bones grow achy, and a chill enters his soul.

Distinctive footsteps are now approaching from behind and growing with intensity as they inch closer. Matt grabs his ears and shuts his eyes, but the ominous sound continues to grow louder. As he cowers in fear, knowing danger is fast approaching, he musters his courage and turns to confront whatever may be pursuing him.

Nothing appears. There's a recently paved blacktop, stretching endlessly in two directions. His eyes return to the pasture, but all he sees is more endless pavement. There is no pasture, no farm, no grass, no fence, no Heliacal Star, and no Kristine. The heaviness in his legs has lifted, and Matt walks. He moves around in a tight circle and looks for something familiar, anything to ground himself, but his action yields no satisfaction.

Matt is alone in the middle of a lifeless intersection, appearing as symmetrical and endless pathways. The roads intersect in the exact spot he stands. Matt chooses a direction and starts walking. As he progresses down the path, Matt prays his decision will somehow return him to the lush pasture, Kristine, and Heliacal Star.

This path of infinity offers nothing but the same endless blacktop road for mile after mile amid an unchanging barrenness, regardless of the distance traveled. There is no change in gradient and no indication of homes, buildings, or civilization. The temperature and air remain constant amid an absence of wind or weather. As he stretches his neck to search for something different or new in all directions, Matt sees only the never-ending road. He's lost any concept of time and cannot distinguish minutes from hours or days since he began walking. Finally, a light wind brings a noticeable and refreshing change, but Matt is unsure if it's a breeze of hope or an ominous gust.

The wind increases in intensity and howls through the oak and maple trees on either side of the road. It quickly escalates to hurricane force, causing the trees to sway and branches to fly as brush, rocks, and broken twigs are tossed everywhere. With only his arms for protection, Matt is repeatedly stung by flying debris until the storm abruptly stops and everything goes silent once again. He checks his arms and body for scrapes and bruises but is surprisingly unscathed. He feels no pain or much of anything except for a bone-chilling achiness, which emanates from beneath his skin.

An oversize man appears from the behind the shadow of the forest and steadily approaches as Matt's trepidation intensifies. Despite his abject fear, Matt again decides to confront the danger rather than flee. He stands his ground and turns. The large man swings a large baseball bat, causing Matt's heart rate to accelerate and his courage to fade. Matt calculates his diminishing odds of survival as Louisville decisively moves toward him. Without breaking eye contact, Matt slowly steps back while Louisville continues to advance and shrink the distance between them. Matt spins around and sprints away as fast as his legs allow.

He dashes away and refuses to turn around or look behind him, until he becomes so exhausted, he can no longer take another step. Visions of the car chase with Louisville are repeating in his head, and he lacks energy to forge any farther. Matt slowly turns to sneak a peek behind him. There is no sign of Louisville, just the familiar-looking blacktop, endlessly disappearing into the horizon.

After catching his breath, Matt walks in the same direction and stumbles upon a solitary, yet familiar-looking house. There are no other houses, streets, or people around, but the residence is unmistakably his childhood home. Worried that Louisville may still be lurking nearby, Matt takes an exaggerated look in all directions until convinced the danger has dissipated. The front door is unlocked and, without knocking, Matt walks inside.

As he enters the house, his mom is preparing breakfast inside the kitchen with the distinctive and familiar scent of sizzling bacon with scrambled eggs. Inside the kitchen, his mom appears younger than she did earlier this morning. Sitting at the kitchen table is a middle-aged man presenting a broad smile and waving to Matt. Recognizing his dad, Matt runs up to embrace him.

Overjoyed yet confused by the scene unfolding in front of him, Matt can finally speak. "But you died when I was . . ."

His dad is barely audible while speaking, and his words sound like a foreign tongue. Matt shrugs and pleas with his dad to slow down and speak English. This has no effect. His dad hands him a betting ticket with the racetrack logo, but unlike a typical voucher, there is no date, race, or amount wagered.

The voucher simply reads, *Go All In. You'll win with Heliacal Star*. Matt pockets the voucher.

The sound of a metal ladle hitting the floor temporarily disrupts Matt's focus. He leans over to pick it up and return it to his mom, but instead finds Kristine where his mom was just standing. She offers a cheerful smile while receiving the ladle and returns to the bacon and eggs cooking on the stove. Matt rereads the voucher and thinks up several questions. What does the message mean? Who murdered his dad? How did he manage to escape the car accident, and how did he end up here? As he looks across the table to ask his questions, his dad is suddenly gone. Both his mom and Kristine have also disappeared. He looks around the room again and discovers there is no table, no chairs, no bacon, no smells, and no house. Once again, Matt finds himself alone in the dark. He lies on the ground, closes his eyes, and screams.

A throbbing numbness permeates his body with an engulfing yet dull pain pounding inside his head. Matt struggles to opens his eyes but is unable to process why there are shards of exploded glass and debris surrounding him.

The air is hot and steamy, and his sweat has soaked through his clothing. The sky appears below him as the pressure inside his head grows in intensity. The pressure across his chest is constricting his air channel as the steering wheel is pressed tightly against his sternum. Struggling to make sense of the situation, he recalls trying and failing to start the car, just prior to the explosion and before things got really strange. Upside down and trapped in place by the compressed steering wheel and a locked seatbelt, Matt realizes he has just survived the car crash with Louisville. He can only manage a slight twist as he looks toward the passenger seat.

He sees Kristine also appears to be locked into her seatbelt. Her eyes are open, and her lips are moving, but he cannot hear anything over an obnoxiously loud humming inside his ears. Unable to move or speak, Matt blinks, hoping she'll see he's still alive. Kristine squirms within her confined space and manages to loosen her safety belt.

The humming dissipates and is immediately replaced by the sound of approaching footsteps, hastening Matt's anxiety. He fears Louisville is approaching. The steering wheel is so tightly jammed into his chest that Matt can hardly breathe, let alone speak. He manages a weak gurgle. Unable to free himself, Matt concedes his fate will be inevitably sealed, and he'll become another statistic in Louisville's coffer. Desperate to wriggle out of his trap, Matt knows he is defenseless. He turns his head and watches Kristine contort her body and lean out through the passenger-side window. He can only see the lower part of her body as she slithers partway out the shattered passenger window.

Suddenly, Matt hears three deafening pops, and Kristine slides back inside the car. She turns to Matt and yells, "I just shot that motherfucker!"

For the first time, Matt notices his gun in her hand.

CHAPTER 57

All attempts to free or loosen himself prove futile as Matt remains wedged upside down and pinned to the protruding steering wheel. The broken glass from the surrounding windshield inflicted multiple scratches around his arms and face, causing a mild burning sensation, an annoyance, but it's secondary to his sheer inability to move or breathe freely.

It takes several moments for multiple police and paramedics units to converge around the area in an impressive array of lights. Lying just a few feet from Matt's overturned car is Louisville Larry Lonsdale, conscious but quivering while bleeding on the ground. The paramedics attend to the wounded man who just took multiple gunshots to his right shoulder.

The paramedic says to his partner, "He's lost quite a bit blood and needs to be moved ASAP." They carefully yet quickly cover the wound and load Louisville onto the stretcher and into the ambulance. Multiple officers are scouring the scene as others take eyewitness reports.

A second team of paramedics simultaneously arrives at Matt's overturned vehicle. One of them asks, "Can you hear me from inside the vehicle?"

Unable to speak or move, Matt grunts as loud as he can, hoping to be heard.

The pair of paramedics remove the remaining shards from the window on the driver's side of the car. One reaches through the opened window, wedges a thin cushion behind Matt's head, and leans hard into the steering wheel, until a small space opens between Matt's chest and the wheel. Without the enormous pressure of the wheel exerting on him, Matt is finally able to take a normal breath.

Finding his voice, Matt finally says, "Thank God!"

The paramedic says, "Sir, please remain as still as possible while we assess your injuries and determine if you're safe to transfer. Can you tell us your name and what happened?"

Considering his circumstances and overall situation while pinned upside down, Matt feels a sense of relief, knowing his assailant has been disarmed and disabled, at least temporarily.

Matt responds to the paramedic, "My name is Matt Galiano. Kristine and I were forced off the road by that other guy. She had no choice but to shoot, as he was going to kill us."

The paramedic says, "Okay good, Matt. We're going to release the safety belt now. To keep you secure, my colleague will grab hold of your shoulders and ease you down slowly. Don't move on your own, even after the belt is unlocked. If you feel any pain or pressure, tell us right away. We don't anticipate any issues since your shoulders appear uninjured from the crash. Once you are released from the seatbelt, we'll pull you out of the vehicle securely. Are you ready?"

"Yes. Please get me the hell out of here," Matt says frantically.

Reaching inside, the first paramedic unlocks the belt while the other slowly lets Matt down and in a single motion, places his arms underneath Matt and carries him through the open driver-side window. Matt lets out a loud groan and lies flat on the ground, stares up to the sky, and takes a deep breath.

"You sustained multiple scrapes and burns across your face and arms, likely from the broken glass and deployed airbag. We'll administer some treatment now, then bring you to the hospital for further examination."

On the other side of the car, Kristine hands Matt's gun to an officer after she crawls out of the car without assistance. She initially refused medical help but eventually allowed the paramedic to perform a cursory exam. As Matt lies down next to his vehicle, Kristine approaches and kneels next to him. Seeing her alive and uninjured provides a massive wave of relief as he feared she could have been seriously injured. As violent as the crash had been, both he and Kristine amazingly and miraculously appear to have escaped without life-threatening or debilitating injuries. Sitting up to greet Kristine, Matt is halted as a piercing pain emits from his midsection. He says to the paramedic, "My side just hurt a ton when I tried to get up. It doesn't feel horrible when I lie down, but I'm afraid to sit up."

The paramedic says, "As you were pinned to the wheel, it's not surprising, as you bruised your sternum from the accident. Since you're not in discomfort while lying down, stay down, try to relax, and breathe as normally as possible. Do you know if you lost consciousness?"

Matt answers, "I definitely blacked out, but I have no idea how long. The last thing I remember is frantically trying to start the car before everything exploded. Next thing I know, I'm locked into my seat, upside down with a steering wheel pressed into me."

CHAPTER 58

After he's admitted to the hospital, there's an endless parade of pokes, prods, and X-rays, along with nurses taking regular blood pressure readings, reviewing his oxygen levels, and doing temperature checks. After what seems like a never-ending saga yet again, the attending doctor enters the hospital room.

"Mr. Galiano, you're a very lucky man! It appears you suffered a head wound, a broken nose, and a couple of bruised ribs. All things considered, this could have turned out much worse. Given the fact you experienced a head wound, we're obligated to hold you here overnight for observation. Assuming no complications, you'll be released in the morning." He points toward the doorway. "Oh, it looks like you also have some visitors outside."

Looking beyond the doctor and toward the door, Matt notices Kristine standing next to his mom on the other side of the entry. Smiling, he says, "Please, bring them in."

Kristine approaches, her eyes moist and reddened. She kisses him gently on the forehead, holding it for an extended moment, and says, "I was so scared after we were rammed by that asshole. I was calling to you and you weren't responding." She wipes her eyes. "I really thought I lost you back there, Mr. Galiano."

Matt gestures for Kristine to come close to him. He whispers to her, "Did you really shoot Louisville?"

Kristine nods. "You bet I did! While you've been here, I've been getting grilled by the cops. By the way, they'll need to see your carry permit. Fortunately, there were multiple witnesses who tabbed Louisville as the aggressor and confirmed my actions were done in self-defense. They're not pressing any charges against me. The only bad thing . . . " She pauses, and whispers so only Matt can hear her, "I suppose I'm not a very good shot 'cause he's going to fully recover."

Matt ponders her words. If Kristine hadn't found his gun and possessed the wherewithal to employ it, neither of them would be alive right now. He is grateful for her decisiveness and quick thinking. His mind drifts to the dream, his childhood home and the vision of his mom and dad. It felt so real. He looks toward his mom, standing at the end of his bed, and a heavy lump forms in his throat. "Mom, when I was knocked out, I saw you . . . and Dad."

His mom walks next to his side and squeezes Matt's hand.

Looking at both his mom and Kristine, Matt continues, "I actually saw you both at the old house, with Dad. I even saw Heliacal Star at one point." He lightly presses his mom's hand as tears form in his eyes. "Dad told me to pursue Heliacal Star. It was really him. It wasn't a dream." Matt remembers one important element of his dream. He says, "Can you hand me my jeans? Don't worry, I'm not going anywhere."

Kristine brings over his jeans, and Matt rummages through the pockets, which are empty. He says, "I know this sounds crazy, but Dad passed me a betting voucher, which had no wagers on it but it read something like, *Go all in and you'll win with Heliacal Star*. I once read that humans are unable to read text while dreaming, so I'm thinking it was more than just a dream. I can still see those words emblazoned in my head right now."

His mom looks at him with compassion and says, "That sounds like something he would say. You know, he always wanted to own a racehorse and act like a big shot, but he never had the means or opportunity." She looks at both Matt and Kristine and asks, "Heliacal Star is a racehorse, right?"

Kristine winks at Matt. "Is this your way of saying you still plan to head Upstate?"

Without any hesitation, Matt responds, "The moment I get released."

CHAPTER 59

Inside his room, Larry is handcuffed to his hospital bed and under police watch with an officer stationed outside his door. He uses the remote to prop himself up as Special Agent Anjero enters his room and closes the door behind him to be alone with Larry.

Chuckling as he notices the shoulder harness and sling, Anjero says, "Good morning, Larry. Looks like you had a rough day."

Larry props himself upright. "Did you come here just to rub it in? What are you doing here? Are you here to save me from this mess?"

Anjero ambles up to the bed, presses a hand on each side of Larry's pillow, and leans forward, close enough for Larry to smell the flavor of his morning coffee. Anjero speaks with an unwavering voice, "Larry, now is the time for you to shut the fuck up, because you're in a shitload of trouble."

Anjero steps back from the bed, looks away from Larry and out the window.

From the third-floor hospital window, he watches the activity on the busy street below. After a moment of silence, Anjero turns to Larry with his hands on his hips and yells, "You stupid idiot! You really screwed yourself for good this time. I can't protect you anymore from your own stupidity. Before this bullshit, the police had already issued a warrant for your arrest for aggravated assault and battery! I could have helped you on those charges, but not anymore. It's not a good look, Larry."

Anjero turns his back to Larry and marches toward the door.

Larry shouts, "Anjero, wait!" Anjero stops. "I've got something for you. It's big, and I have it on tape."

Anjero says, "Larry, I'm seriously done with all your bullshit."

"No bullshit, Agent Anjero. I have Ken Kaufman on tape. You'll want to hear this."

CHAPTER 60

Driving down the gravelly driveway of Happy Trails North, Paula White is moving slowly in her Ford pickup yet manages to kick up a small dustbowl behind her on a sun-filled morning. She is on time for her scheduled meeting with Carol Chambers to inspect the facility and boarding conditions.

Carol greets Paula near the end of the driveway and points toward the nearest of two identical twelve-stall barns, where Heliacal Star is located. Between each barn is an indoor riding arena, currently devoid of any activity. A winding dirt trail slopes down behind the barns leading to several fenced pastures, also visible from the main road.

Inside the first barn, the stalls are empty except for the one holding Heliacal Star, as the other horses have been turned out to their respective pastures for the day. Carol explains how all the horses are walked and turned out to pasture daily, and how meticulous attention is given to every horse, no matter its breed, origins, or ownership.

As she follows Carol down the shed row, Paula pokes her head into each of the stalls until reaching the one with Heliacal

Star. She takes an extended look at the dark bay horse and says, "You know, I've been training horses at that racetrack since the 1990s and have never visited this farm before." She looks through the mesh and into the stall where Heliacal Star seems unfazed by his visitors while grazing on a flake of alfalfa on the ground.

"How long has . . . has . . . sorry, what is the owner's name?"

Carol turns to Paula. "Amanda Casey is the name of the farm owner. She's owned this property for almost twenty years. I'm not sure who owned the property before Amanda, but I can certainly vouch for her. We were both raised in this area, and I've known Amanda since grade school. My daughter's horse also boards here. Her name is Peanut and—"

"Did I tell you I found a buyer for this horse? I have only one day to ensure this horse can manage a long van ride." Paula walks into the stall, unwraps the bandages on his front legs, cautiously lifting his right front leg as her cell phone rings.

Gently placing the horse's leg on the ground, she answers the phone. "First barn. It's just me and the manager here, a gal named Carol." She turns to Carol. "That was my vet. She's here to do an exam on Heliacal Star."

Paula checks Heliacal Star from multiple angles as he continues to feed, showing little interest in the visitors around him. Once the veterinarian arrives, she joins Paula and Carol in the stall and does a cursory inspection, sliding her hand over the horse's legs, fetlocks, and knees.

She says, "His fetlock is loaded with fluid and remains pretty warm to the touch. I can also see he is lame at the walk just by observing him move around inside the stall."

Carol nods.

Paula turns to the vet. "I recently sold him and plan to put him on a van in a couple of days. Keep this in mind in regard to any sedation or pain blocks he may need for the long van ride?"

The vet says, "He should be fine for transport. Give him two grams of bute in the morning and evening and maintain a thick cotton wrap around his fetlock area. I'm going to take a few radiographs to determine if this guy will need arthroscopic surgery."

Paula leads Heliacal Star out of the stall and onto a mat as the vet returns with a portable radiograph and gently shaves the hair around his fetlock. Heliacal Star protests by throwing his head and stomping his hind leg, prompting Paula to tighten her hold on the lead rope and tug it sharply a few times, effectively correcting the horse's uncooperative behavior.

After applying a mild anesthetic, the vet takes several pictures of the fetlock. As the sedative takes effect, Paula no longer needs to apply her tight hold, and she approaches the vet, who is kneeling in front of digital images on her laptop.

"What are you seeing, Doc?"

She points to the screen. "If you look here, you'll notice he broke his fetlock in two spots. The good news is the break appears to be clean and nondisplaced. He'll need a procedure to insert one or two screws, which will reinforce the area and prevent further risk for injury. The sooner I can do this, the sooner he'll recover. I estimate he could return to light activity about three months after surgery, but I don't foresee this guy racing again."

Paula says, "Thanks, Doc. I can see the fracture and have no issues with your evaluation and assessment. I'll need to inform the new owner before we do anything. I've got a—" She is interrupted when her phone alerts her to an incoming text message. "Excuse me for a moment, Doc."

Paula turns away from the vet and pulls up the text message.

> *Hi Paula, this is Kristine Connelly. Matt Galiano was in a car accident today and got banged up a bit. He'll be okay, and I'll drive him upstate. I want to confirm the deal with Heliacal Star is still on, but can we push our meeting till Thur?*

Paula looks up. "Hey, Doc, when can you perform the surgery, and how much will it cost?"

She checks her phone and says, "He'll need to come to the clinic and require general anesthesia, so I'd say we're talking in the neighborhood of $3,500. Tomorrow is super busy. I could take him on Thursday."

Paula nods to acknowledge. "Thursday will be fine."

She peeks into the stall and watches Heliacal Star, who has returned his attention to the remaining timothy and alfalfa as the vet expertly applies a thick cotton bandage and covers it with vet wrap from just below the fetlock and partway up his front leg. As the group leaves the stall and exits the shed row, they observe several horses running as a tight group in the pasture as a light wind picks up, blowing a few leaves in front of them.

Carol asks Paula, "Is everything okay? Do you have any concerns?"

Paula says, "No, no. It was as expected. Can you excuse me for a minute?"

She takes a step to the side and taps out a text.

Hi Kristine. Shit. This horse is pretty damaged and will need surgery on Thursday. It will cost between 3–4K. Assume you knew he needed surgery and will cover expenses. It's ok if you need an extra day. Glad your friend is not seriously hurt.

Paula reaches over and shakes Carol's hand. "Thank you for your time today. I'm satisfied with his accommodations. I'll return here on Thursday and haul him to the clinic for surgery. The new owner will meet us here on Thursday, too."

Carol says, "It was nice to host you. Hey, I have more time if you want to see the rest of the farm."

"Thanks, but no. I really must be going."

As Paula walks toward her car, a loud horn is blaring repeatedly from the small parking area. She approaches her pickup, but a horse trailer is idling in the driveway just behind her truck and blocking her from the exit. A grizzled-looking man rolls down the window of the trailer, points at Paula's truck, and yells out, "Is that your piece of shit?"

Paula slowly walks to the trailer, as the man's head is fully extended out of the driver-side window. "Are you serious?"

He says, "Just move your heap, sweetheart. I need to get in there."

Carol runs up to Paula and frowns. "I see you've met . . . Mr. Nanske. I'm so sorry, Paula." Carol turns to John Nanske. "Amanda is expecting you, although I thought you were coming later. I'm the one who instructed Ms. White to park here. She's heading out now. Please back up and let her pull out."

He grunts. "I'm on a tight schedule."

Nanske backs up his trailer, giving Paula barely enough space to negotiate through the tight opening.

"I'm so sorry about this, Paula," Carol says. "He's a total jerk, but I've never seen him this ornery. I don't understand how Amanda tolerates him. If you wouldn't mind pulling out, it would make things easier for everyone . . . he won't be here on Thursday. I promise."

Paula speaks loudly while staring at Nanske, "Carol, you don't need to apologize for this asshole. I'll leave now." She turns to Carol. "Thank you again for your help today."

As she slowly pulls out, she rolls down her window and extends her middle finger, maintaining the gesture until out of sight.

After leaving the farm, her phone alerts her to an incoming text message.

Thanks Paula! We will see you Thursday. Matt and I will meet you and your vet at the farm before his surgery. We'll cover the cost of surgery. Kristine.

CHAPTER 61

Wake up, Matt!"

Hearing his name, Matt barely opens his eyes from the passenger seat of the car, but it's enough to see Kristine winking at him. The late morning sun shines through the driver-side window, accentuating Kristine's blonde highlights. He has little doubt Louisville would have expeditiously disposed of them right after the accident if she hadn't taken such prompt and decisive action to stop him.

Since leaving Long Island prior to dawn, Kristine has been driving all morning, fully relieving Matt of the task, given his lingering pain and soreness from the car accident. After they left this morning, Matt swallowed three ibuprofen for inflammation and two acetaminophen for pain management. Half asleep for most of the drive Upstate, he occasionally heard a familiar song playing on the radio and would open his eyes and then doze off again.

Matt stretches his legs and arms until an intolerable pain radiates out of his midsection, a rude reminder of various injuries sustained from both the assault and the automobile accident. He adjusts the passenger seat into an upright position, rubs his eyes, and observes the surrounding countryside.

His eyes now fully open, he asks, "Hey, what time is it and where are we?"

Kristine smiles. "It's almost eleven, sleepyhead, and believe it or not, we are only minutes from Happy Trails North. How are you feeling? You ready to own Heliacal Star?"

In spite of his discomfort, Matt is genuinely excited.

"You bet I am!"

A wave of paranoia strikes him as he fires a series of rapid questions at Kristine. "Did you tell Paula White we'll be arriving soon? What time is her vet arriving? Oh shit, where's the envelope?"

The moment the words leave his mouth, he recalls Kristine placing the envelope stuffed with cash inside the glove compartment before they left. He opens the latch, takes out the manila envelope, and peeks inside.

Kristine glances at him. "What's the matter, Matt? Don't you trust me?"

Matt chuckles at the sarcastic jab as Kristine grabs her chirping phone and hands it to him. "Here, please take it. Tell me what it says?"

Matt takes the phone, but instead of reading the notification, he stares at Kristine.

She shoots him a quizzical look. "What? Why are you looking at me?"

"I'm sorry. You just . . . you look especially good in that dress. Also, I appreciate everything you've done for me the past few days. I'm glad we found each other."

Kristine flips back her bangs. "Mr. Galiano, flattery will get you everywhere."

Matt blurts out, "Ah, I knew it. I've seen you in that dress before."

She glances at her outfit. "That's not possible. My entire outfit is new except for the boots. But, hey, thanks for noticing! I bought this dress recently, and today seemed like the opportune time to wear it."

Matt is convinced he's seen Kristine in her outfit before but is unable to recall the time or place. The navigation app on Kristine's phone instructs them to exit the highway in one mile.

Suddenly, Matt remembers and shouts, "I got it!"

Kristine lurches forward in her seat. "You trying to scare me?"

Matt responds, "No, I mean yes, I mean, I'm not yelling about the exit. I remember where and when I saw you in that dress. And I'm one hundred percent positive."

He turns to look out the window, places his fingers on his forehead, and mumbles to himself, "Whoa. This is friggin' weird."

Kristine follows the GPS app and exits the highway. "What are you talking about? Have your meds gotten you loopy?"

The GPS interrupts again with instructions to turn left in one hundred feet and then make an immediate right turn.

Matt says, "I saw you wearing it after Louisville smashed my car. I was knocked out. I was dreaming—kind of. I'm not sure how to properly describe it."

Matt hasn't thought about his dream since leaving the hospital. A chill spirals down his spine as he remembers seeing his dad in the kitchen, passing him the voucher. "You were in the same dress, boots, and everything. We were happy, holding hands and watching Heliacal Star play in an oversize pasture. Then, you disappeared." He closes his eyes and surprises himself with the vivid recollection of so many details. "Until much later, when I saw you again. We were at my house. My mom and dad were also there. My dad liked you and Heliacal Star, too."

As she turns into the driveway, Kristine says, "Holy shit, Matt! I'm convinced each of us has a partner or soulmate we're destined to locate. We're just getting to know each other and don't want to go too deep right now, but perhaps this dream of yours means something."

Matt smiles and nods. "I was starting to wonder the same thing!"

Kristine idles the car at a sign that reads *Happy Trails North*. Matt notices a large horse trailer is blocking much of the driveway. He points to a narrow parking space, left of the trailer, and Kristine maneuvers into the spot with barely enough space to slip through.

After such a long drive, Matt is eager to get out and stretch his legs. As he steps out, the rumbling sound of the trailer's engine diverts his attention. As the trailer roars to life, several horses whinny from the back before it pulls out of the driveway and drives onto the main road.

Opposite the driveway, Matt looks toward the barn area, arena, and pastures situated just beyond the barns at several horses grazing near the fence. It's a bit warmer than Matt expected as he feels a film of moisture forming on his forehead. He tosses his jacket into the car and watches Kristine as she walks toward the barn.

The surrounding grassy pastures also remind Matt of his dream, when Kristine stood alongside him while Heliacal Star snacked on a carrot. The musty smell of horses combined with the sweet smell of fresh cut grass presents a moment of tranquility. Several feet ahead him, Kristine turns around. "Hey, are you coming or what? C'mon, let's go see your new horse!"

Eager to see Heliacal Star and make it official, Matt realizes he's forgotten the envelope. He returns to the car, opens the glove compartment, and grabs it.

They hold hands as they enter the barn. Kristine, "Remember, Heliacal Star is also dealing with a few serious injuries, too. I'll take a look and assess his condition, but I want you to know I'm one hundred percent behind your decision, regardless. If you decide to change your mind after seeing him, remember, you're not obligated to complete the deal."

Matt says, "No cold feet here. Remember, my dad instructed me to get him, besides, Heliacal Star means more to us than just being a great racehorse. We never would've met if not for Heliacal Star. I can't wait to see him."

A few vehicles pull up behind them, and Matt turns to see a sport utility vehicle and Ford pickup coming down the gravel driveway. As there was no greeting committee upon their arrival, Matt presumes it must be Paula White and her vet arriving.

As the pickup comes to a stop, an older women calls over to them, "Are you Matt Galiano?" Matt waves to acknowledge and recognizes Paula White from the racing office at Belmont.

"I'm Paula White. I heard about your car accident and hope you're okay. I'm glad you made the drive. Your horse is just inside; let me take you to him. He's a bit banged up, but hopefully with surgery and time off, he'll feel better soon."

As they are chatting, the utility vehicle pulls up alongside the truck, and Carol Chambers introduces herself.

Holding the manila envelope, Matt says to Paula, "I suppose you're going to want this. You can count it. It's all there."

Paula says, "You should see him first and let your gal friend here give him the once-over before I take that. If you're still interested after you both get a good, long look, we'll make it official." She holds up her handbag. "I've got his official Jockey Club registration papers in here."

As the group moves inside the stable, Matt's excitement grows and his pace quickens. Kristine keeps up as they stride a few steps ahead of Paula and Carol. Entering the barn, Matt overhears Paula talking to Carol. "Can you believe I ran into that asshole again on my way over here? I recognized his ugly mug and that hideously dreadful trailer."

In a flat tone, Carol says to Paula, "I was told unequivocally by Amanda that Mr. Nanske was not coming anywhere near this place today. At least he's gone for now."

Paula chuckles. "Don't worry about it, sweetie. I can handle myself. When I passed him on the road, I showed him how long my middle finger can extend."

Matt turns around. Paula approaches him. "We're talking about this guy Nanske. Let's just say he's a first-class asshole. Let's go see your horse." She points. "He's over there. Second stall on the right."

Matt looks through the stall door, which is partly open, but something looks off. Instead of Heliacal Star, there's an older chestnut-colored quarter horse standing there.

Matt turns to Kristine. "This isn't Heliacal Star."

Paula and Carol approach the stall. Feeling anxious, Matt turns to Carol. "Which stall did you say he was in? This is definitely not Heliacal Star."

Carol looks inside and nods in agreement, then looks into several neighboring stalls. Turning to Matt, Carol's face appears flushed. She says, "I'm so sorry. I don't quite understand this." She points to the second stall on the right and says, "He was right here earlier this morning when I came to check on everything."

Matt's eagerness to see Heliacal Star morphs into a combination of confusion and nervous energy. Matt looks directly at Carol. "Do you lose many horses?" He takes a moment to collect himself. "If he's not in this stall, then where is he?"

Carol does not answer but instead continues to look inside each of the stalls, shaking her head. She asks Paula, "Maybe your vet already took him to the clinic?"

Paula responds, "Not possible. She's not coming till this evening; the surgery is not scheduled until tomorrow. Besides, if she were coming here, she would've called me. She's also aware that Kristine needs to speak with her."

Carol pulls out her phone, excuses herself, and stands just out of earshot to make a phone call.

Matt is growing increasingly uneasy about the entire situation. He inches closer and hears Carol saying, "No, that cannot be possible."

Matt freezes in place as Carol's voice elevates from a near whisper to a raised tone. "No, Amanda, we have his papers right here!"

Carol's words fail to exude any confidence about the situation. Matt fights his instincts and swallows his panic, instead offering Carol a chance to provide a plausible explanation with the hope she has located Heliacal Star.

Carol is shouting now. "You need to bring him back ASAP!"

She hangs up, looks away, and then turns to Matt. "I'm really sorry about this, Mr. Galiano. I will fix this. I promise."

Matt refrains from getting animated after noticing Carol's dejected look and pale complexion. Believing she's not at fault, Matt pivots into problem-solving mode. "So where exactly is my horse?"

Carol speaks without looking up. Her voice cracks. "I'm so sorry about this. I'm going to straighten out this mess."

Kristine steps in front of Carol and points to Matt. "This poor guy just traveled six hours in wretched pain, only two days after surviving a life-threatening car accident, just to see this horse today. You're going to tell us right here and right now what the fuck is going on!"

Carol stands upright as her voice quivers. "Yes, you're right. I was just speaking with Amanda Casey." She takes a step away from Kristine. "Amanda is the owner and manager of the farm. There's been a terrible misunderstanding. Amanda just informed me your horse shipped out this morning."

Matt is speechless as the pain in his side intensifies with every bit of discouraging news. "What exactly does that mean? Who took him? Can't they just send him back?"

Paula now moves into Carol's face. "Matt is right. If he only shipped out this morning, he cannot have gone very far. I don't know what games you people play here, but you and your friend

Amanda need to find and return him immediately. If not, you and your friend are going to face much bigger problems."

Carol gets teary. "I'm really, really, sorry about this. Amanda said it was John Nanske who hauled him out. She promised she'd get him back right away. I'm really sorry about this misunderstanding."

CHAPTER 62

Following her call with Carol Chambers, Amanda Casey promptly phones John Nanske.

Prior to Matt and Kristine's arrival at Happy Trails North, and unbeknownst to Carol, John Nanske arrived at the farm earlier in the day to collect on his quota of livestock per a long-standing arrangement with Amanda Casey.

As part of this arrangement, Nanske pays $500 cash for each horse Amanda offers him, no questions asked. This has resulted in more than one hundred castaway horses being turned over to him in the past few years, exceeding $50,000 of supplemental income, off the books, for Amanda. Of late, Nanske has been showing up more often, thus reducing the pool of available horses. When he arrived with an empty trailer this morning, Amanda initially offered Nanske only two horses, which was well short of his trailer capacity. Hauling a small number of disposable horses has never been a concern before, but Nanske increased his offer by another $1,000 per horse without reason or explanation. With the added incentive, Amanda suddenly found an additional four horses for Nanske to haul, including Heliacal Star.

Amanda Casey, known in the community as an animal lover, has kept her arrangement with John Nanske secret. Regardless of the condition or health of the horse, be it infirm, aging, abandoned, injured, hard to handle, or otherwise, Nanske has always brought cash and never asked questions. He's never shown any interest in the origin or history of the horses he hauls, and Amanda has never challenged his motives. While most transactions involving horse ownership involve a legal or notarized document, Nanske has never required any paperwork, registration papers, or health certifications.

Before partnering with Carol Chambers, Amanda struggled to find horses for Nanske. Amanda leveraged Carol's trustworthiness to gain public trust and promoted Happy Trails North as a reliable equine rescue operation. Carol's integrity and enthusiasm for saving unwanted horses helped establish the farm's reputation as a safe haven and preferred destination for those seeking refuge for horses in need.

Carol's social media profile prominently features her work rescuing horses and her involvement in the day-to-day operations at Happy Trails North. The daily cost of care for any horse is expensive and especially taxing if the horse is no longer active in terms of racing, showing, working, or trail riding. Happy Trails North offers an almost too-good-to-be-true opportunity for owners to escape these ongoing expenses, while being assured that their horse will be safely rehomed with a caring and loving owner.

On her social media profile page, Carol Chambers has posted several photos of horses at Happy Trails North, including one of her daughter riding her rescued Arabian. There are also scenic shots of the farm with horses playing in pastures and captions touting the farm's involvement in rescuing horses. She links to articles with dire warnings describing the fate of those animals sold at agricultural auctions and the inhumane treatment that follows, should these animals be sold to the wrong people. To enhance her profile, she openly shares information regarding her memberships in multiple national rescue groups and animal activist organizations.

Carol's photos have hundreds of likes, solidifying her reputation as a passionate and trustworthy person and someone who's genuinely interested in the welfare of all animals. She shares a lot about her personal journey and how she and her daughter found peace through their involvement with horses after her husband's untimely death. Meanwhile, the Happy Trails North website is sprinkled with positive reviews. One recent reviewer wrote:

> *Carol and everyone at Happy Trails North were super helpful in relocating our retired quarter horse, a former dressage horse, to a safe new home. They provided all the paperwork and kept us updated on her relocation. It's a huge relief to find a farm that cares deeply about these animals. I highly recommend them for anyone seeking a new home for their horse.*

Another reviewer commented:

> *It's a pleasure to work with such a super kind and compassionate individual. We were so happy to discover Happy Trails North and Carol Chambers, who assisted us in relocating our dear RooRoo to a new and loving home.*

Amanda reaches Nanske on the phone. "Hello, John, I've got a problem and need your help. It seems one of the horses I gave you this morning was by accident. I made a mistake and am going to need him back. The owner just showed up and is melting down in front of Carol right now. Can you return him right away?"

Chuckling, Nanske asks, "Which one?"

She answers, "The lame dark bay thoroughbred with a star marking on his forehead. I erroneously assumed he was another throwaway, broken-down horse. When can you get him back here?"

After a short pause, Nanske says, "You do realize I'm on a crazy-tight schedule. I'm already super late with a haul to Canada and need to reach the border before they shut down for the day." His tone sharpens. "You got paid, right?"

Amanda acknowledges, and Nanske continues, "Listen, I'll pull him off the trailer, and you can pick him up at my farm. Will that work for you, my dear?"

Amanda says, "Yes, I'll swing by and grab him in the next thirty minutes. I owe you one, John, and thanks."

CHAPTER 63

After being discharged from the hospital and released on bail, Larry Lonsdale has been alone inside his apartment. His unshaven face is covered by stubble, matching an oily complexion and unwashed hair. Watching television in a pair of unwashed shorts, he adjusts his shoulder harness, as instructed by the doctor, to limit movement and aid recovery.

As Larry flips the channel, Ken Kaufman suddenly appears at his doorway, unannounced, and promptly sits at the kitchen table. He slides a hot coffee in a lidded cup across the table and invites Larry to join him. Larry obliges as Ken says, "Morning, Larry. I must say, you look like shit today."

Larry leans forward slowly and grabs the coffee.

Ken stands, walks over to Larry, and smacks him hard across the top of his head. "I heard you got yourself into a fender bender with your old buddy Matt Galiano. You never showed up at the precinct." Pressing two fingers deep into Larry's shoulder harness, Ken continues, "I also heard his little girlfriend popped you a few right here." Larry grimaces from pain but refrains from retaliating or saying anything.

Ken smiles grimly. "Yep, looks like my sources are accurate!"

Larry lowers his head. "I honestly don't know how that miserable bitch managed to fire three shots at me. I smashed that fucker's car up pretty good. They both should be dead." He shrugs his other shoulder and looks at Ken. "Did you come here to bust my balls?"

Ken moves in close and slaps Larry across the face. "Wash up, you smelly son of a bitch, and get dressed. We've got a job to do. Chop chop, let's go!"

Larry stands up and looks himself over. "I'm not exactly in what you'd call game shape. What gives?"

Ken walks toward the doorway. "When the boss says you've got a job, you do it. No questions asked. Now, move it. I don't have all day."

Larry retreats to the bathroom as Ken ambles toward the window and looks outside at the activity on the street below. Twenty minutes elapse, and Larry reappears washed, shaved, and dressed wearing an oversize jacket, masking his shoulder harness.

They leave Larry's apartment together and settle inside Ken's car, which is parked on the street in front of Larry's apartment. As Ken pulls out, Larry turns on the radio and stops on a local talk show. The radio host expresses his outrage over street crime and bemoans how politicians are perpetuating an epidemic of filth, crime, and homelessness while taking money from the pharmaceuticals and tacitly supporting an ever-expanding opioid and pain-killer industry.

Larry turns to Ken. "This guy on the radio is a crackpot, but he's got a point!"

Ken flips off the radio and places his index finger across his lips. Larry nods, and they drive in silence for another ten minutes until Ken parks on a quiet street in a residential area. He turns off the engine but keeps his safety belt secured.

Larry unbuckles, looks around, and says, "What the fuck . . . ?"

Ken interrupts. "Shh, not a word."

They sit in silence for several minutes until Ken's phone beeps, prompting him to unbuckle. Ken turns to Larry. "It's time. We'll go inside from around the back."

The houses on this block are picture-perfect, with compact front yards, manicured lawns, and quaint gardens. The modest-looking two-story colonial in front of them is indistinguishable from the other houses on the street. A brick pathway leads to a small porch. Encircling the property is a four-foot chain link fence with a *Beware of Dog* sign hanging on the gate facing the sidewalk.

As Ken exits his car, he glances up and down the block. It's late morning, and there's nobody in sight. Two additional vehicles are parked on the street, just ahead of Ken's car.

Ken unlatches the gate, and Larry follows him around the perimeter of the yard until they reach the back door. A charging basset hound approaches while barking, startling Larry and causing him to flinch and scooch behind his partner. Ken leans down, pets the hound, and takes out a stick of beef jerky. "Here you go, boy."

He takes the remaining beef jerky out of his pocket from the partially opened bag and tosses it across the yard. The hound spins around and chases the bag, ripping it open, eager to devour its contents and ignore the two men.

Larry takes a step forward and stops. He gestures toward

Ken. "What the fuck is this place? I just stepped in a pile of dog shit."

Ken says, "Keep it down, Larry." He strides ahead of Larry to the back door. The dog seems preoccupied across the yard. Larry turns away from Ken and scrapes the dog shit off his shoe with a pen. While scraping his shoe, he says to Ken, "This place is weird. What the fuck are we doing here?"

Larry tosses the soiled pen across the yard toward the dog. As he turns to Ken, he finds himself looking into the barrel of Ken's .44 revolver.

A trapped animal is considered the most dangerous of prey, and Ken maintains his distance as he waves his weapon. "No more stalling. Get inside. Go through the first door and down the stairs. You try anything, and I'll blow your fucking head off. Now move it. I'm right here behind you."

Larry's face goes pale. He pleads, "You can't be fucking serious? Hey, Ken, it's me, Larry. . ."

Ken snarls, "No more bullshit, Larry. Now move it, or I swear I'll pull this trigger."

Larry slowly walks through the back door and continues, as instructed, through the first door, which leads to a basement staircase. As he descends, he's met with pitch darkness. Ken instructs Larry to continue all the way to the bottom of the stairs, keeping his weapon pointed on him all along.

Clenching the railing with the hand of his good arm, Larry continues down into the darkness. Ken calls out, "Once you reach the bottom, the light switch will be on your left."

Larry feels for the switch with his left hand and flips it up.

The lights come on, but the wattage is low and the basement is only dimly lit.

A voice speaks in a calm and deliberate tone only a few feet from the landing, but hidden from where Larry stands. "What exactly were you thinking, Larry?"

Larry turns toward the recognizable voice and freezes in place. Tony Kaufman continues, "I was wrong, you really are one dumb son of a bitch."

Larry drops his head, and says, "Tony, I . . . I . . . swear . . . I . . . didn't do . . ."

Ever so slightly raising voice, Tony continues, "I told you to keep a low profile, and what do you do? First, you start a bar fight and bring out an army of cops. Then, you plow into the same guy and his girlfriend with one of my cars. Are you for fucking real? Why is keeping a low profile so fucking hard for you to understand?"

Larry lowers his head. "I did it to protect us. That bitch is going to screw us over because she's in bed with Matt Galiano. I bet he's the one talking to the feds!"

Tony stands up slowly and saunters to Larry, who stands stiffly and holds his breath.

Tony says, "And what makes you think Galiano is the one talking to the feds?"

Larry hesitates. "Didn't you say we had a rat? I figured it must be him."

Tony motions ever so slightly to Johnny and Frankie Fischer, who Larry can now see are standing nearby. They appear from the shadowy corner of the basement and move close to Larry.

Tony says, "Make it good. I want those bullets in his shoulder to feel like afternoon tea with the queen!"

The Fischer brothers are well-known among their associates and by local law enforcement as a pair of ruthless enforcers for the Kaufman clan. As the older of the two brothers, Johnny Fischer lifts weights daily, resulting in his impressive size and bulk. His chiseled physique, shaved head, and tattooed arms underscore his reputation for ferocity. His younger brother, Frankie, is renowned for his hair-trigger temper. It is well-known among the crew that he once tore off a random stranger's ear and forced it down his throat after the poor guy disrespected Johnny.

Johnny is first to act, with a lightning-fast jab right across Larry's nose, staggering him, and Frankie follows with a series of rapid punches to Larry's midsection. As Larry is hunched over in evident pain, Frankie rams his elbow into Larry's exposed face, opening a gash on his cheek and across his forehead.

Johnny grabs his target by the hair and slams his head into the wall, then rips the shoulder harness off, causing Larry to scream in agony. Instantaneously falling to his knees and onto the floor, Larry is gasping for air.

Showing no mercy, Frankie kicks the helpless Larry, causing the man to crumple into a ball and writhe in pain. Johnny signals to his brother to hold up. He grabs Larry by the top of his head and yanks him up and into a crouched position against the basement wall. Johnny launches several more powerful blows across Larry's face and stops after Larry is rendered unconscious and slumps onto the floor.

As Larry lies motionless on the basement floor, Tony speaks without emotion. "That's enough for now, boys."

Frankie rolls Larry onto his back, causing his wallet, cell

phone, and a car key to drop out of Larry's pocket. Picking up the items, Frankie stares at the exposed port at the top of the key, drops the phone, and says, "Oh, fuck!"

He hands the damaged car key to Tony.

Tony looks at the exposed port, stands over a motionless Larry, and tosses it on the chest of the splayed body. He kicks at Larry until he hears a groan, confirming Larry is awake.

Tony looks down at him and says, "You dirty motherfucker. A fucking listening device?"

Crouching down and staring at him, Tony spits at Larry, "Talk to me, rat!"

Larry spits out blood and coughs. "What? I swear, I didn't do anything." He coughs again and spits up more blood. "I don't know . . . someone planted that device on me."

Frankie yells out, "Bull-fucking-shit, Larry! I've been going through your cell phone history. You've been calling a private number from your contact list. Wonder who that can be? Not too bright, Larry!"

Tony signals to Frankie and Johnny.

Frankie does not hesitate in grabbing a lamp from the wall and hands the cord to his brother. Johnny easily fends off Larry's feeble attempt to resist, wraps the cord around his neck, and tightens his grip. Larry cannot escape as he flails and struggles, to no avail. After a minute of struggling, Larry's body goes limp. Johnny maintains a tight grip for several additional seconds before releasing Larry to the floor, lifeless.

Tony says, "Let's clean up this mess."

CHAPTER 64

Carol Chambers is the first of the trio to enter the police station. "Sheriff, we need your help." She turns and points toward Matt, who is hobbling behind her into the station. She says, "This man's valuable racehorse has just been stolen!"

The officer eyes Carol, Matt, and Paula and focuses on Matt. "Is what she says true?"

After her earlier phone call with John Nanske, Amanda Casey fessed up to Carol about Heliacal Star, and then Carol relayed the same to Matt, Kristine, and Paula. In doing so, she also told of Amanda's promise to retrieve and return the horse to Happy Trails North immediately.

After an hour passed without any updates or indications of the horse being returned, Matt lost his patience, and Paula volunteered her opinions regarding John Nanske. Matt genuinely believed Carol was sincere in demonstrating her concern, but she also hadn't done anything to resolve the situation. Increasingly frustrated, Matt decided it was time to act. There would be no more waiting.

Matt insisted Carol phone Amanda. When she was unable to reach her, Carol brought Matt, Kristine, and Paula to Amanda's house to confront the farm owner. Kristine played the role of chief interrogator and pressed Amanda for answers, insisting on a firm timeline for the horse's return. When Amanda only repeated her earlier story about returning the horse, Kristine moved into her face and demanded details. Standing next to Kristine, Paula shouted about taking legal action against Amanda and Carol if they were incapable of resolving the situation immediately.

Kristine shoved Amanda, causing her to stagger and almost fall. Raising her arms in a defensive posture, Amanda reiterated it was Nanske who took the horse in error. Kristine hovered with a menacing look and threatened Amanda with her fist clenched. Amanda finally unraveled and revealed her longstanding arrangement with Nanske. Amanda insisted Heliacal Star was never part of this arrangement and should be returned imminently. Floored by Amanda's admission, Matt determined it would be best to split into two groups. Kristine insisted on accompanying Amanda to Nanske's farm while Matt, Paula, and Carol drove to the police station to file charges against John Nanske for grand larceny of a racehorse.

Inside the station, Matt responds to the sheriff, "Yes, sir. My racehorse was taken without permission or authority from Happy Trails North by John Nanske. I have all the horse's paperwork with me. We believe the horse could be at Nanske's farm right now."

The sheriff asks, "How do you know this Nanske fellow stole your horse?"

Somewhat irritated by the question, Matt takes a protracted breath, knowing it's best to cooperate. "I purchased the horse from this lady over here." He points to Paula and hands the sheriff the horse's Jockey Club Registration papers and a signed and notarized bill of sale document. "That lady," he says, now pointing to Carol Chambers, "is the farm manager. She will also confirm my horse was stolen by Nanske."

The sheriff looks over the registration papers and bill of sale and looks at Paula. "Can I see your identification?"

Paula hands over her driver's license and points to the bill of sale where her name appears. The sheriff now turns to Carol. "Do you corroborate this gentleman's story about his horse being stolen by this Nanske guy?"

Carol says, "Yes! Please, can't you do something?"

The sheriff takes a moment to input data onto his computer. He turns to the group. "Did any of you go to see Mr. Nanske about returning the horse?"

Carol immediately responds, "Yes, of course. We tried calling him multiple times. The owner of Happy Trails North is at his farm now because he wasn't answering his phone."

Matt's phone rings. Kristine's name is on the caller ID. He excuses himself and answers the phone. "Did you find Heliacal Star?"

"No, Matt, he's gone. Nanske hauled out of here with a trailer load of horses about an hour ago. Nanske's wife finally admitted he took off for Canada. Matt, he's hauling Heliacal Star to the slaughterhouse!"

Matt leans over, wheezes, and dry heaves. Prior to speaking to Kristine, he was hopeful they would locate Heliacal Star, have a terse word or two with Nanske, and bring his horse to the clinic for his scheduled surgery. The situation is beyond his worst nightmare.

"Are you sure Heliacal Star was on the trailer when he left?"

"Unfortunately, yes. According to his wife, all the horses taken from Happy Trails North this morning are on that trailer. We even did a quick walk around the place. He's on it, one hundred percent."

Matt eyes Carol and Paula, who are still talking with the sheriff. After processing Kristine's words, his throat tightens from the enormous lump forming as his frustrations turn to despair.

Kristine is talking. "Matt? Are you still there?"

An overwhelming sense of defeat settles in. "Yes, I'm here, but what more can we do?"

"I'm close. I'll see you in a few minutes. I have an idea."

It's just at that moment when the sheriff approaches. "Sir, we've dispatched an officer to the property of Mr. Nanske. We'll speak with him. It will take time to get a signed warrant, but we'll question him about your horse."

Matt turns to the sheriff, grits his teeth, and says, "There's no point, because my horse isn't there. Nanske has already left with a van full of horses, including Heliacal Star. That son of a bitch is on his way to Canada to murder my horse."

Paula places her arm around Matt's shoulders and says unconvincingly, "This is not over, I swear!"

Sobbing, Carol approaches Matt and Paula. "I'm so sorry. I swear to God . . . I never knew Amanda was doing this. I've worked so hard to save horses from people like John Nanske, and Amanda continually reassured me our horses were being shipped to loving homes." She slumps into a chair and looks toward the floor. "So many people trusted us. They trusted me. How could I be so stupid and not have known? Oh my God! I've been sending these poor animals to their death all along!"

CHAPTER 65

Tony and Ken Kaufman walk side by side around the perimeter of the house while the Fischer brothers remain inside with the lifeless body of Larry "Louisville" Lonsdale. The quiet neighborhood contrasts with the violence inside the house. Ken cups his hand over his mouth and whispers, "If he talked . . . then Larry knows about the money, our connections, and the stash. He even knows John Nanske by name and how he transports our stuff. If so, we can be assured they're already looking for Nanske. We can't take any chances and need to reach him before the feds nab him. We also need to put our current transaction on hold and wait till things calm down."

Tony nods. "Get hold of Nanske. Then, I need you to go Upstate and—no, scratch that, I'll send Johnny and Frankie Upstate."

Putting his arm across Tony's shoulder, Ken again cups his hand around his mouth. "Nanske may become a problem. Suppose he's already been compromised by the feds? I must have called him a half-dozen times before you even stepped outside, and I kept getting his fucking voicemail."

Tony looks up toward the cloudless summer sky and shakes

his fists in the air. He stops suddenly and abruptly pivots back to his brother. "Did you try his wife?"

Ken shakes his head.

"Call her now," Tony instructs.

Johnny pops his head out the back door and waves toward Tony. Once he has Tony's attention, Johnny gestures with a thumbs-up. Tony tips his head slightly forward, and Johnny retreats back inside the house. From the top of the stairs, he calls down to Frankie, "We're clear. Let's move this sorry carcass out of here."

The back door flies open, and Frankie and Johnny emerge carrying a rolled-up carpet. It sags in the middle, but Johnny keeps it propped by reaching underneath it with his right arm without breaking stride. He winks while moving past Tony, who stands alone on the sidewalk and near a rusted van parked on the street. Ken stands several feet away while talking on a mobile phone. The rest of the neighborhood remains quiet and is otherwise undisturbed.

After watching the Fischer brothers load Larry's body into the back of the van, Tony enters his car and turns over the ignition. Ken jumps into the passenger seat and turns up the volume on the radio. He moves close to his brother and whispers, "I got hold of Nanske's old lady. She said he left for Canada about an hour ago."

Tony asks, "Have the feds been up there asking questions or looking for him?"

Ken replies as if anticipating the question, "Definitely no agents or cops, but apparently there were a couple of crazed women who roughed her up and accused Nanske of stealing a valuable horse. I don't know what the fuck Nanske is doing, but his wife said these women were scary mad and threatened to call the cops."

Tony slams his fist on the dashboard. "Okay, let me think." He looks out the window for several seconds and turns to Ken. "If he's on his way to Canada, it means the feds haven't nabbed him yet, but we can't ignore the possibility of some local cop pulling him over." He stops and slams his fist on the dashboard again. "Seriously, what the fuck is wrong with Nanske, stealing a goddamn horse. Now I gotta worry about the local Upstate cops in addition to the feds!"

Tony takes a cigar from his pocket, fumbles with the lighter, and almost drops it as he catches it before it falls on the ground. After a few strikes, he lights the cigar, rolls down the window, and blows out a billowing puff. He rolls the window up, turns off the radio, clenches his fist, and smashes it onto the steering wheel. "STUPID FUCKING IDIOT!"

Ken turns up the radio once again and speaks with an unhurried tone, "Let's assume Larry sang about Nanske and our Canadian connection. This means the feds would be interested and potentially closing in. It also means we need to reach Nanske first and retrieve our cash before the feds find him and seize him and our money."

Tony nods. "What do you suggest?"

Ken continues, "I know the exact route Nanske takes to Canada 'cause I used to tail him. If he left about an hour ago, he'll probably reach the border in about six hours. If I leave right now and head north on the throughway, I can inter- cept him before he makes the border. It's about a five-hour drive from here, so there's no time to lose."

Tony taps his fingers on the dash. "When did you last speak to the prick?"

Ken looks at his watch. "Just before I picked up Larry this morning. Probably a couple of hours ago? He told me he was driving to Canada today. He sounded a bit nervous. Let me try him one more time."

Ken gets Nanske's voicemail. "Why won't this motherfucker answer his goddamn phone?"

With an empty stare and sullen eyes, Tony says, "That piece of shit is carrying five million dollars of our money, and yet, that prick can't pick up his fucking phone? Is he trying to steal my money?"

Ken squeezes Tony's shoulder and leans in. "Who the fuck knows? I need to find his sorry ass and stop him before he's nabbed by the authorities and takes us all down. Don't worry, Tony. I'll find this prick, and when I do, I'll ensure he never talks."

CHAPTER 66

Although his van is certified to haul only ten equines, Nanske regularly crams in a dozen or more horses, and this trip is no exception. Leaving his farm just a short while ago, he managed to jam fourteen horses inside the back of his trailer. After locking the trailer doors, there will be no need or reason to reopen them until his arrival at the slaughter facility in Quebec.

Prior to turning onto the main highway and after ignoring repeated calls from Amanda Casey, John Nanske powered down his phone and tossed it into the rear of the cab.

Roughly six hours away is the agricultural checkpoint for the United States at Champlain, where John Nanske's experience will be routine. After verifying his passport and asking the usual questions about his citizenship and purpose, the federal inspector will examine his paperwork for livestock and apply a USDA seal on his van, making it unlawful to break the seal until he arrives at the slaughter facility.

Once he crosses into Canada, $5 million will forever exit the United States. The cash will become untraceable as it disappears from Canada and is wired to offshore accounts where only the Kaufman brothers can access the funds.

For Nanske, the practice of slaughtering horses is considered a necessity to deal with an overpopulation of horses, both wild and domestically bred. They claim the problem is overbreeding, as horse owners lack cradle-to-grave responsibility, especially once the animal is no longer productive. Kill buyers like Nanske insist they provide a valuable service, as such unwanted horses will otherwise live without proper care. He will further defend his profession when confronted by animal rights groups or those seeking to rescue unwanted or abandoned horses.

For John Nanske and his contemporaries, the welfare of the horse is outweighed by a desire for money. He pumps the horses with cheap grain to put weight on and then shoves them onto an undersized trailer. If a horse is bitten, hurt, thirsty, or hungry during the ride, it doesn't matter to John Nanske. He'll still be paid by the pound.

When Heliacal Star arrives at the slaughterhouse, he will be frightened by the smells and sounds coming from inside. He will instinctively try to escape but instead find himself passing through a narrowing gated pathway that will lead him toward an inevitable and premature death. Eventually he will enter a chute originally architected for a bovine head and face the nail gun. If he's lucky, his misery will end with a single shot, but it may require several tries, and he will thrash and cry from intolerable pain before ultimately succumbing.

As Nanske continues along the highway, the rear of the trailer rocks as the horses inside maneuver for space within the intensely cramped quarters. Fear and anxiety have likely gripped Heliacal Star by now as one of many condemned horses on this journey. His injured and unattended ankle is only exacerbating his dire situation as any movement or stress will only intensify his pain.

Heliacal Star cries out along with several other horses. A neighboring horse bites his back, and he fights to preserve his small space. After leaving the sanctuary of a comfortable stall and soft hay floor, Heliacal Star whinnies hopelessly.

Stopping at a red light, Nanske opens his folder with the manifest and health certificates. He counts them up, confirming it matches the number of horses being hauled. His papers are forgeries, but no one knows that but him. He reads the fourteenth and final certificate as the traffic light turns green, places it on the passenger seat, and punches the accelerator. He checks his watch. A little more than five hours until he'll reach Canada.

CHAPTER 67

Carol Chambers is hunched over, hiding her face. "I cannot believe this is happening! All this time, I thought I was saving horses."

Matt's patience is running thin. The sheriff seems unmoved by their situation. Matt says, "With all due respect, enough of this bullshit. It's time you got off your ass and stopped this asshole from getting away with my horse. Don't you understand he's not just stealing him but planning to murder him?"

Matt walks up to Carol. "Knock it off! Your pouting and self-pity is not helping, either. You didn't know! How could you? While you're wallowing over here, that asshole is getting away and laughing at us."

Placing his hand atop Matt's shoulder, the sheriff says, "I appreciate your frustration, but please understand I'm doing everything possible within the confines of the law. I've alerted the state police, but there are hundreds or perhaps thousands of trailers and trucks on the road at any given time. Unless you can share more information, my options are limited."

Matt straightens up to make a last-ditch plea to the sheriff.

Ready to make his case, he catches a glimpse of Kristine entering the station.

Matt's thoughts are thrown back to his first encounter with her. Matt has learned to rely on her and vice versa. They've formed an incredible bond built off an intense trust in each other. He wonders how dramatically different and boring these past few weeks would have been without her. Regardless of what happens next, Matt knows deep in his soul that his life has been touched and he's grown richer as a result of his relationship with Kristine. Watching her enter the station, he wills himself to find a solution to Heliacal Star's perilous situation. Now is the time to fight.

Kristine immediately darts her eyes to the sheriff and says, "Contact US Border Patrol immediately. I know for a fact our horse thief is heading to Canada!"

The sheriff grabs a pen. "Good thought. There are two main agricultural crossings. I will alert them about a trailer hauling horses. Do you have any other details we can use?"

Paula shouts out, "Yeah, tell the customs agents he's a first-rate asshole!"

The sheriff dismisses Paula and returns his focus to Matt and Kristine. "To be clear, I don't have any evidence, just your word, that a crime has been committed. Our agents can only hold him a short while unless or until we get direct evidence of a crime. Also be aware that only Canadian customs can prevent him from crossing into Canada. I'll fax a copy of your registration papers around to the relevant agencies."

Matt turns to Kristine. "You heard the man. They can only do so much. Are we going to have to find him ourselves?"

Kristine says, "I was beginning to think you'd never ask. Let's go get him."

The sheriff interjects, "Hold on there! I understand you desperately want justice, but vigilantism is not the solution. You're only putting yourself at risk."

Matt and Kristine look at each other and laugh. "Risk?"

The sheriff continues, "Trust me, this kind of thinking only works in the movies. The authorities are properly trained and way better equipped to handle this."

Kristine reaches out to shake the sheriff's hand. "Thank you for your help and advice." She turns to Matt. "It's time to go. Nanske has a two-hour head start. We'll need to make up the time."

Paula holds up the keys to her pickup. "I want a piece of that asshole, too."

Paula grabs Carol's elbow and yanks her out of the chair. "C'mon."

Carol wipes her eyes. "I can identify Nanske's van if we see it. I'll know it if we pass it."

The four of them move toward the exit.

The sheriff calls out to them, "I can't stop you from doing this, but let me give you one more piece of advice. If you find him, please call the police. Don't handle this guy alone."

Once outside, Paula leads the group toward her truck.

Paula says, "Listen, I've got a full tank of gas and a radar detector, and this rig can move when I push the pedal, so get in and let's find this bastard."

Paula punches the accelerator and squeals the tires as the truck rushes through the intersection and onto the highway entrance ramp. As they gain speed, she says, "That's our last traffic light for the next two hundred miles."

———

The indicator light pops on the dashboard, warning of low gas as the dial hovers just above empty following three hours of nonstop driving. Ken tells Johnny, "We're making good time. Let's make a pit stop." At the next opportunity, he pulls off the throughway and into a service station.

Since leaving the city, Johnny has been repeatedly dialing John Nanske and consistently getting voicemail. After leaving several urgent messages to return his call, Nanske's voicemail has reached capacity.

After failing to reach Nanske for the umpteenth time, Johnny phones Tony from a burner while Ken is filling the gas tank. Tony picks up quickly. "Any news?"

"Nothing. He's still not picking up. We stopped for gas about halfway up. We should be there in about two and a half hours. We'll intercept him if the others don't find him first."

In his typical monotonic voice, Tony says, "Keep me posted," and ends the call.

Johnny crushes the burner on the ground and returns to the car. Ken grabs the wheel and says, "Let's go!"

CHAPTER 68

Special Agent Carlos Anjero is walking briskly outside of the arrivals terminal at Albany International Airport following a short, turbulent, and late-arriving flight from LaGuardia. In the time it took to drive to the airport, pass through security, and land, he could have arrived by car. An unmarked black sedan pulls up to the curb where Anjero is walking, and the passenger window slides down.

A clean-shaven young professional in a charcoal suit and solid blue tie leans over from the driver's seat. Anjero moves closer to the passenger window. The driver of the car reaches out through the window. "Jason Williams from the Albany branch. I'm your tagalong and your driver."

Anjero extends his hand. "Anjero. Thanks for the help. The flight was awful, and we're already behind schedule." Anjero jumps in the car, and they quickly exit the airport and pull onto the throughway heading north toward Canada.

As they pull onto the throughway Williams asks, "What can you tell me?"

Anjero leans back in his seat and presses his head deep into the headrest. "We need to catch this mother." He exhales and says, "Our office has been tracking Kaufman and his cronies for the past five years. I just learned through an informant about their method for transporting narcotics, and how they're able to move cash out of the country. They've been doing this right under our noses, from the bottom of a horse trailer. I never in a million . . . we're going to nail them for money laundering, smuggling, drug trafficking, and the illegal transport of goods across an international border."

Williams asks, "How exactly are they carrying the money?"

"They load the cash into a false bottom in a horse trailer. According to my guy, they have a partner who sells old horses in Canada for slaughter. When he reaches the border patrol, his load is marked by the FDA as a quarantined load, and he drives straight into Canada. I suppose the animals are preinspected before loading, and he avoids deep inspection at the border crossing. On his return to the States, he collects a different group of horses and brings them back to his farm along with the smuggled paraphernalia."

Williams nods. "Clever."

Anjero continues, "We don't know if Kaufman has one or multiple drivers hauling for them, but we know of at least one."

"Got it, but what brings you here right now? Is something happening?" Williams asks.

Anjero looks at his driver. "They didn't tell you much, did they? I suppose that's good. I don't know the precise timing of their next shipment but if my informant is right, it's any day. I've been in touch with border patrol, and they've added surveillance as of last night at Champlain and Erie, the primary crossings for livestock. Champlain is more likely, as it's closer to the slaughterhouse, but Erie is possible since our guy's farm is located in western New York."

"Got it! We'll reach the Champlain crossing in about two and a half hours, assuming no traffic issues. Has border patrol reported anything unusual?"

"Only a dozen trailers or so have been stopped since last night, but nothing resembling our operation. We need to be cautious, though, as word will spread fast and drivers will tip off fellow drivers if they suspect something. We're only targeting trailers with horses. We don't want to tip our guy off and send him underground. I've been waiting too long to nail Kaufman, and if our guy gets spooked, we're going to miss this unique opportunity."

"And you can connect our guy to Kaufman?"

"Once we grab this piece of shit, we'll throw the book at him. I'll lean so hard into him he'll be pissing out of his asshole before I'm done. We have a warrant ready to search his farm and confiscate his phone. We're holding off on sending agents to his farm right now to avoid tipping him off and sending him into hiding."

"Are you getting any new updates from this informant of yours?"

"He was supposed to meet me this morning but never showed up. I've come to expect this type of bullshit from this bum. He recorded a poor-quality conversation of him speaking with Ken Kaufman earlier this week."

Williams asks, "Suppose this guy gets cold feet, then what?"

"If we don't catch him at the border, then we'll need to shift to plan B."

"Plan B, what's plan B?"

Anjero smiles. "Plan B is we come up with plan B if plan A doesn't work."

CHAPTER 69

Matt is numb as he stares out at the rolling hills, open pastures, and setback farmhouses off the highway. As he looks at the countryside, Matt struggles with the horrific realization that thousands of horses, just like Heliacal Star, may end up facing slaughter. As they drive past a quaint-looking home, Matt's thoughts wander beyond Heliacal Star's fate to more pleasant images as he envisions himself living in a remote place but at a different time and under different circumstances. He pictures an existence without the constant shadow of Louisville Larry or Kaufman.

While Matt has been lost in thought, Paula White has been deftly navigating her diesel pickup at high speed over the narrow and winding two-lane highway. She's slowed only by a warning chirp from her radar detector.

After briefly slowing behind a landscaping truck, the pickup suddenly swings out to pass, causing Kristine to slide across the back seat and into Matt's lap. Snapped out of his daydream, Matt winces as Kristine inadvertently presses against his ribs.

As Matt grimaces, Kristine immediately scoots back. "I'm so sorry, Matt. Are you okay?"

Matt does his best to smile through the stabbing sensation as he recaptures his breath. "I'll be fine, but only because it's you. My ribs still hurt like a mother, but we have bigger issues to worry about right now than my injuries."

Matt points to the scenery around them. "Was it like this where you grew up?"

Kristine rests her head on his shoulder and says, "I must confess, I miss being up here. It's far from perfect and not nearly as busy or exciting as the city, but this will always be home to me."

Turning to Kristine, Matt asks, "Do you think Heliacal Star understands what's happening to him? Do you think he's scared?"

She looks down and away for a moment and gently places her hand on Matt's arm. "Horses are acutely aware of their surroundings. They are one of the few—maybe only—domesticated flight animals, and they're hypersensitive when placed in unfamiliar places or situations. This is especially true of thoroughbreds—they're considered a hot-blood breed. Right now, every animal in the back of that trailer is aware something is wrong."

Matt seethes with resentment for John Nanske. He bristles at the notion of such indignity being thrust upon these once proud athletes.

Kristine taps his arm. "I'm sorry, Matt. I didn't mean to upset you. It's possible Heliacal Star believes he's shipping to another barn or racetrack. I'm not there, so I don't know."

From the back seat, he says, "Hey, Paula, how much farther until we find that piece of shit?"

Paula keeps her eyes on the road and says, "We're doing really well on time. At this rate, I expect to catch that motherfucker within the next hour."

Carol speaks out. "I never liked that guy, but I'm mostly pissed at Amanda. I trusted her and never in a million years saw this coming. How can she be so callous and uncaring? Honest to God, I thought we were saving horses, not sending them to . . . to . . . to be slaughtered!"

Carol uses her sleeves to wipe her face clean and takes a few short breaths. Tossing her head back, she rubs her eyes, turns from the front seat, and looks directly at Matt. "No more feeling sorry for myself. I'm going to help you save your horse." She slurps in a breath and continues, "If there is a God, we are going to catch that bastard, and he's going to pay dearly for his actions."

Paula takes her hands off the wheel for a moment and claps. "Everyone, we all need to focus now. Keep your eyes open. It's only a matter of time before we spot that bastard's trailer!"

CHAPTER 70

Ken Kaufman glances at his watch as he and Johnny Fischer approach the exit for US-11 S, just two miles south of the Canadian border crossing at Champlain. Leaning over, Johnny suddenly blurts out, "Hey, boss . . . yo! Turn off . . . now!"

Ken keeps driving at the speed limit in the left lane. "What are you talking about?"

Johnny reaches across from the passenger seat and pulls on the steering wheel, causing them to skid across the two-lane highway and fishtail onto the exit ramp for US-11. On the ramp, Ken jams his foot hard onto the brake, causing Johnny to lose his grip on the wheel, lurch forward, and take a header into the dash.

As the vehicle stops partway up the exit ramp, Ken slaps Johnny across the back of his head. "What the fuck was that all about?"

Johnny leans back. "Sorry, boss, but you were cruising right past the last exit before Canada, and we'd be screwed if you missed it. While you've been driving, I've been studying this road map. Since our idiot partner is driving eastbound, he has to come through here, on this road."

Ken snaps the paper road map from Johnny's hand and

chuckles. "You know, you could have mentioned this thirty seconds earlier, like, before we reached the exit!" He unfolds the map and stretches it across his lap, looks at it for a moment, and neatly folds it. He glances at his watch. "Nanske left his farm about eleven this morning, so he should be close."

An older-model sedan approaches from behind and pulls into the lane next to Ken and Johnny and up alongside them. Ken looks over at the stopped vehicle, drops the map, and wraps his left hand over the handle of his revolver while keeping it out of sight from the neighboring car. An overweight man with horn-rimmed glances and a well-worn baseball cap rolls down his window. Ken tightens his grip, rolls down his window, and glares toward the driver of the other car.

The man in the other vehicle leans out and says, "Hey there, stranger. I've noticed you've been sitting here for a while. Are you lost? Do you need some help?"

Lightening his grip on the gun, Ken offers an awkward smile and throws out an obviously fake accent. "I appreciate your help, but we're fine. We was a bit lost, but all's good now. Much obliged. Have a great evening."

Still leaning out his window, the driver nods. "Sorry to disturb you. Have a great evening, my friend." He drives off.

Johnny turns to Ken and chuckles. "I guess we're not in the city anymore! That poor bastard has no idea how close he just came to meeting Jesus!"

Ken points at his gun. "Let's get the fuck out of here before I really use this thing." He grabs the wheel, puts the car in drive, taps the gas pedal, and turns left onto US-11 S, traveling westward.

Johnny takes out one of his many burner phones and calls his brother. Having done this drill countless times, Frankie answers with his typical grunt, signaling it is safe to talk.

Johnny says, "Hey, bro, we made it to the meeting spot. I'll be in touch as soon as we bag the bait." Frankie doesn't say anything, and Johnny ends the call.

US-11 S in Upstate New York is a 225-mile two-lane highway that stretches from Syracuse to Lake Champlain and intersects Interstate 87. Ken drives westward for a few minutes and turns left onto a narrow and desolate-looking country road, perpendicular to the highway. Johnny looks at Ken. "Where are you going?"

Ken slows down and does a U-turn. Just shy of the intersection, he pulls the car to the right edge of the road and shifts into neutral. While tapping his forehead, he says, "We're going to camp right here and wait for that prick."

Ken opens his window and exaggerates taking a deep breath. He says, "It don't smell this frigging nice where we live, my friend. Roll down your window and enjoy some country air."

Beyond the trees and to the right of their parked car sits a two-story farmhouse, set back from the roadway, with a wraparound porch and aging paint job. A small grassy lawn in front and large fenced pasture out back are mostly obscured from the roadway by a dense foundation of adjacent trees.

Ken leans past Johnny and looks toward the old house through the trees. "Hey, Johnny, check out the house over there." He points. "We're in the middle of nowhere. What the fuck would you do for fun and excitement up here?"

Johnny looks out his window toward the house. "Not for

me. The air smells nice, but this place couldn't handle me. I'll take the city any day of the week over this country shit."

Ken smiles. "I don't know, Johnny. Give it a few days, and you might fit in with the locals!" His smile erupts into laugher, and Johnny joins him.

Ken glances down at his watch. "It's almost half past six. He's got to be close."

Long ago, Ken and Tony Kaufman spent much of their time together on the street without enforcers to handle confrontations or situations. Ken grabs his revolver, caresses it lightly, and smiles. "This is fun, Johnny. Reminds me a little of the old days when I was on the street with Tony."

As the syndicate grew and the authorities began to watch them more closely, they brought in more protection in the form of hired thugs, like Johnny and Frankie Fischer.

A light rumbling sound approaches from the east, and Ken and Johnny sit upright.

"See anything?" Ken asks.

"Definitely some sort of truck, but I don't see it yet."

The rumbling grows louder as the truck rolls past them. Ken releases his grip. "Nope. Not him."

Seconds later, another truck approaches. Looking left, Ken tells Johnny it could be a horse trailer. As the van passes directly in front of them, Ken smiles broadly. "Son of a bitch! That's our guy!"

Ken shifts the car into drive and pulls out directly behind John Nanske's horse trailer.

CHAPTER 71

Pushing his sedan to within inches of the bumper of Nanske's trailer, Ken Kaufman is dangerously close to ramming the trailer from behind. He glances toward Johnny, who nods, then swings out across the dotted yellow line and accelerates until his sedan is keeping pace with Nanske's cab.

Johnny lowers the passenger window and vigorously waves his arm, gesturing Nanske to slow down and pull over. He turns to Ken, pinches his nose, and says, "If this ain't no shit-smelling trailer."

Nanske looks over, ignores Johnny's instructions, and instead accelerates and moves partway across the dotted yellow line, blocking the sedan from passing.

Ken asks, "What the fuck is he doing?" He punches the accelerator and maneuvers around the trailer. Johnny hangs his head and shoulders out the car window and sticks out his middle finger toward Nanske. He shouts toward Nanske, "Hey, moron! Pull the fuck over!"

Ken accelerates ahead of the trailer, swerves sharply in front of it, and slows down rapidly. A few cars are now approaching from the opposite direction, blocking Nanske from attempting to pass.

Ken turns to Johnny. "I wonder if that asshole just shit his pants." As he further reduces his speed, with Nanske's trailer behind them, Ken says, "Let's do him fast. I don't want to whack any local do-gooder should they happen to come upon us and mistake us for a stranger in need."

The sedan pulls off to the side of the road and stops. Johnny looks over his shoulder at the cab slowing behind them and moving to the side of the road. Ken shifts into park as the trailer abruptly swerves onto the main road and accelerates past Ken and Johnny in the sedan.

Slamming both of his fists across the steering wheel, Ken yells out, "You stupid motherfucker!" He jams his car into drive, punches the accelerator hard, and skids onto the main road, now several hundred feet behind Nanske's trailer. Ken shouts, "I'm going to pull his sorry ass out of that trailer and beat the living piss out of him and then shoot his ass!" Once again, Ken speeds up to the sedan, closing in on the slower-moving trailer. He says, "Once we get close, shoot out his back wheel."

Ken maneuvers the sedan across the dotted yellow line, and Johnny lowers his window, draws his pistol, and fires three shots into the left rear tire. The tire bursts, causing the trailer to swerve and skid from left to right, leaning hard until it's almost tilting over as it slides awkwardly. The trailer jackknifes over the wet grass. As the trailer comes to a stop, Ken parks his sedan.

Nanske leaps out of the trailer and sprints toward the road, as both Ken and Johnny jump out of the sedan.

Ken shouts, "Stop right there, Nanske!"

Nanske stops abruptly, turns around, and says, "Oh, Mr. Kaufman, it's you! Shit, I almost had a heart attack. I didn't recognize your partner when he waved that gun at me from the road. Honest to God, I thought someone was trying to hijack my rig and . . . what the heck is going on? What are you doing here?"

Ken Kaufman saunters toward Nanske, shows his pistol, and says, "John, why didn't you pick up your phone when we called you like a hundred times?" Not waiting for a response, he waves the gun in Nanske's face. "Johnny and I have been calling you for the last several hours, and I gotta say, we're out of patience right now!"

Ken steps up to Nanske's face and snarls. "Now, you're going to listen to me, asshole, as plans have changed. This run"—he points to Nanske's van—"is officially over."

Nanske is trembling and shrugs while keeping his eyes fixed on the gun. He gestures toward the weapon. "Do you really need to wave that thing at me?"

Without hesitation, Ken rams the barrel of his gun against Nanske's forehead and forces him down to his knees. Ken releases the pressure, and Nanske falls forward, face down, his hands splayed on the ground. Hovering above, Ken kicks some dirt onto Nanske and says, "Because of your stupid antics, Johnny and I had to drive from fucking Queens to deliver you this message." He squats down and looks at the shuddering man. "How about you tell me what's going on? Rumor has it you're trying to make fast with my money!"

Nanske lifts his head, struggles to get up on one knee, and places a hand atop his temple to stop the blood trickling down his face. He looks at Ken, who continues to point his gun at Nanske's head. Nanske struggles back to his feet. "Mr. Kaufman, for God's sake, I have no idea what you're talking about! I've always been loyal and would never—"

A cold rain begins to fall, and Ken strikes the gun across Nanske's chest, forcing him to lurch forward, drop to his knees again, and gasp for air.

A seething Ken shouts, "Prove it! You think you're so fucking smart? Get my money right fucking now."

Hunched down on all fours, Nanske cries out, "Why would I ever do something so stupid and foolish? How long have you known me?"

Ken stares down at Nanske as the rain picks up. Johnny Fischer is nearby, looking out for passing motorists.

A cold and steady rain now falls as Nanske pleads, "Please, Ken. You gotta believe me. I've always been a good worker and would never . . ."

Ken continues to point his gun at Nanske. "Look at me, John."

Nanske is shaking, soaked from the rain. "Please! Dear God, Ken! You know me better than that!"

Johnny runs up to them, waving his arms, and grabs Ken's attention. "Cars coming," he says and points to the road.

Ken methodically places his weapon in the rear of his jeans and conceals it with his untucked shirt. He yanks Nanske by the shoulder and pulls him forward. "When these cars pass, you're going to wave and pretend I'm helping you out. You fuck this up, and I'll shoot you dead without thinking twice. Hopefully for their sake, they won't stop to offer assistance."

Three cars drive past, each slowing down and staring at the trailer sitting perpendicular to the road. The first vehicle stops, and the driver rolls down the window. Before the driver speaks,

Ken Kaufman yells loudly through the rain, "We're all good here. My friend's van blew a tire. We already called roadside service, and they should be here any minute." The driver waves to Ken and continues on his way, followed by the next two vehicles, who also drive off.

Once the cars are gone, Ken removes the gun from his pants and points it at Nanske. "We're going to attract too much attention, and this rain isn't helping. Where's my money?"

Nanske pleads, "Please, Ken, don't do this. I'll get you the money. It's inside the trailer, right where you put it a few days ago. For the love of God, you gotta know I've done nothing wrong!"

Ken waves the gun. "The money, John, NOW!"

Nanske walks to the back of trailer, unlocks the back door, and turns to Ken without unlatching the door. "The money is underneath the floorboards, back-right corner of the trailer." He points in the direction of the false bottom. "There's a lot of horses inside. If I open this door, I may not be able to control them."

A strong gust of wind blows as the sky grows darker and the rain transitions into a mix of rain and hail. Johnny returns, indicating another vehicle is approaching. Once again Ken conceals his gun. He says to Johnny, "This is ridiculous. I'm going to shoot this bastard after this next car passes!"

The passing vehicle is a large fifty-foot trailer, hardly slowing down as it drives past the trio. The speed and size of the passing truck shakes the ground and sprays a wave of standing rainwater at them from the roadway. Ken raises his forearm to shield his eyes from the water.

As Ken is momentarily distracted, Nanske drops the keys and sprints across the roadway. Ken fires first, and Johnny follows with several shots in Nanske's direction. Nanske disappears into the woods across the roadway.

Ken yells out, "Shit!" The inclement weather and canopy of trees make it impossible spot Nanske. Throwing up his arms, Ken says, "Fuck this shit. Let's grab our money and get the fuck out of here before anyone else shows up."

Ken and Johnny return to the rear of the trailer, ignoring the raucous sounds of whinnying horses coming from inside. Johnny says, "This smells awful."

Ken says, "I'll open the doors, and you jump in and grab the cash. It's over there in the false bottom." He points to the back-right corner of the trailer and says, "And hurry up!"

Johnny looks at Ken, "What about all these horses?"

Ken says, "I'll only open the doors wide enough for you to crawl inside. You're strong enough to push any horses aside if they're blocking the door. C'mon, before someone drives past. We gotta move now."

Ken opens the unlocked trailer doors, creating a small opening barely large enough for Johnny to slip inside. Johnny crawls through the opening, and a loud bang accompanies a jolting force, which tosses both men sprawling backward. The first horse bolts out, rearing high while leaping out of the trailer, clearing Johnny's head by inches. Johnny staggers backward and falls onto the wet ground, then gets up. A second horse immediately follows, sidestepping Ken. The remaining horses follow out the now wide-open rear door of the van, creating an impromptu stampede on the roadway.

Running to the car, Ken shouts to Johnny, "Grab the money!"

Johnny approaches the trailer from the side and avoids the

ensuing pandemonium. As the horses seem to have all exited, Johnny jumps into the back of the trailer. Once inside, he sees a lone remaining horse standing inside. Johnny lifts the door to the false bottom and grabs the box of cash as the horse snorts, rears up his forelegs, and slams down onto the floor with an earth-shattering thud. He charges at Johnny, who rolls out of the van and onto the ground just before the final horse leaps out to escape the trailer.

Inside his car, Ken kicks opens the passenger door as Johnny sprints toward it, leaps inside, and avoids the bedlam of loose horses running around the roadway. Ken turns the ignition key and revs the engine but cannot pull forward as several horses are blocking the roadway. He shifts into reverse and accelerates backward, slamming on the brake before ramming a loose horse behind them. The car spins onto the roadway, and Ken shifts into drive and slams his foot on the gas pedal as another horse darts in front of the accelerating car. Ken swerves to avoid a collision, causing the sedan to spin over a wet patch of roadway. The vehicle careens off the road and into a canopy of trees. The car smashes into the base of an oversize oak tree and comes to a jarring stop.

Without a safety belt, Johnny Fischer is launched through the windshield and thrown against the tree. Ken Kaufman's head jolts forward into the depressed airbag while the force of the accident jams the wheel and dashboard deep into his unconscious body.

CHAPTER 72

Taking her foot off the gas pedal, Paula leans forward and says, "Holy shit! Look at that . . . straight ahead!"

Matt stretches his neck to look out the front window and is stunned to see several loose horses running all over the roadway. On the side of the road, he notices a horse trailer, spun around and perpendicular to the road.

Kristine declares the obvious. "Those are loose horses!"

"That's Nanske's trailer!" Carol says.

"I'll be damned! So it is," Paula says. "But what in the world is going on out here?"

Carol grabs her mobile and dials 911. The events unfolding in front of them seem surreal, and Matt pinches himself to ensure he's not dreaming again. There are loose horses everywhere, yet not a single person is in sight.

Where's Heliacal Star? Matt wonders where his horse and Nanske could have disappeared to.

Paula pulls her pickup onto the shoulder and parks near Nanske's abandoned trailer.

Matt jumps out from the back seat, ignoring his discomfort. Kristine jumps out from behind him and says, "The horses don't even have halters on them!"

Carol drops her cell phone in her purse. "The police are on their way."

Matt walks with Kristine to the rear of the opened trailer; it's empty except for a thick layer of dirt and waste. The odor is overwhelming, and Matt steps back to search for Heliacal Star.

Matt looks at Kristine. "Do you see him anywhere?"

She shrugs, and Matt looks toward Paula, who is standing beside her pickup. Matt shouts out, "Hey, Paula? Do you see Heliacal Star anywhere?"

She shakes her head.

Kristine joins Paula at the roadside, and they frantically wave their arms to direct the escaped horses off the roadway. Several of the horses settle on a grassy area off the road, but a few others ignore them and continue to wander across the pavement.

A car pulls up and parks behind Paula's truck, followed by a second and third vehicle.

Matt walks to the front cab of the trailer and props himself onto the driver's seat, as the door has been left ajar. His hopes of locating Heliacal Star fade. He spots a partly opened folder on the seat and looks inside.

Reading the contents of the folder, Matt thumbs through the individual health certificates for each horse. He sees Nanske's name signed at the bottom of each one. He reads another certificate showing an FDA seal. A chill vibrates down his spine as he contemplates what was in store for these poor horses.

Climbing down from the cab, his energy wanes and he slumps to the wet ground, propping his back up against the large front tire of the trailer. He vows to get up and continue his search for Heliacal Star but first needs to catch his breath and regain his strength.

When Matt finally staggers toward the back of the vacated trailer, the surrounding scene remains chaotic as Paula and Kristine lead several others who have now gathered to control the horses and keep them off the roadway. Matt hears hooves clomping behind him. He turns around and sees a large dark bay thoroughbred limping toward him. As the horse moves closer, Matt immediately recognizes the distinguishable white star marking on the forehead of the gelding.

CHAPTER 73

Trucks and trailers are backed up for a quarter mile at the Canadian border, as the FBI and state police continue to carefully inspect all livestock trailers before allowing them to proceed to Canadian customs. Any approaching truck or trailer with livestock on board is now required to unload before it enters Canada so a team of Federal Drug Enforcement officers and trained dogs can inspect inside every trailer.

Agent Anjero sips on a black coffee as he walks up a ramp and into one of the trailers being inspected. He turns to the officer holding the dog. "Anything to report?"

"No, sir. This van is clean."

"Was this guy hauling horses?" The officer nods affirmatively, and Anjero continues, "Where is the driver now?" As directed by the officer, Anjero walks inside a makeshift tent and finds the driver being interviewed by another officer.

He shows his badge and says, "I'm Special Agent Carlos Anjero. Can I see your license and any documentation you're carrying to identify your cargo?"

The unshaven driver, in a weathered yellow baseball cap that says CAT, stands up and hands over his license and documentation. He says, "What's going on? Here you go, but I already showed this to the officer."

Anjero quietly inspects the documentation. He looks at the driver and returns to his paperwork. The driver removes his cap and wipes his head. Anjero looks at him and then at the photo from his license and then one more time at the driver.

Anjero returns the documentation to the man and says, "It looks like all your paperwork is in order and your trailer is clean, although the inspectors are still finishing up their work outside. I also noticed you have a USDA certificate and are planning to haul these horses to a slaughterhouse in Canada."

Accepting the papers, the driver responds, "Yes, sir. That's correct, but there's nothing illegal about what I'm doing."

Anjero dismisses the comment. "I'm looking for someone hauling horses to the same facility in Quebec. We have reason to believe he's smuggling drugs and cash into Canada."

"No, sir. I'm just hauling horses and doing my job. Nothing sinister in my trailer."

"I know. Point is that most of the trailers we've seen so far don't transport horses, and I cannot imagine there are many trailers carrying this USDA designation, if you know what I mean."

The man throws a puzzled look and Anjero continues, "Okay, let me spell it out. I assume this is a small world, and you all know each other. Our guy may be an associate of yours because he also hauls horses with the same USDA designation. Get it?"

The man shrugs and says, "I mind my own business. How the heck would I know? Don't you government guys work together? Why don't you just call the USDA and ask them yourself?"

Anjero stares at the man for a few seconds but offers no additional comment. His cell phone rings, breaking the silence as Agent Williams runs toward him. He whispers to Anjero, who in turn says to the man in the yellow cap, "You're free to go."

The pair of agents speed walk to Williams's car. Williams brings him up to speed about the abandoned trailer and the loose horses a few miles away.

Anjero slides into the passenger seat as Williams drives. "What makes you think it's our guy?"

Williams says, "We phoned in the license plate of the van, and it belongs to a guy named John Nanske. We then called the USDA—"

Anjero interrupts, "Good, I was meaning to ask you to call them."

They pull onto the interstate. "Turns out this Nanske guy recently received a set of certificates from the USDA to haul horses into Canada. We're close!"

As they arrive on scene, Agents Anjero and Williams meet with the State Police officer. "I'm Special Agent Carlos Anjero, and this is Agent Williams. What's the story here?"

"We only arrived a few minutes ago. I've got some officers en route, and there are some locals trying to round up the horses. The trailer is registered to a guy named John Nanske, but he's nowhere to be found. The first group of witnesses on the scene haven't seen him or anyone else associated with the van."

A voice comes over the police radio. "We've just located a disabled vehicle crashed in the woods, beyond the shoulder of the roadway. It's about five hundred feet from the trailer. The driver is unconscious, possibly deceased. There is also one other passenger, seriously injured, but appears conscious and lying on the ground next to the vehicle. We are approaching with caution."

A few minutes pass, and the same voice comes over the radio. "We believe the driver is Kenneth Kaufman from New York City, based his identification. He is deceased. The second passenger has been identified as John Michael Fischer. He is conscious but critically injured. We've called for an ambulance."

Anjero and Williams move to the rear of the abandoned horse trailer and observe two officers tearing apart the floorboards.

Anjero turns to one of the officers. "What have you found?"

"We found a false bottom inside the floorboard. I suspect it was used to smuggle items into and out of Canada. When we opened it, I thought we would find pay dirt for sure, but it was empty. Completely empty."

Anjero stares at the officer, kicks his feet over the mess on the floor, and asks, "What do you mean, empty?"

The officer points to the floor and repeats, "I'm sorry, sir, but it was empty, completely empty."

EPILOGUE

SIX MONTHS LATER

Wearing a snug, fitted safety vest and tightly strapped helmet, Matt sits stiffly atop a horse for the first time in his life. Brushing a finger over his pants pocket, he nervously feels for the object stuffed inside. Reassured, he takes a deep breath and turns cautiously toward Kris. "You sure I'll be okay on this horse?"

A light winter breeze sweeps through the open arena situated about fifty miles east of Belmont Park in Suffolk County, Long Island. Matt instinctively tightens his legs, inadvertently signaling the horse to lurch forward. He yanks the reins hard, halting any initial momentum as his legs go rubbery.

Kristine quips back, "Try not to panic, Matt. Calm down and soften your legs."

Matt struggles to relax his legs and settle his nerves, feeling increasingly uneasy about his decision to take a riding lesson today from Kristine.

Admiring Heliacal Star while perched in the saddle, Matt

reflects on the past several months. Following their dramatic reclamation of Heliacal Star, several news outlets and social media platforms picked up their story and introduced Matt, Kristine, Paula, and Carol to the general public as horse rescue heroes. Disturbed by Heliacal Star's nearly fatal encounter within the callous world of horse slaughter, Matt leveraged his newfound celebrity to promote several national and local horse rescue charities and gained widespread support from the local racing authorities.

He also reconnected with Alex Sherman shortly after Heliacal Star's dramatic rescue. Sherman expressed shock at the dire circumstances that befell the horse and remorse for his own failure to protect him. Alex joined Matt in visiting several farms and financially supported multiple rescue charities. Sherman subsequently elevated his own charitable involvement by purchasing Happy Trails North from the legally entangled Amanda Casey. He renamed the farm Victoria's Place in honor of his late daughter and began to rebuild and rebrand the place as a charity-endorsed horse rescue operation.

Carol Chambers apologized on her social media channels for her previous association with Amanda Casey. She then outed several known kill buyers, including John Nanske, and joined Alex Sherman as the full-time farm manager. Kristine, Matt, and Paula all endorsed her for the job. For their criminal activity, Amanda Casey and John Nanske were both indicted on multiple counts of animal cruelty, fraud, and theft. Amanda was arrested and jailed, but Nanske disappeared after escaping across the highway last summer and hasn't been seen since.

Bolstered by the positive media coverage, Kristine effectively grew her track presence, training higher-quality racehorses with a burst of interest from several owners expressing a shared interest in animal welfare. She relocated her stable at the racetrack to be adjacent to Bouchard's stalls, and he acted as a mentor.

After initially being rescued by Matt and Kristine, Heliacal Star began his rehab on Kristine's family's farm, just south of Albany. The couple often drove the three hours together from Long Island to Upstate New York to check on him. As the horse's health improved and he grew stronger, Matt and Kristine became inseparable. Following a final veterinary exam, Heliacal Star was deemed healthy and fit for training. Kristine transferred the horse to a farm on eastern Long Island to start him with light exercise.

Kristine smiles toward Matt. "Hey, guess who I spoke to today?"

Appreciating the distraction, Matt replies while desperately clinging to the reins. "Let me guess, was it Ted Bouchard?"

Kristine nods affirmatively.

Matt, still rigid in the saddle, offers a sly grin. "Of course."

"You remember that Bouchard told me Ron McGee lost his training license a couple of weeks ago, right?"

Matt nods.

"Bouchard now thinks McGee's going down for race fixing!"

Matt pats the horse and says, "How does he know?" Wanting to believe the rumor, he thinks to himself, *It couldn't have happened to a more deserving person.*

She smiles. "I don't know, but Ted's been around a long time and knows a lot of people. Of course, it's only a rumor, but a girl can dream, right?"

Kristine smiles. "Okay, that's enough stalling, Mr. Galiano. Time to get to work!"

Matt double-checks his helmet and ensures his protective vest is tight. He grabs the reins in his left hand and checks his feet in the stirrups. Kristine gives him a reassuring nod.

He takes a nervous breath and tells himself to relax and stay calm.

Kristine stands at his side, to the right of the horse. "You're doing great. You two look great together, like it was meant to be! Now, take regular breaths and remember to relax your legs."

He shouts back, "I am relaxed!"

Heliacal Star looks back at his rider. The horse turns forward, bobs his head up and down. A surprising calmness suddenly envelops Matt. He realizes this must be the time. With courage and confidence, Matt keeps one hand on the reins and slips the other deep into his pocket. He pulls out a small box, dips his head, and flips it open, revealing a diamond engagement ring.

ACKNOWLEDGMENTS

Writing this novel required an unexpected level of patience, perseverance, and commitment, which far exceeded my naïve expectations. My most important and ardent supporter throughout this endeavor has been my wife, Ann. I am indebted to her for her unwavering enthusiasm, upbeat encouragement, and creative thinking, which enabled me to propel forward and reach the finish line. This manuscript would not have been written without her staunch confidence, love, and faith.

My earnest gratitude extends to horse trainer Tim McCanna. Tim's friendship and mentorship has educated me about the inner workings of racing, training, and horse conformation. He's consistently prioritized the health and welfare of the racehorse for every horse in his care. Tim's feedback was critical to ensure the racing and backstretch scenes are presented as realistic and plausible.

I also am appreciative of the many engaging conversations with trainer A. Ferris Allen III, who also helped shape my views about racing. Both Tim McCanna and A. Ferris Allen III are superb examples of positive influences within racing through caring horsemanship and responsible ownership. As much of the media about racing seems fixated on the occasional bad actor, this has not been my experience during my twenty years of involvement. Tim and his wife, Jan, along with A. Ferris Allen III, breeders Debbie Pabst and Jane Allen, bloodstock agent Claudia Canouse, and horse trainers Paul Barrow, Austin Trites, Woodbury Payne, Abigail Adsit, and Jimmy Toner have only shown me their passion, care, and love for the horses, always putting the health and welfare of the equine above all else.

I also acknowledge my lifelong friends who courageously volunteered as early beta readers. John Previti is the finest horse-racing handicapper I know, and Theodore Keyes is an outstanding pedigree and turf expert. I also appreciate the ongoing support of lifelong friends from our "Saratoga group," Terence Sheridan, Kenneth Kruger, and Michael Grekin.

I'm equally grateful and humbled by the feedback, insights, and encouragement from Laura Anderson, who enthusiastically cares for and loves her off-the-track thoroughbred. An additional shout-out to R-A Mazzola and everyone affiliated with Tashunka in western Washington, for boarding and providing daily care for multiple horse breeds, including multiple retired thoroughbreds, and teaching me proper grooming and riding techniques.

As a debut author with limited experience in line editing, copy editing, typesetting, design, and publishing, I am indebted to the guidance, professionalism, and expertise provide by Lindsey Alexander of The Reading List. She skillfully edited the manuscript to capture the essence of the story while emphasizing speed and flow consistent to the thriller genre.

Lastly, I'm so grateful to my mom, Joan, and dad, Victor Sr., for their lifetime of love and support, and for sharing their values, which have helped shaped my life.

ABOUT THE AUTHOR

Heliacal Star represents Victor Bahna's debut novel. The fictional tale draws upon his two decades of experience owning, breeding, and retiring racehorses. Victor was raised on western Long Island, a few miles from Belmont Park. He first attended the races during his teenage years with several high school friends. After relocating from New York to Seattle and while employed at Microsoft, Victor purchased his first racehorse in a claiming race at Emerald Downs in 2005. He bought his first yearling at auction the next year and currently manages a modest racing partnership and races under the stable name Royal Victory Thoroughbreds. Victor enjoys spending time with his retired thoroughbred, Rooster City. He is passionate about the welfare and health of racehorses and promoting second careers for retired thoroughbreds. He lives in Washington State with his wife and two children and visits Belmont and Saratoga annually with his lifelong friends from high school.

Printed in Great Britain
by Amazon

48056120R00233